I0662628

THE MANUSCRIPT MURDERS

Tony Cerminaro

ISBN: 0692470034
ISBN 13: 9780692470039

DEDICATION

For Fred and Lucia Frontera, lifelong friends, for always being there for me...especially through those dark days...

CHAPTER ONE

Paul Dickinson loved to have a good time, and he loved to go to a club named Hot Rod. No one knew why the club was called Hot Rod since it had nothing to do with cars or racing. Someone told Paul the original owner from the fifties, loved hot rods, hence the name. Another person told Paul the first owner was a tough guy and gangster wannabe. The guy loved to carry a gun, show it to people, and tell them he was packing his rod. As the story went, one night the guy killed someone who to tried to rob him when he was closing up. The next day, the guy changed the name to Hot Rod. True or not, Paul liked the second version better.

It was a Wednesday night and even though Paul was technically working, he still went to Hot Rod. He had a couple of hours to kill so why not do a few shots of tequila, and maybe, if he was lucky, lick some nipples too. That's the kind of club Hot Rod was; something for everyone. It wasn't a sophisticated place but it wasn't a dive either. It had two big bars, and besides tables, a lot of little alcoves lined with various styles of couches where people would often make out. All the bartenders were young, sexy fe-males who really knew how to make a drink, pour a brew, and keep their mouths shut about what went on between patrons. They also had great bar foods, including an amazing tasso and pulled pork sandwich with spicy coleslaw.

Anyone and everyone could go to Hot Rod, and they did. On Wednesdays, they had double down on drinks. You paid for two drinks at full price and they gave the third drink free but to someone else. At first, it sounded confusing as to who got what but it was a new twist on the old two for one and ladies night com-bined. That's because most of the male patrons, who ran from professionals in suits, to hard core bikers, bought the two drinks for themselves, and usually gave the other to a female. Knowing the female you were giving the drink to didn't matter, in fact, that was the point. They wanted to give the drink to a female they just had met or wanted to meet.

Paul never had that problem though since Paul was a la-dies man with a capital L, and you better make all of the letters in bold. Despite being in his early fifties, he looked ten years younger. He was short statured but kept himself in top shape. Dark thick hair with matching eyes and a handsome face, he commanded attention and he got it. He wasn't Italian, but he should have been.

Paul was a retired police officer and had been a private in-vestigator for four years. Twice divorced, he had one daughter and two beautiful grandkids which he usually saw once a week for dinner. He didn't have much time for family when he was on the job, but now since going private, he made the time, at least a couple of hours a week. The way Paul thought, if he had a couple of hours a week for licking tequila off some college girl's tits, he had time for family. What a guy!

Hot Rod was packed tight this Wednesday with the midweek special and that's the way the crowd liked it. Hot Rod had a big dance floor as well but on these nights it wasn't big enough. The people loved to dance, and that was another big plus sign Paul had next to his name, he could dance to anything from the Texas Two Step or an East Coast Swing to a very sexy Argentine Tango.

The other noteworthy thing about Paul was his insatiable attraction to Asian women and ironically their insatiable attraction to him. Maybe it was his looks, charm or humor but probably it was more the way he spent money. Initially, Paul thought Asian women had a special knack for making a guy feel like he was the biggest stud in the room, but rethinking it, Paul knew all women had that knack.

Whatever it was, it worked for Paul, and tonight he was in rare form. Only at Hot Rod forty minutes, he was already on his third shot of tequila and the twenty year old Asian girl he was with had both of her small breasts exposed. Sitting on one of the couches, he had two double downs in front of him plus the two free ones, that made six. Paul had his limes slices stuffed into the girl's empty bra cups, he didn't know her name but he didn't care. She was beautiful, young and had nipples that could poke an eye out if you weren't careful. He often thought he should be wearing welder's glasses when he played this game but why draw more attention than he was already getting.

"Easy, easy," she said with a big wide smile. "Do not bite them, at least not yet."

Paul laughed and took a suck a wedge of lime.

"What's your name?" He asked, glancing at his watch.

"Pi," she replied, finishing her first shot of tequila.

"Pi, like pie you eat?" He said, licking her left nipple that had to be an inch long, well, at least three quarters of an inch.

She nodded, giggling. "Yes, Pi, like pie you eat."

Paul pushed another shot of tequila toward her. "Here, drink up. These two are yours."

She giggled again showing perfect teeth.

"I cannot drink as fast as you can," she said in a heavy accent. "I get drunk."

"It's cool," Paul replied, finishing the third shot. "I don't have a lot of time anyway."

The Asian girl hesitated and Paul pulled a thick roll of cash from his pants pocket. He peeled off two one hundred bills and laid them on the small coffee table in front him.

Pi smiled, took the second shot of tequila and drank it. When she reached for a lime wedge Paul grabbed her hand.

"Let's go to my car," he said, looking at his watch again. "Leave the lime and take the hundreds. I got something else you can suck on."

Pi smiled, picked up the two C notes, got up and followed Paul to the rear entrance. Half way there, a big, mean looking biker got up from a table and put his huge hand on Paul's chest.

"Little young for you, don't you think pops?" The much taller guy said looking down at Paul. "You better leave her with me and you catch a bus back to the nursing home."

Paul said nothing and didn't even flinch, he knew any sign of fear and this guy would have him. Paul had been in this situation many times before by real tough men, and this guy wasn't one of them.

"Well?" The biker pushed on Paul's chest. "What's it going to be?"

Paul stared back but said nothing and the big guy pushed him again.

"Are you stupid man?" He asked this time with a nervous laugh. "I'll really bust you up, you little fuck!"

Paul finally smiled after another long uncomfortable minute.

"You know there's a line Robert DeNiro says in one of his movies, GOODFELLOWS or CASINO, I'm not sure which one but it doesn't matter."

4

"Who cares, asshole." The man said cutting him off. "Walk away now or I'll drag you outside and maybe, just maybe, you'll be able to crawl away."

"Just let me finish first," Paul said nicely in a low voice. "Then, once I'm done you can do whatever you like."

The guy who towered over Paul, perhaps at six three or four laughed, then looked at his three buddies who were sitting at the table for support.

"Go ahead, asshole, finish your stupid story," he said still with his hand on Paul's chest. "Then I'm going to break you into pieces."

"…So DeNiro is describing the Joe Pesci character, who, for all intent and purposes, is a complete psychopath. Well, for you, that's a crazy person. Anyway, DeNiro says, and don't quote me, that if you come at him, Pesci's character, with your fists and beat him, he'll come back with a bat, if you beat him with a bat, he'll come back with a knife, and if you beat him with knife, he come back with a gun."

"Yeah…and that's supposed to be you, this tough dude in the movie?" The biker asked, beginning to lose control and feeling intimidated.

Yeah, asshole! That's me exactly," Paul replied in an ice cold voice. "Only thing with me is, I skip right to the gun and I'll kill you."

The man's smirk suddenly left his face when Paul pulled back his leather jacket to reveal the butt of his Beretta.

Paul continued, "I'm also a retired police officer and you just assaulted me several times in front of witnesses. You also threatened bodily harm, which all are felonies. Those assaults, coupled with threats of violence have put me in fear for my life."

"…And?" The man asked trying to hold his ground, but it was obvious this standoff was over and he had lost.

Paul did not reply, just stared and another long uncomfortable minute passed.

Suddenly, as fast the man had put his hand on Paul's chest, he removed it.

"Fuck you!" he said, walking away. "You're not worth the sweat!"

The man went back to the table, picked up his beer and drained it. He was visibly shaken.

"I got about fifteen minutes," Paul said, turning to Pi.

Pi smiled. "Plenty of time, and after seeing that, I really in the mood for you."

Paul smiled as Pi put her arm around him, and they left Hot Rod for his car.

Exactly fifteen minutes later, Paul was heading out of the parking lot, and back to work.

Twenty minutes after leaving Hot Rod, and getting Pi's phone number, he pulled into the far end of a parking lot which faced the rear of an apartment complex. The apartments were one and two bedrooms units. They were high end and not something a student or someone just starting out would rent. They were, ''I've made it'' apartments for those younger, successful singles or perhaps a professional couple with a new baby or with out of town parents. Someone who didn't want to own a house or a condo but still wanted something nice in a better neighborhood. A place you could bring a new date home to and they would be impressed; impressed right into bed impressed, Paul thought.

It was late April, in Raleigh, North Carolina and unusually cool for this time of year, but Paul could still feel the warmth of the tequila and Pi's expert mouth. She was from Viet Nam and only in this country for a year. She worked at the Best Done Nails Salon down the street from Hot Rod, taking English at night and living with her older married sister. Pi, he thought with a satisfied smile, as he slid down in the seat of his SUV. He always had a taste for a good piece of pie.

It was almost 8:00 pm and in a few minutes Billy Burk would come out of his apartment and get into his new car, just like he had done every Wednesday night for the last three months. Paul had been watching Billy Burk in some form or another, on and off, for the last five years. Ever since Billy Burk had killed his newly married, pregnant wife and made it look like a hit and run accident. A phony hit and run accident that Paul Dickinson and his fellow detectives spotted right away as staged. Only thing was they could never prove it and especially in a court of law. No one believed Billy's version of the event. His early morning phone call from Heather saying her car broke down on some lonely stretch of road was the first tip off. They checked her cell phone records and the call was made at the time he said, but there was no way to verify it was Heather who made the call. He could have made the call himself, when he arrived at the scene. He said he found her lying in the road. Her family said there was no way Heather would have been on that road, especially at that time of night. No way.

Every interview Paul had with anyone close to Heather all said the same thing. She was a sweet, smart new teacher and happy to be a wife and soon to be mother. Also, they all said, no one could understand what she saw in Billy Burk. He was the "total opposite" of Heather her cousin would say over and over as Paul recalled those exact words. The cousin was very sincere and distinct about her description of Billy Burk. He was a prick with ears and she disliked, no hated him, from the first time she met him. Paul could hear the tone her in voice like it was yesterday. 'Billy killed Heather' were the next three words out of her mouth right after prick with ears, she didn't know how he did it, but she knows he did it.

She went on to tell Paul in detail how disinterested Billy was in being married, let alone having children, since he had a son from a previous marriage. Billy the bully, she called him right to Heather's face and Heather would defend him. She would tell her cousin you just don't know him like I do. Paul can still see the anger in Heather's cousin's eyes. 'No, Heather, it's you that doesn't know Billy.'

Then there was that five hundred thousand dollar life insurance policy that Heather signed a month before her death. It took years for Billy for collect on that policy even when the official cause of death had been ruled multiple trauma related to a vehicle accident. Finally, Billy took the insurance company to court, and only recently were they forced to pay.

The cousin's anger was mild compared to the anger felt by Heather's parents, especially her father. He was obsessed with seeing Billy charged with her murder, go to court and be found guilty. Before Paul retired, Heather's father would call almost every day begging for justice for his daughter. Paul tried his best but all he could tell the poor man was that there was nothing new, and unless someone came forward with solid evidence there wasn't anything more he could do.

Paul always had second thoughts about the loss of someone's life and it wasn't something he took lightly. In fact, the four people he killed, or somehow had caused their deaths, were painstaking decisions. Well, there was the one guy he pushed off a roof that tried to push him first; Paul guessed that could be classified as self-defense. Hell, he really thought all but one of those deaths could be classified as self-defense since he was clearly saving the life or lives of other potential victims.

It wasn't like they didn't try to catch Billy Burk in a lie. Paul tried and tried even after he retired as lead detective, he dogged Billy Burk on his own time. The guy just kept telling the same story over and over: He got a call from Heather around 2:00 am that her car had broken down and she needed him to come and get her. Billy drives out to where she was and finds her lying dead in the road some distance from her car. He calls 911 and calmly tells the dispatcher what happened. An ambulance and the police arrive and find Heather's body. Oddly, when they start her car, it works perfectly. Furthermore, there isn't anything about the entire scene that is consistent with a hit and run.

While Paul waited, he ran the whole thing in his mind like a video from start to finish. He was just about to rerun it again when he saw Billy Burk appear. Billy looked good, just like he always did when he was going out. He was thirty three, single and had lost about twenty five pounds since he got the insurance money.

"The man is partying hard." Paul said out loud to no one since he was alone. "Well, the party is over."

The time delayed fragmentation anti-personnel hand grenade is the most common type of grenade used in all wars since WWII. It has a chemical delay mechanism and is surrounded by explosive material. Most people think you just pull the safety pin on a grenade and count to three then throw it in the direction you want it blow up. Simply put, that's about right but actually pulling the pin is just step one. The actual firing mechanism is triggered by a spring loaded striker inside the grenade.

Now, the striker is held in place by the striker lever on the outside of the grenade which is held firm by the safety pin. So, once the safety pin is removed there is nothing to hold the striker lever in place unless you keep your hand on the lever tight against the grenade. Once you let go and toss it, the striker hits the percussion cap which ultimately ignites the detonator. Boom.

Paul, who had many ways of killing someone at his disposal, never liked the up close and personal approach if it could be avoided. Too many things could go wrong and too many chances to leave valuable evidence behind.

Besides, Paul always felt the punishment should fit the crime and in this extremely heinous crime Billy Burk's punishment should be as extreme. Paul could easily get out of the SUV and just throw the grenade at Billy's feet. If the grenade landed perfectly Billy would most likely die from the explosion or be severely maimed. But, what if the fuse was a second or two late or Paul tossed it too early in his haste to retreat. Billy could escape with minimal damage, even unscathed, and not only would Billy be alarmed someone was trying to kill him, but he would have a good idea who was behind it.

Paul lifted the small but powerful binoculars up and placed them to his eyes, then audibly gasped. Someone else was with Billy. Paul shot upright in the seat and dropped the glasses in his lap not believing what he had just seen.

"Oh shit!" He said. "He never went out with someone on Wednesday night. He came back with someone but never went out."

Paul thought of the grenade duct taped right below the steering wheel in Billy Burk's expensive new car. It had been so simple and easy to install. Quickly, with a Slim Jim down the outside of the window to unlock the door then enter the car without slamming the door, and turn off the interior lights. Maybe fifteen seconds. Firmly tape the grenade under the steering wheel, then attach a precut wire coat hanger to the inside door handle and crimping it tight. Now, move across to the passenger seat and take the other end of the coat hanger and carefully hook the curved end, which just reaches, around the safety pin on the grenade. Relock the doors as you exit out the passenger door. Oh yeah, before leaving the vehicle, remove two pint sized glass bottles filled with gasoline and place them right below the driver's seat.

Paul reached for the door handle when he saw the person was definitely with Billy Burk. A pretty, sexy, blonde kissed Billy and they lingered at his car for more groping. Billy's hand slipped down into her tight jeans and he squeezed her ass. There was no way Paul could let this innocent, young girl be killed. He would have to intervene before Billy opened his car door. He watched as they continue to kiss and Billy's hands roamed all over the girl's body from one end to the other in quick succession. Ass, tits, crotch and that's when she broke free with a shy smile. Paul put the binoculars back to his eyes and saw the girl shake her head then glance at her watch.

"Yeah, next time you get more asshole, only thing is there isn't going to be a next time." Paul whispered.

Billy Burk laughed and the girl turned away.

Paul watched with one hand holding the glasses and the other hand on the door handle. If he had to he would shout something to Billy, and call him away from the car. He would bust his balls even piss him off or if he had to pick a fight with him. Anything, he had to do to keep Billy from opening that door if the girl went to the passenger side.

The girl walked to the other side of the car and just when it looked like she was going to get in, she moved across the parking lot to another car. She hit the key fob in her hand, the lights came on, and the doors unlocked; but before she could open the door, Billy shouted something about her ass and she laughed.

By this time, Paul was already out of his SUV and Billy glanced up at him when the interior lights came on. Billy was far enough away from Paul that despite the lights coming on he didn't recognize him since he was dressed in a large camouflage jacket and had a black ball cap pulled down over his eyes. The girl turned back as Billy unlocked his door, opened it, slid into the driver's seat and closed the door. It took about five seconds.

The door, the hanger, the safety pin and the striker handle. Oh yeah, and the gas too.

CHAPTER TWO

Andersson had already been at the scene for over thirty minutes when Stefani got there, and he wasn't happy. They were both called at the same time, Andersson a minute before Stefani. Stefani actually lived ten minutes closer than Andersson, but still she was late. It was cold for North Carolina, fifty degrees, and he was lucky to have a hot cup of fresh coffee to sip on while he waited.

Nicklaus Andersson was smart, tough, well-disciplined and he was the lead investigator, a lieutenant by rank, in the North Carolina State Police, who worked directly for the Governor. A former Army Ranger and only in his mid-forties, he was second generation Swede and looked every bit of it. A Viking without the horned helmet and razor sharp sword. Rather impressive at over six feet, he was well muscled and carried a large caliber Glock instead of the sword.

He pulled out his cell phone and was about to call Stefani when he saw her red Corvette fly by and land in the next parking space. Andersson took another gulp of the still warm coffee and got out of his Hummer H3. This is going to be good, he thought.

"Sorry I'm late, Nicklaus." Stefani apologized, as she walked quickly toward him.

"You got the fastest car in the state and you live ten minutes from here and you're thirty minutes late," he said taking another sip of coffee. "Lucky for you I have some of Hank's special coffee otherwise I'd really be pissed."

Without a word of defense, Stefani stood there and let Andersson scold her. At five-ten and over six feet with her always have on, trademark high heels, she was breathtakingly beautiful.

The police flood lights were up and on full blast so the parking lot looked like the middle of the day. Several people were milling about the burned out wreckage of what once looked like a car. The thick, acrid smell of blurt flesh and bone hung in the air. A fire truck was still standing by just in case.

Andersson looked at Stefani in anticipation of one of her smart come backs to his rebuke but none came. She had on a skin tight black pair of leggings and matching long sleeved top, also skin tight, a black leather motorcycle jacket and stilettos. She also had full makeup on but her brunette hair looked mussed up, as if she had just got out of bed, but hadn't been sleeping.

Andersson smiled at her. He just couldn't be mad at Stefani, well, not for long. Even though he wasn't old enough to be her father, he often thought of her as another daughter.

"Celebrating with Hank?" He asked with a grin.

She nodded shyly. "It's been a year for us since we met. He made me dinner and I had some champagne. We were in bed and..."

Quickly, Andersson put his hand up. "I get it! I get it!"

"I just couldn't leave him like that, Nicklaus..."

"I get it, Roxanne," he repeated and they walked to where what was left of Billy Burk was being photographed by one of Dr. Breshay Abisi's forensic assistants.

"Shay, thanks for waiting to remove the remains until Roxanne got here," Andersson said as they approached.

Shay Abisi was a forensic pathologist and Chief Medical Examiner for Wake County. Originally from Kenya, she was a classic representative of that African culture. She was exotically beautiful with high cheeks bones, six feet tall and extremely thin.

"I wouldn't dream of letting Investigator Stefani miss out on this one," she replied as she stepped back from the open car door and revealed what was left of the interior. The smell of char and gasoline were so pungent it made you gag. You could also still feel the heat from the horrific fire.

"Go ahead and take a look inside," Andersson said, stepping back to allow Stefani access.

The interior of the car was completely gutted and was totally blackened from the flames and intense heat. It was merely a burned out shell of what was once a plush, finely appointed cabin of a very expensive automobile. Everything that could burn was gone, incinerated, the little that remained was melted and outlined in its previous shape, and that included Billy Burk.

"Is that all that's left of the victim?" Stefani asked, standing up from a crouch.

"That's all that's left of Billy Burk," Shay said. "If you want to call Billy Burk a victim. We won't know one hundred percent it's him until we do some DNA testing. I don't think what's left of his jaw and teeth are enough to use for a positive identification. The heat was so hot it nearly cremated him. We do know the vehicle is licensed to him."

They all looked inside the car at the crispy, blackened figure which had been reduced in size by half and was beginning to curl up. Billy's arms and legs looked like he was trying to tuck himself into a small ball, but he was long dead before this curling phenomenon occurred.

"He's fused to the seat from the blast and fire." Shay stated with a hint of awe in her voice which was rare.

"Any idea yet what caused the explosion?" Andersson asked. "A pipe bomb?"

Shay shook her head. "Not sure, but it could have been a pipe style device, whatever it was it was inside the vehicle and not under it."

Andersson looked at the floor of the car which was still intact and noticed the huge hole in the steering column.

"Something was attached to the steering wheel huh?"

"Yes, something very powerful..." Shay began when they were approached by a deputy.

"We're doing a canvas of the neighbors, the apartments and surrounding buildings. See if anyone saw anything," he informed.

Andersson looked around the back of the apartment complex and out to the street in a wide circle.

"I don't see any cameras, do you?" He asked the deputy.

"No sir, not in the immediate area," he replied. "I checked too and we're going to look across the street at some of the businesses on the block which face the parking lot."

"Good idea," Andersson said turning back to the car and the deputy walked away.

Andersson bent over and stared into the car for a long time as if he was looking for something.

"What?" Stefani asked when he finally straightened up.

"This car is parked in plain view where everyone can see it," Andersson began and pointed as he spoke. "I don't see someone spending a lot of time wiring an explosive device to the ignition or setting something up with a timer."

"How about a remote detonator using a cell phone?" Stefani offered.

"It's possible," Shay said. "Wait for the victim to get into the car and then trigger the bomb."

"That's a good idea and a favorite trick of terrorists too," Andersson said. "but the person would have to have electrical knowledge and be able to assemble a fairly sophisticated unit."

"We'll have the ATF take a look and the FBI too if we find any pieces of wiring or a timer," Andersson said. "They're both great at putting back together or telling us the origin of any kind of bomb ever made."

Andersson looked carefully at the car doors. "This vehicle is so well built that the reinforced doors kept most of the explosion inside the car," He said walking around to the passenger side with Stefani and Abisi in tow. "See how both doors bulged and of course all the windows blew out but a great deal of the explosive force stayed contained which was directed at the victim."

"So it had to be timed to go off the moment he got in and closed the door," Shay said.

"That means the timer concept is out but the remote control detonation is still possible," Stefani said.

"The remote control is possible, but I'm thinking booby trap," Andersson finally concluded.

"You mean something with a trip wire?" Stefani said, going in Andersson's direction. "Billy gets into the car and somehow he trips a wire when he sits down behind the steering wheel."

"Yes, that could work," Shay agreed with a smile.

"It could, but the best way for a booby trap bomb to go off is make it so the victim doesn't know it's a booby trap until it's too late." Anderrson said. "He might have spotted the wire before he sat down or what if he didn't strike the wire just right with his body."

"That's true." Stefani said, her mind whirling with ideas. "How about if somehow it was wired to the door and that started the triggering process."

Andersson smiled. "That's what I'm thinking and it's exactly one of the ways we learned to improvise a bomb in the military."

"…And how was that?" Shay asked.

"A grenade." Andersson replied.

"A grenade! Yes!" Stefani said. "Very simple, easy to use and install."

"But how did he rig it so Billy pulled the safety pin?" Shay asked confused.

Andersson went back around to the driver's side of the car and the two women followed him.

"He wired it so when he opened the door the safety pin was pulled and by the time Billy slid in and sat down, he was gone. Maybe four or five seconds …"

"Boom!" Shay said excitedly. "It's brilliant!"

"I'm sure it was very quick to set up too," Andersson said. "Not more than a couple of minutes."

"So it could be someone with a military background," Stefani said.

"Maybe, or someone who just knows the booby trap business," Andersson said, moving out of the way so the forensic team could try and remove as much of Billy's remains as they could while still keeping him intact.

"I'll be doing the post first thing in the morning," Shay said to her assistants as they moved the gurney next to the car.

"Let's see what the canvas turns up," Andersson said. "Maybe someone saw something that could help us."

"How hard are we going to look for the person who did this?" Stefani asked bluntly. "After all, the victim is Billy Burk."

Andersson nodded knowingly. "Hard enough. I want to make sure someone's not suddenly tying up loose ends and they're starting with Billy Burk and going down a list."

"Then I better pull Reynolds and Culpepper in to start checking on the streets," Stefani said, stepping further back from the car as the assistants began to remove Billy. "They can find out if any-one has been talking about the case recently or looking to buy a grenade."

"Good idea and get Harper going on Billy's background too." Andersson said as he glanced at Billy Burk being moved onto the stretcher noting the sharp contrast of the stark white sheets against the horridly burned body. "Let's make a list of anyone directly involved in the case and what everyone has been doing the last few months, including our late friend here."

Andersson, Stefani and Abisi watched as the assistants fin-ished arranging what look like burnt meat into something more to resemble what was once a human being.

"It'll be a long time before I eat another toasted marshmal-low," Stefani said, as they covered Billy and moved him to the nearby van.

CHAPTER THREE

Kira Lake had been a successful corporate attorney for five years after she graduated from law school and had passed the bar. She was super smart, super ambitious and superhot. She also knew how to use all three of those assets to their fullest extent.

Pushing past thirty-five, three years ago, Kira realized two things, make that three things. One, life was boring on the straight and narrow, two, money, a lot of money, made things better, and three, knowing she had an outstanding body, beat one and two by a mile.

Changing careers and becoming a literary agent and legal counsel to those who could write books was not only more interesting than corporate law but made her a very good living. She had a small stable of successful authors who wrote mostly murder mysteries or light romance novels. She also handled a few writers who wrote self-help and cooking books but those were authors she gained when she first began and held on to them.

Kira had lived in New York City for years and adored the big city, non-stop lifestyle, but two years ago she moved back to Raleigh, North Carolina. Born and raised in Raleigh, she could now divided her time between the fast business of New York and the more genteel charm of her southern roots. She felt happier these last couple of years, but she still felt restless. She was always restless for more life and especially for more money.

Never married and with no kids, she enjoyed dating as many men as she could and often was juggling two or three at the same time. For Kira, in Raleigh, it was older, very successful men, one on the way in and one on the way out. In New York she kept her boy toy far away from prying eyes.

Now, though, Kira was crowding forty and she knew people, especially in Raleigh, were talking. In a way, Kira was glad they were talking about her. It made her feel important and she knew most of the talk stemmed from jealousy. She also knew the names they called her. The names people whisper about any woman who had not been married or had a child. Lesbo, dike, old maid, tough bitch, even slut and worse. Did it bother Kira? Fuck no! Nothing bothered Kira except making sure her ass was tight enough to bounce a quarter on it!

Today, she felt wonderful, and she wasn't going to let anyone spoil it despite the fact she was meeting with her most success-ful, but least favorite client, Henry Harris. Henry wasn't rude or insensitive and physically, he was just average height, weight with a bland appearance. He was someone you would probably walk by a dozen times a day and not even notice. The quote "larger than life" was Henry in complete opposite. He wasn't even there, at least not in reality, but, on paper, in print, he was amazing be-cause he wrote under another name, Gina Wells.

As Gina Wells, Henry wrote sexy, trashy books for females from a female perspective and women loved them! Kira called Henry's sexual writing style, sleaze with ease. Now, Henry as

Henry would make any woman's skin crawl but when he wrote as Gina Wells, his books were sold with a pair of oven mitts.

He just had a way with the openly sexual genre. He did porno for women on paper. Sex with a beautiful story and Henry as Gina Wells had the erotic view of sex that a woman would have if a woman was writing the books. Kira knew this the moment she read the first chapter of his first book. In fact, she often said, he had her at the first page, but she had to change his identity and create Gina Wells.

With six smut filled novels to his credit, and no one knowing Gina Wells was actually a man, both Kira and Henry made money. They weren't breaking any world sales records but the number of units sold were steady and over the years, Gina Wells had gathered a loyal following. Gina Wells could keep turning out stories about sweet soccer moms by day who prowled for young men at night or who would find it exciting to sleep with her husband's boss to get him that promotion. Whatever the topic, if Gina Wells penned it, it sold.

Kira always wore the same type of outfit when she had to meet with Henry. Pants, loose and shapeless as possible, a long sleeved blouse buttoned up to her neck and a blazer. The shoes had to be flats and she wore the only pair she owned, she normally wore were high heels. She hated to dress like this but she had no choice. Henry had X-ray eyes and if she could, Kira would have worn lead lined underwear. Henry didn't just undress her with his eyes, he literally had sex with her over and over with his eyes.

Henry was a creeper. A watcher. A sneaky peeper. Henry's that one weird guy who lives in the neighborhood and why you keep your blinds down at night. But, Henry was really harmless and as Gina Wells he had a channel for his sexual thoughts. An outlet that kept him in check, all except for Kira. Nothing could stop his desires for Kira, it was her leverage over him and she knew it. A way to control him and more importantly, a way to keep him under those lucrative contracts. As the door opened, she took in a deep breath and forced her best smile.

"Henry!" She cooed as her stomach heaved. "It's so nice to see you again!"

Henry smiled shyly at her greeting and for a second his smile waned when he saw what she was wearing.

"Sit down, Henry." She said, nudging him away from her toward one of the Stickley chairs. "What's the matter? Aren't you happy to see me?"

Henry flopped down in the chair like a school boy in the principal's office and set the worn brown briefcase down on the floor beside him.

"I'm always happy to see you Kira," he said, staring at her. "I just liked it better when you wore those short skirts and sexy high heels. You were my muse for much of my work. Now, all you wear are baggy pants and those ugly blazers."

"Henry, now, don't mince words. Just tell me how you feel" Kira said, flashing her big smile.

"I'm not mincing my words, Kira!" Henry replied, gripping the arms of the chair so tight his knuckles were turning white. "I was right to the point!"

"I'm sorry, Henry, I was just trying to make a joke." Kira said, as she retreated to the safety behind her desk. "It's just that I've been diagnosed with iron deficiency and lately I'm so cold all the time."

"Oh my god!" Henry cried. "I'm so sorry. I didn't know you were ill. How insensitive of me."

Kira sat down behind her desk and waved him off. "Don't be silly. I've started on some iron pills and I should be fine in no time. I see the doctor in a couple of months for a recheck of my levels."

"Oh thank god you're going to be all right!"

Kira was lying but she didn't care. She wasn't going to have visual sex with Henry no matter what it took.

"Well, I hope when you're better you start to dress more appropriately for me, or should I say more inappropriately, and he licked his thick upper lip several times. Kira watched transfixed on his tongue as it swept back and forth across his lip like a windshield wiper blade. Back and forth. Back and forth. She couldn't tell if he was licking up his excess salvia to prevent drooling or he was demonstrating his his tongues performance for her.

"So, Henry, I must say you're last book did very well and you should clear around six hundred thousand."

"I don't care about that anymore, Kira." Henry said, relaxing his grip on the chair with a loud, long, exasperated exhale.

"You don't care about making money anymore, Henry?" Kira asked, as her heart began to race.

She wished now she had worn the short skirt after all. "I'm not sure I understand."

Henry slapped the sides of the chair sharply twice and it scared her. Kira always wondered if he would have his big meltdown in front of her and as she watched him act out, she hoped it wasn't going to be today.

"I'm sick and tired of writing that trash!" Henry said flatly.

"But why Henry?" Kira said softly, eyeing her cell phone sitting on her desk as she calculated how fast she could call 911 and run out of the door. "You do such a wonderful job and all those women adore you for it."

"They all adore Gina Wells!" Henry said, as his eyes grew darker and his eyebrows furrowed into one sinister line across his forehead. "I'm done with being Gina Wells!"

"But, Henry, she's the MILF's MILF! Just think of Gina Wells as the star in a play and you're acting her part." Kira said, as she fiddled with the cell phone.

Henry stood up and when Kira thought he was going to lunge at her, she grabbed her cell phone but before she could call for help, he suddenly stopped. For a few seconds they stared at each other.

"Henry, are you okay?" She asked in a soft whisper. "Henry?"

"Yes, I'm fine," he finally said. "But I'm totally done, finished and over with being Gina Wells."

Kira took in a deep breath, let it out slowly as she watched Henry sit back down. The room was eerily quiet for about thirty seconds.

"So, Henry. Now that you've made that major decision," she began hesitantly, as she set the cell phone back down on the desk. "What's next?"

When Kira asked that simple question, Henry's demeanor had gone from agitated to elation as if someone had flipped an emotional switch.

"Next?" he repeated. "Next, is my first manuscript by Henry Harris; what did you think Kira, that I would cease to write? To slither away and never breathe again my very existence?"

"No, Henry, I didn't." Kira began with a small smile of hope.

Henry laughed and Kira thought it was the first time she had seen him really laugh. A happy laugh. Henry smiled at her many times and she had seen his creepy grin all too often, but never, I'm feeling good, laugh. "So Gina Wells is dead!" Kira blurted out without thinking of her choice of words. "I meant to say so you'll still write but under your own name."

"You're absolutely right on both counts, Kira," Henry said. "Gina Wells is dead and yes, I will write under my own name. In fact, I've been writing for quite some time under my own name."

"Oh?" Kira said surprised and even a bit offended. "I thought I was your agent Henry, and I haven't seen any of your other work."

Henry didn't really need an agent since most of his Gina Well's novels were uploaded to a website and purchased from there. Henry crossed his legs and folded his hands in his lap.

This was his good little boy posture Kira had seen many times. It was Henry's I've-pleased-you-position.

"Of course Kira, it's all been unpublished." Henry said with a smirk. "I wouldn't dare think of working with another agent behind your back."

Kira sat back in her chair with a satisfied look on her face. Once again she was back in control of Henry Harris. For a terrifying minute or two she thought she had lost him and a great deal of her affluent livelihood. She watched as he carefully removed a thick stack of papers from his briefcase.

"This is it, Kira." Henry gushed another rare, wide, happy, smile. "My first Henry Harris novel and this book I want to see lined twenty hard covers wide in every major book store in the country! No! The world!"

Henry stood up and presented the manuscript to Kira with a slight bow. "I can't wait for you to tell me what you think," he said, as he laid the stack of paper down in front of her and sat back down.

When Henry leaned over her desk, Kira caught a whiff of him. She never was quite sure of his odor. It wasn't quite mildew or moldy smelling, but rather earthy, like patchouli. Whatever it was, it wasn't working for her and in fact, tended to make her nauseous.

"Well, Henry that looks quite ambitious," Kira said, staring down at the tall pile of paper looming up at her. "It's what, four hundred pages?"

"Four hundred and thirty-eight to be exact. About one hundred and forty thousand words, give or take." He replied proudly.

Kira could still smell the patchouli like scent coming off the paper from Henry's hands.

"I want you to start it tonight and let me know first thing in the morning how much you like it." Henry said confidently, and almost singing the words. "I can't wait. I wish I could sit right here while you read the entire book!"

Kira cringed at the very thought of having Henry in her office for even five more minutes let alone all afternoon.

"Henry I'd love to have you sit right there and watch me read your manuscript," she said as she felt the all too familiar twinges of a migraine percolating behind her left eye. Soon she would be nauseous, even more than she was already. "But I have several meetings this afternoon which I absolutely cannot reschedule."

"Oh I know, Kira," Henry said, in a pout. "You're always so busy."

Kira stood up and with the burning pain surging in her left eye came out from behind her desk. "I promise I'll start the first Henry Harris book tonight and I double promise to call you first thing in the morning."

Henry stood up as Kira grabbed his arm, lifted him out of the chair and pulled him toward the door.

"So until then my favorite author, enjoy your day." Kira said, opened the door and kissed him on the cheek. "That's goodbye from me."

In disbelief, Henry touched the spot on his cheeks where Kira had kissed him and hardly noticed she had pushed him out the door.

Kira quickly wiped her lips on her sleeve and tried to forget the kiss, but it was all too late. The pain her in left eye was pounding like a burly railroad crew rhythmically hammering spikes. Slam. Slam. Slam. One after another. The nausea was overwhelming now and too late for a migraine pill. Only one thing left to do Kira knew. Purge. She ran to her private bathroom, closed the door, assumed the position and began to vomit.

That evening, around 11:00pm, with her migraine gone and after leaving Henry's manuscript outside in the cool air to rid it of the last of his smell, Kira snuggled down in her bed to read.

It was 3:00am when she took her first break and noticed the time. God! Where had she been? Four hours of reading Henry's manuscript and she had been totally absorbed from the first page. It was amazing! The best work she had ever read even compared to all the great works. Every word, sentence and paragraph were crafted into a story unlike any before. The characters were so real with a twisting hypnotic plot that gently but completely pulled the reader in until you were part of the story. An observer watching real life.

Kira was physically exhausted but mentally she wanted more of Henry's story. He had captured a woman's modern day struggle without the cheesy, predictable aspect of a romance novel. Henry's insight was brilliant as if he were that woman in the book. Kira had set the manuscript aside and shook her head in disbelief. How could someone like Henry write something like that? Something so delicate yet powerful and then fragile at the same time. An updated version of Gone with the Wind, Kira said to herself as her diabolical mind churned. She looked over at the pile of paper and thought; "I should have written that!" She had always wanted to write something like that! Besides, she lived that book and it was really her he was writing about.

Kira smiled to herself as her evil mind came out from hiding and she reached for her cell phone.

"Chris? It's Kira," she said softly.

"It's 3:00 am, Kira," Chris said, waking up. "Are you okay?"

"I'm fine, baby. Never been better," she replied with a rasp in her voice. "But, mommy's got an itch that needs scratching. Are you alone?"

"Of course I'm alone," he replied knowing what she wanted. "Who would I be with when I got you?"

Chris Fields was ten years younger than Kira and constructed like a male underwear model. The kind you see on a six story high billboard in Times Square. Handsome face, twelve pack abs, and no need to airbrush in anything between his legs. Chris already had the obvious, big bulge nicely tucked in those latest designer briefs.

"Oh, I can think of a dozen beautiful, young women off hand who would love to be in your bed right now," Kira moaned, as she slid her hand down into her panties. She always kept her nails long and filed round at the tips and never with any sharp edges. "Tell mommy how her bad boy wants her."

And Chris began ten minutes of dirty talk just the way Kira loved it.

"That's it baby, hurt mommy so good with that big dick..." Kira cooed as her long index fingernail rubbed the pea in the pod. "I'm almost home."

CHAPTER FOUR

The wedding was a month away and Roxanne had everything all set. Usually a wedding took a good year of planning in advance but Roxanne did it in six months. Of course, she had plenty of help from her mom and money wasn't an issue. The real key to success with planning a wedding is keeping the guest list short. Hank wanted around one hundred people but they whittled it down to sixty. It was going to be simple yet elegant and it would be in Raleigh. The overseas destinations to Europe or a tropical island were the vogue, but Roxanne and Hank wanted to keep the traveling to a minimum. Neither Hank's parents or Roxanne's needed to be impressed. They were all down to earth, hard working people.

It's Hank's second marriage and Roxanne's first. Hank's only sibling, a sister who had become close to Roxanne over the last six months, would be her maid of honor. Hank's daughter, Maggie and Shay Abisi would be bride's maids. Hank had a roommate from college standing up as his best man. Roxanne had never met him but she was fine with his choice since Hank picked Nicklaus and Nicklaus's son as ushers. Nicklaus would partner with Shay and his son with Hank's daughter.

The marriage would be a civil union followed by a Catholic blessing and mass. They had secured a beautiful, old fashioned, Southern hotel with a grand ballroom for the reception. Everyone would have plenty of room, an incredible variety of cuisines, and a big, roomy dance floor. Roxanne's wedding dress, the photographers, limos, flowers and even the cake were all ordered. Everything was all set, in place and ready to go.

Roxanne was never happier nor so sure of any decision she ever made in her life. She wanted to be Mrs. Hank Milson. She just needed to know one thing. Who shot Shadow? She already knew the answer to the question that kept nagging at her from that very day, she knew it wasn't her father. It had to have been Hank and she just needed to hear the words come out of his mouth. This was the one i that needed dotting.

Her father Rocco was an FBI agent and the agent in charge of the Raleigh office. He could have been much higher on the ladder of success but he was satisfied at the rung he was standing on. He was well respected within the law enforcement communities and Roxanne knew he was an extremely capable man, but given all that; he still did not make that shot. Rocco Stefani was an excellent marksman with pistols of various makes and calibers. He was also very good with a rifle, especially since Hank had designed, converted and hand built a Weatherby .300 into a premier sniper rifle.

Roxanne had asked Hank several times in conversations about that day on the roof of the hospital where he worked and every time Hank cleverly sidestepped the real answer. He held firm to the official version which was Rocco Stefani had made the shot that saved her life as well as the lives of Andersson, an FBI agent and the agent's undercover operative.

A few other people in law enforcement, including Andersson, wondered about the shot that saved the day and how anyone could have made that shot in the first place. If Rocco Stefani, a well-known, highly decorated, agent with an impeccable record said he made the shot, then Rocco Stefani made the shot. It was as simple as that and call it; case closed. Which it officially had been since shortly after it happened.

Roxanne didn't want to threaten Hank or somehow make him feel she didn't trust him or that he would intentionally lie to her. At least not lie without some very special reason. That wasn't what she wanted between them now and especially in their upcoming marriage. She had loved Hank from the moment she met him and he had that same instant attraction to her as well. It was a one in a million chance encounter you only hear about, and that's if you're lucky, once in your life. Its two people meeting and everything around them stops as their minds, bodies and souls meld into one being from that moment forward. That's how crazy in love these two people were with each other, inseparable and totally absorbed. Still, Roxanne would have the answer and then, as she often thought about after Hank told her, more questions.

Roxanne was on time this morning for the autopsy on Billy Burk, in fact, she was early and so was Andersson.

"Good morning, Nicklaus," Roxanne said, brightly as they met outside the autopsy room.

"Well, good morning," he replied opening the door for her. "Looks like you finally got some sleep."

"Thank you," she said, passing through the doorway. "Right after we finished up last night, I went straight home and right to bed."

Andersson smiled but did not say anything else and the two of them walked into the room.

"Perfect timing!" Shay Abisi said as she took a big bite out of a large, freshly fried, scratch donut. "I wanted to get started early!"

"Oh god!" Roxanne whispered to Andersson. "She's back on the donuts!"

"Easy, Roxanne," Andersson said, smelling the burnt flesh combined with the smell of the greasy donut. "Just hang back from the table and breathe through your mouth."

Roxanne who had been through many autopsies always struggled with the smells, but nothing made it worse than when Shay ate one of those heavy, fried cakes. It just gagged her.

"Come on over," Shay said, waving the donut at them. "There's something interesting I want to show you."

Andersson and Stefani moved up to the autopsy table where Shay and two of her assistants were stationed. The two assistants, standing on the far side of the table were both clad in the usual protection suits complete with heavy rubber gloves and face shields. Shay, without any protective gear, was standing on the other side of the table and holding that stupid donut like a conductors baton waving it over the burnt corpse of Billy Burk. Andersson moved up closer to Shay and Stefani stayed behind him.

"Now, the fire department was there at the scene about six or seven minutes after someone called it in," Shay began. "A good response time and under some other set of circumstances with a routine car fire, they would have easily put it out in no time."

Shay stopped, took a big bite of the donut and chewed for a minute.

"I have to eat my donut now with you two here," she said between chews. "The ATF and FBI agents will be here at ten and I don't want to be eating my donut in front of them. Anyway, as I was saying, this fire was superhot and as you can see by this crusty, blackened skin and subcutaneous tissue, Billy boy was hit as if with a giant blow torch. Plus, and I'll know for sure once I open him up, that his lungs were liquefied from the concussive blast."

"Did you find any metal fragments embedded in him?" Andersson asked.

Shay held up her hand with the remaining half of the donut ready for another bite.

"Yes, we did and I'm sure we'll find more pieces of metal once we cut away the rest of this char," She replied."

"It was grenade wasn't it?" Andersson asked eagerly.

Shay nodded as she chewed, unable to reply and Stefani inhaled some of vapor rub she had smeared under her nose.

"You were right," Shay replied after swallowing. "Some of the small bits of metal look consistent with a grenade and I think whoever did this also put some liquid soap with the gasoline to make it stick to whatever it hit."

"Another old trick," Andersson said knowingly. "A poor man's napalm."

"Exactly," Shay said, as she contemplated her remaining piece of donut. "We'll see if the ATF or maybe the FBI can determine what era the grenade came from. Some of these babies can go off no matter how old they are, even ones from Viet Nam or as far back as World War II."

"Great!" Stefani said. "I hope he doesn't have any more of these lying around anywhere."

"Thanks, Shay." Andersson said, turning to leave. "We would appreciate it if you'll send to us a full report when you're done."

"Just like always, Nicklaus." Shay replied with a smile and began to suit up.

Andersson and Stefani left and stood outside in the fresh air for a few minutes.

"You want to get some breakfast before we go in?" Andersson asked.

Stefani thought for a few seconds. "Sure," she replied. "Anything but donuts."

CHAPTER FIVE

Kira Lake slept in for the first time in years and sleeping in for Kira was 6:00 a.m. She was usually up at 4:30 a.m., worked out, showered, and was in her office by 6:30 a.m.. This morning was different. Not only had Chris, her boyfriend, relaxed her twice, but she also read more of Henry Harris's new novel before she finally passed out.

Stepping out of the shower, she glanced at the time. It was 8:30 a.m. and she had better call the office and tell her staff she was on the way. Otherwise, if she wasn't there sitting behind her desk barking orders when they all got in they would be calling the police in a panic.

She had just finished toweling off and she still couldn't get Henry's manuscript out of her mind. She was about to reach for her cell phone when lit up. It was her work.

"Good morning," she answered, then calmly listened for a moment to the relieved voice on the other end. "Yes, I'm fine."

More questions from the caller.

"No, nothing's wrong," Kira replied, as she admired her nude body in the large bathroom mirror. "No, no car trouble either, I just stayed up late last night and I felt like sleeping in this morning."

Kira listened to the shock and disbelief as she turned around to check out her ass.

"I know, it's not like me at all and I'm glad you called me to see if I was alright," she said, turning back with a satisfied smile. Her ass still looked great and no noticeable changes since she last viewed it yesterday. "I should be in about thirty minutes."

Kira hung up and her thoughts returned to Henry's manuscript, then she had an idea; a life changing idea. Suddenly, she was laughing uncontrollably.

Dr. Hank Milson had just finished making his hospital rounds on the small number of patients that remained in his practice. Hank loved being an Oncologist and loved to see patients as well, but after discovering Pulminab, which was a cure for most lung cancers, he had accumulated enormous wealth.

He had continued with cancer research, and tried to see patients all the while he was in an ongoing litigation with a powerful tobacco company who was marketing his cure as a way for people to continue to smoke. Not only could people continue to smoke but it was felt that Pulminab acted as a prevention to getting lung cancer.

Hank would never have made such a deal with a them but at the time he got involved with the research company that was funding the project, he was unaware they had also made the tobacco company a partner.

The slow, time consuming legal process was going nowhere and Hank had had enough. He needed more time for his newly formed research company, which was run on a day to day basis by his former head nurse in Oncology, Karen Mellow. Karen was smart and held a Master's degree in Nursing and business. She was hard working and dedicated to the same ideals as Hank. She also agreed they were fighting a very steep, uphill and most likely unwinnable battle.

Hank was about to leave the office and head to Rocco Stefani's gun range where they had been meeting at least once a week for several hours. Rocco was determined to improve his long distance marksmanship. He had practiced and had improved especially at the distances up to a thousand yards. Beyond that distance, he still had a lot more work to do. He knew he would never be in Hank's class but he still needed to try to reach his personal best. On the other hand, Hank's previously non existent handgun skills had greatly improved. Hank also knew he would never rise to the world class level of his soon to be wife, Roxanne.

Hank opened the door to leave just as the phone on his desk rang. It was his outside line and he thought since he was already late he would let the machine pick it up. He walked out, turned around, went back in and answered it.

"Hank Milson," he said.

It was his friend, Luis, from Guatemala calling about his father who had been a patient of Hanks with prostate cancer. The friend's father was diagnosed many years ago and had had a successful, robotic prostatectomy in New York City, which Hank had arranged. The father had done well since the surgery and did not require any further treatment, he was being closely monitored by an local Oncologist in Guatemala.

The father was a very successful coffee grower and also owned a processing plant which distributed his coffee to specialized markets worldwide. One of the best coffees, if not the best he produced, sold for over fifty dollars a pound was shipped to Hank on a monthly basis. Hank's access to this prized coffee was well known in his circle of friends and had been the cause of some good natured banter between Roxanne and Nicklaus. Hank could now easily purchase the coffee but Luis insisted the free shipments continue indefinitely.

"So his PSA levels have been creeping up..." Hank repeated. "...and they can't find any source of the cancer with scanning?"

Luis told Hank they had done a bone scan and PET-CT which were all negative. They also did a special more sensitive scan that was specific for finding any prostate cancer within the body and that was negative.

"The Oncologist is right, he's probably having a bio chemical relapse and although the PSA is rising they can't find the source of the cancer activity."

The friend asked if there was anything they should consider doing in the United States. The Oncologist in Guatemala suggested either watchful waiting with continued monitoring of the patient and the PSA or starting on a hormone therapy to block the production of testosterone. Neither of the options, in this particular instance, has been proven by science to be a better choice than the other.

The friend's father, who was very active and fit, had decided to keep an eye on the PSA every three months and deal with those results.

"It's a very acceptable approach especially if your father doesn't want to experience any potential side effects of the hormone blocking agent," Hank offered. "Of course, in the future, if he developed symptoms or the PSA kept rising he would need repeat testing and perhaps treatment."

Luis agreed and was satisfied he had gotten in touch with Hank for his second opinion.

"He seems like he's in good hands there in Guatemala," Hanks assured. "I don't see any need for him to come to the United States."

Hank and his friend went on to talk about their private lives for another fifteen minutes, and when they got done, Hank had invited Luis and his wife to the wedding. Two more guests to the list. When Hank was finally able to end the call, he called Rocco right away.

"You're late buddy," Rocco said first thing when he saw Hank's number come up on his phone. "Are you afraid I'm getting better thank you with the .300?"

Hank laughed, he and Rocco had become very close friends, especially since the shooting. They were so comfortable with each other they often talked like college roommates instead of soon to be in laws.

"I don't think I have to worry about that happening for the next fifty or sixty years."

Rocco laughed and Hank went on to tell him about the call from his friend.

"If his father is the guy who sends you that coffee we all love, call him back and talk to him for another hour. We don't want to do anything to upset him."

"That's what I thought too when I knew I was going to be late, and besides Luis needed to be reassured."

"Well, get here when you can," Rocco concluded. "I'll be practicing with my .300 and we can do some pistol time later..."

"Sounds good."

Hank and Rocco hung up and Hank's cell buzzed immediately, he laughed to himself thinking he was never going to get to the range today. It was Roxanne this time and the call was brief. She wanted to tell him she would be a little late tonight since she had a meeting in the afternoon about the Billy Burk case. Hank told her he was late meeting Rocco but was on his way and should be home at the usual time. Hank also told her about the phone call from Luis in Guatemala and inviting him and his wife to the wedding. He thought she would say something about the added guests but she didn't and in fact, was happy they were coming.

"I need to talk to you tonight, Hank." Roxanne said, seriously. "So let's plan on a later dinner, okay?"

"Sure. You sound serious," Hank said with a catch in his stomach. "Is everything okay?"

"If you mean between you and I, always…no matter what…" she replied. "I just need to ask you something and I want to do it in person."

"Okay, see you later," Hank replied, knowing what the question was and what his answer would be.

CHAPTER SIX

K ira had called Henry right after the call from her staff and that call to Henry had gotten her a lot of points. Henry told her that he hardly slept all night wondering what she thought of his manuscript. He also thought, knowing Kira, he would be calling her, but her phoning him first thing had him elated. Kira told Henry she loved the book and that she was going to read more at the office and call him around noon with an update. That sent Henry into orbit.

Kira did spend much of the morning reading through another hundred pages and finding Henry's manuscript, as hard as it was for her to believe, getting even better. She thought it was near perfect last night, but this morning she found it flawless and she had to have it. No matter what she had to do to get it; she had to have this book and call it her own.

At noon sharp, Kira called Henry and he picked up before the first ring had ended.

"Kira!" Henry said. "I can't breathe! Tell me! Please tell me you love it!"

"I love it, Henry!" Kira said and she meant it. "It's the best novel I've ever read and I'm not even finished!"

"Oh my god!" Henry swooned. "You're fucking kidding me, Kira! I mean I've never heard you say that about any book! Even books that made you a lot of money!"

"That's because I've never read anything so well written. It's a masterpiece, Henry. A true work of art that will not only be award winning, but will be a fantastic commercial success."

"You're fucking kidding me!"

"No, I'm not fucking kidding you and Henry when did you start saying the word fuck?" Kira asked pointedly. "I don't think I've ever heard you say that word."

"I just started Kira when you told me you loved my book!" Henry replied, dancing around his living room. "Somehow the word fuck came into my head!"

"Oh my Henry," Kira said, thinking how Freudian that was to her. "You're something!"

"I am Kira. I really am something."

Kira paused for a few beats.

"Kira?" Henry asked and stopped dancing. "You still there?"

"I'm here, Henry. "Kira finally said. "Why don't you come to my house this evening for dinner? I can read more of the book and we can discuss it afterward. Unless you already have some other plans, how does that sound?"

No reply.

"Henry?"

No reply.

"Henry are you okay?"

"I...I...can't even talk, Kira." Henry stammered. "I'm just so happy."

CHAPTER SEVEN

Andersson and Stefani skipped lunch since they had eaten at Binky's. Neither one of them were hungry and probably wouldn't eat again until dinner. Binky's was a small neighborhood place that Stefani had first gone to with Vanina. Vanina worked at the State Forensic Unit and lived about four blocks from Binky's.

Stefani and Vanina were out late one night for a bachelorette party, when late turned into early morning. Vanina was hungry and so was Stefani so she took them to Binky's. Nothing could beat Binky's homemade biscuit breakfast sandwiches. Everything and anything you could want for breakfast on a huge, crusty on the outside and fluffy on the inside biscuit. There was thick cut bacon, smoked ham, or sausage, even chorizo, if you wanted to spice things up, add a couple of eggs, any style and top it all off with thick cap of melted cheese. But eat a Binky's breakfast sandwich at your own risk because they were messy business especially if you were a rookie with that first bite. Many a dress, shirt or suit jacket were easily stained from the fall out. When Andersson and Stefani got to Binky's the place was already crowded so they ate in the car.

Next, they went to their office for a few hours, finished some paperwork and got ready for the meeting. When they got to the meeting, everyone was already there. Andersson and Stefani sat down next to Sergeant Craig Reynolds and his partner Jefferson Culpepper, the younger brother of the late Tom Culpepper who was killed in the line of duty. Although Jefferson was a new police officer, Craig Reynolds, who was the former partner of Tom's formed an immediate bond with Jefferson. Lilly Harper, who previously worked in Missing Persons and had helped Andersson and Stefani solve past cases, had become a State Police Officer at Andersson insistence. This small group made up an elite task force which worked very well together utilizing their special talents. Also at the meeting was Shay Abisi and two County Sherriff detectives, one male and the other female.

"I think everyone here knows the Billy Burk story," Andersson began as he walked to the front of the room. "So let's start the time line from right before Billy's car blew up and then we can move backwards into his life."

The male County investigator began.

"We interviewed the girl who was with Billy right before he got into his car, she witnessed the explosion. So far, what's she's told us has checked out. She had just met Billy at the gym the day before and knew nothing about his past, but she liked him and agreed to go out with him. She also told Billy upfront she wasn't going to sleep with him on the first date, or maybe not the second or third."

"Is that why she had her car there at his place?" Stefani asked.

"Yes," the female investigator replied. "She didn't want him coming to her place to pick her up and not have a vehicle of her own in case things went south"

"Smart girl," Lilly added.

"Right", the investigator agreed. "Anyway, she went to Billy's place but didn't go into his apartment.

Billy kissed her a couple of times in the parking lot. She was already getting a caution light with him but was still attracted to his bad boy side."

"Aren't we all," Lilly whispered to Stefani who smiled and nodded.

"Only thing with Billy was that bad boy side was the only side he had," Stefani whispered back.

The investigator continued. "The girl said she was originally going to go in Billy's car but changed her mind when he kissed her and began to grope her as well. She was walking to her car across the parking lot when Billy shouted something to her and she turned around."

"I'll bet you he said something about her ass…," Lilly whispered again to Stefani.

"Did she say what he said? Did she hear him?" Andersson asked.

The investigator smiled sheepishly. "It was something about her ass."

Lilly and Stefani bumped fists and they all laughed.

"So Billy shouts to her and she's about to get into her car when she turns back, but Billy's already opened the car door, slid into the driver's seat, and closed the door," the female investigator concludes.

The male investigator picks up. "The girl said the blast nearly knocked her off of her feet."

They all pictured that in their minds, then Andersson asked. "When the girl was walking to her car did she notice anyone else in the parking lot?" Andersson asked.

The male investigator shook his head. "No, the girl said it happened so fast and with Billy all over her before the bomb went off, she wasn't paying attention to the rest of the parking lot."

"What about the canvas in the neighborhood?" Stefani asked. "Did we get lucky there?"

"We got one hit on a lady who was looking out her bedroom window at Billy kissing the girl. She said the same thing the girl said up until the bomb went off, but she did notice a man had gotten out of his SUV at the end of the parking lot."

"Before or after the bomb went off?" Stefani interjected.

The investigator looked puzzled. "What do you mean?"

"Did the woman see the man get out of the vehicle before or after the bomb went off?"

Neither investigator knew the answer to that question.

"We don't know," the female admitted. "We'll have to go back, re-interview her, and see if she can remember."

"Please do," Stefani said. "Because if the man was already out of the vehicle, he might be less likely to be involved than if he was sitting in his vehicle and drove off after the bomb went off."

"Anyone, if not involved," Andersson stated. "would have at least gotten out of their vehicle to see what had happened, call 911 or even to see if anyone needed help."

"Either action, or both for that matter, didn't necessarily mean he was or wasn't involved," Stefani said. "But it's a small detail that needs answering."

"Since we're brainstorming, there's another possible angle on why the man might have been out of his vehicle," Andersson offered.

"He was going to warn the girl not to get into the car with Billy," Reynolds said, wisely.

"Exactly!" Andersson said. "Let's pretend he was out of the vehicle just before the bomb went off and was going to warn the girl."

"Why would he do that and miss the opportunity to get Billy, and give himself away?" The male investigator asked. "You think somehow he suddenly got a conscience?"

"It's a possibility." Andersson replied. "You said the girl had just met Billy the day before, right?"

"Right."

"Well, the guy who put the bomb in Billy's car must have been watching him for quite some time in order to get his pattern and pick the best time and place to do it."

"Give me the neighbor's phone number and I'll call her right now," Harper piped up. "I'll tell her I'm confused on the detail whether the man was already out of his vehicle or got out after the bomb had gone off. I'll tell her I'm calling to clarifying that point."

"Good idea, Harper," Andersson said looking at her and then back to the two county investigators. "It will also save you the trip back unless either of you prefer to make the call?"

Neither of them wanted to admit they overlooked that detail and gave Harper the lady's phone number. Harper called the lady and asked her in her best southern drawl, then after a few minutes more chat about the woman's new kitten, Harper hung up.

"The man was out of the vehicle before the bomb went off," Harper said. "She's sure since she had noticed the interior light go on when the girl moved to the other side of Billy's car. She said the man was dressed in big, bulky jacket and a baseball cap."

"So, it was possible he was going to warn the girl, or it's also possible he was just an innocent bystander who just happened to be there at the right time."

"But he didn't stay around to speak to the police," Shay said. "That sounds suspicious."

Andersson nodded. "To me too and I have some ideas on that we'll explore later, but since you've spoken up Shay, what do you have on the autopsy so far?"

Shay opened a thin folder that was sitting on the desk in front of her and began to read. "The blast killed him instantly. It was like I thought about the shock wave; it was devastating. It destroyed his lungs as well as his heart immediately. I'm sure he never knew what hit him. The fire afterward was over kill or perhaps symbolic."

"How so?" Reynolds asked.

"It could have been personal as well a professional job since someone wanted Billy burned," Shay replied. "Like they were sending him to hell."

"We're looking at the family," the male investigator chimed in like they already had a prime suspect.

"You mean Heather's father?" Stefani asked.

The female investigator nodded.

"Yes, he's been very vocal in the past about seeing Billy dead," the male investigator defended.

"You think the father planned this, followed Billy, built or bought a bomb and planted it himself?"

"Yes, it's possible or he could have hired it out too."

"Heather's father has a small heating and air conditioning business and he has no military or law enforcement training." Harper spoke up reading from her notebook then glancing up at Andersson. "I took the liberty of checking the father's background since I figured he would be suspect numero uno."

Andersson smiled at her and so did Stefani.

"What else did you find out," Andersson asked with a tease. "Do you know his favorite color?"

Harper looked back at her notes. "No, I don't sir," she replied, seriously. "But I can find out if you think it's important."

Andersson laughed.

"It's not important, Lilly." Stefani said. "What else have you got?"

"Despite the fact Heather's father wasn't in the military or a police officer, he was very good with his hands."

"So, again, it's possible he could have built a bomb." Andersson stated.

Harper nodded. "I really think it's possible for most anyone to build some type of an explosive device, especially since many varieties of bombs with how to instructions are posted online."

"But, having said that," Shay said. "The FBI and AFT took some sample fragments of Billy's bomb and will make a determination as soon as possible, but they 're already leaning toward a grenade."

"That means Heather's father would have had to purchase a grenade and somehow rigged it in Billy's car," Reynolds concluded.

"But there's nothing in Heather's father's history that lends itself to him even owning a gun. Now, if you can get me a warrant, we can check his computers at home and at his business for unusual searches for explosives and bomb making instructions."

"Again, all that doesn't mean he couldn't have gotten someone else to do the job for him." The female investigator reiterated.

"That's all true and were not discounting anything at this point but it's been years since Heather died so why wait until now for revenge?" Stefani said, getting up for another cup of coffee.

"We also did a canvas of the immediate area for any surveillance cameras and we got two located in businesses at opposite ends of the street of Billy's apartment complex." The male investigator continued with their report. "We have someone reviewing the tapes right now so we might get lucky with picking up his vehicle leaving the scene."

"I hope so," Andersson replied skeptically. "But there are several cross streets between those cameras where he could have turned off so it's going to be a long shot at best."

"That's all we got for now," he concluded. "We're still going over Billy's car and then the FBI and ATF will have a go at it too."

They both stood up to leave.

"Thanks for all your help," Andersson said, getting up with them. "We'll keep you posted from our end and you do the same."

"Sure, will do," the female said, shook hands with Andersson and they left.

"Anyone got any other ideas?" Andersson said, getting more coffee.

"I think we should press the family anyway," Reynolds stated. "At least we can eliminate them if nothing else."

"I agree," Stefani said. "I don't think the father's at the top of the list but we don't have any other candidates for first place."

Andersson nodded. "We'll brace the father and her other family members but not too hard, then we'll need to look at any one else who might have wanted Billy Burk dead."

"We're also going to need to look hard at other enemies Billy boy might have incurred over the last four years," Stefani said. "Especially anyone with a military or law enforcement background or who had a connection with the case."

"That's going to be a lot of people," Reynolds said glumly, yet knowing what Andersson was going to say in return.

"Then I suggest you get started right away and begin to whittle that long list down to a more manageable size," Andersson said. "Harper can give you a hand so that should make it much easier on you two."

Harper smiled like Andersson just told her she got a big raise in her pay.

"While you sort through the list of possibilities, Stefani and I will interview the family, with particular attention to the father and see where that goes," Andersson said. "Keep me posted if you turn up anyone interesting, otherwise we'll plan to meet back here in a couple of days."

Everyone left except for Andersson and Stefani so they could plan a strategy and schedule a meeting with Heather's father, hopefully for the next day.

CHAPTER EIGHT

That same afternoon around 4:30 pm, Paul Dickinson was lying in his king sized bed starting up at the ceiling and he wasn't alone. Pi was there lying next to him. They had just finished round one and Paul was reviewing his performance in his head. That's how Paul was with everything he did, including sex. Plan, perform, review and make changes where needed to improve. Always thinking and always trying to improve.

The ultimate goal was perfection and some things could be perfect, or at least perfect at times. Maybe not every time but it was those times when everything came together that was simply perfect.

That's how this first time was with Pi. It was perfect when he met her; he had sensed a real attraction between them. Sure, he was older and she was younger, okay, Pi was much younger, but thinking back to those fifteen minutes in the car, plus what just happened, Pi really enjoyed him. He was sure of it now.

Paul looked over at Pi who was lying on her side with her back to him and she looked perfect. Especially her ass, perfect. Like everything about Pi her ass was small, exceptionally round in shape and incredibly firm. Sure, her ass crack was standard issue but to Paul it was more than a natural fold. It was two gates of flesh that with the right foreplay and finesse opened to another world of naughty pleasures. He smiled to himself as he stared at Pi's ass. Plan, perform, review, but let's not get too far ahead of ourselves. This is was just the planning stage.

Just like he had done with Billy Burk. Plan. A lot of planning right down to the smallest detail. Paul thought of everything that could go wrong, except for that girl. That was almost a mistake, no, make that a disaster. He should have thought of that possibility and he rechecked his mental list. No, he didn't have that on his mental list but maybe that's why he stayed there and watched, maybe he unconsciously planned that contingency.

Paul always used a mental list when he planned and never wrote anything down. Make a mental list since writing things down can always leave a paper trail some can follow. Words were so permanent when words were written down. Thoughts could be permanent too but at least no one could find your thoughts lying around some place. Thoughts like grenade. Now, that thought as a word written down on some list, on some piece of paper, that might be difficult to explain.

Paul laughed to himself as he imagined trying to explain that to some hardnosed, seasoned detective. Oh that? The grenade word, on that piece of paper you found in my garbage, it was just something I wanted to pick up for a friend. Not a real grenade of course, just a toy one. A gag gift.

Something a guy might give another guy as a fun thing; a prank.

While lost in these thoughts, Paul's index finger had found its way to Pi's ass and he lightly traced the perimeter. He laughed again as he thought more about those stupid lists that people write down who are going to commit a crime. Like that brilliant college professor who murdered his wife. Now, he was really stupid and Paul laughed again as his finger circled the outside of Pi's right cheek. Pi didn't move so he kept tracing her ass.

Those damn written lists. The college professor, complete with a hard earned PhD no less, writes down: rope, duct tape, hammer, large, heavy duty, plastic bags and a good quality shovel. He hits her on the head in the garage, just once, as she gets out of her car. Ties her up and duct tapes her mouth and stuffs her into two of the plastic bags. Next, he loads her limp body into the back seat of his car, drives fifteen miles to a remote piece of property that his wife's grandfather owned and removes her from the car. Still breathing, but unconscious, he simply rolls her into a grave he dug that morning and buries her alive.

The next morning, he reports her missing to the police with some crazy story she was in a midlife crisis and had run off with a boyfriend. Just as Paul's finger made a complete circle around Pi's ass, he couldn't help but to remember the look on the professor's face when Paul pulled the trash bag from the garbage can that was sitting at the curb waiting for pickup. No warrant needed and thank you very much. Those damn lists.

"Are you having fun?" Pi asked with a giggle referring to Paul's finger.

The professor confessed and cut a deal for 2nd degree murder if he showed them where he had buried her body. The family wanted her back at all costs and was agreeable to twenty five to life instead of life without a chance of parole. When Pi spoke, Paul's finger stopped tracing.

"Yeah, I am. In fact, I'm really enjoying myself," he replied and gave her a light slap. "You have a perfect ass!"

"Thanks," Pi replied, rolling over with those white teeth flashing at him. "I thought you were a boob man even though mine are not that big."

Paul smiled at her. "I love boobs too, especially for doing tequila shots, but a perfect ass is more a fetish to me."

"Fetish?" Pi repeated. "What is that word?"

Her English was very good and getting better every day but she was still discovering new words all the time.

"It means a special attraction to something. An overwhelming desire," Paul said, as he leaned over and kissed her full lips. "It's usually something sexual and some people even have odd arousals with feet, feathers, even tickling."

"Oh, I see," Pi said, kissing him back. "It's like I have a fetish for older men."

"Well, yeah, I guess," Paul replied, pulling her body to his. "That could be a fetish if older men were a big turn on for you, a turn on you couldn't resist."

"Yes, it is and I have a big turn on for you, Paul." Pi said with that giggle as her hand slid deftly between his legs.

Paul almost recoiled at her touch since it had only been twenty minutes and he would usually need about an hour to recover. Pi giggled again and kissed him passionately as she squeezed her hand tightly while moving it rapidly. Paul winced at first, it almost felt painful but stopped short of protesting when he felt himself responding. Pi kissed him again with even more passion and more rapid jerking.

"See," she said triumphantly. "My fetish for you is working."

Paul could not reply as he focused on what her hand was doing to him. A few more seconds and Paul was ready and Pi knew it.

"Stay on your back," she said, as she slid over him and began to buck up and down. "How you say? Giddy up, cowboy!"

CHAPTER NINE

Hank had been home for over an hour when Roxanne pulled into the garage and came into the house.

"Sorry, I'm late," she said, kissing him. "Nicklaus and I got into the Billy Burk case after the meeting and the time flew by."

Hank hugged her tightly like she was going to leave and never come back. Finally, after holding her so close she almost lost her breath, he released her.

"I made the shot!" He blurted out the words as he stepped back from her. "I know you knew it wasn't your dad and I knew you wanted me to tell you the truth. I also knew it was what you wanted to talk about when you called me earlier."

"I just needed to know, Hank," Roxanne said, seeing the concern in his eyes for her. "It wasn't only the distance that told me he didn't make that shot, although that alone would have been enough, but it was the way he looked at you after it had happened."

"The way he looked at me?" Hank repeated, confused.

"Yes, that look of respect and pride," Roxanne said. "I love my father very much, Hank and I know you know that. I also know how long and how hard I struggled for that look. That look of approval. I really had to earn that."

"Your father and I have gotten close, Roxanne and I thought you would be happy we did," Hank said, as they both instinctively moved to the couch and sat down close to one another.

"I am happy you and my father are close," Roxanne said, putting her head on his chest as words spilled out in a long held confession. "I knew he wanted a boy, a son, but they only had me and he never mentioned that disappointment."

"But then you developed your talent, your gift to shoot and things changed, didn't it?"

Roxanne nodded as tears fell freely from her eyes.

"I just wanted to please him so much!" She cried and Hank put his arm around her. "...and I know there's more you're not telling me Hank, much more besides you taking that shot."

Hank held Roxanne in his arms as tight as anyone could hold someone and their feelings of love flowed freely back and forth.

"Your father is a very smart man, Roxanne," Hank began succinctly. "He suspected it about me when he first saw me shoot long distance that day were both at his range."

"Suspected what?" She asked, after he paused.

"That I was part of an early citizen cell against terrorism..."

"What? A citizen cell...I have no idea what you're talking about," Roxanne said, wiping her tears and lifting her head from his chest. "What's a citizen cell?"

"You were probably just starting college when 9 11 happened and I'm sure you remember that time very well," Hank stated.

"Of course," Roxanne said. "Who could forget that tragic event and the fear we all experienced in the aftermath."

"Exactly the word, fear." Hank said, as he lightly stroked her hair. "I was finishing my Fellowship in Oncology when it happened, and the Anthrax scare was added to the mix a couple of months later. The whole country thought we were on the brink of a global war. I was living in New York City at the time and the military was occupying Battery Park and Governor's Island. At one point, Manhattan was hours away from being shut down and placed under martial law. The FBI, as well as the other government law enforcement agencies were on high alert and training around the clock preparing for what many thought was an inevitable invasion."

"I remember my dad was away for weeks at a time right after the airliners hit the Towers," Roxanne said, recalling those chilling days like it was yesterday.

"Well," Hank hesitated. "That's when I was approached by the FBI, at least I think it was the FBI, to be part of a covert, last defense, citizen cell."

"I'm not sure I'm following you, Hank," Roxanne said. "You think the FBI approached you? You didn't know?"

"I was never at any formal office of the FBI and the individual who approached me said he was working for the Federal Government at the direction of the President. I assumed he was from the FBI but I never saw any credentials or ever knew his real name. But, he sure knew a lot about me and some things I had even forgotten, he reminded me."

"The country was under attack and when the Anthrax began, many in the government thought things would rapidly escalate. We, and I mean the various agencies, found out many so called students with educational visas, simply disappeared into our society and had gone undetected," Hank said.

"…any by then the government wasn't sure if any these cell groups that existed were planning follow-up attacks," Roxanne said.

"Exactly!" Hank said as more than a decade of secrets were suddenly exposed to all the world. "The FBI knew of my skills with a rifle and when the citizen cells were being activated, I was called upon to serve in the event of a large scale invasion."

"Why use civilians in small groups instead of the military?" Roxanne questioned the tactic.

"They did use the military in many places around the country especially since martial law was close to being invoked."

"So why the secret cells of people?"

"The FBI knew if these small, hidden groups of terrorists could insert themselves into normal, every day life in the United States and bring about such a devastating blow to our country, then how many more such cells existed and were awaiting orders to attack various other targets."

"So, the citizen cells were hidden backups? Roxanne said, as she tried to recall all the times her own Father had been absent from their lives during the year that followed 9 11.

"Yes," Hank said. "The FBI felt there would be no way any foreign terrorists would know of these secret cells especially if no records were kept and only a limited number of officials knew they existed."

"And you could act against a so called United States citizen too, if necessary. Roxanne said, as she began to understand the drastic concept.

"Yes," Hank said. "The military, according to the Constitution, is prohibited from taking any action against a US citizen unless certain changes are enacted under the law such a marital law or the National Guard is activated."

"You think my father knew of these citizen cells or maybe was directly involved in them?" She asked citing all the possibilities.

"Yes, I do, but he hasn't told me that directly and I haven't asked him," Hank said, truthfully. "You're the first person outside of my cell that knows about this and my involvement."

"Cell. You keep using that term. Why did they call them cells?" Roxanne asked, as she began to feel months of anxiety begin to leave her not to mention the panic attacks she endured which fortunately through counseling have improved but still plague her.

"It was the term taken from Al-Qaeda," Hank replied. "If that's how they were going to operate then we were going to fight back in kind using their own tactics."

"So really it was another way to maintain a certain balance if an all-out internal attack did occur within our country."

"That's the way it was told to me at that time and I felt it was my duty."

"And now?" Roxanne asked, taking advantage of the free flowing conversation. "What do you think about that concept?"

"I think it was the right thing at that time and I still do today. I may not agree with taking the fight to foreign soil and getting bogged down in a protracted war..."

He let that topic drift off since it was too complex to discuss right then and that wasn't what Roxanne wanted to hear.

"These cells Hank," Roxanne stated, instead of asking as a question to eliminate any doubt. "They weren't just death squads, I know."

"No, they weren't," Hank replied. "They were everyday people with specialized skills. Some were teachers, contractors, doctors, nurses, engineers and yes those who had weapon training as well. Each was then trained to function as a team in case we were needed to prevent anarchy. Each cell or group, to my knowledge, was made up of from five to eight people."

Roxanne was almost done with her questions and none of what he had told to her had made any Difference in the way she felt about him, in fact, and she didn't think it was possible, she loved him even more.

"How many Hank?"

"Two," Hank replied, as he also felt the relief of the burden of these last six months. "My first was a college aged, Middle Eastern man, who was carrying a very powerful bomb in a backpack."

"A suicide bomber?"

"Yes. A fairly new concept for our law enforcement at that time, but we got lucky and were tipped off at the last minute that one of the larger, Jewish Synagogues very near where I was located was going to be bombed on a Jewish holiday. The City was still on edge from 9 11 and my cell was placed on alert. had a roof top position with a view of the Synagogue we were monitoring at about a thousand yards from the entrance."

"We? Someone else was with you?"

"Steve, he was my spotter and back up."

"Steve, your best man?"

"Yes. We were both recruited at the same time. Both doctors, he was also in Oncology and our supervising attending physician was also in our cell. We were supposed to be part of a medical unit but Steve and I were trained to also function as a sniper team if needed."

"Like the Special Forces are trained where no one person has the only skill needed to maintain the team's ability to complete the mission."

"That's right. We had a communication and computer expert who also worked in our hospital as well as two nurses and a lab tech who were in our cell."

"These cells were formed nationwide?"

"Eventually," Hank said. "At first, with the more immediate threat, they were just in the bigger cities like New York, Chicago and Los Angeles. New York, since it was hit first at the Trade Centers and had so many other possible targets, had hundreds of cells."

"It's amazing no one has gone public with being a part of these cells."

"I know," Hanks said. "We feel it's because there's no documented evidence that they even exist. It was designed to be unbelievable."

"Seems impossible."

"I know, but in the past, large numbers of people have known about many top secret projects all over the country and have gone largely undetected. Look at the hidden missile silos that were scattered about and had normal looking houses built right over them."

"You're right Hank, and I'm sure now my father had a part in those cells as well."

You're probably right," Hank said. "He was likely suspicious of me from the first time he saw me shoot at his range."

Roxanne nodded and they both were quiet for a few minutes as they got more relaxed and snuggled down together.

"Did the bomb go off?" Roxanne finally asked.

"No, It didn't," Hank said, kissing her head. "We had a very accurate description of the bomber and Steve spotted him several blocks before the synagogue. He was already acting nervous and when he took both hands out of his pockets, I got the green light and took the shot."

"There was no dead man's switch?"

"Yes, he had one but the bomb also had an activation switch which was off since he was still a fair distance from the synagogue."

"He didn't want a premature detonation either, I'm sure."

Yes, and he also didn't want to look more suspicious than he already did by having his hands in his pockets as he walked into the building."

"I have more questions Hank and I know you know that," Roxanne said, wearily. "Many questions for not only you but for my father too."

"I know and I want to answer them all."

"But, I've had enough for now," She said, and moved up to kiss him. "Let's have something to eat and go to bed."

CHAPTER TEN

Normally, Henry Harris was in bed by 9:00 pm and up around 4:00 am so he could write most of the morning. So, when Kira invited him to dinner at 7:30 pm, he took a long nap in the afternoon. He wanted to be full of energy and not yawning or nodding off during dinner.

While Henry got ready, he had some second thoughts about why Kira had invited him to dinner at her home in the first place. He tried not to entertain those suspicions but with his nature and knowing Kira so well, he still wondered.

When he got to Kira's house at precisely 7:30 pm he was even more pleasantly surprised when he saw how she was dressed. Not that he was complaining, since Kira looked incredible. A white silk blouse, opened generously, was tucked into a black spandex mini skirt that off her probably could have fit into his wallet. The skirt was stretched so tight over her ass it left little to the imagination but still enough to keep you staring, and with Henry's X-ray vision it was a delight to behold. The high heels were over the top, literally, since Kira was already taller than Henry in her stocking feet. Still, no complaints but just much more desire. Kira, his fantasy goddess, towered over him and made him feel all the more worshipping.

"Come in Henry," Kira greeted him holding a glass of champagne. "I just opened a wonderful bottle of ice cold champagne."

"Oh my, Kira, champagne?" Henry said, walking into her home with his jaw still hanging open. "I don't think I've had champagne since I sold my first book."

"I know Henry," Kira said, taking a long swallow of the bubbly when she caught a whiff of his patchouli. "We had some in my office as I recall."

"Yes, we did," Henry said, as he walked further into the expansive great room and looked around. "Wow, Kira, your home is lovely. It's so big, especially for one person…"

Kira closed the door, poured Henry a glass of the champagne and handed it to him. She ignored his compliment about her home.

"Here's to us, Henry," Kira toasted, drank the rest of her champagne and refilled the glass.

"To us?" Henry questioned, before he sipped the champagne.

Kira drank more before replying. "Yes, Henry, to us. Not only is this a new beginning for your writing but for our relationship as well."

Henry took a sip of the champagne.

"To us!" He said, smiled widely and drank more and more.

After his first glass of champagne was quickly gone, Henry sat down on the couch. He and Kira toasted various other things to toast and by that time they had finished, it was a good thing Henry was sitting down since his head was spinning.

"I think I need something to eat," he said. "I'm getting drunk."

Kira stood up adjusted her skirt and finished her third glass of champagne before announcing.

"Organic prime rib roast, garlic mashed potatoes and baby spring peas await you, Henry!"

Henry tried to get up and staggered back down into the couch.

"Oh my!" He said, with an embarrassed laugh. "I think I need to sit down for a minute, Kira."

"Are you okay?" Kira asked, helping to steady Henry as he tried to sit. "You stay right there Henry and I'll get you something to eat."

"No! Kira! Please don't bother," Henry pleaded, as he tried to get up but slumped right back down.

"It's no bother, Henry," Kira said, walking away into the kitchen. "I really think you need something to eat before you pass out."

Henry laid his head back and focused on the ceiling.

"I think you're right, Kira," he said, as he mentally floated.

Kira was came back with a large china dinner plate laden with roast beef, mashed potatoes and buttered peas.

"Here Henry," Kira said. "Let me help you eat…"

Kira set the plate down on a heavy dark teak coffee table, cut some of the meat into smaller pieces and fed Henry.

"There you go," Kira coaxed, like a new mom with her baby. "Eat that all up now…

Henry had no more than swallowed the meat and mumbled something about how good it was when Kira came back with a forkful of mashed potatoes.

"Here Henry," she said, holding the fork to his mouth. "Try some of these mashed potatoes."

Henry ate the potatoes, then more meat and some of the peas as well. In a few minutes, he felt less dizzy and sat up.

"I feel much better, Kira," he said, taking the fork from her. "My head has stopped spinning and I think I can feed myself."

Kira smiled and patted his face. "See, I knew you just needed something to eat and you would be fine."

"I'm sorry to be such a pain, Kira," Henry said, cutting more of the roast beef.

Kira slid back on the couch but angled herself so that when he faced her, he could see right up her skirt.

"You eat all you want, Henry. I'll sit right here and watch," she said, making no effort to pull her skirt down which would have made little difference anyway.

Henry had already spotted her black silk thong which barely covered her mound. Henry tried to act nonchalant at that glorious sight but he almost choked when she saw his downcast eyes and she opened her legs even wider.

"Aren't you going to eat anything Kira?" Henry asked, as he moved to the edge of the couch so he could reach more food and also to get a better view between Kira's legs.

"I'm fine Henry," Kira lied. She was famished, but her hunger had suddenly turned to nausea. Henry's patchouli aroma had mixed with the smell of his nervous body odor and the two together made for a noxious combination; a kind of sweet and sour with a touch of well-aged, cheddar cheese. It was definitely not appetizing.

The plate of food she had fixed for Henry was enough for two people but Henry pressed through it all in record time. He ate and gawked at Kira's crotch between bites. Some food, some gawking and over time the gawking got longer and longer as Henry got full. Once he was done eating and had cleaned the plate, he sat back but still facing Kira. He was sweating profusely and his odor was rank.

"All better?" She asked with a smile although she could hardly contain the bile that surged from her empty stomach.

Henry burped loudly before he could reply.

"Oh I'm sorry," he said, putting his hand to cover his mouth. "I guess I ate too fast."

Kira reached for more champagne and filled her glass. If she was going to get through this, she would need to be drunk.

"Henry, I know you feel better now that you had something to eat," she began, carefully measuring her words. "But, I think you really got faint for a few minutes and might have even passed out."

"I did?" Henry asked. "I passed out and I don't remember it?"

Kira nodded her head. "Yes, you can pass out and when you wake up not recall it."

"I think you might be right, Kira," Henry said. "...and I feel so sweaty too."

"Yes, in fact, you're very sweaty," she said, with a big smile. "...and I think you would feel better if you had a bath..."

"Really?" Henry replied, not sure he was more shocked he was sweating so much or that Kira said he needed a bath. "I'm sorry, I must smell offensive."

"Oh no, Henry," Kira said, quickly as she took his clammy hand in hers. "I didn't mean to offend you. I only mentioned it since the evening is so young and I thought you might like to get more comfortable."

"Oh...oh...oh..." Henry stuttered. "Would you rather I take a quick shower?"

"No, Henry," Kira replied, standing up and pulling Henry to his feet. "I don't want you to take a quick shower. I want you to take a long bath."

Henry was standing closer to Kira than he had ever been and it was an amazing feeling to stand in her aura.

"But, I don't want to impose, Kira," Henry protested, weakly. "I think a bath would be too inconvenient."

Kira kept pulling Henry by his hand to the far side of the house where she had to two guest bedrooms with two full bathrooms. There was no way he was going to use her bathtub or let alone even see her private bedroom. Kira went into the first bathroom she came to, turned on the water and the bathtub began to fill.

"Let me help you, Henry," Kira whispered in his ear as she began to unbutton his shirt. "I can undress you while the water fills the tub."

"Undress me?" Henry said, and suddenly he felt faint again. "You want to undress me?"

"Why not Henry?" Kira said with her best sexy smile usually only reserved for her boy toys. "I wouldn't want you to pass out and hit your head or something."

Henry watched passively as Kira finished unbuttoning his shirt and removed it. Next, she unbuttoned his pants and slid them down.

"I feel so embarrassed, Kira." Henry whined, looking away from her eyes as his pants came off. "I mean, I'm standing here in my underwear ready to take a bath and you're fully dressed."

Kira laughed. "I'm not sure you noticed, Henry, but I wouldn't call this fully dressed. I don't think it even qualifies as partially dressed."

Henry nodded, but before he could reply Kira unbuttoned her blouse and took it off. Her natural, firm breasts heaved in the skimpy, lace bra that only barely contained them. Henry could see her long, red nipples peeking over the top which seemed to say hi to him.

"I don't want you to feel embarrassed, Henry, so I'll get more comfortable too." Kira said, easily without the hint of modesty.

She turned around, slid down her spandex skirt and set it down on the vanity. She smiled in the mirror at him knowing damn well he was staring at her ass and what an ass it was! Henry gasped at the sight and felt weak in the knees.

"Kira, you're so beautiful!" He exclaimed. "I always knew you had an amazing body, but now to actually see like this. Well, it's very erotic and stimulating."

Kira laughed and turned around. "It must be very stimulating, Henry, from the look of the briefs you're wearing; you've got the hard on of your life!"

Henry blushed. "Yes, I guess I do."

"Take off those briefs, Henry and get into the tub! Now!" She ordered, knowing instinctively how to handle him.

Henry nodded obediently, licked his lips like a lizard that just ate a big, juicy fly, took off his briefs and stepped into the warm, sudsy water. Kira pulled up her thong tightly which only accented her camel toe and felt completely disappointed as she looked at Henry standing nude in the tub. Henry was the two things she didn't like in a man; smaller and thinner than average. If anything, at least be thick! She could deal with the lack of length if she had to, but please be thick enough to stretch her out and fill her up!

Henry saw her smile dip slightly into a frown.

"I'm sorry," he whined, the humiliation almost seemed like it turned him on even more. "I know I'm below size..."

Looking at him now, Kira wished she brought the bottle of champagne with her, especially since what she was seeing standing before her definitely had harshened her mellow. Her smile recovered in a fraction of a second as she realized, on the positive side, it was simply the less she would have to deal with.

"You're fine, Henry," she said, dismissively, as she moved to him still with the snap of authority in her voice. "You know what they say Henry, it's now how much you have, it's how you use it that counts!"

Henry smiled like a schoolboy who had just played show me yours and I'll show you mine.

"Sit down in the water, Henry!" She barked loudly. "Now!"

Henry quickly lowered himself into the tub and moaned how wonderful the warm water felt.

"You like that, Henry?"

He nodded and the lizard tongue ate another fly.

Kira did not kneel at the side of the tub but stood, looming over Henry in a motherly fashion. She did not say anything and began to wash him. Soon, at her touch, she could feel him relax as she scrubbed away most of his anxiety, not to mention his odor.

"Feel good, Henry?" She asked as her right hand massaged his back and her left hand went down under the water between his legs.

"It feels very good, Kira," Henry said, with his happy smile. "Both of your hands feel good."

Kira laughed and she increased the tempo of her left hand. She knew he wouldn't last long and as the end happened for Henry it was like an ending he had never experienced before. It was much different with Kira and his body shook as he humped with the rhythm of her expert hand.

When he finally stopped thrashing and was still, he took in a deep breath before turning to her.

"I'd love for this evening with you last forever, Kira, and I would do anything to have that happen," he said, sincerely, and his tongue ate another fly.

CHAPTER ELEVEN

The next morning, Andersson was pulling out of his driveway when his cell phone rang with an old fashioned ringing. He had tried putting his phone on vibrate but he had missed too many calls. He put the car in park, retrieved the phone from his breast pocket and looked at the number. It was Reynolds.

"Good morning, Nicklaus," he said, cheerfully. "Where are you?"

"I'm at home. I mean, I'm in my car ready to back out of the driveway," Andersson replied when he spotted a box of Chiclets sitting in the console. "What's going on?"

"You won't believe what just happened," Reynolds said. "Willy Burk just walked in or should I say staggered into the station and he was either drunk or high or both."

"Who? Billy Burk? Billy's dead!" Andersson said, as he fumbled to open the box of gum.

"No, not Billy Burk," Reynolds repeated. "Willy Burk, his older brother.

"Willy and Billy?" Andersson said when the flap on the box of Chiclets suddenly popped open spilling Chiclets all over the front seat. "Oh shit!"

"That's what I said too when I saw him," Reynolds replied. "Oh shit!"

Andersson picked a couple of Chiclets off the seat and put them in his mouth.

"I don't think I remember Willy," Andersson said, chewing. "Is his real name William?"

"No, it's Willy," Reynolds said. "Just like Billy is, or was, only Billy. He wasn't a William either. The father was William and he wanted both of his sons to have his first name but he didn't want them both named William."

"So instead of one of them being named William he gives each of them a version of William. Couldn't he have at least named one of them William?" Andersson asked, trying to pick up the other Chiclets and put them back into the box.

"Who knows or even cares for that matter, but I do know the father was a mean prick," Reynolds said. "I busted him a couple of times when I was in uniform for domestic violence. He kicked my ass once and I kicked his ass the next time. I never reported the beating he gave me and he didn't report it when I beat him up! Anyway, after I stomped him good, he stopped hitting his wife and eventually she ran off with some other guy."

"What did Willy want?" Andersson asked offhandedly, as he kept sliding one Chiclet after another back into the box.

"He wanted us to arrest Heather's father because he's sure her father is behind Billy's death. He said if we didn't arrest him and put him in jail, he would handle it himself."

"Oh yeah?" Andersson said, defiantly, since he was already annoyed that he had lost some of his Chiclets on the floor. "Did you tell Willy boy that we're working on it, and if he goes even close to Heather's father, we'll arrest his stupid ass."

Reynonds nodded in reflex to Andersson's raised voice. "Yes sir, I did. In fact, I told him if he didn't leave the station right now we would arrest him for disorderly conduct and public intoxication."

"Good!" Andersson said, starting his car. "Call Harper and tell her to look into Willy's background and the old man's too."

"The father's dead, Nicklaus," Reynolds said. "He had a heart attack about two years ago."

"Okay, then have her concentrate on Billy and Willy, and speaking of Heather's father, I'm going to meet Stefani in about an hour to talk with him at a job site. I spoke with him yesterday afternoon and he said he didn't want us coming to the house and dredging it all up again in front of his wife. He said he can't come into the office since he's been backed up on a job plus he's been working shorthanded. So, to save us all the grief we're going to him."

"Okay, I'll call Harper and get her going on the Burk brothers and I'll also have Culpepper pull Heather's files from the cold cases," Reynolds said. "He and I can start going through all that stuff…"

"Alright, Craig, that sounds good and also find out who the lead detective was on her case," Andersson said, backing out of the driveway. "I'd like to talk to him too …"

"I don't have to look that up, Nicklaus, I already know…" Reynolds shot back. "It was Dickinson, Paul Dickinson."

"Super Dick? That's right come to think of it," Nicklaus said, shifting into drive. "I haven't seen him since his retirement party and it's strange to equate Paul with a case that went unsolved."

"You're friends?" Reynolds asked.

"Not really friends, more like professional associates," Andersson said, driving away. "He was an extremely good detective but his style was, shall we say, on the fringe."

"Was he called super dick because of his last name or because he solved so many cases?" Reynolds asked.

Andersson laughed. "I never called him super dick, well, not to his face anyway. It was an inside joke with a few of the old timers and Paul didn't like it."

"That's too bad, I thought it was a compliment."

"Not really, Paul liked the ladies a lot, Craig, even when he was married," Andersson said. "He always was juggling a couple of them at a time."

"Okay, I get it," Reynolds said. "Sorry now I asked…"

"Anyway, keep an eye on Willy and see what he's up to," Andersson said, "at least for the next couple of days."

"Will do," Reynolds said.

"I have to go," Andersson replied. "The traffic is picking up."

Stefani sat in the new Corvette that Hank had given her for an engagement present and watched Heather's father help unload some ducting from one of three vans which were parked in front of a business. She could have approached the father by herself but she wanted to wait for Andersson. Five more minutes passed and she noticed his car turn the corner and pull up behind her. She got out of the Corvette, and walked to his car, his window was already down when she got there.

"I know I'm late," Andersson said," But I got a call from Reynolds just as I was about to leave my house."

"I didn't say anything," Stefani replied with a grin.

"You didn't have to say anything," Andersson said, opening the door and getting out of the car. "You talk to him already?"

Stefani looked down the block at the three men unloading the van.

"No, I thought we would do it together since neither of us have ever met him before," She said.

"That way we can both get his reactions at the same time."

"Good idea," Andersson said, walking toward the men. "Nice and easy."

"Only way I know," Stefani quipped.

"Yeah right."

Heather's father saw them approaching, said something to the other two men and he walked towards them.

"Albert?" Andersson said with his hand outstretched. "I'm lieutenant Andersson and this is Special Investigator Stefani. We spoke on the phone yesterday."

"It's Al," he said in a friendly manner, shaking hands with them both. "I like to be called Al."

"Sure Al," Andersson said, as the three of them huddled neat the curb in the cool morning.

"Like I said on the phone last night," Al began, touching the brim of his ball cap that had the logo of his business on it. "When I heard Billy Burk was dead I danced in the street and I mean I danced for real."

"From what we heard and know about Billy Burk, I'm sure you weren't dancing alone," Andersson said in support.

"Are you kidding? I bet if all the people who are happy that piece of crap is blown up; we could have had a block party." Al replied, touching the brim of his hat again.

Andersson watched Al closely as he spoke and could see years of genuine anger still simmering below the surface. The man was as tall as Andersson, but very wiry and had, big thick hands from years of hard work.

"I never liked Billy from day one and I told Heather too," Al kept talking and touching the ball cap like he always did when he got anxious."

"We just have a few questions for you Al," Stefani said, sympathetically. "We know talking about this is very emotional."

Al nodded. "That's why I didn't want you to come to my home."

"It's fine Al," Andersson said. "We're comfortable right here."

"I never understood what Heather saw in that loser."

"Heather was a school teacher, wasn't she?" Andersson asked.

"Yes, she was," Al broke a small smile. "Brand new and a damn good one too. She loved to teach."

"I bet she did and I'm sure she loved kids too," Stefani added.

"She did," Al said as tears welled up in his blue eyes. "Heather was five months pregnant when that fuck killed her. I only had two daughters and now there's just Heather's sister."

"One more question Al and we'll let you get back to work," Andersson said, touching his shoulder.

"You know I had Billy working for me after they got married," Al continued. "I tried to teach him the business and I thought if he made good money he would be a good husband, but things only got worse."

Stefani moved her position around Andersson to face Al directly when she asked him.

"We have to ask you Al," she began softly. "For the record, what time did you finish working and where were you from say six pm on…"

"I was right here," he replied, without hesitation, shooting his thumb over his shoulder at the job site.

"We finished up around seven and the three of us had a beer over at Duffy's. You can ask those two."

"We believe you Al," Andersson said. "What time did you get home?"

"Around eight-thirty," he said. "This is a rush job and if we finish ahead of schedule we get a big bonus."

"Okay Al," Andersson said, with his hand outstretched. "Thanks for your help."

Al shook Anderssons hand then Stefani's and as they walked back to their cars Al began to shout.

"I'm glad Billy's dead and I hope you don't ever catch who did it!"

Andersson and Stefani turned back and saw Al with his hands cupped around his mouth.

"In fact, if you do find the guy who did it, thank him for me," Al said, as loud as he could. "...and if he needs a lawyer let me know. I'll be glad to pay for it!"

Andersson got into his car while Stefani walked to the Corvette and neither of said anything to Al.

"Hey look! I'm dancing in the street! I'm dancing in the street!" Al said, and kept it up as they both drove away.

CHAPTER TWELVE

Kira slept in again the next morning but this time she had called her assistant and left a message for her before she went to sleep. It had been a very long time since Kira slept in two days in a row, but she needed the time to rest and to think. The night before with Henry was very traumatic for her. It took all the courage she could muster to invite him into her home, let alone have to do what she did with him.

After Henry left, Kira cleaned every surface and piece of furniture he had touched or occupied, especially the bath tub; which she cleaned three times and finished wiping it down with pure bleach.

She didn't know how long sperm could survive but she was definitely going to find out and she wasn't going to allow anyone to use the tub until she was sure it was safe. The thought of one of Henry's little fish wiggling around in someone's bathwater made her skin crawl.

With all the cleaning done, Kira made coffee, and decided to make scrambled eggs and toast. She usually didn't eat anything before lunch and then it was always something light; either fruit or a yogurt. This morning, since she didn't, nor could she eat any dinner with Henry, she was famished.

She took out the eggs and after whisking them into a froth, poured the liquid into a saute' pan which was swimming in melted butter. Kira ate scrambled eggs maybe three or four times a year but when she did, she pulled out all the stops. Next, while the eggs cooked into a light pile of yellow fluff; she toasted two thick slices of dark bread and spread them heavily with strawberry jam.

When the eggs were done to perfection, she sat down at the table and wolfed them down with a slice of toast before she took her next breath. She laughed out loud at how hungry she was as she pushed a glob of jam, resting on her upper lip, into her mouth. God, she needed to have a breakfast like this more often, but the thought of all the calories made her decide the three times a year was enough. Well, maybe she would add Christmas and her birthday.

In a few more minutes, she finished the other slice of toast, put her dishes into the sink, but took the whisk she had used with her. Leaving the kitchen, she grabbed her cell phone and went back up to her bedroom. With her hunger satisfied, she needed to have her bell rung a couple of times.

Henry aside, the atmosphere of her sexually dominating someone was a huge turn on. It wasn't like being with Chris, her young, model stud, now there was a man who knew how to measure up in every way. With Chris, control took on a whole new meaning unlike the control she had used with Henry. Henry was direct authority; telling him what, how and when to do it and his reaction to that style was exactly what he needed. She laughed as she thought of them both and licked the sticky whisk like a lollipop.

Control with Chris was more subtle but still she was the mistress and sex was the way she wanted it. She appealed to Chris's ego with the excitement of sexual exploration and she made him climb that mountain over and over again with her orgasm being his summit. Kira always knew from the time she was in high school that she could control any male she wanted and that included many of her much older teachers.

The kitchen whisk was Kira's first and still favorite sex toy. Knowing her mother searched her room daily since she was in middle school; looking for weed, booze or cigarettes, when the time came, Kira knew a vibrator was out of the question. Her mom fancied herself as a gourmet cook but in reality was at best mediocre. Still, the woman had every utensil a chef could want including an array of whisks of various sizes.

At first glance, someone, especially someone who was male, might think a whisk was the last thing they would use, but Kira knew better. The baby whisk was out unless she was using two at once; the next size for the inside and the baby for her outside. Now, that was really cooking!

Kira looked at the clock on the nightstand while she speed dialed Chris. Five rings later, and almost heading for voice mail, he answered.

"Baby, it's me," she moaned, as the whisk easily rotated around her. "Where are you? Can you talk?"

"I'm at Rockefeller Plaza shooting a commercial."

"You're on a shoot, now?" She said. "It's only eight o'clock in the morning."

"I know and we've been here since six," Chris replied, annoyed. "Aren't you at the office?"

"No baby," she said, as she felt the familiar curved wires slide around. "I'm home and I really, really need your help."

"Now?" He said, incredulously. "Kira, I'm outside with ten other people standing around me and besides that it's very cold."

"Oh Chris, please honey," she begged. "Mommy's cooking up something for her baby boy and it's not in the kitchen."

"Oh shit, Kira! Not now!" Chris said, moving away from the crew while they adjusted the lights for the next shoot.

"Are you doing more underwear pictures honey?" Kira asked, softly as the whisk found its way inside.

'No, I'm not," Chris replied, remembering the show Kira put on for him with her set of whisks. "I'm actually dressed in a tuxedo doing a new designer perfume ad…"

"Oh goodie, being me a sample…"

"I will but tell me …how does that whisk feel?" Chris asked, testing the fabric strength of his pants.

"Oh honey, you can't imagine what mommy can whip up with her whisks!"

"I bet!" He said, grabbing onto himself for a fast tug. "I've seen firsthand what you can do with those things."

"You have now…haven't you?" Kira gushed, finding her spot as she spun the whisk. "Are you in the ad with a young, hot female?"

"Of course," he answered, gliding along the wall that surrounds Rockefeller Plaza. "The perfume is supposed to lure guys who look like me."

"Like those superhot models need perfume to lure any guy," Kira said, moving the whisk in and out as well as with the spinning motion.

"The perfume is for woman who don't look like super models…"

"Are you going to fuck her for me?" Kira asked, as she neared the end. "Like you did before with that other one and tell me all about it when we're together."

"If you want me to," Chris pulled on himself as he sensed her finishing and the friction of the pants brought him dangerously close to the end. "I can't cum with you baby. I'll have a huge wet spot and I'm going to be here another couple of hours."

"That's okay, Chris. Save it for the bitch and really ruin her for me," Kira rasped, and she heaved violently in the bed thinking of him with the model.

"I will," Chris replied, letting go of himself before the point of no return.

"Good," Kira said, shivering with aftershocks as she pulled out the whisk. "Does she look like the type of woman that might like it rough?"

Chris looked back at the young, beautiful, thin model. "Could be," he said, smiling at her. "She's got that sweet, innocent, doe eyed look…"

"Oh my…sounds like a prospect. Try to spank her ass when you're fucking her and slap her face with your dick when you're done," Kira ordered. "See if she likes any of that…then let me know."

"I will," Chris replied, walking back when he saw the director waving him over. "I have to go baby, they're ready for me."

"Okay Chris," she said. "You made mommy very happy…"

"I'm glad," he said. "When are you coming back?"

"Tomorrow morning," she replied. "See you then and don't forget what I told you about the model."

"I won't," he said and disconnected.

Kira smiled to herself as her left hand massaged between her legs and she licked the whisk.

CHAPTER THIRTEEN

A big, gooey cinnamon bun is probably one of the most decadent things someone can eat any time of the day; no matter what meal, breakfast, lunch or dinner or even as a midnight snack, a cinnamon bun fits the bill.

Stefani left the street meeting with Heather's father but didn't go to the office. She headed for a nearby mall and although most of the stores were still closed; the cinnamon place had just opened and were putting out a fresh, hot baked supply of buns. She bought one of the buns and sat down at a small nearby table to eat it. She didn't get coffee since nothing could replace Hank's brew and she had finished the cup she had brought to the meeting.

She needed some alone time and some time to think about what she and Hank had talked about last evening. She had just taken a bite of the cinnamon bun when she sensed someone standing behind her. She chewed the bun and glanced up over her shoulder to see Buster.

"Hey Buster," she said, but the words barely came out since her mouth was full.

"Hey Roxanne," the retired Navy SEAL replied. "Not playing the game this morning?"

Stefani swallowed as she shook her head. "I'm always playing the game with you Buster…"

"Well, you had me fooled," he said, sitting down opposite her. "I've been following you since you left your house this morning and all through that meeting with Andersson and some guy. I don't think you ever even saw me, let alone take some evasive action."

For years, Buster was Stefani's personal trainer, fitness/ hand to hand combat coach and overall general military style life advisor. A former highly decorated Navy SEAL, he operated a successful private security agency and took on a very limited number of special clients for training. He was tough, unyielding, hardnosed and unorthodox in his methods and he was always on duty.

"You know the deal with me," he began, reaching over and breaking off a large piece of her cinnamon bun. "You're my top student and we're on a twenty-four seven training schedule. That's what you wanted when you signed on."

"I know," she replied. "And I saw you about two minutes after I pulled out of the drive way."

"Bullshit!" He said, eating some of the cinnamon bun. "You didn't see at all even when I was standing behind you just now."

"Okay, I didn't see you," she admitted, dabbing some of the cream cheese frosting off the bun and putting it into her mouth. "I just feel overwhelmed."

"What's wrong?" He said, sympathetically, which was out of character. Buster didn't care what excuse you had; there was no excuse for failure. "Still having trouble with the panic attacks?"

"Sometimes," she said, pushing the rest of the cinnamon bun away. "But lately, for the most part, they've been better."

"So what's the problem?" He asked, reaching for the rest of the bun. "You're a beautiful woman who can almost kick my ass plus you're marrying a guy that's filthy rich! Yet, you were so detached that you didn't notice me following you when the three blind mice could have seen me."

Stefani laughed. "It's personal…and there's no almost about it…I can kick your ass!"

Buster laughed and ate the rest of the bun before replying.

"Bullshit! Nothing is too personal between us, you know that by now."

She nodded, but still did not elaborate.

"It's the shot, isn't it?"

She looked up at him with a look of shock clearly on her face.

"How did you know?"

Buster shrugged. "It's a no brainer, Roxanne. Besides, I've known you for ten years and with all due respect to Rocco's weapon skills; he didn't make that mile shot."

"It was almost two thousand yards, Buster," she corrected.

"Even more reason he didn't do it and what's so bizarre is there's only maybe eight or nine guys in the world who could have made that shot and four or five of them are living in other countries. I know two or three are in Russia and the other one is in Israel. The rest are in our Army and Marines, two each at best. So, you have to ask yourself, where did a guy like Hank, who's never been in the military, learn to shoot like a world class sniper."

"He's trained himself since he's been a young boy," she said. "He's learned to master it all; the breathing and the exceptionally low heart rate, coupled with the ability to remain completely motionless. Plus, he has a rare gift for shooting accuracy and therefore is in a class by himself."

"Like you do with a pistol," Buster interjected.

"I guess…" Roxanne replied, while her mind milled a hundred more questions.

Buster picked at the rest of the frosting on the empty plate and wiped his mouth with a napkin.

"Did you enjoy my cinnamon bun?" she asked. "And would you like me to get you another?"

"As a matter of fact, I did, and thank you for offering, but one was enough."

Roxanne smiled at him. "I'm glad you followed me. I needed to talk more than I needed to eat."

"So what's the big deal about Hank shooting a guy who was trying to kill you?" Buster asked seriously. "Seems like Hank's a good guy to have around, especially since he's saved your life twice since you've met him."

"You're right and I'm very grateful he did or most likely I wouldn't be sitting here now and I get that."

"But?"

"But," Roxanne paused. "I just want to know everything about him."

"Such as?"

"Have you ever heard of Citizen Cells?"

Buster's posture stiffened and he glanced around before nodding.

"Yes, I have," he said, leaning in closer to Roxanne so he could lower his voice but not to the point he was whispering. "I was on active duty when 9 11 happened and I was a handler for several groups in Chicago."

"Hank was part of one in New York City where he was doing his Fellowship in Oncology."

"So this is about Hank being in one of the Citizen Cells?" Buster asked, leaning back.

"I just want to know where we stand with all this, for now and in the future," Roxanne said. "We both know they're threats on a daily basis in our country and we see new terror groups forming all the time in the Middle East. They're beheadings on television and now those same groups are calling for home grown terrorists in our country to strike out."

"I understand those concerns and where you stand is just where you are now," Buster said confidently. "You're doing what you should be doing every day. You're working to protect people and to help maintain the strong layer of security we have in our country."

"Are those cells still active and do you think Hank is still involved?" Roxanne asked. "I just want to know so I can support and perhaps even be a part of it."

"Have you talked with your father about this?"

"Not yet, but I intend to," she said, looking at her watch. "I have to go, Nicklaus will be wondering where I am."

"Okay, Roxanne," Buster said, standing up. "I can tell you some of the cells are still active and since the Boston Marathon bombings most of the old ones are coming back online too."

"Really?" Roxanne said, getting up and picking up the empty plate and napkins. "I don't think Hank has been contacted, at least he hasn't mentioned it."

"Well, he might have been contacted and is just on standby."

"And you." Roxanne asked, directly. "What's your status?"

Buster's features grew tight like Roxanne had seen before, especially right before he was going to strike.

"I'm active and I've always been active."

"I'll call you," Roxanne said, and walked to a nearby trash container, deposited the used plate and left the mall.

CHAPTER FOURTEEN

Craig Reynolds and Jefferson Culpepper dug out the cold case file on Heather Burk and set it all out in the conference room. There were several boxes of evidence, including witness statements, police reports and photographs; none of which led to an arrest let alone a conviction. After they did a preliminary look at what they had, they began to read everything in chronological order.

"You'd think with all of this stuff they collected, someone would have been charged," Jefferson said, leafing through one of first deputies report who responded that fateful night.

"That's how it is with a lot of cases, Jefferson, and especially in a murder when no one gets charged." Reynolds replied, picking up the next file from the stack. "…you saw all those boxes lined up in that room."

"To tell you the truth, Craig," Jefferson said. "It was intimidating to see so many boxes of what were once people's lives and are now just pieces of paper with very little chance of ever being solved."

"You're right and probably half of those cold cases, maybe more, have the perpetrator identified but for whatever reason, the prosecution could not move forward to trail…"

"It shouldn't be like that," Jefferson said, idealistically. "Justice should be swift to those who are guilty."

Craig laughed. "You sound like your brother now. He was always ready to go out and arrest someone who he knew was guilty, whether we could prove it or not."

"As it should be!"

"And a lot of the time it is," Craig replied, pawing through Heather's autopsy report and photos. "But A lot of the time when the DA sees what we have, he or she says it's not enough for a conviction."

Jefferson wanted to continue to talk about the criminal justice system but it was too early in the morning to get upset about something he had little control over. Besides, he knew the bottom line, had heard it all his life. First from his dad and then from his older brother Tom, who were both police officers before him. 'Someone is innocent until proven guilty in a court of law.' It didn't always work perfectly, not for the accused or especially the victims, but it was the best system we have and much better than no system at all.

About two hours later, Jefferson asked Craig if he wanted a fresh cup of coffee, which he accepted, and they both took a break. After they settled back with their coffee, Jefferson asked who Paul Dickinson was and if he had known him.

"I did know Paul well, he's been retired now for a number of years, but when he was here, he was an outstanding detective," Craig began, sipping the hot coffee. "Solved hundreds of murder cases, many no one thought could be solved, but the Heather Burk case was the only one that got away. In fact, your brother, who idolized Paul, would tease him in a good natured way about never closing it out."

Jefferson, who was in mid-twenties, was tall like his brother, but leaner and much less mean, so hearing what Reynolds had just said, he somehow could not picture his brother being good natured about anything. Tom Culpepper was a state champion football player who was thick muscled and could be down right aggressive if you rubbed him the wrong way or even the right way for that matter.

"Tom must have really respected him because there weren't many men he admired that much to be good natured about," Jefferson said flatly.

"Well, Paul Dickinson is a guy you don't mess with," Craig said, in Tom's defense. "He's not a big man physically and although he's in very good shape, there's just something about Paul that scared people."

"What do you mean, scared people?" How?" Jefferson asked.

Craig shrugged. "Just some rumors about him…that's all…"

"What kind of rumors?" Jefferson pressed Craig since he really wanted to know the man who could impress his brother that much.

"You didn't hear this from me," Craig said, hunching over his coffee cup. "But some people said Paul was connected to several suspicious deaths."

"Suspicious how? Line of duty deaths?"

Craig shook his head. "No, not line of duty, not directly anyway, but people he thought were guilty but could not prove, somehow ended up dead."

"…and he was thought to have killed them?" Jefferson said, then joked in disbelief. "Maybe we should look at him for Billy's death…"

"Geez, kid…I know…" Craig laughed nervously. "But anyway… it's difficult to say with the other deaths since he was never formally investigated let alone charged with any wrong doing."

"How many deaths are we talking about?" Jefferson asked.

"Three or four but two of them were determined to be accidental and there was only one we could say Paul was directly involved with…"

"Like how?" Jefferson was freaking out and wanted to know everything.

"The guy was a suspect, he was dirty and we all knew it," Craig said. "But he was an engineer and really smart."

"Who did he kill?" Jefferson asked, wide eyed with excitement. "This is crazy shit man, so tell me bro. I won't say anything."

Craig put up his hand. "Easy dude, we're just talking and I'm just saying…and I'm not sure he killed anyone…"

"I got it! I got it!" Jefferson replied, with his thumb and forefinger making a zipping motion over his mouth.

"Long story short and I don't want to talk about this again…" Craig said sternly and he waited for Jefferson to calm down.

"I'm cool, Craig…go ahead."

"We feel the guy killed his business partner, another engineer, with a poison. A heavy metal."

"That's sick, man…poison is evil…"

Craig nodded. "Not slowly either. He just gave him a one-time dose and the guys suddenly sick, goes to the hospital and dies."

"Why did he do it?"

"For the money…like always. He was tired of half."

"So did you ever figure out how he did it?"

Craig shook his head. "We're not sure, but we think he did it right before they got on a plane to come back to the States. These two were big time international structural consultants and went all over the world."

"Where did it happen?"

"Tokyo," Craig said. "They have a huge problem with space over there. Too many people trying to occupy too little of it. Someone wanted to build a large building on a tiny piece of land so these guys went over to take a look at it and tell them how to do it."

"Tokyo police are pretty sharp, aren't they?"

"Sharp yeah, but both of the guys were back in the States when the partner gets sick and dies."

"I see what you mean. What are they going to do…"

"The kicker is, the engineer we think killed the partner has got some heavy metal in his system too."

"Fuck me!"

"Exactly, and of course it's just enough to make him a little sick but not kill him."

"So Tokyo thinks someone else tried to poison them both, but who knows where and when…"

Craig nods. "There you go Sherlock…case closed. "Tokyo says it was probably the competition for the building project, which was worth tens of millions in consultant fees alone."

"What happened with Paul and the engineer?"

"Paul's on the guy all the time, even to the point of harassment, so when the guy balks, Paul pulls the friend card."

"Shaming him…like don't you want to find who killed your partner?"

"Right and it's hard for the guy to deny Paul face to face time," Craig said. "…and Paul keeps on feeding him little bits of information."

"How did he do that? Didn't Tokyo close the case out?"

"Sure they did. They closed it out a few weeks after the guys dead, but Paul tells the suspect he's got a cop in Tokyo still working the case and he's close to finding the source of the poison."

"So by now the guy's getting paranoid and really feeling the pressure."

"Big time," Craig said, "…and Paul's really got some in cop in Tokyo hooked on the case and he's poking around on his own time and sending Paul emails."

"But the case is really going nowhere..." Jefferson concludes.

"Worse than that. It's a total zero, but Paul, who has a sixth sense about people, confronts the guy on the roof of a building, pisses him off and the guy attacks him."

"Witnesses?"

"Three other people that were with the engineer."

"What did Paul say to the guy that pissed him off so bad?"

"We don't know, not exactly anyway. The witnesses, who were some distance away, said they were talking when suddenly the engineer attacked Paul hitting him with his fists and trying to choke him."

"Self-defense and Paul had to shoot him."

"Nope. Paul breaks free of the guy and moves back from him, but the guy's so mad now that he just blindly charges."

"...right off the roof..."

"They were ten stories up and the guy pulls a Humpty Dumpty right on the sidewalk."

"Fuck me!" Jefferson said, with a whistle.

CHAPTER FIFTEEN

Stefani left the mall and went to work. Once she arrived, she headed to Andersson's office on the opposite side of the building. They both had corner offices as a small reward from Governor Forbes for a job well done, although Andersson never let Stefani forget his office was a little bigger. Andersson's door was open so Stefani tapped once on the outside and walked in.

"Where were you?" Andersson asked, looking up. "I thought you were right behind me."

Stefani sat down on the small leather couch.

"I was but I had to make a stop," she said, crossing her legs.

"For what, and I know it wasn't for coffee since we got the best coffee in the world right here," he said, pointing to the coffee machine on a table near his desk.

"No, it wasn't for coffee," she said. "I wanted one of those cinnamon buns they only have at the mall."

"You're kidding me right?" Andersson said, surprised. "Those buns are huge! A family of four could share one and still have some left for the dog."

"I know but I had some thinking to do about the wedding and I wanted to window shop at the same time," she lied about the wedding and she knew he knew it.

"So why didn't you bring me the other two thirds of the bun you didn't eat?"

"I was going to but Buster showed up right after I sat down and he ate your part."

"Buster? What the hell was Buster doing at the mall and eating my share of a cinnamon bun?"

"He was following me…"

"You two still playing that crazy twenty-four hour a day game?" Andersson asked. "I thought you two quit that psycho stuff months ago."

"I tried to quit Nicklaus but that kind of training keep you sharp, and besides; it's fun."

"Fun? With Buster?" Andersson shot back. "The only thing Buster should be doing twenty-four seven is wearing a straightjacket and being heavily sedated in some mental ward. He's crazy, Roxanne."

"You're just pissed because he beat your ass once," she said. "Speaking of crazy, I didn't tell you, a couple of months ago he got in our house at two in the morning, and neither Hank or I heard him."

"What? In your house? At two in the morning." Andersson said, pointing his finger at her. "See, crazy! Who does that?"

Stefani scoffed. "He didn't do anything, just moved some things around and left a note so we knew he got in. I still don't how he got past the alarm system."

"That's a burglary! He committed a felony!"

"No, he didn't," Stefani retorted. "As part of the game rules, it's not a crime if I gave him permission."

"See, that's what I mean and on second thought you ought to be in a straightjacket too and sitting in the room right next to Buster's."

"Well, no worries partner," Stefani said, proudly. "I got him back a couple of weeks later. I got a call from a friend who told me Buster was taking a new date to his favorite restaurant, so I put on a blond wig and surprised him when he went into the men's room."

"You really didn't do that now, Roxanne, did you?" he asked. "Tell me you didn't."

"Okay, I didn't," she said with a sheepish grin. "But you should have seen the look on his face when he saw me standing behind him. I thought he was going to pee all over himself."

"Okay, you win, Roxanne," he said. "I'm the crazy one for even listening to you…"

A sharp rap on the door stopped Andersson in mid-sentence. It was Mary Gordon, Governor Forbes chief of staff and campaign manager for his upcoming Presidential bid.

"Oh good, just the two people I wanted to see," she began, walking into the office and straight to the coffee.

"Good morning to you too, Mary," Andersson said, watching her pour herself a cup.

Mary Gordon was in her early fifties but looked ten years younger despite her hard veneer. She was blond, five-two and barely a hundred pounds and like Stefani, she always wore a great pair of high heels.

"First things first," she said, after tasting the coffee. "What's going on with this Burk thing? I'm already seeing the mad bomber on the loose stories in the newspapers."

"We're on it, and we just talked with Heather Burk's father about an hour ago," Stefani piped up.

"Oh really?" Mary said, turning around to her. "You think the father had something to do with it?"

Andersson shook his head. "No, we don't. We think he's the type of guy that would have done something to Billy Burk a long time ago."

"So why not now? Why couldn't he have waited all these years and killed him anyway?"

"He seemed too happy that Billy was dead," Stefani said, looking down at Mary's high heels. "New heels?"

Mary smiled and shook her right foot. "I got them in D.C. last week when I was on a fact finding trip for the Governor and did some shoe shopping too."

"Looks like more shoe shopping than fact finding," Stefani said, offhandedly.

"Like them?"

"Love them!"

"Thanks," Mary replied and the two of them bumped fists. "So, you were saying that the father was too happy..."

"It was like he had just heard the news and was reacting for the first time," Andersson cut in. "If he really had something to do with it he might have been more evasive or not want to talk to us at all."

"So he's off the list?" Mary asked.

"No, not off the list," Andersson said. "He has an alibi we have to verify, but I don't think he did it."

"He still could have paid someone to do it," Stefani said. "It's too early to eliminate anyone."

"Who's next?" Mary asked, looking from Andersson to Stefani and back to Andersson. "I have to tell Forbes we have a prime suspect."

"We don't have a prime suspect Mary," Andersson said benignly. "We're just getting started. Reyonolds and Culpepper are going through the cold case file to see if there's anyone else that might shake out but that case is related to Heather Burks murder. The Billy Burk bombing might not even be connected to her death at all, so we don't want to develop tunnel vision before we look at all the possibilities."

"Well, that's not good, Nicklaus," Mary said dismayed. "If I tell the Governor that, he might think we really have a mad bomber running loose."

Stefani laughed. "We don't think Billy's bombing was random. From the circumstances we know of the crime scene; he was carefully targeted."

"In fact, we feel this crime was very personal," Andersson said. "Therefore, we need to go through his past with a fine toothed comb."

"Then I can assure Forbes that we don't have to push the panic button and call out the National Guard."

Andersson nodded. "No mad bomber, no panic button and definitely no National Guard."

"Good!" Mary said, jumping up and setting her coffee cup on Andersson's desk. "Now, that that's settled, I can get on to bigger and better things."

"Mary, can I ask you a political question?" Stefani said.

"Sure, go ahead," Mary replied, checking her time. "But I only have a minute and I have to run."

"Hypothetically, what would be Governors Forbes's Presidential policy on the growing threat from home grown terrorism?"

Mary looked at Andersson who shrugged his shoulder.

"That's a very broad topic because terrorism has been tied to so many facets including our foreign policy and the ongoing wars in the middle east."

"I know," Stefani said. "But is he ready to fight terrorists on our own soil? Here in America and not some far off country we only see in a news report."

"I'm not sure where this is coming from and I don't have a lot of time right now," Mary said, clearly taken aback by Stefani's question. "But I can tell you the top three things on our agenda. The economy, jobs, and our national security."

"Our national security, here, as well as abroad?"

Mary nodded, smiled and looked directly at Stefani before leaving. "Yes! Absolutely here! Definitely here! Now, does that answer your question?"

"Yes, it does and thank you."

Mary waved to Andersson and left the office.

CHAPTER SIXTEEN

Paul Dickinson walked into the Raleigh Police Headquarters right before noon and he couldn't have gotten a warmer welcome. Many of his old friends were still there and even those who were new on the job seemed to be in awe that he was back for a visit. There were handshakes and even a few back slaps all around. One of the uniformed officers stuck his head into the conference room where Reynolds and Culpepper were finishing up right before leaving for lunch.

"Hey Reynolds," he said. "Guess who just came into the station and is looking for you?"

"Who?" Reynolds asked, setting one of the empty boxes down.

"Paul Dickinson," he said, with a big smile. "Can you believe that?"

"No, I can't," Reynolds replied, slightly jolted. "What's he want?"

"He said he heard about Billy Burk and he thought you might want to talk with him since he was the lead detective on his wife's case."

Reynolds looked at Culpepper. "The guy's a mind reader."

Culpepper closed the file he was reading. "First Willy Burk comes in and now Paul Dickinson," he said, sarcastically. "This is our lucky day. Maybe we won't even have to leave the building to catch who did this…"

Reynolds shook his head. "You sound more and more like your brother every day."

"Thanks, I'll take that as a compliment," Jefferson said, deadpanning. "I think."

Reynolds looked back to the young officer. "Have him come in."

"Okay," the officer said. "I'll get him. He's still shaking some hands but I'll snag him before the war stories begin."

"Better hurry," Reynolds said. "Or he'll have us waiting all afternoon."

A few seconds after the officer left, Paul Dickinson walked into the conference room.

"Hey Craig," he said with his hand outstretched. "Been a long time…"

They shook hands vigorously.

"Too long Paul," Reynolds said, releasing Paul's hand and looking to Culpepper.

"I don't think you know Jefferson Culpepper, he's Tom's brother."

Paul and Jefferson shook hands.

"Sorry about your brother," Paul said, sincerely. "He was a great cop."

"Thank you," Jefferson replied, and moved back so Reynolds could take the lead.

"What brings you in Paul?" Reynolds asked, point blank.

"The Burk case of course," Paul replied, spreading his hands wide to all the files and photographs lying out. "I thought since I was the lead detective, sooner or later you would want to talk to me. So, here I am."

"You're right," Reynolds said. "We do want to talk to you and I'm sure you can shorten our search through all of this stuff. No one knows the case better than you."

"You aren't kidding, Craig," Paul said, touching some of the files that were stacked on the conference table as the memories flowed back. "I lived and breathed this case for years."

"Sit down Paul," Reynolds directed, pulling out a chair and sitting down himself.

Paul sat down next to him and Culpepper sat down behind Reynolds so Paul could see them both at the same time while they talked.

"I know you did. Tom and I worked this one for a while too," Reynolds recalled. "I think at one time or another the entire force was involved."

Paul nodded. "This was high profile for sure. A young mother to be in a hit and run. Everyone wanted it solved and we were under a lot of pressure to bring it in, but it just wasn't meant to be."

"It was the time element wasn't it?" Reynolds said, as if he had to remind Paul.

"It was a lot of things, Craig," Paul answered, staring at the files. "We just couldn't put Billy at the scene of Heather's fake hit and run until after he got the call from her."

"That's right. Billy was home and Heather was broken down on that lonely stretch of road."

"A road anyone who knew Heather said she had no business being on and would never have driven to in the first place."

Craig looked back at Jefferson and said. "The cell towers confirmed Billy got the call from Heather's phone and that he was at their house when the call came in."

"I remember Tom talking about the case," Jefferson added. "He said somebody else have to had helped Billy."

"Exactly," Paul confirmed. "No way Billy could have staged the scene and made the call on her phone and be home to receive the call at the same time. We think, or should say we know, it was his brother Willy who helped him."

"Speaking of Willy," Craig said. "The asshole was just here. If you were here a couple of hours earlier you would have bumped into him."

"You're kidding." Paul said. "Willy came here...for what?"

"Yeah. Can you believe it?" Reynolds said.

"He was drunk, even high," Culpepper rang in. "He was demanding we find who killed his brother."

"Did you arrest him?" Paul asked.

"No way man," Reynolds replied. "No one wanted his sorry ass around here. We threw him out and put a couple of our guys on him."

"Okay, I get it," Paul said. "Better to keep an eye on him until he sobers up and see what he does than be cleaning up puke..."

"You got it." Reynolds said. "Not that we think he's really going to do anything stupid."

"Stupid was Billy and lazy," Paul said and you don't have to worry about him anymore. "Now Willy was actually the smarter of the two but his quick triggered temper always got him into trouble."

"I've run into Willy a couple of times on domestic calls and we got into it pretty good," Reynolds said.

"I remember that," Paul said, with a big smile. "He sucker punched you or something like that and the next time you went out there, you were ready for him."

"Yeah, I sure was," Reynolds replied, putting up his fists. "He tried to make the same move on me but I gave him a couple of solids to the nose and he never got off a punch. You should have seen it...I beat him down to the floor."

Paul and Culpepper laughed as they watched Reynolds air fight.

"Whoa partner," Jefferson finally said, holding out his hand like a referee. "Don't give yourself a heart attack."

Reynolds stopped punching and laughed breathlessly. "You're aren't kidding, I better get back to the gym."

After they had a good laugh, Reynolds got serious and looked around at all the stacks of paperwork around them.

"Save us some time Paul, and tell us what really happened that night."

"You know the story Craig…"

"But my memory is fading and I know Jefferson would rather hear it from you…"

"Okay," Paul said, clearing his throat. "Billy wanted out of the marriage two weeks after he said I do and a few months later Willy came up with a plan to not only get rid of Heather but to make some real money as well."

"The insurance money." Reynolds said.

"Yes, like over a half of a million," Paul said. "Willy could steal any car ever made and that's what he did best. When he wasn't drunk, high or beating on his girlfriend, he was stealing high end cars and selling them to a dealer who shipped them overseas."

"He stopped beating his girlfriend after I put him down," Reynolds reminded, with a quick jab.

"He did, that's true and she had a chance to get away from him too," Paul said.

"Is that how you think they worked it?" Jefferson asked, trying to keep Paul on track. "Willy stole a car, hit Heather and set up the scene…"

Paul pointed his finger at Jefferson. "Very good kid, that's exactly what happened but I think it was a pickup truck and not a car. She was hit about waist high and she had a lot of internal injuries, so I think he used a pickup truck with one of those huge metal bumpers. He could have hit her just once and not sustained much damage to the vehicle, if any at all."

"Nothing that would have brought any unwanted attention..." Reynolds said.

Paul nodded. "That's right. See, Willy's waiting on this lonely stretch of highway in nowhere when Billy drives up with Heather. Somehow, after they get out of their car for whatever reason, Willy hits Heather and they both stage a hit and run accident."

"How does Billy get back to his house to establish an alibi when the call comes in from Heathers cell?" Jefferson asks.

"Easy, Willy brought a crotch rocket with him in the pickup. They both had them back then and that's another reason why I think they used a truck."

Jefferson summarizes it. "Willy hits Heather, they stage the scene and Billy heads home on the cycle then Willy calls Billy like he's Heather calling for help."

"Yeah, real simple," Paul said. "Billy drives out there and finds Heather lying in the road. In fact, she's some distance from her car which is parked off on the shoulder with the flashers going."

"Why would she walk away from the car if she knew Billy was coming to help her?" Jefferson asked.

"She wouldn't but I guess they had to make it look like she was going for help when she got hit.

Otherwise, if she stayed in the car she wouldn't have gotten hit in the first place."

"What I don't understand, if it's connected at all to Heather's death, is why someone would wait until now to kill Billy ..." Reynolds stated.

"Good point," Paul said. "It might not be connected at all and you guys will be chasing your tails looking at the Heather angle."

"True, but we still have to look at the obvious motive," Reynolds reminded him. "The revenge aspect."

"Revenge for Heather's death is a great motive," Paul agreed. "But outside of the father and me no one else wanted him dead for that reason."

Reynolds laughed. "You? The father I can see, but why you?"

"Come on, Craig," Paul said, with a bit of swagger. "We all know that Heather Burk was my only real big case that I never closed."

Reynolds shook his head. "But like the father, why wait all this time?"

"I don't think it's got to do with Heather, not now," Paul said. "I think it's about the money."

"The money huh?" Reynolds stated. "You think it's about the insurance money."

Paul nodded. "Follow the money, that's what I'd do and besides, I was at Hot Rod Wednesday night getting a BJ in the parking lot."

Reynolds turned back to Culpepper again. "See, Jefferson, that's a good detective for you. He knows we want to ask him where he was Wednesday night, but he saves us the embarrassment and he tells us up front."

"I'm learning, Craig, I'm learning."

"Good, because you're learning from the best…"

"Alright you guys, you can stop waxing my carrot," Paul said, standing up. "I have to go since I have a lunch date."

Reynolds and Culpepper got up when Paul did.

"I'll walk you out Paul," Reynolds said.

"Okay," Paul replied, putting his hand out to Culpepper. "Nice meeting you kid. You're going to go far."

"Thanks," Jefferson said, watching Reynolds put his arm around Paul's shoulder. "Nice to meet you too."

Reynolds steered Paul to the door and asked him one last question before they left.

"Is your lunch date the same girl who with you in the parking lot?"

"Yes," Paul said, with a laugh. "She is, and why not come along with me, that way you can verify my alibi and get a free lunch, all at the same time..."

CHAPTER SEVENTEEN

"I can't this weekend Henry, I'm on my way to the airport, I'm flying up to New York for a couple of days," Kira said. "I'd love to see you again, we'll definitely make a date for when I get back."

"I understand Kira," Henry said, graciously. "I know you have business in New York but I wanted to get together not only on a personal note but for my new manuscript."

"Of course Henry," Kira said, sweetly. "I haven't forgotten the manuscript and I surely haven't forgotten the other night either."

Henry blushed as he recalled that night and despite being drunk he remembered every detail vividly.

"I know Kira, it was the best night of my life!"

"You flatter me, Henry," Kira said. "And if I didn't have business there, I would rather stay right here in Raleigh with you."

"Really?" Henry said, skeptically. "I just can't believe that."

"Why Henry…," Kira said, defensively. "Are you calling me a liar?"

"No! No, I didn't mean it that way!" Henry screamed, almost as if in pain. "I just meant I can't believe this is happening to me. I would never call you a liar..."

"Well, that's nice to know Henry," Kira replied, dismissively. "You better not call me names because you know what happens to little boys when they're bad, don't you?"

Instantly, Henry's heart leapt at her threat. "I'm not sure..." he stammered. "Do they get a spanking?"

"That's right Henry," she replied, switching into her dominating role. "Mommy gives them a spanking on their bare bottoms."

"Oh my!" Henry murmured in anticipation. "I guess if I deserve one for calling you a liar then I guess I should receive one."

"We'll see Henry...we'll see. When I get back we'll see what you deserve..."

"Okay Kira," he said, wishing she would tell him what she would do to him.

"I'll call you first thing when I get back," she said. "I promise."

"Alright Kira," Henry said saddened. "I'll be waiting."

A couple of hours later Kira was riding in a limo heading into Manhattan tucked up against Chris.

"You have no idea how much I've missed you baby," Kira said, looking up at him.

"I think I have a pretty good idea," Chris replied, kissing her lips. "Especially after that phone call yesterday."

"Yesterday was just a warm up for what's coming today and that pun was intended," she said, and she parted her legs for the driver who was watching them in the rear view mirror.

Chris laughed at her pun and looked down at Kira's provocative pose. "I'd tell him to keep his eyes on the road, but I know it's turning you on to give him a little show."

"That's right, I love a little public fun to get things going..."

Chris laughed and kissed her lips again.

Another fifteen minutes of playing grab ass in the backseat, plus a couple of near misses with pedestrians as the driver tried to keep up viewing Kira's ever changing positions, and they were there.

The apartment where Chris lived, which Kira owned, was new, and after Chris tipped the limo driver, they went inside the building. Kira wanted to mention to Chris, just casually, that she had written a manuscript but right now she didn't want to spoil the mood with business. She would save laying the groundwork for that until later at dinner, then she laughed out loud at another of her puns.

"Something funny?" Chris asked.

"Just another little dirty thought I had..." she replied, yanking him by the hand.

Chris made a feeble attempt to resist her pulling, but relented up to his apartment door.

"None of your dirty thoughts are little," he said, kissing her and moving his hands over her body. "By the way Kira, I have a surprise for you."

"Oh," she said feeling between his legs. "That's no surprise but I'm not complaining either."

Chris licked in both of her ears, which drove Kira crazy, and whispered in one of them when he finally stopped.

"No, that's not the surprise," he said, opening the door which was unlocked. "But this is..."

They walked into the entrance way which led into the living room and at the end of a short hallway was the young model from the photo shoot. She was kneeling, nude from the waist up, but you could hardly tell she was female since her chest was nearly flat, except for two extremely long, almost black colored nipples.

"This is Radhika, she's from India," Chris said, presenting her proudly. "In Hindi, her name means fulfiller of desires."

Radhika stayed on her knees as Chris and Kira walked over to her.

"Oh Chris," Kira said, gleefully as she walked around the girl. "Now, this is really a surprise..."

Chris beamed as he watched Kira slowly inspect his present.

"She's just turned twenty-three and almost old for the modeling world," Chris began.

Kira leaned over, and smelled the girl's hair, she remained motionless as Kira continued to waltz around her.

"She's beautiful Chris," Kira said, after several minutes. "So exotic and I love her jet black hair cut short like that, almost boyish. She's remarkable."

"Yes, she is," Chris replied excitedly, knowing he had pleased Kira beyond expectations. "She's five seven but looks taller even without the high heels."

"Her skin is amazing," Kira said, leaning over and licking the girl's face. "...and no makeup either."

"No, I thought since Radhika had such incredibly large eyes and sensuous lips, that leaving her in a natural state for you was the way to go."

Kira pulled hard on one of the girl's bullet shaped nipples and then on the other, twisting it painfully. The girl did not flinch nor utter a sound.

"She's so delicate looking, yet I sense an inner strength like she's going to be able to take a lot."

"She will," Chris said, his voice began to tremble. "She has limited experience but what's she's done already is impressive."

"Have you had her yet?" Kira asked almost afraid Chris was going to say yes.

Chris shook his head and the trembling in his voice began to spread down over his body.

"No, I haven't," he replied, but quickly added. "I know you told me to take her but when we got started in the vanilla way and I realized what a potential find she was; I stopped. I knew you would have wanted to experience that with me firsthand."

Kira sauntered to Chris and he wasn't sure if she was upset or not since her face was expressionless.

"You did the right thing despite your disobedience," she said, striking his crotch which made him buckle. "Now take off your belt and drop your pants!"

Chris caught his breath in short gasps and did as she demanded. He unfastened his belt, handed it to her and let his pants fall to his ankles, exposing himself. Kira stepped back, smiled that he wasn't wearing any underwear, then walked back to the model who was still motionless and staring blankly.

"You see that big, angry, dirty thing between his legs?" Kira said, loudly to Radhika, who nodded slowly. "Crawl over there and make it all better!"

Radhika opened her mouth in an exaggerated motion and leaving it a gaping hole, she arched her back and began to crawl. Her crawling wasn't timid or choppy in movement, but like a big cat. Her hands worked as large paws, slapping the floor with her body writhing in an erotic rhythm. She was suddenly transformed from the kneeling boy waif into predator after prey.

"Oh I love that!" Kira praised. "She's really hungry and knows how to show it."

The girl stopped at Chris's feet and tightened her body into a coil ready to spring on command.

"That's it! That's it!" Kira said moving to her as she looped the belt into a collar. "I better get control over this one; she's like a wild animal."

Kira took the belt, swung it around the girl's neck, pulled it tight and reeled her back.

"There! Now take everything off Chris. I want you naked for this wild cat."

Chris slid off his loafers and stepped out of his pants, kicking them to the side. Next, he took off his jacket and shirt. His bare, lean body was glistened with a light coat of sweat and clearly defined the ridges between his twelve pack.

"See how beautiful he is," Kira whispered in the girl's ear as she tightened the belt around her neck. "You want him I know but you're going to have to earn it…"

Kira pulled back on the belt and the loop grew even tighter.

"Lick him!" She ordered, pulling Radhika's head to Chris.

The girl tried to move her open mouth to him but Kira steered her away.

"No! Not yet! Lick his body first! Taste him everywhere and show me how much you want him before I give you the reward."

The girl did as she was told and began to attack Chris's body. First, she made long, wide licks up his thighs, all around him and up his abs as far as she could reach with Kira pulling her back in restraint.

"That's it, you wild bitch…fight me…fight me!"

Chris stood still and did not touch the girl as she slithered all over and around him. Her tongue was never dry and feverishly lapped as she replaced his sweat with her salvia. After what seemed an endless dream, she finished and all three of them were extremely aroused.

"Take him now! Take it all and suck!" Kira shouted and felt the swelling surge between her legs. "Suck him down your throat while I pull the belt tighter!"

Radhika immediately lunged at Chris, totally engulfing him while Kira pulled back on the belt just at the point of strangulation.

"Not yet Chris…Don't rush it…we're not there yet…" Kira urged, as she kept the pressure on the girl's neck while moving back and forth with her bobbing head. "Give her another few seconds and she'll be ready to pass out…"

Chris nodded and concentrated on the pleasure while still keeping his control. Radhika continued to suck at a furious pace and Kira finally felt a slight lag in the movement of her head.

"Now Chris! Now!" Kira shouted, and released the belt from around the girl's neck just as Chris exploded into her mouth.

Chris screamed, took hold of Radhika's head and jammed himself down her throat.

"That's it! Keep it going Chris! She's there…she's there…"

The girl put her hands up to Chris's thighs to steady herself as her body began to shake in a very intense orgasm.

"Hold on to her Chris…easy…easy…don't let her pass out…"

Kira watched them as she began to feel her own tremors pass through her body.

"Let her breathe Chris…or you'll choke her…" Kira said, barely able to get the words out; the belt falling slack in her hand.

Another thirty seconds with more climatic aftershocks between the three of them and foreplay was over. Now, on to some real sexual fun.

CHAPTER EIGHTEEN

Later, that Saturday morning, back in Raleigh, Hank had just arrived at Rocco's gun range and was getting out of the Jeep when Rocco approached.

"I already know about your conversation with Roxanne," Rocco blurted out. "I just got off the phone with her."

Hank continued to the back of the Jeep and removed his modified Weatherby .300. He was already carrying his Glock on his person.

"What did she say?" Hank asked.

"Not that much, just right to the point," Rocco replied. "She knew I didn't take that shot and she was disappointed we didn't tell her."

"I know, we talked quite a bit about it the other night and she's still got a dozen questions for me."

Rocco closed the rear door of the Jeep for Hank and they both walked to the indoor pistol range.

"I wouldn't worry about it Hank, I think we both know she knew you took the shot but she just wanted to hear one of us say it."

"I know and now in hindsight, I wish I had told her that day it happened."

"She also mentioned you told her about the citizen cells," Rocco continued, and unlocked the door.

"Yes, I feel at this point lying about any of this is only going to complicate things for her and I in the future."

They both walked through the open door and into the range. Rocco turned on several switches and the entire mechanized range came to life like an amusement park.

"You're right, and even if Roxanne wasn't the super detective that she is; I think it would be impossible to hide what's going to happen in the near future."

"Rocco, you really think we're all going active again like right after 9 11?"" Hank asked, setting the rifle and ammunition case down on one of the nearby tables.

"No Hank, I don't think, I know," Rocco informed. In fact, many of the units, especially in the larger cities, have already gone active."

"You're kidding?"

"The threat is very real in this country and we're already encountering more homeland terrorists."

"I thought on the drive out here you might have something more positive to say..."

"I wish I could say life is fine and there's no risk to anyone in this country but the world situation is way out of control Hank," Rocco replied. "While we have many of the protective agencies within our government tending to our security in foreign countries; it's going to be up to the FBI, state and local law enforcement to prevent any attacks from within the country."

Hank pulled his weapon from his waist holster and loaded it while Rocco moved into the new sophisticated control area which operated the gun range.

"How about trying the gold challenge again?" Rocco asked. "You did pretty well on it last week and that was your first time."

"Sounds good," Hank replied, getting his ear protection on. "I'm all set when you are and my weapon is hot."

"Okay," Rocco said and he shut off the power to all the doors locking them so someone was unable to enter during a live fire. "Here you go!"

Hank instinctively moved to his left even before the targets began to pop up in various combinations and threats. Many of the human form targets were civilian silhouettes mixed in with the criminals as well as other law enforcement personnel. Hitting one of the good guy targets brought severe penalties and lowered your score.

Hank fired in rapid succession all the ammo that was in the clip, ejected it and reloaded another fresh one in a split second. In less than a minute he was done firing and the place smelled of gunpowder.

"How did I do?" Hank asked, emptying the weapon and holstering it.

Rocco held his thumb up. "Wow!" he said, coming out of the booth. "Great score and you're getting near beating the record times too."

"You're kidding?" Hank said, looking at the print out in Rocco's hand.

"No, I'm not. There's only a few scores and times better than yours."

"Let me guess," Hank said, sarcastically. "You, Roxanne and a couple of your top FBI guys."

"Yeah, well you're close to my best score and to the two guys on my team but we're all light years from Roxanne."

"Let me see that," Hank said, taking the score sheet from Rocco. "How can that be? If I'm shooting so well how can she be that far ahead."

Rocco laughed. "I guess it's because her scores are consistently perfect and she does it in amazingly fast times."

"So, in other words I'm never going to catch her let alone beat her."

"Yes, that's right," Rocco agreed. "It's the same principle with you and me on the rifle range. You're always going to be better, more accurate and faster than I am. Why? Because you're probably the best rifle shot in the world and that's the way it is."

Hank sat down on the edge of the table and set the score sheet aside.

"I don't want to lie to Roxanne or keep anything from her again…ever," he said, flatly. "I know it was my idea to say you made the shot, but I was wrong. It only ended up making things worse by lying about it."

"I know you just wanted to keep your past quiet Hank but that can't happen," Rocco replied. "Not any more it can't…"

"I know Rocco and I guess I knew it the moment I pulled the trigger," Hank said, getting off the table. "But I also know Roxanne and I will work together on it and somehow make it all work."

"You will…I'm sure you will…"

Hank picked up the Weatherby .300 and the ammunition.

"Let's go outside and shoot some long distance targets," Hank said. "…and just to let you know, I'm feeling particularly confident today."

"Is that your nice way of saying I'm going to get my ass kicked out there?" Rocco asked, his ego already crushed.

Hank smiled. "Yes, I guess it is."

CHAPTER NINETEEN

It was around five thirty in the afternoon when Pi showed up at Paul Dickinson's place. He expected her at a little after six when the nail salon closed but she had left early.

"I thought you got done at six on Saturday?" He asked, letting her in.

"I usually do but my last client come early and she just want pedicure," Pi said, hugging Paul at the same time. "I miss you."

Paul hugged her tiny frame and kissed her. He loved Pi's lips from the moment he saw her at Hot Rod and he knew she was for him. Well, he noticed her ass too but he saw her lips first and that was unusual for Paul since he always noticed a woman's ass first. He squeezed her tight and swallowed her up in his arms.

"I feel safe with you Paul," Pi said, between kisses. "I know we just meet..."

"It's met," Paul corrected. "We just met."

Pi put her hand up to her mouth. "Oops...Yes, I forget. We just met is what I mean to say."

"Meant to say..." he said, laughing.

She giggled. "I'm nervous and my English gets worse when I'm nervous."

Paul released her from his bear hug. "Why are you nervous Pi?"

"I don't know but I feel different with you…from the first few minutes…"

"Maybe you mean you're excited to see me and said nervous …"

Pi nodded. "Yes! I mean excited. Good excited!"

"Me too," Paul said, hugging her again and despite their vast age difference, they both felt a genuine attraction. "…and here I thought you just liked to collect Franklins…"

Pi thought for a moment, then pushed at Paul but the push didn't budge him.

"No! That's not true!" she said, angrily. "I'm not whore! You were the one who put the money down. I never ask for it!"

Paul looked at Pi and could see more hurt in her eyes than anger.

"I'm sorry Pi," Paul said, sincerely. "I didn't mean to hurt your feelings."

"Well, you do…" she pouted with her lips even fuller.

He smiled down at her. "…it's you never asked for it…not ask…"

Pi looked briefly confused at what Paul had just said but when she realized what he meant, she quickly slapped his chest.

"I want you to correct my English but not when I'm mad at you or we make love…"

"…or when we make love…," he corrected again.

Pi slapped his chest again and giggled. "I'm still mad at you Paul so do not correct me!"

Paul took Pi in his arms, kissed her again and tasting a tear he knew she was crying.

"I'm sorry Pi," he said, looking at her. "I really am. I thought we were just going to have some fun…and…"

"What? You give me Franklins and everything okay?"

He nodded.

"I know we not same age or even close but I would not be here with you if I did not really want to…"

Paul nodded again. "You want to get some Italian food and maybe see a movie?"

Pi nodded, wiping her tears. "Yes, I very much do and we come back here and make love…"

"Yes…and no corrections," Paul said, smiling.

"Yes…make love and no corrections…" Pi replied, with her giggle.

Back in New York, Kira, Chris and Radhika were doing everything but making love. Love wasn't part of what they were doing, at least for each other, but it sure was fun. After Kira's idea of foreplay in the entrance way, something to drink and a short rest, Kira pushed them to round two which made her the center of attention.

Sure, she was the dominant one but Kira not only wanted others doing whatever she demanded; she wanted a lot of attention for herself. Most people would find having more than one person at a time sexually, distracting, but for Kira it was a matter of multiple simultaneous stimulations. Her areas of sensitivity were numerous and having them all aroused at the same time just increased her pleasure.

Radhika was a natural submissive who not only learned rapidly but anticipated her dominant's needs. She was agile and her slender frame made her accessible, and more importantly none of her body was off limits.

Into round two, Chris was taking turns on them when Kira wanted to lick Radhika while Chris did her from the back at the same time. Kira tied the models legs by the ankles into two large iron rings above the headboard which Chris had previously secured into the wall. When Kira had finished, Radhika looked like a beautiful butterfly pinned opened in someone's collection and Kira began to gnaw on her like a beaver on a young tree trunk. There were teeth marks all over the girl and at one point Chris pulled back on Kira's hair fearing she was close to drawing blood.

Kira eased up but bucked back even harder with each of Chris's movements until he knew she was nearing the end. He was exhausted from giving her the incessant pounding but there was no way he could stop until she was satiated; then just as she groaned as if in pain, her cell phone rang.

Everyone stopped and at first no one knew what was happening. There were enough bells and whistles already going off and at this point the new ones only added to the confusion. Still, they all finished before Kira removed herself from between the two of them and retrieved her phone. Chris went to untie Radhika from over the head board when Kira interrupted him.

"Leave her up...I'm not done with her ..." Kira said, looking down at the caller ID. "What the fuck?"

"Kira she's passed out..."Chris said, reaching for the rope tied around her ankle.

"Okay, take her down and bring her around..." Kira said, trying to catch her breath before answering the call. "Henry...what a pleasant surprise..."

Kira? You sound all out of breath..." Henry said. "Are you jogging or working out?"

"Yes, as a matter of fact, Henry, I'm working out after a long day of endless meetings."

Henry listened to her rapid breathing until she became uncomfortable and knew it was turning him on.

"I don't mean to rush you Henry but I need to shower and meet some clients for dinner in an hour."

Henry listened another few moments before he replied.

"I just wanted to see how your trip was going and I was going to wait until you came back but I'm just busting at the seams to tell you!"

"Tell me what Henry?" Kira asked, watching Chris untie Radhika and gently slap her face as he tried to bring her around.

"Give her some water," Kira said, spontaneously.

"Are you with someone?" Henry asked.

"Yes, well not really together," Kira said. "I'm in the hotel gym and of the woman who was on a treadmill next to me felt faint."

"Oh, at first you sounded like you were all alone..."

"I am...So what's the big news Henry?" Kira asked, steering him back on track.

"I've completed my third manuscript and I'm so excited, I just had to tell you."

"Your third manuscript?" Kira asked, wiping her sweaty forehead with her hand.

"Yes, my third," Henry replied, elated. "Didn't you sense after reading the first manuscript that I left the door open for a second book?"

"I did, but I thought it was something in the future," Kira said, astounded. "You mean you've completed a trilogy?"

Henry nodded with his happy grin and she knew it but was glad she could not see it.

"Yes!" Yes!" He said, jumping up and down. "I've been a busy little bee, Kira."

Kira could hardly reply. "I...guess you have Henry..."

"I've been writing, ten or twelve hours a day, seven days a week. I wanted the trilogy to be a surprise but I didn't want to miss any of my Gina Wells deadlines..."

Well, I must admit Henry, you've really surprised me," Kira said, sliding off the bed when she heard Radhika moan softly as she began to come around.

"Henry, does anyone else know you've written this trilogy?"

"No, no one. I said that I brought you the first manuscript."

"Yes…you did," she said, leaving the bedroom in case Radhika said something and Henry heard her. What about your mother Henry. Does she know?"

"No, of course not," Henry said, firmly. "You know I love my mother dearly and she's all I've got for family, but she would have told all her friends, and my secret would have been out"

"Good, I'm glad. It's very important to keep this between us," Kira was thinking as fast as she could and her mind was a mile ahead of her mouth.

"I know Kira and I plan on keeping it secret just between us."

"Henry, I'm taking an early flight Sunday morning; why not meet me for lunch when I get back."

"Lunch? Tomorrow?" He repeated. "Just you and I?"

"Yes Henry, just you and I at my house again," she tempted.

"Yes, of course, I'd love that."

Kira could hear Chris talking to Radhika and telling her something about passing out and that she would be okay.

"Henry, I want you to come to my house at noon and I want you to bring the other two manuscripts."

"Okay, if you want me to Kira…sure…"Henry could hear the pitch of her get deeper. She wasn't asking him to bring the manuscripts; she was telling him, ordering him and he liked that.

"…and Henry," she said furthermore, "No one and I mean no one is to know about these manuscripts until we're ready to publish."

"Okay, Kira," Henry squeaked. "Whatever you say…"

Kira smiled at herself in a large mirror that hung over a deep maroon, leather, love seat. She admired her nude body and did her little pirouette to check out her ass.

"Yes, Henry…whatever I say and anything I say…whenever I say it…"

Kira hung up before Henry could reply but it didn't matter; he was speechless and his tongue did the lizard lick.

CHAPTER TWENTY

Hank stayed late at the gun range with Rocco so Roxanne worked into the afternoon with Andersson. They used the extra time to put together some of the briefing for Monday morning with the Wake County DA, Michael Carson. They didn't have a lot of earth shaking information but Andersson wanted to keep Carson in the loop since he knew Carson was a detail person and didn't like surprises.

Roxanne and Hank had a standing dinner date for Saturday, seven o'clock, at one of their favorite restaurants. She kidded Hank when they first agreed to keep their Saturday dinner date open for themselves that they would start their dates at seven o'clock, so as they got older the time would get earlier until they reached the early bird special.

Roxanne felt much better after her talk with Hank about the shooting. She was still having panic attacks on occasion and with her pattern; they happened when she least expected one, but overall they were getting much better.

Roxanne had a couple of hours before she had to meet Hank and that meant she had time to get some wedding gifts; not for Hank but for the two women who would be her maid of honor and lone bridesmaid. It was something she had been putting off since having a lot of money to spend still gave her an awkward feeling.

Despite living comfortably before she met Hank and having their new found wealth, she never realized how much responsibility went along with it. Not that she didn't enjoy it or love the feeling of security, we all want that; it was the purchasing power. Like buying the wedding gifts for Hank's sister, Erin, his daughter Maggie, and Shay Abisi. She wanted to buy them something exceptionally nice, and something very special.

Roxanne wanted to spend a lot of money on them but then she thought they might think she was showing off and trying to over impress. But, both Shay and Erin, were well off in their own right, and they might not feel an expensive gift was over spending, but then again, would Hank's daughter realistically use an expensive gift? Of course she would, when she was older, it would be a treasure.

It was all relative Roxanne decided, and despite a drop in popularity, a watch was still a beautiful piece of jewelry as well as a practical timepiece. Roxanne settled on three designer watches which were personally engraved to commemorate her wedding but foremost their friendships. She was always fond of Shay Abisi, and now Erin Milson was like the sister she never had.

Speaking of time, Roxanne had over an hour before she was to meet Hank for dinner, so why not go for a spin in her new Corvette. A spin to Roxanne meant taking the sports car out on a lonely road she had found and really letting it go. She loved the speed and she could drive like a professional even while wearing high heels.

She was about twenty five minutes out into her run and had slowed down to head back when she spotted the lights in her side mirror. Shit! She was busted! It never happened before on this isolated stretch and it was always a good place to open up the Vette and let her run, or so she had thought.

Immediately, Roxanne pulled over and shut off the engine just as the North Carolina State Police SUV pulled in behind her. Despite the fact she was with the State Police herself, it was very shocking and intimidating to be pulled over for speeding, not to mention embarrassing. Her side window was already down and her empty hands in plain view when the Trooper carefully approached.

"Good evening," he began, staying slightly back from the open window.

"Good evening Officer," Roxanne replied, turning to face him while keeping her hands on the steering wheel.

"Do you know how fast you were going Ma'am?" he asked.

"I'm not sure but it was fast," Roxanne replied. "I was so busy with the clutch and shifting; I really wasn't paying attention."

"Well, if you didn't slow down on your own I probably wouldn't have caught you this time either," he said, with a note of pride. "I clocked you at over one hundred and twenty three miles an hour on the straight part when you went by me."

"Really, that fast?" She said, but knowing she was going well over one hundred through that part.

"Are you trying to kill yourself or worse, someone else?"

"No sir, I'm not," she said, now noticing how young the Trooper looked. "You said you wouldn't have caught me this time either if I hadn't slowed down. You tried to catch me before?"

"Three times before and I've been waiting for you for two weeks to come back," he said. "You seem to always favor this time of day too, so I staked out the road every evening..."

"I'm sorry, I would have stopped if I saw your lights..."

"I'm sure," he said, unconvinced. "Let me see your driver's license and registration."

Roxanne complied and the Trooper looked at them then handed them back to her.

"Here you go, Ma'am," he said. "You're free to go but please keep your speed down."

"I'm free to go?" Roxanne asked, looking up at the Trooper. "But, I was speeding...real fast. You said so yourself"

"Yes Ma'am, you were," he said, disappointed. "But you're Roxanne Stefani and you're one of us..."

"You know me?"

"I know of you Ma'am," he said, proudly with a smile. "Everyone in law enforcement in North Carolina knows you. You're the only female to have ever been awarded the Medal of Valor and they rarely have given them out to anyone in the State's history."

"But I deserve a speeding ticket..."

"Heck Ma'am, you deserve a bunch of tickets but I'm not going to write a single one," he said, getting nervous. "My girlfriend is a Trooper Ma'am, and she even has your picture on her locker receiving the Medal of Valor; she would kill me if I wrote you a speeding ticket. Besides, I know you work directly for Governor Forbes."

Roxanne stuck her hand out the window handing the license and registration back to him.

"Here! Take these and write me the ticket or tickets! She said, forcefully. "I broke the law and got caught!"

The Trooper looked dumbfounded, but took the license and registration from Roxanne.

"Are you sure Ma'am?"

"Very sure!" Roxanne replied. "No one is above the law no matter who they are!"

"Yes Ma'am," he said, and went back to his vehicle.

Ten minutes later he returned with one ticket.

"Here you go," he said, handing her the ticket.

Roxanne read the violation.

"Eighty in a fifty-five mile an hour zone?" She asked. "You said I was doing one-twenty..."

"One-twenty-three, Ma'am," he corrected. "If I put that speed down, you'll probably get your license suspended not to mention your insurance rates will double."

Roxanne looked at the ticket. "What's your name?" She asked, trying to read it where he had signed.

"Pritchette Ma'am," he replied, with a tip of his hat. "Randy Pritchette."

"Thank you Trooper Pritchette," she said. "I'm not going to speed again like this. It was a dangerous thing to do on a public highway."

"Yes Ma'am, it was," he said. "You should find a track to take this baby out on..."

"You're right," Roxanne said, setting the ticket down on the seat. "I'll take it to the track."

"Have a good evening Ma'am," he said, and started to walk back to his vehicle.

"Two weeks you were out here waiting for me?" Roxanne called back to him.

"Yup...two long weeks..." he called back.

"Send me your supervisor's name to my office email," she said. "I want to inform him or her about your outstanding police work."

"Ma'am?"

"You heard me..."

"Yes Ma'am." And he walked away shaking his head.

Roxanne picked up her cell phone and called Hank to tell him she was going to be late.

CHAPTER TWENTY-ONE

The phone call from Henry Harris was a real game changer for Kira in more ways than one. She was completely flabbergasted that he had completed three totally amazing manuscripts and she was the only person who knew about it. The phone call also put an end to her sexual fun but it didn't matter especially since she saw how tired both Chris and Radhika looked. Furthermore, she was now too excited about the manuscripts to think of little else except for a nice, thick, prime steak.

Like a marathon runner, Kira always lost three or four pounds with her hours of vigorous activity so she always rewarded herself with a great steak and there were few places in the world better for steak than New York City.

They all showered, got ready and went by limo to one of the finest steak houses Kira knew and they ate. Kira had a huge bone-in Delmonico, medium, with a loaded baked potato the size of a football, and a side of creamed spinach. Chris and Radhika, being models, had a small salad with Balsamic vinaigrette and a four ounce filet to match; but they were famished and split a baked potato without anything on it. After dinner, they dropped Radhika off at her apartment and Kira and Chris went back to his place to sleep.

The next morning, Kira was up early and off to the airport. She was so eager to get back to Raleigh that she didn't even wake Chris to say goodbye. These manuscripts were much too important to her and she would have them at all costs.

Back in Raleigh, it was still early and she had plenty of time to shop and prepare lunch for her and Henry. She wasn't going to have anything elaborate just some Panini's, fresh fruit and plenty of ice cold champagne. Henry wasn't a big eater and anyway, she knew he wasn't coming to her house for just the lunch.

Henry was right on time at precisely noon. The doorbell rang and Kira opened the door with her best gushing greeting.

"Henry!" She said, hugging him in the doorway. "I'm glad you could make it."

Henry loved her greeting and especially the feel of her body against his.

"Oh Kira," he said, kissing her cheek but missing her mouth as his intended target. "I've been counting the minutes from the time we hung up yesterday."

"Come in, Henry, come in," she said, taking his arm. "Now, it's just a simple lunch, nothing fancy, mind you."

"Whatever you have Kira will be fine, I'm sure," Henry said, moving to the kitchen with her. "You know I'm here to see you and not to eat..."

Kira spun him around and right into of her highboy chairs.

"Here Henry, sit down," she said. "The Panini's are all ready for the press and you can have a nice cold glass of champagne while I make them."

"Oh, champagne again?" He said, with his happy smile. "It must be another special occasion."

After Kira poured Henry a glass of champagne, she took the two sandwiches of roast chicken, pesto, roasted red peppers and Provolone cheese and placed them into the Panini press. She closed the lid and while they grilled flat, she poured a full glass for herself.

"Here's to us, Henry and to the trilogy that will rock the literary world!"

Henry watched Kira drink the wine and committed to his long term memory exactly how she swallowed. He was fascinated with the mechanics of how a woman's mouth worked and the slight variations when compared to a man's. He noticed tiny things about people in general but especially about women and his writings reflected it.

When he wrote as Gina Wells, he was Gina Wells and it was why his erotic novels written by her were so good. Henry could convey to women as only another women could. He wasn't confused sexually nor a woman trapped in a man's body; in fact despite his very limited experiences with women, he was a solid heterosexual.

"Aren't you drinking Henry?" Kira asked, showing some dismay. "You know its bad luck not to take a drink after someone has made a toast."

"Really?" Henry said, putting the glass to his lips. "I didn't know that and I had every intention to complete the toast but I was just observing you swallowing."

Kira cocked her head to on side; even for Henry that statement was bizarre.

"Well drink up Henry," She prodded, while shaking her half full glass at him. "It's bad luck on the person who doesn't complete the toast."

Henry quickly took several sips of the champagne with the third sip going up his nose resulting in a minor choking spell.

"Sorry Kira," Henry said, after a couple of coughs and some sniffing. "I think the idea of something I didn't do right causing me bad luck, scared me."

"Are you okay now Henry?" She asked, downing the rest of her champagne and refilling the glass.

"Yes, I'm fine, Kira," he replied, drinking more.

"Good, now that the bad luck curse has been lifted, let's have some lunch," she said, playfully but leaving Henry still shaken.

"They smell delicious and I actually have the same Panini press at home," Henry said, walking over to the enormous granite covered island. "It's so much easier for me to make a sandwich that's a meal, especially when I'm writing."

"I bet," Kira said, lifting the lid to reveal the massive, perfectly grilled sandwiches.

"They look great," Henry said.

Kira took the Panini's from the grill, cut them each in half and set them down on two large, white, square plates.

"Here you go Henry, enjoy!"

Henry picked up a half of Panini, took a bite and sat back down. Kira did the same thing, they ate the first half of the sandwiches in silence.

"I didn't realize how hungry I was," Henry said, picking up the other half and taking a bite.

"Me either," Kira said, reaching for the other half of hers.

They ate the rest of the sandwiches with little more than a few comments about how great they tasted. When they finished eating Kira poured another full glass of champagne for each of them.

"To Panini's!" Kira said, holding her glass up high.

"To Panini's!" Henry said, clinking his glass to hers.

They both took long swallows while all the time Henry kept his eyes on Kira's throat.

"So did you bring the other manuscripts Henry?" Kira asked, glancing around. "I didn't notice you carrying anything when you came in."

Henry nodded, as he felt the bubbly working and his head moved back and forth affirmatively.

"Yes, I did," he replied. "I did exactly as you told me Kira, they're in my car."

"Very good Henry," Kira said, touching his face with her hand.

Earlier, she had ignored Henry's familiar unpleasant odor and was even able to enjoy her lunch in spite of it, but now with the smell of the sandwiches gone, she began to feel nauseous. Kira took an exaggerated slide off her chair and Henry's eyes fell to her thighs which were generously exposed. Her black leather mini skirt was soft and hugged every part of her.

"See anything you like Henry," she asked, as she began to feel the effects of her third glass of champagne.

"I like everything I see," Henry replied, following her with his eyes as she moved behind him.

She lay her head on his back and fought the urge to retch.

"I think it's time for another bath Henry," Kira said, softly as her hands glided over his crotch.

"I've been thinking about another bath with you since my first one," Henry swooned, leaning his head back and closing his eyes as he recalled it. "It was the best time of my life."

Kira squeezed him tightly and felt the Panini in her stomach begin to rumble.

"Let's get more comfortable Henry," Kira said, moving back to catch her breath.

Henry slid off the chair and followed her down the hallway to the same bathroom they had used the first time.

"Oh my god!" Henry said, almost losing his balance when he entered the bathroom.

Kira smiled, spun around and presented the room as if someone had pulled the cover off a vintage car for the first time in years.

"Viola!" She said. "Everything is ready as you can see. I even pre-filled your bath with very hot water that should have cooled by now to the perfect temperature."

Henry took in the entire fantasy scene that Kira had created for them. There were lit candles everywhere with shimmering shadows in the otherwise unlighted bathroom. The tub was full of thick soapy water that looked like whipped cream and there was a heady odor of incense that was worthy of any ceremony.

"Undress now Henry!" Kira's voice snapped like a bullwhip across his back. "Now, I said!"

So shocked, Henry shook from her verbal assault and spilled the rest of his champagne on the floor, splashing onto her high heels.

"I'm sorry! I'm sorry!" He cried out.

"Look at what you have done Henry!" Kira scolded, ignoring his apology. "You stupid, clumsy, little boy."

"Shut up!" She shouted, wide eyed in real anger that frightened Henry. "Shut your mouth and look at what you did."

Slowly, Henry lowered his eyes to her shoes.

"Do you see what you've done?"

He nodded with his eyes fixed on her wet shoes.

"Get down there and lick it off!" She screamed, pointing.

"What?" Henry said, suddenly feeling the urge to pee his pants. He had never seen Kira like this and she had changed in an instant.

"I said get down on your knees and lick my shoes clean!" Kira snarled through her teeth like a rabid dog.

Henry was so afraid of Kira that he didn't know if he could move. Was she just play acting, he thought or was she really mad at him. Either way, it was as if she had flipped a switch in him and now, he was extremely sexually aroused. One part of his brain wanted to protect him and was telling him to run while another part of his brain was telling him to stay.

Kira shouted at him again and again, as she came straight at him.

"Lick it off! Lick it off!"

Henry lost control and peed his pants, but at the same time he was so terrified, he dropped to the floor and began to lick Kira's high heels.

"That's it, you little worm, lick them nice and clean," Kira's voice had changed to a sing song tone he had heard before and it only made his tongue go faster.

After a minute of licking, Henry began to cry when he felt his warm, wet pants and realized what he had done.

Kira kneeled down, straddling Henry's head between her knees. "Is mommy's little boy crying?" She asked.

Henry did not reply, looking up at her looming face and she thumped the sides of his head sharply with her knees until he nodded.

"Yes...I did..." he murmured.

"...and did mommy's little boy pee-pee in his pants?"

No answer and more thumping.

"Did he?" she asked again.

"Yes," he finally whispered after another thump that made his ears ring.

"Get undressed and get yourself into the bathtub," she ordered, standing up. "Do you really think I want to touch a dirty, little boy who peed his pants?"

"No...no...I don't..." Henry said, getting up, totally humiliated.

"Then clean yourself while I watch!"

Henry nodded, completely broken and yet completely turned on at the same time. He had never felt so sexually alive in all his life. He wanted to think about what had just happened and more about why, but he was so captivated with what was still going on that right now, he didn't care. He just wanted, no needed, more of it.

"Hurry up, you bad little boy," Kira said. "Get out of those dirty clothes so mommy can wash them while you clean yourself."

Henry undressed as fast as he could and folded all of his clothes into a neat bundle and handed it to Kira.

"Good boy," Kira said, taking the clothes. "You know if I touched any of your pee-pee I would have had to punish you."

Henry nodded, standing in front of Kira, naked and fully erect.

"Now get into the tub and wash up you little piggy and I'll be right back."

Henry got into the bathtub and washed himself; five minutes later, Kira was back wearing nothing but panties and a pair of high heels.

"All clean now?" She asked, with a big smile; her mood had done a one-eighty.

Henry had his head down expecting the worst from her or maybe he was hoping for the worst; but he looked up.

"Yes, I'm all clean now," he said, with the happy Henry grin. "You look beautiful Kira, so natural…"

Kira took the opportunity to accept Henry's compliment and look at herself in the mirror. Her bare breasts were still firm with hardly any sag, perhaps a lift in a year or two, but she definitely didn't need or want implants.

"Thank you, Henry," she said, after staring longer than she should have, but Kira could have stared all day. "Did I ever tell you I love to scuba dive?"

Henry's sexual thoughts of Kira were rudely interrupted. "What? Scuba dive?" He replied, and he stopped touching himself under the water. "No...I mean we never talked about it...but I have seen several pictures of you in your office which looked like you were on vacation."

"Yes, that's right," she said, with her hands on her hips as if she was going to scold him. "I do have some pictures in my office of me wearing my gear..."

"I noticed them the first time I was there and I could tell you looked like you knew what you were doing. You even have one showing you underwater in a bikini."

"Funny, you never mentioned seeing them, Henry," Kira said, kneeling down besides the tub.

Henry stared at her breasts, especially the nipples, and Kira leaned over so they would bounce on the side of the tub.

"I never said anything about the diving pictures since most of the time you were always in such a hurry..." He said, watching her bounce her breasts.

"You should learn how to dive Henry," Kira said, scooping up some sudsy water and massaging in all over his back.

"Me? Scuba dive?" He said, falling into a dreamy state, the moment her hand touched him. "I don't think so Kira, since I don't even like the water."

Kira's hand rotated over Henry's skinny back and she continued.

"You do know how to swim, don't you?" She asked, whispering so close to his ear he could feel her breasts slide against his arm.

He nodded, replying weakly. "Yes, I can swim some...but I'm not what you would call a strong swimmer..."

"Okay Henry, I understand your reluctance," she said, suddenly disinterested. "I just thought since I'm a certified Master diver, that I could teach you the basics."

"You're a Master diver Kira," he said. "…and you could teach me how to dive?"

"Yes Henry, I could teach you, but if you're not really interested in learning, and since you hate the water…"

Kira let the sentence dangle as she moved her other hand under the water and took hold of him. Henry closed his eyes as the blissful sensation of her skillful hand spread over his entire body.

"I didn't say I hated the water," he pointed out, concentrating on the movement of her hand between his legs as he forgot all about the one on his back. "Maybe I should learn how to dive, especially if you were the one willing to teach me."

Kira pulled a little faster on him. "It would be one on one lessons Henry. Just you and I, like we are now, you might say in a very hands on approach…"

Henry smiled at her obvious double meaning and asked hopefully. "Would it? You mean like the hands on approach we're having now?"

Kira licked in his ear and made sure he could feel her nipples as well.

"Very much like the hands on we're having now," she said, between licks. "In fact, I don't see why the hands on approach couldn't advance to your hands on me…"

Henry opened his eye wide with anticipation. "You mean I would touch you too?" He asked, needing to hear her answer.

"Yes Henry," she said, as her hand jerked faster. "You could touch me too…if there were those opportunities."

Henry whined as he felt the end nearing, for he wanted this time with Kira to last forever; it was more important to be with her no matter what it took. Still, his cautious nature wanted answers to so many questions, but now, he could never risk ending, what he could never have imagined even beginning. He was caught and on some level he knew it; he was falling helplessly and just couldn't stop it.

CHAPTER TWENTY-TWO

Willy Burk had sobered up after a nonstop, three day, drinking binge; but it wasn't like he was stone cold, zero blood alcohol sober; Willy was never that sober. But, Willy had to sober up, at least back to base line, since he had important things to do. First, he had to bury what was left of his brother now that the ME had released the remains. Secondly, and more importantly, he had to find, and somehow kill the guy who blew Billy up. Not an easy task on the second one, especially since the guy that did it was a retired police officer named Paul Dickinson. He knew it was Paul Dickinson since he knew Paul Dickinson never stopped harassing Billy; never stopped trying to prove Billy was behind Heather's death. He also knew no one else wanted Billy dead, at least not that dead. Besides that, it couldn't be anyone else Billy knew, since no one Billy knew was smart enough to even build a bomb, let alone plant one in his car.

Willy had a two bedroom apartment a few miles from Billy's new place and he also had a girlfriend but he chose to live alone.

Willy had tried living with someone but they always ended up in a breakup.

He didn't want to be married and he didn't want any kids so why live with someone. He just wanted his freedom to what he wanted, which was pretty much anything.

Willy did a couple of years in the Marines after high school and he was a good one until he tested positive for cocaine; but coming home was even tougher than being in the Marines. His mother had left years earlier and now his father was meaner than ever. If it wasn't for his younger brother Billy he would have got on his motorcycle and headed for South Florida.

Willy got arrested a couple of times for drug possession and then he got wiser, he stopped the drugs and the penny ante dealing. He kept using alcohol but learned how to steal high end cars and fix motorcycles. Willy was very careful about the cars he stole and the people he worked for, since he hated jail and was determined never to go back. He got very good at stealing cars but he got even better at fixing motorcycles, so he quit stealing cars and opened the repair shop.

It was Sunday morning when Willy crawled out of bed, showered and put on a fresh pair of his best jeans, a clean, black muscle shirt and a worn brown leather jacket. Willy was tall, good looking in a rough way; with facial stubble of a three day growth. He was more like his father in a lot of ways where Billy was more like his mother. Now, he was on his way to the funeral home to say goodbye, the services would minimal; no frills and no calling hours, since no one would be calling. The way Willy thought, why spend the money when none of it would matter. What mattered was finding a way to get to Paul Dickinson and not get caught.

But Paul Dickinson knew what Willy was thinking and he was waiting for him when he came out of his apartment. At first Willy couldn't believe his eyes when he saw him leaning on his motorcycle. The sun was bright in his eyes and he thought at first sight he was seeing things.

Willy wanted to charge Paul and rip him to pieces; not only for calling his dead brother an asshole, but more for leaning on his motorcycle.

"You got a death wish leaning on my motorcycle?" Willy said, with his big fists balled up tight.

"Maybe I do," Paul replied, grinning. "Know anyone who wants to see a nice guy like me dead?"

Willy relaxed and unclenched his fists. "Oh I get it," he said, walking closer to Paul. "You're wired up and think I'm going to say something stupid because I'm pissed at you."

"No, not really Willy," Paul said, standing up from the motorcycle. "I'm not wired and I already know you'll say something stupid since everything you say is stupid."

Willy growled inside himself, but walked past Paul and carefully checked over his motorcycle.

"Don't worry, I didn't scratch it and there's no bombs on it either…"

"Very funny," Willy said, still looking over the motorcycle. "I'm not going to fall for that…"

"Fall for what?"

Willy got on the motorcycle, started it up and revved it loudly several times.

"Where's your buddies?" Willy asked, looking around. "You got Reynolds hiding in that panel truck over there with a video camera, just waiting for me to beat your ass…"

Paul laughed. "Reynolds wouldn't even get out of bed for a piece of shit like you and as far as the ass beating goes; I'd shoot you before you threw the first punch."

"Yeah, right old man…if I started hitting you, you would be lucky to wake up in the hospital, if ever."

Paul walked up close to Willy and stared him in the eyes. "You're going away Willy boy for what you did to Heather, and we both know how much you hate prison."

"Keep it up dick head…" Willy said, slowly rolling off on the bike. "You got yours coming…"

…and so do you dick head!" Paul said.

Willy popped up his middle finger, drove off and Paul shouted after him.

"Say goodbye to Billy for me…!"

Andersson had just got back from church with his family, they didn't go every Sunday and his daughter Gretchen balked at even once a month, but she went. She said she didn't need organized religion since she was spiritual. Andersson told her you can be spiritual when you're living on your own; once a month you can be spiritual as a family in church.

Andersson usually ate something with his family before church and later had a late Sunday lunch around two. Lately, Gretchen had missed the lunches and now even, his son, Nicklaus Jr., was having excuses to miss them. He was at the age when he was always heading someplace or meeting someone, and the meal time was inconvenient. The joys of teenagers.

Andersson really didn't mind their absences since it gave him an opportunity to go into the office for a couple of hours; especially when he needed some quiet time to think. He could think at home, or anywhere for that matter, but he always thought better at work, at his desk, and he needed to think about the Billy Burk case.

The briefing scheduled for tomorrow was pretty much a formality. Michael Carson, the Wake County DA, would want some answers, some direction, even a solid suspect or two would be nice. Right now, they had a lot of rumors, phone tips and one eye witness to not much of anything.

Several things bothered Andersson about this case and the main one was timing. Why blow up Billy Burk now and not two years ago or a month after Heather was killed. Why now? He thought again about Heather's father and had pegged him for a prime suspect, but when he met him that morning with Stefani, the guy was just too happy. He wasn't nervous at all that the police were there to talk to him, but moreover Andersson could see the relief in his eyes, a father's eyes, and of course, no one could miss him dancing in the street.

The father was just too obvious, too genuine; Stefani so thought as well and she had a knack for someone who was lying, especially about a murder. There were little things she looked for as opposed to what the person said, rather it was about how they said it or how they reacted after they spoke. She looked for a tick, a twitch, or eyes that darted around, even a tiny smirk. Some people who were guilty had all the answers and others didn't have any; funny thing was it could go that way for someone who was innocent too.

Andersson made coffee, it was his second cup of the day, and he was trying to limit himself to three. This new stuff from Hank's connection in Guatemala was addictive and he found himself drinking more coffee than ever so he decided to cut back.

A few sips of the fresh brew and he felt that soothing feeling pass over him. Yeah, he was addicted, but he kept on sipping it anyway.

He was just about to jot some names down on a piece of paper when his cell phone rang; must be Meredith, but when he looked at the caller ID, it was Mary Gordon.

"Got you!" Mary said, her voice gleeful like had caught him doing something wrong.

"Hi Mary," he replied.

"I bet you're in your office too…"

Andersson looked around the office as if someone was watching him. "You got a camera in here I don't know about?"

"Maybe…after all your office is state property and putting a camera in your office wouldn't be illegal."

Andersson thought for a moment since it was hard to tell when Mary was joking with you, or she was dead serious; the line was that fine.

"So what can I do for you Ms. Gordon?" He asked, avoiding her camera statement all together.

She laughed. "Ms. Gordon indeed! Good tactic, change the subject, but I know you'll look for the camera later."

"Damn right I will!" He said with a laugh. "I must admit Mary, you're good…"

She snickered. "I'm not good Nicklaus, I'm the best…"

"Modest too," he shot back.

"Listen my friend," she began. "We have a small problem and I couldn't mention it the other day when I was in your office."

"What's the small problem?" Andersson asked, knowing there were no small problems where Mary Gordon was concerned mainly because it always involved the Governor.

"Stefani's wedding," she answered. "it's next month and she didn't invite the Governor or me for that matter…"

Nicklaus sat up and looked out the window; suddenly he noticed the bright sunny day had thick, dark storm clouds rolling in.

"The Governor wants to go to Stefani's wedding?"

"Yup…and so do I!"

"Why?" Andersson asked. "I mean no offense to either of you, but it's going to be a low key event and frankly, that's the way Roxanne wants it."

"I'm sure she does and we're not looking to crash it or upstage the bride; no one could upstage Stefani."

"So you want me to ask Roxanne for you?"

"Would you please Nicklaus…," Mary said, in one of her rare, nice person, no politics involved voices.

"The Governor really wants to go to her wedding? You too?" Andersson did a reality check.

"Yes! We do!" Mary replied. "You want me to have Governor Forbes call you himself? You know he thinks the world of you and he's always bragging about Stefani."

Okay…okay…you don't have to flatter me…," Andersson said. "I'll ask her but I can't make any promises."

"Great!"

"But no fanfare Mary," Andersson added to the deal. "No press coverage, just two guests at a wedding."

"Well, let's plan on four of us. The Governor and his wife, plus me and my escort. No fanfare, I promise."

"Stefani is going to kill me," Andersson said. "She just told me Hank added a couple more people they hadn't planned on. Why didn't you ask me this a month ago?"

"Heck Nicklaus…we thought she would have invited us…"

Andersson cleared his throat. "You know Stefani wasn't going to play that game."

"I know, that's why we waited last minute so to speak," Mary said, cleverly. "This way it looks like we just showed up to congratulate the new bride and groom."

"Enough spin, Mary. I got it and you knew I would…"

"Thanks Nicklaus," she said, sincerely. "I'll tell the Governor it's all set."

"Wait Mary! Let me talk to Roxanne first…," he said, but she had hung up.

CHAPTER TWENTY-THREE

Monday morning came and with it the usual Monday morning bullshit. The weather got warmer but those storm clouds Andersson saw were not just his imagination. The April rain was falling, DA Carson was going to be late for the meeting, which was unusual since he was always on time, and Andersson had just asked Stefani if the Governor could come to her wedding.

"Hell no! No way Nicklaus!"

"Calm down Roxanne!" Andersson said. "Let's look at the positive side."

"There is no positive side Nicklaus," she said, marching up and down in front of his desk. "You know he's going to show up with the press too…and who knows how many staffers…"

"Sit down a minute Roxanne," Andersson said. "Mary Gordon promised me none of that will happen.

They're just coming to your wedding as everyday guests."

Stefani sat down. "Oh that's a good one Nicklaus. You know he's coming because we're his babies and are high profile; not to mention he can always say a few words about his upcoming Presidential bid..."

"I know Roxanne, but I really don't think that's going to happen."

"Well, I do..."

"Roxanne, I know we differ on the politics of our positions but you have to accept that we work directly for Governor Forbes and very possibly he will be the next President of the United States..."

Roxanne sat still and did not reply. She was practicing her new technique for maintaining her cool when she was stressed. She tried to think of the end result, the answer to the problem or issue before she got angry and wasted the energy. She would picture herself at the decision, the right answer; the what's actually happening best solution answer and make it.

"Okay, sure, let's invite them," she said calmly. "If you would like it, I will call Mary myself."

Andersson was stunned. "You will?"

"Yes, I will," she replied. "I'd be happy to and I'm sure Hank will be delighted to have the Governor at our wedding as well..."

"He will?"

"Why not?" Roxanne said, smiling. "He wanted a bigger wedding anyway."

Andersson smiled back. "Yeah, he did, didn't he?" Thanks Roxanne."

"My pleasure Nicklaus," she said. "Now what about the briefing? We got anything new to tell the DA?"

Andersson looked down at some notes he had written yesterday, after his phone call with Mary Gordon.

"Not that much, I'm afraid," he said. "I'm hoping Harper, Culpepper and Reynolds came up with something of value. I held off from pressuring them until they had a chance to review the Heather Burk case. I'm convinced Billy's death is somehow tied to her death and he wasn't killed for some other unrelated reason."

"I agree, Billy's death is tied to Heathers."

"I did have some time to think about the case and some co-incidences I felt were odd," Andersson said. "Well, I mean, I had some time in between being your wedding planner."

"Very funny," Stefani said, but she did laugh. "What coincidences do you mean?"

"Paul Dickinson for one, as well as Willy Burk, both of them showing up at Raleigh Police Headquarters."

"But Dickinson worked the case and was the lead detective," Stefani pointed out.

Andersson took out his Chiclets, popped a couple into this mouth and offered them to Roxanne but she declined.

"You don't know Paul Dickinson like I do, I know him as much as anyone can know him. He's the kind of guy that is willing to not only cross the line, but is willing to move the line way up field first, and then cross it."

"You think he would blow up Billy Burk?"

"I'm not sure, but if he did, I wouldn't be surprised."

"But why? Why would he do that?"

"Two reasons; revenge for Heather and Paul wasn't going to let Billy enjoy the insurance payoff."

"What about Willy Burk?" Stefani asked. "Doesn't he benefit from his brother's death?"

Andersson shrugged. "I don't know, but I guess he might. It's something we need to find out and I'm sure Harper will know."

"If you think Paul Dickinson is a possible, then that's fine with me; we'll talk with him, but I think we need to look at Willy too."

"Sure, I agree and anyone else that might have wanted Billy dead…"

The meeting finally got started at 11:00 am and Michael Carson apologized for the delay. The conference room at Raleigh Headquarters was nearly full, there were County Deputies, State Police forensic personnel, including Shay Abisi and Vanina Cruz. Culpepper and Reynolds, plus a few other Raleigh Police officers sat at the table opposite the County folk. Harper, who was now a State Police officer sat with Andersson and Stefani. DA Carson sat at the head of the table and spoke first after his apology for being late.

"The Heather Burk death was big news, not only around here, but nationally, and it still is, especially since the case went unsolved," he said. "We all know this, and we're constantly reminded about it on the news, as well as on many crime investigative television shows. Everyone thinks her husband did it and so do we, although we didn't have the evidence to prove it. Now, our prime suspect is dead, in fact, he's blown up in a spectacular fashion, which of course the news media just loved. Therefore, we're back on the hot seat to solve this and perhaps even bring some closure to the Heather Burk saga."

Carson paused and Andersson took his cue to begin.

"Thank you DA Carson," he said. "Right off we think the motive or motives for killing Billy Burk was revenge and or greed. We're not going to mention one of our suspects by name since it's too early and needless to say, everything discussed in this room is confidential. We all know the preliminary report on what happened to Billy Burk; so what have we learned about him since?"

"Thank you Lieutenant Andersson," Harper began formally. "For one thing, we originally thought Billy got a half of a million dollars from the insurance company, but actually he got a million minus the three hundred thousand to his lawyer."

"Now how in the hell did that happen?" Reynolds asked, perturbed.

"An accidental death clause in the policy paid double on the original amount and Heather's death, after three autopsies, was finally ruled accidental."

"Three autopsies?" One of the County Deputies asked. "Why did it take three?"

"The County did the first one," Harper replied. "In fact, it was done by Dr. Abisi who is here today."

"I ruled multiple traumatic injuries with undetermined circumstances," Shay said. "The investigation was ongoing and I wanted to reserve the right of possibly changing it to a homicide."

"Thank you Dr. Abisi," Harper said before continuing. "The second one the insurance company had performed when Billy filed the claim. Their investigators thought the same thing that we did; that the scene of Heather's hit and run appeared staged. But, without an arrest or any evidence to support those allegations, the insurance company ended up in one legal maneuver after another."

"How did Billy support himself during his legal wrangling with the insurance company?" Stefani asked.

Culpepper took a turn replying. "From what we could find out from reviewing his bank statements and Income tax filings, he lived with his brother Willy, and worked some legitimate jobs for short periods of time."

Harper picked it back up. "The way the pattern appears is Billy would work in labor based jobs, such as landscaping or putting up sheet rock and he did some roofing too in the spring months."

From what you're saying it was much like the work that his father-in-law started him out doing, but Billy quit after a couple of months," Andersson said.

"Yes, it was," Culpepper replied. "We feel it was just a cover, something to make him seem more like the struggling, sympathetic widower who had just lost his young wife and unborn child."

"From what I saw in the follow up search of Billy's apartment, there wasn't anything incriminating," Reynolds said. "In fact, it looked pretty normal for a single guy his age who just came into some money and left living with his older brother."

"It was," Harper agreed. "We only found the remains of one joint he probably smoked with the girl before they left his apartment. There wasn't any other illegal substances, drug paraphernalia, or firearms."

"Lilly, did you get a chance to see if Billy had a storage unit?" Stefani asked.

"Yes, we did and we couldn't find anything listed in his name or any receipts, or storage facility contracts that indicated he had a unit somewhere."

"So we don't think Billy was doing anything illegal that might have gotten him killed?" DA Carson asked, getting impatient.

"No sir," Reynolds answered from across the table. "We talked to several of his known associates and no one had anything negative to say which might lead us in that direction. He didn't seem to have any enemies besides Heather's father and Paul Dickinson."

"Paul Dickinson." The DA said, perking up. "I thought he was retired a long time ago?"

"He is retired," Reynolds said, "but he came in to see us the other day and offered his help. You know, give us a refresher on the cold case since he was the lead detective."

"I don't want Paul Dickinson anywhere near this case!" The DA said, pointing his finger. "That guy is crazy and we have locked horns many times on previous prosecutions; especially with his tactics in obtaining evidence."

The room was quiet for a few seconds after the DA's outburst of anger that obviously went a lot deeper toward Paul Dickinson.

"What about mistake in identity?" Stefani proposed, breaking the awkward silence. "What if who ever blew up Billy thought they were getting Willy."

"That's a possibility we looked at as well," Harper said, reading through her notebook. "Willy certainly runs with a more much dangerous population of friends than Billy. Plus Willy has a criminal history and who knows what he was into we don't know about."

"Willy's been off the radar for a long time as far as we can tell," Reynolds said. "He used to be quite the car thief before Heather died, then all of a sudden he stopped."

"We also checked Willy's employment record when we were checking Billy's and he's been squeaky clean," Culpepper said. "He mainly made his money fixing motorcycles but he also did some body work for a repair shop."

"Seems like the two brothers got real cozy," Andersson said. "Let me guess, I bet Willy is Billy's only heir and he stands to collect the rest of Billy's insurance pay off."

Harper nodded. "Yes sir, he does. Billy's mom is alive but Billy filed a will right after Heather died, and named Willy as his sole heir."

"So what happened…," Stefani concluded. "Willy got stiffed on his end of the insurance money and killed Billy?"

"Sounds good to me," Reynolds said. "Maybe Billy got greedy after he had the insurance check in his hands and decided to cut Willy out."

"It's possible," Culpepper agreed. "The only thing we could find as far as payment to Willy was a new pickup truck Billy bought for him about a week after he got the money."

"…and nothing after that?" Andersson asked.

Harper shook her head. "No sir, we can't find any large withdrawals, not even for the new pickup, but Billy was making the monthly payments."

"Most of the money is just sitting in the bank," Culpepper said. "Billy bought his new car and moved out of Willy's place into that fancy apartment, but again, everything is paid by the month. No big spending sprees to our knowledge."

"Where would Willy get the grenade?" Shay asked, out of nowhere. "I'm sure somehow he could have bought it, but did he have any knowledge with explosives? You would think anyone who could use a grenade in the way it was used on Billy, knew what they were doing."

"That's a good point Dr. Abisi," Harper said. "...and we found out that Willy was in the Marine Corps for a short period of time before getting kicked out. He did a year in Iraq and saw some action according to his military records."

"I'm sure if he didn't throw any grenades in battle, he at least learned how..." Andersson said. "We all learned how to toss a few live ones when I was in the Army. It doesn't take much to learn the basics."

"I like it!" Carson said, checking his watch then looking at Andersson. "Talk to Willy and see what he's got to say about all this. Brace him hard and let him know we think he's our prime suspect. Point out, he's got means, motive and opportunity unless he can prove otherwise."

"Okay, we'll go see him today," Andersson said.

Michael Carson stood up. "I have to leave," he said, but first leaned over and whispered to Andersson. "Let's have a talk with Paul Dickinson too. I don't want anything happening to Willy."

Andersson nodded and Carson left the conference room.

"One more question for you Craig," Andersson said. "...and we can wrap it up. Did any of the surveillance teams you put on Willy come up with anything?"

Craig shook his head. "Nothing suspicious," he replied. "Willy biked around with his buddies and hit the usual bars.

One of the rookies we had out there saw an older guy who was well dressed have what looked like some words with Willy early Sunday morning."

"Words with him?" Stefani asked. "You mean an argument?"

"Not an argument according to the rookie just words back and forth. He couldn't hear what they were saying since they were parked across the street, but the well dressed, older guy shouted something to Willy when he rode off on his motorcycle and Willy gave him the finger."

"You think it was Paul Dickinson?" Stefani asked.

Reynolds nodded. "Sounds like it."

"Show the rookie a picture of Dickinson and let me know ..." Andersson said.

"Okay, I'll catch him this afternoon when he comes off shift."

"That's it everyone, unless someone has anything to add," Andersson said. "Thanks for the hard work over the weekend."

Everyone got up to leave and Stefani leaned over to Andersson.

"Let's go talk to Willy, and we better go see Paul Dickinson too."

CHAPTER TWENTY-FOUR

While Andersson and Stefani were heading out to find Willy; across town Kira Lake and Henry Harris were just getting into a swimming pool for Henry's first private diving lesson. Diving is like most sports with different degrees of difficulty and challenges. Someone may fish in a small stream or pond right in their own backyards and still catch a fish. Others need the best rods and reels, to charter a boat, and fish in the Gulf of Mexico but they all still enjoy the sport of fishing.

Mountain climbing depends on the skill of the climber, their equipment and of course the size and location of the mountain. There's running, biking, kayaking, hiking, camping and hunting to name a few more. Not to mention the professional teams that are a world apart from what the everyday person or family enjoys or can afford; even as a spectator.

Diving is has all those ingredients, as any other sport, but the one thing you absolutely must have in diving is oxygen. It's not snorkeling or being able to hold your breath for a couple minutes, it's SCUBA diving and by definition it's a self-contained underwater breathing apparatus and without that you drown. Safety is another big factor in diving and most beginners learn in a pool, which is closed water diving as opposed to lakes or the oceans which are open water diving.

Diving in a pool is pretty easy compared to diving in a large, open body of water. Open water takes some experience and knowledge since they are various depths, currents, temperatures, and the physical size of the diver to consider when planning a safe dive. All of which depend on another extremely important factor; time. How much time do you want to spend underwater; which in turn, will dictate how much air you will need. The average dive for the casual diver in forty feet of warm water is about forty-five minutes before you have to surface.

The equipment for diving is also pretty standard and that's what Henry was finishing putting on with the personal help of Kira.

"Here you go Henry," Kira said, standing next to him in the smallest of bikinis one could possible wear and still be able to say you're wearing a bathing suit. "We have the entire pool and staff at our disposal for the next two hours. We went through the safety procedures, now let's get to know the equipment and get into the water."

"You think I'm going to be okay with all this stuff on?" Henry asked, already feeling overwhelmed.

Seems like a lot of weight…"

"It is a lot of weight but that's what you need to stay underwater," Kira said, as she helped with his outfitting. "This is a BC or buoyancy compensator, your face mask, snorkel, fins and air tank. All this will feel much lighter once you're in the water."

Henry stood still while Kira and one of the pool staff finished putting the equipment on him. He tried to concentrate his fears on Kira's body which he found very motivating.

"Don't we need those wet suits too?" Henry asked stepping into the fins.

"No, not for the pool or for most shallow, warm water dives, but a lot of people wear them anyway. I will usually wear one to protect my skin and stay warm if I'm going to be out on a boat all day or I'm planning a deeper dive."

"Where's your gear Kira? Aren't you wearing all this equipment too?" Henry asked.

"No, I don't need to since you're just getting used to the breathing and feeling comfortable underwater," she said, stepping back after they finished suiting up Henry. "There, you're all set!"

"I'm just like a Navy SEAL!" Henry proclaimed, "...and I'm all ready for my first dive!"

The young man who had helped Kira, looked at Henry, then back at Kira, rolled his eyes and walked away.

It wasn't difficult to find Willy Burk; Andersson and Stefani used the two addresses along with a recent photo Harper had provided. One of the addresses was his home and the other a small garage where he fixed motorcycles. Since it was late morning, Andersson and Stefani thought they would try his place of business first and it turned out to be right where Willy was.

"That was easy," Stefani said, looking down at the picture and back up to Willy. "He's right outside working on a motorcycle."

Andersson pulled the state vehicle to the curb and shut it off.

"That's our boy," he said, looking down at the picture Stefani was holding.

"You want to be the bad cop, as usual?" Stefani asked, slipping the photo back into her black notebook.

"Me...the bad cop?" Andersson shot back. "You're always the bad cop..."

Me? I'm always as sweet as apple pie," Stefani replied.

"I don't know where you get your apples, but let's both be good cops and throw him off," Andersson said, and they both got out of the car.

It was a beautiful, sunny day but the temperature was still on the chilly side and Willy spotted them coming up the short driveway.

"Morning officers," he said nicely. "I've been expecting you."

"I'm Lieutenant Andersson and this is Special Investigator Stefani…," Andersson said, but couldn't finish the introductions since Willy interrupted him.

"Must be from the State," Willy said, watching Stefani slowly move off to his left side. "I know a lot of the local cops like Reynolds. You know Reynolds?"

"You're right, we are from the State Police and we'd like to talk to you about the death of your brother," Stefani said, ignoring his question about Reynolds.

"Sure, I'm happy to talk about that," Willy said, wiping his greasy hands on a rag. "Let's go inside."

Willy had a tiny office in the back of the two stall garage. Once inside, things looked a lot neater than Andersson or Stefani had expected. The garage was very clean and all the tools were hung up on peg board.

"It's not much, but I'm working on building up my business before I move to a bigger location," he Informed them, as they walked into the office, which barely held a small, cheap desk, a few chairs and a phone. "Have a seat."

Andersson and Stefani sat down and they were all so close they could almost touch one another.

"We have to be clear about something Mr. Burk, right from the start," Andersson acknowledged.

"You don't have to talk to us and in fact, you have the right to remain silent or have an attorney present…"

Willy laughed. "Number one, call me Willy and number two, I don't need you to read me my rights.

I didn't do anything wrong."

"We didn't say that you did Willy," Stefani said, crossing her legs. "We just want to cover all the bases since there's a lot of money involved with your brother's death."

Willy had a flash of anger. "So because I stand to inherit his money, I'm a suspect in his death?"

"We're just looking at all the possibilities of who might benefit from your brother's murder," Andersson said, tensing up in case Willy took a swing at him. "You know the routine; we always look at those people who are closest to the victim, which starts with the family."

"I know and you're right...," Willy said, still clearly agitated. "I know from the inside too...like prison and I'm not planning on going back...ever."

"That's a good attitude to have," Stefani said, distracting Willy's attention from Andersson. "Be positive and upfront with us so we can cross you off the list."

Willy leaned back in the wooden chair while he waited for the burn to pass through him.

"I didn't have anything to do with Billy's dying," Willy struggled to contain his emotions. "Yes, he just got a lot of insurance money and in fact he bought me that new pickup truck settin out there..."

"That was real nice of him," Andersson remarked. "I saw it coming in...a real nice truck."

"Damn straight it's a nice truck," Willy said, defensively, leaning forward again. "That's the kind of brother he was; we were real close."

"That's a good brother," Stefani said. "To me it shows you and him were close. That you two would do anything for each other."

"Damn right we would!" Willy said, forcefully. "Anything that one of us needed we would do and besides all that, Billy was very generous with his money too. Why would I kill him?"

"Good question Willy," Andersson said, bewildered. "Why would you kill him?"

"Why would he?" Stefani asked Andersson. "I mean Billy bought him a nice truck and all."

"I wouldn't that's why!" Willy said, pointing his finger at Stefani. "I wouldn't have killed Billy for twice all that money...or three times the money he got!"

"I guess you don't have any reason to have done it," Adersson said. "What do you think Stefani?"

"I agree, if you didn't kill him for the money; there's no motive," she said as if arriving at some conclusion. "No reason...no motive..."

"That's true," Andersson said. "...and I'm sure you want to cooperate and all...you know, help us find Billy's killer since you didn't do it."

Willy felt cornered for a second. "Help you...how? I don't know anything..."

"Well, you could let us search your apartment and this garage," Andersson offered. "Seeing you didn't do anything wrong and want to be cooperative."

"That would probably take you clear to the bottom of the list if we didn't find anything suspicious,"

Stefani said, looking at Willy then over to Andersson. "Don't you think so Lieutenant?"

Andersson nodded. "If we didn't find anything incriminating...yeah, it would put him at the bottom of the list...maybe even clean off of it..."

"See Willy," Stefani said, smiling at him. "Clean off the list and we could go find someone else to investigate."

Willy thought about the search and thought if he had any-thing in his possession that might be incriminating but he knew he didn't.

"Yeah sure, go ahead, search my place and look around here too..."

Andersson nodded to Willy. "Good, but let me ask you one more question before we get going on our searching and just for the record."

"What's that?"

"Where were you around seven-thirty to eight-thirty on the evening your brother died?"

Willy thought back. "I'm not sure, not exactly right now, but I know I went out that night, and I was supposed to have met Billy, but he had met that chick."

"Okay, think about the timeline for that evening and let me know if you were with someone or went someplace we can verify..."

"It's important Willy," Stefani added. "The timeline is impor-tant...especially to keep you off of the list."

Willy nodded at her. "Okay, I'll think about it and get back to you."

"So Willy," Andersson began, drawing his attention back. "do we have your permission to search your places and we don't need a warrant?"

Willy nodded his head, stood up, and spread his long arms out wide.

"Search all you want...I have nothing to hide."

Andersson looked back at Stefani.

"You heard the man," he said, with a big smile. "Let's call out team in here and get Abisi and her crew to join us and then we'll all go over to the apartment."

"Right away," Stefani said, getting up and taking out her cell phone.

Andersson got up too. "Now you can't go anywhere until we're done so just hang around here if you would."

"Can I finish the work I started on the bike?" He asked, like he was bored already.

"Yes, you can work on the bike but stay in plain sight and don't remove anything from the premises."

"I won't," Willy said, stepping out from behind the desk to head back outside. "Just be as fast as you can and then take me off the list."

"We will," Andersson said. "It won't take long to search this place since it's so compact."

"Good," Willy said. "The sooner the better since I got things to do and a life to live."

CHAPTER TWENTY-FIVE

It only took a couple of hours to search the garage and Willy's apartment, not counting travel time for all of them, and they didn't find anything incriminating or suspicious. They even searched his nice, new pickup truck that Billy bought him, with Willy watching their every move, and they didn't find anything.

Nothing. No signs of any explosives or material to build a bomb. There were no guns, or weapons of any kind or even any drugs.

"He must have a stash somewhere," Stefani said in frustration. "This guy can't be this clean."

Shay Abisi and her crew of technicians were all packed up and ready to leave.

"We checked his garage, apartment and pickup truck from top to bottom and even used the dogs, and metal detectors and found nothing. No drugs and no residue of drug use in any of the three places we searched. This guy is not using any illegal substances in any of those places nor has anyone else."

"What about a friend's place or a friend's storage unit?" Stefani asked, everyone in general but looking at Harper.

"A friend's place is always a possibility but it's unlikely someone would hold explosives or illegal substances unless they were somehow benefitting from it. Plus, Willy's going to be very careful about having his stuff in someone else's care. He would worry if they got busted for something they would use his illegal activities as leverage for a deal with DA."

"As far as the storage unit goes, we checked and rechecked," Culpepper added in support.

"He's got to have something...somewhere," Reynolds said, in frustration. "I know this guy and he can't be that far from his pot stash. He loves to smoke, he must be doing it somewhere else, where he feels safe."

Everyone stood still dumbly looking at one another before they all moved outside of the garage into the bright sunlight where Willy was leaning up against his truck.

"All done?" He yelled over to them, as they filed out of the garage. "Find anything?"

Reynolds was the first to reply.

"If we did you would be the first to know."

Willy laughed mockingly. "I'll take that as a no, Reynolds"

"That's Lieutenant Reynolds to you dog breath."

"Oh excuse me, lieutenant sir," Willy said, snapping to attention with a sharp salute. "By the way Craigy...how do you like my new truck? I was going to get black, which I thought you might like, but I went with the red."

Reynolds wanted to go over to Willy when he made the remark about being black, but instead walked the other way toward his car.

"Looks like a girl's truck to me and not like something a big, tough asshole like you would drive."

Willy laughed louder and cupped his hands around his mouth.

"Speaking of assholes Reynolds sir," he shouted. "Why don't you go search your buddy Paul dick head's place like you did mine. He's the crazy fuck that belongs at the top your list. He's a real psycho but you already know that since you were hiding in that panel truck across the street when he was baiting me yesterday."

"What's he talking about?" Andersson asked Reynolds.

"I don't know," he said, with a shrug. "I told you the guys a big pot head and he doesn't know what he's talking about himself..."

"You weren't at the stakeout watching him right?" Stefani said, out of ear shot of Willy.

"No, I wasn't going to pull a Sunday morning stake out," he said. "I had a couple of rookies do it...

They were all I could get and we shut it down at noon anyway."

"Dickinson must have paid Willy a visit," Andersson said.

"Maybe he did...who cares?" Reynolds said. "He was probably just rattling his chain."

"Maybe, but this guy Dickinson keeps showing up and it's another coincidence," Andersson said.

"Let's go talk to him and see what he's really been up to..."

Henry Harris had spent so much time in the pool that his hands and feet were shriveled and he smelled like chlorine which Kira thought wasn't such bad thing.

"I'm done Kira and I mean it!" Henry balked. "No more diving!"

Kira pulled off her facemask. "Okay Henry, we're done for today, but I want you back here tomorrow morning at nine!"

"Tomorrow?" Henry screeched. "I thought this was going to be a fun thing. Something you said we could do together and remember; it was supposed to be more hands on."

The pool assistant went to help Henry take off his equipment but Kira waved him off.

"Let him do it himself," she said, her temper flaring. "You need to learn the basics Henry so you can be ready for the open water when we go to the Keys."

The assistant stepped back from Henry and watched as he fumbled with his BC vest.

"We're going to the Keys?" Henry asked with even more shock on his face than was on the pool assistants. "You didn't mention that before…"

Kira flipped from anger to disappointment. She had been in the water just as long as Henry had been, but where Henry looked like he was the last surviving rat off a sinking ship; Kira looked like she had just stepped out of the shower.

"It was supposed to have been a surprise Henry," she said. "It's all planned in fact. I figured a few days in the pool and we would do a few days at the Keys."

"Oh Kira, I had no idea we were going to go away," Henry said, shivering.

The pool assistant saw Henry was shivering, looked at Kira, who nodded, and he moved off to get a couple of warmed terry robes.

"It was my way of thanking you for letting me agent your new manuscripts," Kira said, softly moving closer to Henry so no one else could hear her.

"Kira no one else would manage my work but you," he said, as matter of fact. "You know that."

"I know," Kira said, giving him a peck on the cheek. "it's okay, the trip was easy enough to put together since I always use the same yacht service and I can just as easily cancel it."

The assistant returned with the warmed robes and they both slipped into them. The robes fell good and Henry immediately stopped shivering.

"You chartered a yacht for us?"

Kira nodded and began to walk away from the pool side.

"Take care of our gear and see me before we leave," Kira said to the assistant. "I have something for you."

Henry followed her over to a small plastic table and chairs that were stacked with towels.

"You're going to cancel the trip now?" Henry said, almost in a panic. "Why?"

Kira sat down, picked up one of the towels and patted her face dry.

"You need to have the dive basics down Henry and if you don't want to spend the time in the pool, well, I don't want to take you diving in open water..."

"But, I'm willing to learn Kira," he said, sitting down across from her.

"I know you are Henry, but we both have busy schedules..." Kira spoke to him like the trip was already an afterthought. "We can continue with the diving when we both are available."

"But we're both available now and you have the trip all planned," Henry pleaded. "Let's not cancel it."

Kira pulled her wet hair back into a pony tail with a tie.

"Are you going to make it here for the next couple of days and practice with me?" She challenged him.

"Yes, of course I will. I promise."

Kira was silent for a long time, painfully long for Henry, before she replied.

"Okay Henry, let's see how the training goes and if I think you're ready when we're done...we'll go."

"Oh god Kira, I'm so happy! Thank you!"

Kira smiled and patted his face. "Don't thank me just yet..."

CHAPTER TWENTY-SIX

Andersson, Stefani and Reynolds left Willy's garage and decided to get something quick to eat before they went to see Paul Dickinson. They wanted to stay in the part of town where Paul had his office but they didn't know any place special to eat so they went to a nearby pizza shop. The place was basically take out with a large walk up counter and two huge pizza ovens on either side of the room. The counter also had two cash registers on either end so people could order, and pay, then pickup.

An area off to one side, had a couple of wooden tables and four sets of chairs near a large self-serve soda cooler. The place was busy with in and out traffic so they each had a large slice of cheese pizza and a can of soda; the pizza was good and the soda cold.

When they finished, outside of the pizza shop Reynolds re-read the address to Paul Dickinson's office.

"It's not that far from here," he said. "I was there a couple of times when he first opened. Are you sure you don't want me to call him first and tell him we're coming?"

"Yes, I'm sure," Andersson said. "If Paul Dickinson is the kind of guy who can walk into Raleigh Police any time he wants; I'm sure he won't mind us walking in on him any time we want and not call ahead."

"No offense to you two," Reynolds said, looking at Andersson and Stefani. "We're really looking at Dickinson like he's a suspect?"

"Yes we are," Stefani said before Andersson could speak. "Next to Heather's father, he's second on on the list for the revenge motive."

"That's true," Reynolds said, still not convinced. "But why just blow up Billy and not Willy too or for that matter why didn't Paul kill Willy first and then go after Billy some other way? Willy is definitely going to be on his guard now and he's going to be much tougher than Billy to get."

"We're not sure of anything Craig," Andersson said. "We just need to make sure that a decorated, retired police officer wasn't involved."

"We'd like nothing better than to clear Dickinson and move on to someone else," Stefani said, walking to their vehicle.

"Okay, I'm in," Reynolds said, getting into his car. "Follow me."

Andersson and Stefani followed Reynolds to Dickinson's office, which was about ten minutes away and housed in a two story, turn of the century home. The brick house, which was situated on a corner, had been completely restored. The old fashioned red brick was methodically sand blasted so it really popped and the foundation as well as the roof was totally replaced.

Andersson and Stefani got out of their official vehicle and waited for Reynolds to park.

"Wow!" Stefani said to Reynolds as he approached them. "The private eye business must be very good."

"It is," Reynolds said, looking at the beautiful structure. "The place has been completely restored inside and out in every detail.

Paul even had the house raised so they could remove the crumbling foundation and replace it with a new one which was up to code."

"He must have sunk a fortune into this place," Andersson said, staring at the impressive building.

"He did," Reynolds said, walking toward the entrance. "But he bought the place when it was condemned by the city and they were going to tear it down. I think he got it for a dollar as long as he was going to completely restore it and he had to live there too."

"He lives here too?" Stefani said, as Andersson held the front door open for her.

"Yup," Reynolds replied. "He has the entire second floor."

They all went inside and walked into an elegant setting; it was like a very rich persons living room from 1900. There were tall windows, exposed brick walls, heavy beamed ceilings, and original hard wood floors polished to a flawless gloss. Period furniture was everywhere including several Victorian era couches; all set on three gorgeous carpets.

Sitting right in front of them as they walked in, was a very attractive mid-forties woman, seated at an enormous roll topped desk that was dog legged and connected to an ornate, hand carved wooden desktop. The desktop housed all the modern electronics but kept them out of view from anyone as they entered.

"Good afternoon, welcome to PD Investigations and Security, how may I help you?"

Andersson took the lead and walked up to the desk; his identification was already out in his hand.

"I'm Lieutenant Andersson from the North Carolina Bureau of Special Investigations and this Special Investigator Stefani and Lieutenant Reynolds from Raleigh Police. We're here to see Paul Dickinson."

The woman who was immaculately dressed, smiled at Andersson, and nodded knowingly.

"Yes, of course," she said, standing up. "Mr. Dickinson's been expecting you. Please follow me."

Andersson looked at Reynolds thinking he had called ahead.

"Wasn't me, Nicklaus," Reynolds said. "I didn't tip him off."

The woman walked to a large wooden door that looked like it had been hand carved and had huge brass doorknobs. She knocked once lightly on the door then opened it.

Paul Dickinson was sitting next to another roll topped desk just like the one that was in the outer office and he was on the phone. He waved to them to come in. The female assistant, who was as tall as Stefani asked them if they wanted anything to drink and they all declined. Just as she directed them to sit down, Dickinson hung up and stood up.

"Nicklaus Andersson!" Paul said, walking to them with his hand outstretched. "It's been a long time."

"You know Craig," Andersson said, turning to Stefani. "I'm not sure you've ever met Roxanne Stefani."

When Paul saw Stefani he walked past Reynolds like he wasn't even there.

"No, we haven't met but I know of her," he said smoothly, and they shook hands.

"Nice to meet you Paul," Stefani said with her dazzling smile.

Paul was shorter than she was; he was shorter than everyone in the room for that matter, but he had a presence that commanded your attention.

"Please sit down," he said and they all moved to a cozy area off to one side of the room near a lighted gas fireplace. There were two, deep maroon colored, soft leather couches which faced each other and only one chair between them. It was obvious that the chair was for Paul and the couches for everyone else. Once they were all seated and his assistant left, Stefani spoke first.

"I must say Paul, this house and all the renovations are amazing; it's beautiful. Did you do any of the work yourself?"

Paul beamed at Roxanne then glanced down at her legs. "Well, thank you Roxanne, and yes I did a lot of the work myself. Of course, I had help with replacing the foundation and the roof, as well as with the electrical and plumbing."

"It must have been a massive undertaking," she replied. "Craig said the property was condemned when you purchased it."

"Yes, it was," Paul said, finally taking his eyes off her legs and looking up at everyone. "In fact, I used to live here when I was kid. We didn't have the whole house back then and actually four families occupied the building. We all had half of a floor with a few tiny bedrooms, a small living area, a kitchen and one bathroom. Originally, it was a turn of the century mansion owned by a very rich couple who had four children. Over the years, after the couple died, the place was sold seven or eight times and finally fell into disrepair. When I saw the city was going to bulldoze it, I bought it and began to restore it to it's original glory."

"You sure did that Paul," Andersson said. "It really looks great."

"Thank you," Paul said, spreading his hands out. "I have several of my main staff here as well, but their offices are all on the other side so that way they can share a great view of the park. I'd give you a tour but I'm sure you're not here to see my house."

"No, Paul, we're not," Andersson said. "But I'm sure you do know why we're here…"

Paul smiled. "Of course I do," he said, crossing his legs and relaxing his hands on the arms of the chair. "I thought you would be here this morning bright and early waiting on doorstep, but then when you didn't show up, I figured you went to see Willy first."

Andersson smiled. "Yes, we did and Willy was very cooperative. He even let us search his apartment and place of business without a warrant."

"...And you found nothing, right?" Paul asked.

"Right," Stefani replied.

"Okay, so what do you want to know from me?" he said and began to rattle off the answers to his own questions. "Did I kill Billy Burk? No. Where was I the evening he died? I was at Hot Rod and I was with someone until after eight o'clock which I believe was around the time Billy went boom. Will I permit you search my place of business and home? No. Not without probable cause and a search warrant which is specific to what you are seeking in that search. Why won't I let you search voluntarily, because I have clients private information to protect, and because I don't want to since I've done nothing wrong."

"I guess that sums things up for us now, doesn't it?" Andersson said after a long awkward moment.

"Yes, I guess it does!" Paul said, smugly, staring back at Andersson.

"Paul, can we get the name of the person you said you were with at Hot Rod that evening?" Stefani asked.

Paul turned to her and his smiled came back. "Of course you can Roxanne," he replied. "I have all that information written down for you and you can get it from my assistant on the way out."

Andersson stood up and so did Stefani and Reynolds. They all knew they weren't going to get any more voluntary information from Paul Dickinson nor would he tolerate further questioning.

"Paul can I ask you one question before I leave," Andersson said.

"Sure Nicklaus," Paul said, standing. "Just one."

"It's hypothetical of course…"

"Of course…"

"If you were going to get Billy and Willy for revenge; for what we all know they did to Heather and her unborn baby. How would you do it?"

"I'll kill Billy and frame Willy for it!"

"Me too!" Andersson said, and he shook Paul's hand and they all left.

CHAPTER TWENTY-SEVEN

Hank Milson was a busy guy that got a lot done and got a lot done every day. He also made getting a lot done look easy. He was disciplined and consistent but still took time for himself and the others in his life. His new found wealth from the lung cancer treatment he discovered kept pouring in and even for a man of his intelligence it took some time to comprehend it all.

The flexibility of his ideas, his broad scope of goals and his future married life with Roxanne were now paramount. His education, medical training and experience made him able to juggle ten things at once; but lately, the ten things had become twelve.

The lawsuit with R. Wight Tobacco was over and aside from the money it cost for the legal battle, it was still a victory of sorts, or at least a stalemate. Hank wasn't happy that the treatment he had created was being used, mainly in China and Russia, to keep people smoking and to get others, especially young people to start smoking. The positive side to the bizarre equation is the cancer victims Pulmimab is saving.

Karen Mello, the former head nurse of the cancer center, who was now Hanks right hand and daily operational officer of his research company, had continued to prove herself invaluable. With her MBA and superior managerial skills, she kept the research company running smoothly and focused on specific targets coupled with an exact plan of how to reach positive results. They hired the best people possible, paid them well, and gave them the finest, most up to date equipment.

Hank still saw patients in his hospital based practice four days a week and although he usually didn't see Roxanne during the day, like most couples, they talked on the phone frequently.

"How's the Burk case going?" Hank asked, taking a break in his office after seeing the last patient on his schedule.

"Slow," she replied, disappointed. "We got a couple of good suspects but so far no real evidence."

"Sorry honey, but I have confidence in the Stefani girl," he said, cheerfully. "Something will break."

"I'm not sure at this point but Andersson and I have a few more interviews," she said.

"What time will you be home tonight?" He asked.

"Probably around six, six thirty..." she said. "I'm going for a long run shortly, I'm changing here then coming home after I'm done."

"You want some pasta tonight and maybe a couple of your mom's meatballs?" He tempted. "You're going to need to carb up after your run and I got her meatball recipe down pretty well."

She laughed. "Sounds good and I'm glad one of us can cook otherwise we'd have to hire someone or eat a lot of takeout..."

Hank checked the time. "Six thirty sounds better for me," he said. "I wanted to stop and see your father before I went home."

"Lately, you two have become thicker than thieves," she said. "Not that I mind but I know my dad, he's always got something in the works..."

"You know us both so well..." Hank said, remembering his promise not to keep any secrets from her.

"He's got some ideas about what you and I were talking about the other day."

"Ideas?" Roxanne asked, knowing Hank did not want to discuss anything in detail on the phone.

"Just ideas or is he moving forward with those ideas into reality?"

Hank hesitated. "We'll talk about it soon, it's just in the preliminary stages, but emerging off paper and it's definitely no longer table top stuff. It's been approved and going real world. It has too."

"Okay Hank," Roxanne said, with a small sigh. "I understand and I love you."

"I love you too," Hank replied and he hung up Kira Lake finished with Henry's first dive lesson and side stepped any of the numerous offers he had for them to get together afterwards. She had other plans and she needed time to prepare if they were going to the Keys this weekend. She said no to a late lunch or a dinner with Henry and he wasn't happy with or willing to take no for an answer.

"What about if I come over to your house around eight?" He begged. "I'll even bring the best champagne and since we already spent hours in the water already today, we can skip the bath and perhaps try your bed."

Kira was furious with Henry and it was a good thing they were talking on the phone. She was very upset with him; this was his third phone call to her, and she was tired of his persistence.

"Henry honey," she said, squeezing the receiver tightly wishing it was Henry's neck. "I'd love to do something like that but the truth is I'm exhausted, not to mention all the preparations I need to make for our trip to the Keys this weekend."

"I know Kira, but all the time at the pool today was spent talking about diving or actually having me underwater when I'd rather be under you."

Kira shook off the wave of nausea that just went through her with that vivid thought.

"I know you would Henry and frankly, my special little boy," she purred, choking bile back down.

"That's where you're going to be this weekend; underwater and under me."

"Really Kira?"

"Of course really!" She replied, trying to relive in her mind the time she just spent with Chris and Radhika; where she really would want to be. "I'm going all out on this Henry; a private plane, chartered yacht, the diving and the especially the time alone."

"OMG! OMG!" he repeated, sounding like some teenaged girl asked out on her first date. "I didn't know you were going to so much trouble for us…"

"It's no trouble, it just takes planning but fortunately I use the same people for my dive trips and pay very well for short notice," Kira said, sounding weary. "A quick flight to Miami and then I have a private sea plane which takes us right to the yacht."

"A sea plane?" Henry said, stopping in his tracks; the high school squeal gone from his voice. "You mean the planes that can take off and land on water?"

"Yes Henry," she said, lying back on the couch. "A plane like that…why?"

The oh-so-familiar wave of fear that had been Henry's constant companion all his life returned. Something new and something potentially fatal. From the first time he rode a bicycle as a kid, even with the training wheels, he felt a fear something would happen; something bad. It was an exaggerated perception for Henry, well beyond the normal. His intensity to observe, assess, concentrate, evaluate, and understand anything, was phenomenal. Henry was a savant' – a Rain Man – without the idiot part. It was why he wrote so well without actually experiencing whatever he was writing. He could watch people; study them, listen and learn but participation took on a phobia like fear. Therefore, all his gathered knowledge, made him rethink doing whatever he was about to do.

It's why he created Gina Wells and she was much more than a fake name on the title page of a book. She was someone real to Henry someone that could create a sexual life for him, a life he could enjoy well beyond the scope of fantasy.

"Can't we have the yacht you chartered pick us up in Miami instead of taking the seaplane? He asked, his hand shaking so much he could barely hold his cell phone.

"Henry, the yacht we use is busy with other charters, especially this time of year," Kira said, sensing his fear and finding it suddenly arousing. "They're on a tight schedule and I had to work some magic just to get this weekend."

"Well, why not cancel this weekend and plan something for a couple of weeks or a month from now," he said, knowing she would say no. "We could take our time with the diving lessons and I'd feel a lot more comfortable...especially about the seaplane."

Kira couldn't even imagine the thought of having to spend two more weeks with Henry, in any capacity.

"No, Henry, no!" She said, dominantly. "You're going to finish the lessons and go on the trip to the Keys this fucking weekend like we planned!"

The use of the word fucking and the way Kira said it, sent Henry into orbit. Kira's orbit and he began licking his lips frantically. That word...that fucking word...it was so Freudian and

Henry knew it. She used that word to emphasize what kind of weekend this would be for them; a fucking weekend...not a diving weekend, but a fucking weekend!

"I'll be safe?" he asked and despite the rampant flood of sexual thoughts he was experiencing, his fears were in full force. "Nothing bad will happen to me?"

Kira smiled to herself, how quickly Henry had responded to her; he was so Pavlovian, so well trained.

"No Henry," she finally said, her voice as smooth as eating fine chocolate. "Nothing bad will happen this weekend; that is, unless you want it to..."

CHAPTER TWENTY-EIGHT

Paul Dickinson was in a world of his own and there wasn't anything to do but enjoy it. Everything was working as planned and all he had to do was sit back and let it happen. Besides a perfect plan in motion, which was enough in itself; he was with Pi, but he had to be careful. Pi was a distraction, a positive, exciting and thoroughly ego building distraction, but she still was a distraction.

The bigger concern for Paul was the feelings he was beginning to develop for Pi. He was usually able to keep them well in check but not this time, and he wondered if she was somehow playing him? She was different than all the rest. She really seemed interested in him and their sex was more like the sex he had felt with his ex-wife when they first met. It was a connection, a bonding feeling, well beyond the physical; and that idea buzzed around his head like a mosquito in the night. Was he falling for Pi and did he purposely leave out the word love in his assessment or even worse he thought, was she falling for him?

He glanced over and saw her lying next to him. It was natural, her lying there asleep, and that bothered him even more than the feelings he felt. He never let any of the women he saw stay over night. It was tacky at times and sometimes even downright rude; but that rule always kept him from getting involved. The next thing you knew she was bringing over some of her stuff. First, it was just makeup, nothing special, some lipstick, or a curling iron to fix her hair after sex and before they went out. Then, an extra pair of panties or a bra followed, no worries, they won't take much room in your sock drawer. Then, as they closed the deal, a few clothes in your closet and it was over, they were moving in and marriage was on the horizon. What the fuck happened?

Paul sat up and carefully slid out of bed and the first thing he noticed was that her clothes were neatly piled on a chair which was good. Pi was neat and Paul was neat; he liked neat. He scanned the room and spotted her lipstick on his dresser. He rushed to the closet, opened it quietly and saw her black beaded jacket hanging in there. He shot to the bathroom and peeked through the door at the vanity. No curling iron and he breathed a sigh of relief but there was a hairbrush and it wasn't his.

He thought again trying to quell a surge of panic; Pi didn't use a curling iron, she had straight black hair. She was Asian and didn't use a curling iron to his knowledge.

Paul flopped down on the bed mumbling. "I'm done…I'm done…" Which woke up Pi.

"Paul?" She called out to him. "You okay?"

Paul sprang out of bed before she could fully awaken.

"Pi, you have to leave!" He said. "You have to leave now!"

"What?" Pi said, not sure she had heard him correctly. "I have to leave?"

"Yes, please get up and get your things," he said, acting not himself.

Pi rolled over and sat up. "Paul what is wrong? You look like ghost scare you."

Paul wanted to correct Pi and tell her – I look like I saw a ghost – but there wasn't any time for that; he had seen a ghost any way you said it and it was his. His ghost of relationships past and he had to put a stop to this one immediately.

"Please Pi, just get up and leave. I'll take you home. Something has happened and I need some time to think."

Pi got out of bed without saying another word. She was nude and Paul watched her walk to the neat pile of clothes and begin to dress. He looked at her ass as she stepped into her panties, he wanted to stop her, but he didn't. When she finished dressing, she got her black jacket out of the closet and her brush from the bathroom then stood at attention in front of him with a hurt look on her face.

"I ready," she said, as the tears rolled down her cheeks.

Paul felt sick looking at her face, her obvious pain and those tears now flowing freely. He wanted to stop himself but he couldn't.

"The police will come to see you Pi at the nail salon, soon, perhaps even today," he said. "A male and a female cop for sure, possibly a black one as well. They will ask you if you were with me last Wednesday at Hot Rod."

"The police?" she said, sniffing and wiping away the tears. "Are you in trouble?"

"No, I'm not in trouble Pi, but you need to tell them you were with me," he said, as he put on his pants, shirt, socks and shoes. "Like, as you know, we really were..."

"I tell what happens in parking place?" she asked, shyly.

"Yes, if they ask...tell what happened in the parking lot...in my car..." he said. "But, let them ask you, don't volunteer the information."

"How this volunteer?" She asked, puzzled.

Paul grabbed his jacket. "You know, don't tell them you were in my car giving me a blow job at eight o'clock…let them have to ask you for every detail…don't just say it before they ask…"

"But, it was eight o'clock," Pi said, managing a giggle. "I do give you blow job…"

"I know," Paul replied, putting on his jacket and fishing out his car keys. "Just remember you will get anxious when they ask you so you might say something that I would correct but don't worry…say it anyway…it will seem more natural…"

"I will," Pi said, wiping more tears. "I will make them ask me long time…"

"Good Pi," Paul said, moving to the door. "Let's go."

"Paul?" Pi asked, stopping when he went through the doorway. "Will you come back to Pi? See me again?"

Paul nodded, unsure he would. "I promise…I will…"

But when they left Paul's house it was still very dark and when they were driving in the car, Pi felt completely alone. She felt Paul had opened his heart to her and suddenly, for no reason she could understand, had closed it.

The next day, when the nail salon opened at ten o'clock, Andersson and Stefani were waiting for Pi, but she was late. The owner of the salon was a mid-forties woman, also from Vietnam and also like Pi very petite and attractive. She told Andersson and Stefani Pi was never late even though she took the bus to work. The owner was talking about selling the salon and it was just a few minutes after ten when Pi walked through the door.

"Here Pi now," she said.

Pi apologized to the owner for being a few minutes late in English and then the two of them spoke in Vietnamese for another couple of minutes. Both Andersson and Stefani felt the owner was telling her the police were here to talk and was wondering why.

"We talk back here," Pi said, leading Andersson and Stefani to a small room in the back of the salon which served as both a kitchen and break room for the staff. They all sat down at a table, Pi offered them tea or coffee and they both accepted some tea. Pi got them the tea while Andersson made the formal introductions and showed Pi their credentials.

"Pi, you know why we want to talk to you?" Andersson asked, sipping the strong tea which was very good.

Pi shook her head. "Tea good?"

"The tea is very good, thank you," they both replied.

Pi smiled.

"We're looking into the murder of someone who was killed last Wednesday evening," Stefani said.

"Someone who was blown up in their car not that far from here. Did you hear about that?"

Pi nodded. "I hear from customer...but I not read..."

"Do you know Paul Dickinson?" Andersson asked.

Pi nodded slowly. "Yes."

"How do you know him?" Stefani asked, sipping her tea.

"I meet him at Hot Rod," she replied, casting her eyes down with some embarrassment. "It a big bar very close to salon..."

"Yes, we know it." Andersson said. "Were you there last Wednesday evening?"

"Yes, I do go to Hot Rod Wednesday most always..." she replied. "...after work."

"What time was that?" Stefani asked.

"Seven o'clock...when close here..."

"Did you meet Paul Dickinson last Wednesday?" Andersson asked.

"Yes, I meet him," Pi said, smiling for the first time. "He very nice to me...buy drink..."

"How long were you with him at Hot Rod?" Stefani said. "Do you remember?"

"About hour…maybe more…"

"So you were with Paul Dickinson at the Hot Rod until around eight?" Andersson said.

Pi nodded.

"Did you leave with him at eight?" Andersson followed up.

"Yes, we leave together."

"Where did you go?" Stefani asked.

"To his car" Pi said, showing more anxiety.

"Where did you go after you got into his car? Andersson asked, sensing Pi was either having a struggle with the language or she was purposely holding back information.

"We stay in car."

"You didn't leave the parking lot…you just stayed in the car?" Stefani asked.

"Yes, we stay in car and we talk."

Andersson looked at Stefani and Pi put her head down again.

"Okay Pi, how long were you in the car talking?" Andersson asked dubiously.

"Not long… but I not know…"

"But Paul Dickinson left alone after you talked in the car?" Stefani said.

"Yes, I go back in Hot Rod."

"Was it after eight o'clock?" Andersson asked, trying to pin down an exact time line.

"Yes, it after eight…"

"Okay Pi, thank you," Stefani said, as she finished writing the information down in her black notebook. "We'll need your home address and we're done for now."

"For now?" She asked. "You come back?"

"Maybe," Andersson said. "We have to go to Hot Rod and talk to some people."

"Okay, I there Wednesday..."Pi said, again. "They tell you."

"Yes, we're sure they will," Stefani said. "Thanks for the tea."

They left the Best Done Nails Salon and walked down the long block to Hot Rod.

CHAPTER TWENTY-NINE

Hot Rod didn't open until eleven for lunch but the place was unlocked, the lights were on, and the bar was open. Hot Rod looked big even when the place was full of people; now, when Andersson and Stefani walked in, the place looked gigantic. The dance floor was large enough for a professional basketball game. No one was sitting at any of the over one hundred tables, or twenty private alcove areas that lines the walls, all around the other half acre. Someone was behind the bar and there was one guy sitting on a stool with a large, cold mug of beer In front of him.

"The restaurant opens at eleven-thirty," the young woman behind the bar shouted to them and her voice echoed around the empty room. "You're welcome to have a drink at the bar..."

Andersson and Stefani walked up to the bar and the young girl came over to them.

"What can I get you?"

As fast as those words came out of her so did Andersson and Stefani's credentials.

"We're from the State Police," Andersson said, not saying their names, but they each held up the creds long enough for her to read them.

"I may not look it, but I'm twenty-three, and we proof everyone..."

"We're not here about serving minors or checking IDs," Stefani said, moving up closer to the bar and standing between two stools. "Were you working here last Wednesday or know who was?"

"I was here last Wednesday. I'm here every Wednesday and I'm here every day but Sunday." The girl was cute, feisty, and talked so fast the words ran over one another. "I go to school part time and don't owe a dime."

"That's great," Andersson said, also moving up between two stools. "Do you know a guy named, Paul Dickinson? I have a picture of him..."

"Forget the picture," she said, wiping off the bar. "I know Paul, everyone in here knows Paul. He's a private eye and he's loaded. He's the best tipper we got and as far as I know; we ever had..."

"Was Paul in here last Wednesday evening," Stefani asked, watching the girl wipe the same spot over and over.

"Sure he was," she said, looking up with her first smile. "He was back in one of our more private booths, drinking tequila shots with some young Asian, who I think works down the street at the nail salon."

"You mean Pi?" Andersson asked.

"Yeah Pi," the girl replied and she stopped wiping. "What's this all about?"

"We're checking where everyone was when that bomb went off around eight o'clock last Wednesday," Stefani said. "We think Paul Dickinson left before eight with Pi and might have seen something important."

"Did you ask Paul if he saw something important?" The girl asked and her smile disappeared. "Or are you checking his alibi?"

"We're checking a timeline of events and we need your cooperation, young lady…," Andersson said, leaning over the bar in her face.

"Okay…sure…," she said. "He was here around that time… but I'm not exactly sure the time he left.

His server was Cassie, and she would know what time he left."

"Why would she know," Andersson asked, softening his approach.

"Because Cassie is the lucky bitch that gets to take care of Paul when he's here, which is three times a week," the girl said, annoyed. "He always wants that booth in back and he always wants Cassie to be his sever. Heck, she can just take care of Paul and make more in tips than any of us do all night."

"Okay, thanks," Stefani said. "We'd like Cassie's full name and phone number."

"Sure," the girl said. "But, you could come back on Wednesday after six and she will be working…"

"Maybe we will come back, but we'll take her full name and number before we leave," Andersson said, leaning in again.

"Okay…okay," she said, stepping back. "I just thought you might want to catch Ollie at the same time."

"Ollie?" Stefani asked. "Who's Ollie?"

"Ollie is Oliver. I don't know his last name but he's an outlaw, biker, wanna be. We got a bunch of them who come in and sit back there at the large round table and check out the girls."

"What happened with Ollie last Wednesday?" Andersson asked.

"I didn't see it since the place is crazy on Wednesday with our drink special, but Cassie told me Paul got into with Ollie just as Paul was leaving."

"What do you mean…got into it with Ollie?" Stefani said. "They have an argument or was it more?"

"It wasn't a fight but Cassie said it was definitely heated…at least on Ollie's part. Cassie said it was over Pi but she didn't hear what exactly was said about her. Cassie said Paul was as cool as can be up against Ollie who's as big as a tree but about as smart as one…"

"Did this Ollie follow Paul outside?" Stefani asked.

"Cassie said Ollie didn't go outside right then, but he could have left shortly after he sat down."

"How do you know Ollie didn't leave right then?" Andersson said.

"Cause Cassie told me when Ollie came back to the table where his buddies were sitting, he was real pale and looked like his had shit his pants…"

"Paul backed him down real good, huh?" Stefani said.

"Big time," the girl replied. "Cassie said Ollie was talking tough, all mean and bad ass like …and Paul's standing there talking about some movie he saw way back when…"

"What movie?" Andersson asked. "Did Cassie mention the name?"

"I don't remember it all since I was pouring drinks back and forth, but she did mention DeNiro was in it. One of those Mafia types…I'm not sure. I probably wasn't even born or maybe I was in kindergarten when it came out."

Stefani laughed, but Andersson just broke a smile.

"Okay thanks," he said. "Maybe we will come back Wednesday and we would appreciate it if you would point this Ollie out to us but don't mention to anyone we will be coming."

"Sure, I won't say a word," the girl replied. "Now can I get you something to drink or would you like to stay for lunch?"

"No thanks, we have more stops to make," Stefani said. "Maybe some other time…"

"Sure, I'll be here unless I've graduated."

Anderson and Stefani laughed and left.

Henry was still sucking air like a new born guppy.

"You're breathing too rapidly," Kira said. "You need to stop think-ing about taking a breath and just try to let it happen normally."

Henry took the regulator out of his mouth and pulled off the face mask.

"How can I breathe normally when I'm underwater?" He sputtered. "It's not normal to breathe underwater Kira, so con-sequently, I keep thinking about taking that next breath."

"I understand Henry, and I know it's not normal to breathe underwater, that's why you have the air tank but you're almost hyperventilating and sucking through tank after tank."

"I know! I know!" He said, in frustration.

Kira wanted to lose her temper and go off on him, but the pool assistant was just a few feet away.

"Look Henry," Kira began calmly. "When you're underwater at the Keys you will have so much to look at that you'll forget all about taking a breath…"

"That's what I need," he said. "I need something to take my mind off my breathing."

"Okay," Kira replied. "I'll put my gear on and we'll both dive together. You're doing okay so far and It will give us a chance to practice those hand signals I taught you."

"Thank you very much Kira," Henry said, walking to the pool ladder and getting out. "Let me get a fresh air tank while you get your gear on and we can go back in."

The assistant left to get Kira's dive gear and a couple of fresh air tanks.

"You'll be fine Henry," Kira tried to be encouraging knowing Henry was very close to quitting.

"I'll be fine when all this is over...," Henry said, removing his BC. "I'm not sleeping well and I'm having nightmares when I do get to sleep."

"Nightmares?"

"Yes, nightmares about diving and about that seaplane too," he replied. "I'm a wreck."

"I'm sorry honey," Kira said, touching Henry's wet arm. "You wait, it's going to be a wonderful time and all this work is going to be worth it."

Henry felt a chill pass through him when Kira touched his arm and he put his wet hand over hers.

"I feel better when you touch me," he said, feeling some relief. It makes me feel safe, like when my mother used to do it."

Kira sandwiched Henry's hand with her other one and rubbed it lightly.

"Like this, Henry," she said. "Did she do it like this?"

"Yes, she did and my forehead too," he replied, falling immediately into a dreamy state. "I was afraid of everything, and her comfort made it all go away."

"Your mom is in a private nursing home now, isn't she?" Kira asked, taking her hand off his and placing to the side of his face.

"Yes," he replied, closing his eyes and pressing his head to her hand. "She's eighty and very sharp mentally but very frail from osteoporosis. It's a very nice place with a lot of excellent staff, and they provide the specialized care she needs. Fortunately, I can afford to keep her there..."

"That's a good son Henry," Kira said, sliding her index finger down to his lips and gliding over them.

"You've provided well for her in her later life when she needed you the most; just like she did for you when you needed her most."

Henry's eyes were closed and Kira steadied him with her one hand as she stuck the tip of her finger into his mouth.

"There you go Henry, show me how you're going to please me," she teased, rolling her finger tip around his tongue. "That's it, honey, suck, nibble, lick and chew on it…"

Henry's tongue went after her finger just like she had told him. He grabbed at it and pulled it deeper into his mouth; wrapping it up just like a good lizard would. Watching his little mouth work on her finger tip like this, would normally have made Kira vomit if it wasn't for her twisted fascination of seeing him do it.

"That's it baby boy," she whispered close to his ear when she spotted the assistant approaching. "You work mommy like that this weekend and I can promise you I'm going to mess my little guy's face all up."

Henry started to make guttural noises with his mouth and Kira could feel him go weak.

"Easy honey, easy," she said, barely able to remove her finger from the grasp of his tongue. "My gear is here, and the extra air tank."

Henry had his eyes closed when the assistant saw him and he was still slightly swaying.

"Is he okay?" He asked, setting the gear down next to Kira.

"Yes, he's fine now," Kira said, with a reassuring smile. "He just felt a little faint since he forgot to eat breakfast this morning."

Henry opened his eyes and was surprised at his surroundings. It was if he had been somewhere else and had just returned; definitely an out-of-body-experience.

"Does he want some orange juice or a power bar?" The assistant asked, staring at Henry with the creepiest feeling he had ever experienced in his life. "Miss Lake, is he really okay?"

"Yes, he's fine," she replied. "Low blood sugar will sometimes make people act like this and yes, some orange juice would help…"

"Sure, I'll get some right now," the assistant said, turning away, then adding. "I hope I never get low blood sugar…"

CHAPTER THIRTY

The next couple of days went slowly for some and too quickly for others; for Andersson and Stefani the days were dragging. They went back to Hot Rod on Wednesday and spent three hours waiting for Ollie to show up, but he never did. No one knew why he wasn't there; when he was always there on Wednesday, and no one knew or would say where he lived or worked.

They did get a chance to talk with Cassie, the server, who took care of Paul Dickinson and had witnessed the verbal altercation with Ollie. Cassie was sure Paul and Ollie got into it before eight o'clock since she checked the time right after Paul and the Asian girl left Hot Rod. She remembers saying to herself two more hours and I'm done. Usually, she was there until 2:00 am, since the tips were so good on Wednesday, but she had a date, and was meeting the guy at ten.

Cassie also was sure that Ollie had started the confrontation by saying something to Paul about being with such a young woman. Stefani pressed Cassie for every detail she could recall and Cassie told the story five times and each time she remembered a little more detail of what happened. After Cassie had finished telling the story, for what Andersson promised was the last time, the facts remained.

Ollie had confronted Paul over Pi and after some words, he threatened Paul. That's when Paul recited something about DeNiro from one of his movies, which Cassie was sure Ollie had no clue what he was talking about since he stood there looking dumber than usual. Andersson and Stefani laughed when Cassie said that and it made Cassie feel like she was really helping them. Cassie went on to say; things got real tense at the end and she was positive Paul said, 'I skip right to the gun and I'll kill you.'

Andersson whistled when Cassie said the words …'and I'll kill you…' She said it was really something to see. She said Paul stood there as cool as could be and Ollie just backed down. Stefani remembers her saying Ollie looked really scared when he sat back down at the table. There was no hiding it despite the fact he tried to. She wasn't sure where Ollie went but after a few minutes he was gone.

The days went too fast for Kira and Henry too even though the time dragged for both of them when they were at the pool. They both dreaded the upcoming three day weekend and for different reasons.

Henry was still not sleeping well even though he had gotten a small prescription for sleeping medication from his primary doctor. He did get several hours of sleep using the medication, but his nightmares of of dying in a plane crash were more vivid than ever.

The seaplane would take off from the dock after they boarded and everything seemed to be fine. The plane would accelerate and skim over the surface of the water as it tried to become airborne. Everything seemed to go well until the plane got ready to lift off; and Henry had two versions of the take off crash. One version, which played more frequently than the other, was the seaplane losing power right as it left the surface. The plane would rise and then start to bounce over the water until it began to cartwheel.

In the cartwheeling crash, the plane would struggle again and again to lift off giving Henry the hope the plane would be able to get into the air; but really he knew that something was going terribly wrong. The cartwheel crash would tear the seaplane apart piece by piece, and as it broke up, the passengers inside would be subjected to tremendous crushing injuries. Henry always was flung free of the plane as it disintegrated, but was still strapped into his seat on impact, and drowned.

In the other nightmare crash version, Henry was airborne, and the seaplane was climbing to its designated altitude, when suddenly both engines quit, and the plane plummeted into the water, Again, despite the horrific crash, he survived the crash, securely buckled in his seat, only to drown again.

Kira wanted the weekend over even before it began, only from one standpoint; she despised Henry's touch and she knew she was going to have to have some physical contact with him to make her plan succeed. She wasn't sure yet how much contact they would be having; and as far as she was concerned she already had had way too much. But she kept thinking of her goal, and that always kept Kira on track no matter the obstacles. The finish line was all that mattered to her, and winning; how she ran the race was of no consequence.

Her success and accomplishment on this weekend with Henry depended on flawless planning, and flawless planning is what Kira Lake did well, always. The other part of her perfect plan would come after she returned from the trip and for Kira that time couldn't come fast enough. Those manuscripts would be hers and all the success and glory that went them.

CHAPTER THIRTY-ONE

It was around two o'clock in the afternoon on Thursday, and Harper had worked through lunch, when she hit pay dirt. Her office, which was formerly Stefani's old office, was equally distant between Andersson's and Stefani's, when she called them to come to her office as soon as possible; both, Andersson and Stefani, could hear the excitement in her voice, and went immediately.

"I found the storage unit!" Harper said, jumping up, as both came through the door.

"What storage unit?" Andersson said.

"Willy Burk's storage unit," Harper replied, picking up some papers.

"I thought you checked that out already and he didn't have a storage unit," Stefani asked, trying to read what Harper was holding in her hand.

"I did, I checked it thoroughly, but I didn't check under his old, live in, girlfriend's name," Harper said, smiling and holding up the paper for them to see. "After the briefing the other day, I got to thinking about who else might have a unit Willy was using, and I found it under Angela Pardee."

"Why would she let Willy use her storage unit?" Andersson asked. "I thought we also said Willy was too careful to trust someone else that might have access to his stuff."

"We did and that's still true," Harper replied. "Willy's had the unit for several years and has been paying for it with money orders. Here, I got the storage company to fax me over the contract and payment slips."

"Did Willy forge her signature? Stefani asked.

Harper shook her head. "No, I spoke with the owner of the storage company and he keeps a copy of her driver's license, and from what I can tell, it's her signature."

"So, after they break up, Willy just keeps paying the monthly rental for the unit...," Andersson said, looking at the rental agreement.

"Yes, and he pays by money order so there wasn't a paper trail from his bank back to him when we went looking," Harper said, picking up copies of the money orders. "Now, these signatures on the money orders are just scribbles and these are obviously done by Willy."

Stefani took the copies of the money orders and looked at the signatures, then at Angela Pardee's signature on the rental agreement.

"You're right, these signatures aren't even close," she said, handing the papers to Andersson.

"...especially when no one would really care or check since they had the monthly payment...," Andersson added, taking the papers.

"Exactly what I thought too," Harper said. "I've got all the payment receipts and they all look the same. Willy paid every month on time and paid with a money order."

"All we got to do now is get Angela Pardee to give us permission to open the storage unit since technically she's the person who has rented the unit," Stefani said. "We don't need Willy's permission."

"No, we don't," Andersson said. "but we need to find Angela Pardee and we need to get her persmission."

Harper smiled again. "I've found her and when I talked with her, at first she didn't remember having the storage unit."

"Is she willing to let us search it?" Stefani asked.

"Yes, she is," Harper said. "Especially after I told her were looking for evidence in a murder case."

"We better get someone over to the storage place and sit on the unit until we call the DA and make sure everything is kosher with the search," Andersson said. "We don't want any glitches, and lose anything we might find in a bad search."

"No rush," Harper said. "I sent Culpepper over already and Angela's going to be leaving work and be there at three."

Andersson smiled at Harper. "Good work," he said. "This could be a big break for us."

"Thank you sir."

An hour later, after Andersson had called Michael Carson and Stefani talked with Reynolds; everyone was standing outside number fifteen storage unit while a light rain fell. Carson had looked over the original rental agreement carefully and it said nothing about Willy Burk on it nor did it state that Willy Burk could have access to the unit. Carson whipped up a short document, which gave the State Police permission to search the unit, for anything that might be deemed illegal or suspicious evidence in any criminal charges. The document also gave immunity to Angela regarding anything they found in the unit. Carson also brought along a notary from his office to witness her signature.

"Okay, everything looks good," Carson said, after explaining the document to Angela and getting her signature. "Let's open it up."

The owner took a large bolt cutter and snapped off the lock, Culpepper removed the lock, and slid up the garage door. The unit, which was the size of a narrow one stall garage, had four large plastic containers neatly lined up on one side of the unit and three motorcycles parked in tandem on the other side.

"I'll bet those babies are stolen," Reynolds said, walking over to the bikes, while Andersson headed to the plastic containers.

"Open them up," he said to Culpepper. "Let's see what we got in these."

"You have cameras on these units?" Stefani said to the owner, while Culpepper began to take the lids off the containers.

"No," the owner said, trying to work his way over to where Culpepper and Andersson were standing.

"Too much trouble and I like to respect my client's privacy..."

"What about their belongings?" Stefani asked, blocking him from getting any further.

"They store at their own risk," he said, craning his neck to see what was in the first container. "I got the security gate and each tenant gets their own entrance code and I have a fence all around the place too. So, we don't get many complaints of a break in and the camera systems are a pain in the ass.

"Looks like a lot of tools and more motor cycle parts, probably from other stolen chopped up bikes,"

Culpepper said, moving to the next container.

"We're going to need to see any a list of other tenants in your facility." Stefani said to the owner.

"Why don't you go back to the office and start getting those for us, please."

The owner looked Stefani then back over to Andersson and Culpepper.

"Okay," he said, reluctantly. "Stop by the office when you're done here…"

After the owner had left, Stefani helped Harper check the third container and they found Willy's pot stash.

"We got some weed over here," Harper announced, took some pictures of it, and carefully removed the plastic bag with her gloved hand.

Andersson turned around and looked at the bag Harper was holding.

"Tag it for the lab," he said, "Have them check for any of Willy's prints but that doesn't look like more than a personal use amount unless you find more."

Harper and Stefani removed the rest of the stuff from the container and set it down on the floor. Aside from the small amount of weed, the rest of it was all brand new motorcycle parts still in their original boxes. The last box they saw in the bottom of the container wasn't anything commercially packaged like the other boxes they found, and when Harper went to touch it she thought twice about removing it.

"Take a look at this one Roxanne," Harper said. "It's not like the other ones that were in this container and it's got some funny writing on it that looks Chinese."

Roxanne leaned over Harper's shoulder and peered into the container at the unusual box.

"Don't touch it Lilly," Stefani said. "Andersson, you better take a look at this."

Andersson left what he was doing with Culpepper and went to her.

"I'm not sure what it is," Stefani said. "but I think we should call the bomb squad."

After the bomb squad arrived and had their robot remove the box from the container, they found it was simply made of cardboard and the Chinese writing indicated that the box contained one inch screws. When the cover of the box was finally removed, there wasn't screws of any size in the box but there were two hand grenades and the box looked like it could have held four.

"Go pick him up…murder one…and read him his rights…," Carson was the first to speak after seeing the grenades. "I'll get the warrant for his arrest."

Michael Carson scurried off to start preparations for another sensational, media crazed, photo-op and press conferencing, high profile case. But he would need to have all of his ducks in a row and that included all the baby ducks walking a straight, unbroken line with no stragglers. He knew all of Heather Burk's case was going to be resurrected and re-analyzed over and over. Like only a few cases of this nature, where they contained all the ingredients for national attention, it could go either way; very positive or very negative.

All of the failures, of not having been able to bring those responsible for Heather's death and her unborn baby's death to justice, were now within his grasp to correct. Michael Carson had a second chance, another bite at the apple, to fix what was broke and carry his name to victory. It was the big break, the half-court shot with two seconds left in the game or a grand slam hit to win in the seventh game of the World Series. He could make this work and not only wipe clean the slate that had injustice written in Heather's blood on it, but rocket himself into the political spotlight. He could garner more praise, and foremost, serious consideration by Governor Forbes, soon to be President of the United States Forbes, for any possible White House position. Thoughts of National Security Advisor, Head Legal Counsel to the President, or and dare he even think in those terms; Attorney General, made his pulse quicken and gave his testosterone a wakeup call.

You're only as good as your last win...kept ringing in Michael Carson's ears and he wasn't going to lose...not this time; and not for anyone or anything.

PART II

Crime and punishment should meet in a medium in favor of sanity… and usually it does…but sometimes it does not…

CHAPTER THIRTY-TWO

On second thought, Michael Carson wanted Willy Burk arrested in spectacular fashion. He wanted a SWAT team called in and he wanted Willy taken into custody with all the media coverage he could muster in thirty minutes.

Michael Carson, the DA of Wake County, would be standing, waiting, when they brought him in; when Willy did the walk in front of all the cameras; in front of the whole world. Good thing Michael Carson asked Andersson and Stefani to make the formal arrest before he called the media.

"I don't think we're going to need SWAT Michael," Andersson said, calling Carson by his first name and making his request sound more personal. "We just finished searching where he lived and where he worked, plus his truck and we didn't find anything remotely criminal let alone any weapons. Why not just pick him up like you said in the first place.?"

"But we just found two grenades in his storage unit...and you said there might be another one... "

"I know and we have those two grenades and if Willy does have the fourth one hidden somewhere, I don't think he's going to use it on Stefani and I if we just knock on his door. He's more apt to use a grenade if we surround him with SWAT and it looks like he has no way out...," Andersson said.

"But I wanted a media covered arrest Nicklaus and a lot of attention this case should get," Carson lamented, as he took out his cellphone, knowing he had told all of his staff drop everything and start to work on prosecuting Willy Burk.

"This also might be an elaborate setup," Stefani said, point blank, like slapping Carson right in the face.

"What? Are you crazy?" Carson said, freezing in motion and holding his cellphone up like the Statue Of Liberty. "We found the fucking grenades in his storage unit for God's sake! They came in a box that would have been gift wrapped if it had a bow on it."

"That's just my point," Stefani sprang back. "Why would he need more than one grenade and why would he store them in the unit...for what a rainy day."

"I don't know...maybe they came four to a box and you had to buy all four...maybe it was buy three and get one free....I don't really care," Carson said, sarcastically.

Stefani was ready to spar but Andersson put up his hand to her and the other one to Carson.

"Let's just think a minute before we react and live to regret it," Andersson finally spoke, defusing what could have turned into a fist fight and ending up with Carson wearing his ass for a hat. "Why not bust Willy for what we know are going to be stolen motorcycles, some parts, and the weed. We'll save the grenades and murder charges until we have him securely in custody."

"Good idea," Stefani said. "He's still on parole and we know he will lawyer up right away."

"She's right Michael," Andersson said, checking his watch. "Let us drive by his garage and see if he's there…"

Carson was still standing like Miss Liberty with fast fading visions of himself talking tough on the six o'clock news but then he began to really think.

"Okay," he finally relented. "We'll arrest Willy for the weed, and parole violation, while we sort out the stolen motorcycles and parts; before we hit him with the murder charge."

"Sounds good," Andersson said, like Carson had just thought of it all by himself.

While Andersson and Stefani, with Reynolds, Harper and Culpepper were on their way over to arrest Willy; Henry Harris was at his mother's bedside watching her as she began to eat her dinner.

"That looks good mother," Henry said, as he looked over her food tray. "But we could have gone to the dining room as well and been with your friends."

Henry's mother, now several inches under five feet tall, and weighting barely ninety pounds, was sitting in a large, overstuffed chair, looking like a child who was dressed up to play an old lady. An old lady who was so weak she could hardly pick up the fork to feed herself.

"You want me to help you mother?" Henry offered, as her bony hand began to tremor.

"No Henry," she replied. "I think I can do it but could you cut up my chicken for me."

Henry picked up the knife and took the fork from her hand and sliced the roasted chicken breast into small pieces.

"There you go mother," Henry said, with the happy Henry smile. "Just like you did for me when I was young."

Henry's mom smiled with the same tiny mouth and identical happy Henry smile.

"That's right," she said, taking the fork from him. "I used to cut up your meat for you so you wouldn't have to do it yourself. You always had your nose in a book and I didn't want you to stop reading."

"I know," he said, as he watched her taste the chicken. "I always loved to read even when I was eating and I didn't want to stop and take the time to cut my meat."

"Those were wonderful days Henry," she said, slowly chewing the tiny piece of chicken and swallowing it. "It was just you and I and your books."

"I know and life was so easy for me," he said. "Not like it is now…now I have to make decisions for myself. Now I have to go on diving trips that I don't want to go on…"

"Just don't go Henry," she said, tasting some of the buttered rice and sensing his growing anxiety.

"You know you don't like the water anyway; you never did."

"I know mother," he replied, softly. "But Kira insists we go and you know I've never been able to say no to Kira."

Henry's mother nodded and then pointed with the fork at him.

"You've always been obsessed with that woman and frankly I can't for the life of me know why," she said, the dislike in her voice was obvious, her dislike for Kira Lake was always obvious.

"Oh mother, please, let's not argue about Kira again…"

"I know…I know," she said, eating more chicken. "but she makes you write those dirty, disgusting books and I don't like it!"

"Well mother, those dirty, disgusting books, which I prefer to call erotica, make a lot of money," Henry sniped. "Money that keeps you in this exclusive nursing home, where the staff fawn all over you, and serve you delicious meals at your bedside."

Henry's mom smiled at him. "You're so right Henry, and let's not talk about Kira Lake anyway, let's talk about your new manuscripts…"

CHAPTER THIRTY-THREE

Andersson was right, and when they got to Willy's garage he was still there, but he wasn't alone. He was with someone, a woman, and they had caught him literally with his pants down and the woman bent over his desk. Willy wasn't embarrassed and he wasn't as mad about the arrest as about the fact that he didn't get to finish.

"I don't know anything about any storage unit and I want a lawyer," he said, even before Reynolds could finish placing him in handcuffs.

"You better change your tune Willy," Reynolds said gruffly, as he snapped the cuffs on tight. You've violated your parole and you're going back to jail to finish the other year of your sentence."

"Big deal," he lashed back. "I can do a year in County on my head."

"Well, you won't be going the time for those stolen motor-cycles on your head," Andersson said, walking Willy out of the garage to the patrol car. "That time for those charges are going to be done in a North Carolina State Prison and all we know how much you enjoy the state system."

Willy was defiant in front of the woman he was with who looked every bit as frustrated as Willy did about being interrupted.

"I'm not going to any state prison since I didn't do anything wrong."

Andersson packed Willy off with Reynolds and Culpepper while Stefani finished talking with Willy's companion who had nothing to offer and was let go.

"It's a good thing we didn't show up with SWAT and the media," Stefani joked after the woman drove off. "All the noise those two were making I don't think they heard us walk in until they saw us standing in the doorway."

"I know and I don't think they cared even then…" Andersson said, taking out his box of Chiclets and popping a couple into his mouth.

"The way I saw it…they got started right away…"Stefani said, taking a couple of the Chiclets Andersson offered, then pointing to the doorway. "Willy met her right inside the door and neither one of them thought to lock it. Her top and bra was off a few seconds later …"

"Okay Roxanne…okay," Andersson said, putting away the Chiclets. "I get it…"

"What?" She said, smirking. "I was just trying to show you my deductive skills and tell you what I think happened…"

Andersson shook his head. "I know how the scene unfolded, and you know it, since we both saw how it ended…"

"No, we didn't see how it ended," she said, poking more fun at him. "We almost saw how it ended…"

"Roxanne if you're trying to embarrass me…you've succeeded."

Paul Dickinson would have done a high five to someone, when he heard Willy Burk had been arrested, but he was alone in his office at the time. There was a brief mention of it on the six o'clock news, no video, and the only reason the arrest was reported at all, was Willy's family connection to Billy and Heather Burk. Just a couple of quick lines about the brother of the late Billy Burk whose wife, Heather, died under suspicious circumstances, was arrested on parole violation and alleged possession of stolen property. No mention of a murder charge or any grenades being found.

Paul wondered why they hadn't mentioned the grenades and that immediately concerned him. He would have bet Michael Carson would have made a big deal out of the Willy Burk arrest but everything seemed low key. Maybe they didn't find the grenades; could it be possible? No way, he thought, the storage unit wasn't that big nor did it contain that much stuff that they could have missed them. They had to have found the grenades and for some unknown reason they weren't releasing the information, but why? He knew they found the storage unit the same way he did, by remembering Willy's ex-girlfriend, Angela Pardee. He thought it would have taken them a couple more days to think of her...maybe Reynolds remembered her.

Paul needed to think and not panic and most of all, beyond all else, he needed to remain quiet. Do not talk about this new development to anyone because that would to be a mistake. Talking or asking any questions about Willy Burk would be his downfall. He wanted answers, but he needed to be quiet, even invisible, and let this whole thing play itself out. He had done everything right, the way he had planned and so far it was working perfectly; almost.

Even if they suspected, in the remote, almost non-existent, possibility that Willy was being framed, without any real proof of it, Michael Carson was still going to prosecute him. Now, with Paul needing another distraction from all this, something to take his mind off negative thoughts, he wondered if he had been premature in his breakup with Pi.

CHAPTER THIRTY-FOUR

It was early Friday morning, when Henry Harris arrived on time at the airport in Raleigh. Kira was already there at the gate, and Henry didn't mind the non-stop flight to Miami. But, when he boarded the seaplane; he screamed all the way up on takeoff and all the way down on landing. Kira didn't know who was happier they had landed; Henry or the pilot.

"It wasn't that bad Henry," Kira said, getting off the seaplane and stepping onto the dock. "I don't think you had to scream like that. I've flown with this pilot many times, but I don't think he will take me again after that performance."

"I'm sorry Kira," Henry said. "But that take off and that landing were exactly how I saw them in my nightmares right before we crashed and I drowned."

"That's the silliest thing I've ever heard," she said, waving to a man dressed in a white uniform who standing on the yacht, which was docked about thirty yards from where they landed. "There's our yacht Henry…let's go."

"What about our luggage?" Henry asked, suddenly feeling hot dressed in a long sleeved shirt, sweater and tweed jacket.

"Don't worry about it," Kira said, twirling around in the bright sunshine. "Someone from the yacht will get it for us so let's just board and have some ice cold champagne."

Once on board the sixty foot yacht, Henry realized the entire boat and crew were completely at their disposal. The Captain, who was the same man Kira had waved at, was dressed in a white uniform and had four gold strips on his shoulder boards. To Henry he looked like the Captain of a Navy ship not a pleasure yacht. He was tall, tanned with blue eyes that matched the beautiful blue water all around them; his short cropped white hair and matching closely trimmed beard, was the finishing touch. His entire crew, three men and three women, all young, gorgeous and like him, dressed in white, starched uniforms.

"Sam, how are you?" Kira gushed, hugging the Captain and kissing him on both cheeks; Hollywood style. "I'm so glad you could take us for the weekend on such short notice. Thank you."

Captain Sam hugged Kira so tight their bodies touched which Henry thought a little too close and lingered a little to long for a casual greeting. Kira let the Captain hug her for almost an awkward moment then she broke free and turned to Henry almost as an afterthought.

"Captain Sam," Kira said, looking slightly embarrassed which was something for her, since she rarely felt embarrassed. "I'd you to meet a dear friend of mine and an incredible author, Henry Harris."

Henry looked like he felt after the seaplane ride; he was pale, weak and a little green around the gills.

"Henry, pleased to meet you and welcome aboard the ESCAPE," Captain Sam said, with a curious eye. "Are you okay? You're not getting seasick already, are you?"

Henry did feel a little nauseous although a lot better than when he landed.

"No, I'm not sea sick," he said, forcing the happy Henry smile and shaking Captain Sam's hand. "I just don't do well on seaplanes."

The Captain laughed and gave Henry a light slap on the back. "I don't like seaplanes either, but you can rest easy on the ESCAPE, my friend; it's going to be smooth sailing for the next couple of days."

"Oh good, Captain," Henry said, thinly. "I can't wait for my first dive…"

Captain Sam laughed again, flashing what Henry thought were the whitest teeth he had ever seen.

"No worries, my friend," he said, turning to Kira with an obvious wink no one missed. "You're in good hands with Kira. She's one of the best divers I've ever had the pleasure of having aboard the ESCAPE."

Henry heard his words, pleasure of having, but not in any way connected with scuba diving.

"I'm sure she is," Henry replied, gawking at the six crew members standing behind Captain Sam, who was focusing all his attention on Kira.

"Sam, I remember a couple of your crew members," Kira said, as she tried to divert his attention away from her. I recall Hanna, your first mate, but I think you have a couple of new ones since I was last here."

Captain Sam turned away from Kira and looked back at the crew like he had forgotten they were even there.

"Oh yeah…Kira…we do have a couple of new crew members…," he said. "I was just going to have them introduce themselves to you and Henry."

Following their Captain's lead, each crew member introduced themselves in turn, giving their rank with duty function. They did so fast, that Henry only remembered two of the crew members names and both of them were very attractive.

"Now that everyone has been introduced," Captain Sam said. "Would you and Henry, like a glass of champagne on the aft deck while we get ready to depart?"

"Of course Sam," Kira said, coupling her arm around his. "I thought you would never ask."

Henry watched as Kira walked away with the Captain and felt hurt, lost and not sure of what to do.

"Henry would you like some champagne too?" Hanna asked, walking to him with a cheerful smile.

"What?" Henry said, his eyes still fixed on Kira and Captain Sam. "Oh yes, I'd love some."

Hanna who was genuinely friendly, offered her arm to Henry. "Shall we?"

Henry smiled the happy smile and they followed Kira and Captain Sam to the aft deck.

The other crew members quickly dispersed and began making preparation to leave. Two of them went and brought the luggage on board while two others cast off the lines which secured the yacht to the dock. The last member went to bridge and started the engines.

Henry sipped the champagne Hanna had given him and although he was sitting with Kira on the aft deck; she was concentrating all her attention on the Captain. When Hanna left for other duties, Henry felt like the third person on a date. He did notice that Captain Sam did not have any champagne and only drank sparking water. Henry was happy to see that at least the Captain was going to be professional in how he operated the boat.

"I'm afraid I have to leave Kira," Captain Sam said, apologetically and standing. "The engines have started and I need be up on the bridge…"

"I understand Sam," Kira said, in a tone of voice Henry had never heard Kira use before and what Gina Wells would call 'sultry'. "Duty calls."

Captain Sam did a slight bow to Kira, Henry thought, as if he was going off to some maritime battle.

"I'm sure I'll see you later," he said, noticing Henry. "Once again Henry, welcome aboard…enjoy yourself…"

Captain Sam left and went to the bridge leaving Kira and Henry sitting alone.

"He seems like a very capable man," Henry said, refilling both of their glasses with champagne.

"He's just how Gina Wells would write a stud of a captain of a pleasure boat. Tall, handsome, confident, with a tight, muscular body, that fits so well in his crisp, white uniform; of course, Gina would go on to describe, in detail, his obvious, thick bulge that was between his legs…"

Kira laughed, sipping more champagne. "Don't be so jealous Henry. Captain Sam did me a huge favor getting us down here on such short notice and the least I can do is give him a little attention for his efforts."

Henry felt that familiar knot tighten in his stomach, as it always had done since he could remember.

It was that uncomfortable, unwanted, left out, and rejected feeling of not belonging.

"Did you ever have sex with him Kira?" Henry said, sounding even more like the jealous lover.

Kira shifted around to face Henry and her whole demeanor had changed in an instant.

"So what if I did?" She said, challenging him. "Would you want to hear all the gory details? Or better yet, Henry, why not have Gina Wells tell me how she would have written our sex scene; she's so good at being naughty."

Henry's tongue started to poke out of his mouth but he caught it in time and pulled it back inside.

"Gina Wells would have her Captain Sam come to you in the middle of the night when everyone was asleep or so he thought," Henry began, as his personality transformed into someone else. "He would be wearing his white uniform stretched tight over his masculine body, looking every bit like the real man and sensual lover. Someone in control, an air of authority; a man that got what he wanted or he just took it and that included his women."

Kira let out a long coo. "Keep going Gina, you're turning me on fast…"

Henry ignored her comment, since he was now Gina Wells, and describing what she would have written.

"You would be waiting on the bed for him; instinctively knowing he would come to you, since he had no choice and couldn't resist. You would have something sexy on, but a little trashy, even slutty, nothing subtle or romantic; this wasn't about love; this was about lust. You want him to know what this was all about, and what he was going to get, but how he was going to have to take it."

"Rough?" Kira asked, feeling that all too familiar tingle between her legs.

"Really rough…two alpha dogs going at it…but not right away," Henry replied, not engaging Kira.

"You would be lying there, uncovered when he entered, an offering in stockings, and garter belt with a matching panties and bra set and the obligatory high heels. Nothing exposed but everything available; if you dare."

"Yeah baby…take me if you can…"

"No champagne or small talk, in fact, no talk at all; the mood and the passion said it all. Gina Wells' Captain would move around the cabin like one of the big cats in a cage; pacing back and forth as he stared at you, his quarry. Let me at her! Let me at her! He undresses in front of you to pique your arousal. Not a male stripper show but as if he was slowing unpeeling a very large banana. A thick, slightly curved, perfectly ripe banana."

"Oh fuck yeah!" Kira said, sliding closer to Henry and licking her lips. "I just love big, thick, ripe bananas!"

"The Captain slides out of his clothes piece by piece, like removing the peel on either side while exposing the banana, little by little," Henry continued. "Soon, and with great anticipation, he's nude before you, with all the sides of the peel down, and the big, thick, slightly curved banana fully exposed."

"Oh baby…come to mama…" Kira moaned, sucking back a mouthful of salvia. "I'd take that beautiful banana right down my throat and never stop eating it…just hold my head and hang on tight…"

"That's exactly what Gina's Captain would do," Henry said, softly moving closer to Kira as she was mesmerized by his words. "He would give the banana just the way you wanted it!"

"…And no one eats a banana the way I do," Kira whispered, opening her mouth to the imaginary banana. "It's like my mouth is a one size fits all…and the bigger the better…"

"Yes…and the Captain knows that, as your tongue swirls around it lightly at first, simply to feel the texture…the meat of the banana and the distinctive flavor."

"I love the taste of banana too!" Kira said, and her tongue licked the air as tiny droplets of spit sprayed from her mouth into the bright sunlight.

"Gina's Captain would remain silent as he watched you devour the banana; a woman starving to death and finally able to eat something."

"Yes! That's how I'd be eating that banana all up, like it was my first meal in a week!" Kira said, dropping her hand down between her legs and squeezing. "...And I know Gina's Captain could hold on for as long as I needed...for an hour or more... even all night, until my hunger was satisfied."

"Of course he could," Henry said, as he touched his knee to hers and felt the vibration of her movement. "Gina's Captain could last forever and finish in a torrent when he was damn well ready."

"Yes...he could hold back but no man can hold back when I'm ready...Gina's Captain or not," Kira said, closing her mouth and sucking as hard as she could while she squeezed her hand tighter between her legs. "When I want it...I want it! I'd rake my teeth over that banana and turn that baby into mush!"

Just then, Hanna, Captain Sam's first officer, was coming up the stairs to the deck, she stopped suddenly as Henry and Kira came into view. She froze on the stair case, her vision just breaking over the deck level, so neither of them saw her. She stood there on the stairs, transfixed on what was happening, and she watched as Kira shuddered and shook, violently at first, then a five second pause, then another long series of rocking spasms before she finally stopped. When it was over, Hanna slowly took the couple of backward steps down the stairs as the yachts horns sounded several times and the boat began to slowly move away from the dock.

CHAPTER THIRTY-FIVE

Henry Harris's screams on the seaplane were nothing compared to the screaming from Willy Burk when he heard Michael Carson add the charge of murder at his arraignment. Willy was shouting and cursing at everyone; Carson, the judge and even his own lawyer. No one could say anything to Willy to calm him down, it took two bailiffs and three additional deputies to physically remove him from the court room.

Carson used Willy's outburst and display of his violent temper to bolster his request to the judge that Willy be remanded without bail; which the judge quickly granted. Andersson and Stefani, along with Reynolds, Harper and Culpepper were there to witness it and the following news conference which took place on the court house steps.

Michael Carson was in rare form when he was met by a throng of news media and at least a half dozen television cameras; all labeled with the various national news outlet logos. Questions were peppered at Carson from the moment he opened the court house door and they came faster than baseballs from an automatic pitching machine in spring training.

Carson dodged the questions and led with a statement.

"Willy Burk was charged today with capital murder in the death of his brother Billy Burk," he began.

"The State of North Carolina will prove beyond any shadow of doubt that Willy Burk planned and carried out the execution of his brother for profit. We have motive, method and opportunity..."

Carson barely finished the brief statement when the questions started again, fast and furious. The two most popular questions Andersson and Stefani could hear asked over and over were about the grenades found in the storage unit and if Billy's death was somehow connected to his wife's death. Carson side stepped any questions about Heather's death; stating no comment, but he did respond to questions about the grenades.

"The grenades found at the storage unit are currently undergoing metal analysis with the ATF in an effort to match their metal structure to the metal fragments found at the scene of Billy Burk's explosion."

More questions followed on top of more questions, and Andersson, Stefani and Reynolds, Harper and Culpepper slowly faded out of camera range, down the court house steps to their cars.

"Welcome to Barnum and Baily's big top," Andersson said, glancing up at the circle of men and women that were tightening around Michael Carson like a hangman's noose. "He better be right about Willy Burk or the news media will ruin him."

"He seems pretty confident up there," Reynolds noted, as he watched Carson point to one reporter after another for more questions. "And as far as I'm concerned, I'd like nothing better than to see Willy Burk be the forty-fourth execution in North Carolina since 1977."

"If those two grenades match those fragments from Billy death; he's done," Culpepper said. "That's super strong forensic evidence and juries love that. It's so easy for them to convict someone when the evidence says they did it."

"You think after all the evidence against him is made available to his lawyers, he'll plead out?" Harper asked.

"I'm not sure Carson will accept a plea deal even if Willy wanted one…," Stefani said, looking up at Carson in front of all the media. "I can smell blood in the water."

"I think you're right Roxanne," Andersson said, leaning against their car. "Carson wants Burk, and he wants him not only for Billy's death, but unofficially, he'll get him for Heather's death as well."

"You mean in the court of public opinion?" Harper asked.

"Exactly," Andersson replied. "If he gets a conviction on Billy's death, people will naturally think it was related to the insurance money as motive, ergo, Billy and Willy killed Heather."

"Nice and slick too," Reynolds said, with a satisfied smile. "Just like the Burk brothers deserve."

"That's if Carson wins his case," Stefani said.

"You sound skeptical," Reynolds said. "You think there's a chance he could lose?"

"There's always a chance he could lose," Andersson said. "But, you're right Craig, Carson's got what looks like an air tight case against Willy."

"Amen to that brother," Reynolds said. "Anybody want to go to Binky's for breakfast?"

Everyone agreed, and piled into the car, leaving Carson all alone on the court house steps, still gabbing away.

CHAPTER THIRTY-SIX

In the Keys, after the Escape left the dock, it quickly got up speed out into the ocean, but it wasn't that far offshore when it reached its destination and anchored. The best diving was near reefs or old ship wrecks which were often located in relatively shallow water. Therefore, the Escape would stay a safe distance from any hazards while Kira and Henry were ferried back and forth using the yachts dingy.

Captain Sam had everything in the way of equipment they would need and all they had to do was suit up and dive; only Henry wasn't happy with the sleeping arrangements.

"I thought we were sleeping in the same cabin!" Henry said, with an angry face, when Kira opened her cabin door. "Besides that, Hanna's got me clear down at the other end of the boat."

"Come in Henry," Kira said, closing the door once he had entered. "We have separate cabins Henry, since we're supposed be down here as business partners getting some sun and some diving. As far as anyone knows, including the Captain, that's the extent of the relationship. I saw no need to give them any other indication."

"But you said I would be with you and that we would have time together, special time Kira," Henry said, suddenly feeling deflated in her presence.

Kira said nothing, but simply unbuttoned her silk blouse, removed it, and took off her lace bra.

"Do you think my breasts are beginning to sag Henry?" Kira asked, showing them to Henry as if he were making a determination on whether she should have cosmetic surgery or not.

Automatically, Henry looked at her breasts and shook his head. "No, they're still remarkably full and look very firm to me."

Kira slid her hands around her breasts from the outside inward, cupping them.

"They do feel good and my gynecologist says I have very dense breasts, which should keep them very firm into my twilight years."

"That's good Kira," Henry said, wanting to move his hands up to touch them as her long nipples tightened in the cool air conditioning.

"Here Henry," she said, holding them up to him. "Feel them and see what you think."

"Feel them," Henry asked, quickly forgetting his anger. "You want me to examine them?"

"Yes, silly boy," she said, offering them. "First, take them both in your hands, and get a good grip on them too; they're heavy."

Henry moved his small, delicate hands up, and carefully replaced hers.

"That's it Henry…squeeze them tightly and lift them up at the same time…"

Henry followed Kira's directions and lifted her breasts one at a time as if he were judging melons at the supermarket.

"What do you think?" She asked, barely able to tolerate the clamminess of his hands. "They can wait a couple of more years?"

Henry's tongue started to dance around the outside of his lips.

"Yes...at least two more years...maybe longer...," he replied, moving both of his hands to her right breast and caressing it. "They're perfectly round and so symmetrical too."

Kira laughed. "You want to kiss that one Henry? Get a little taste before our first dive."

"I'd love to kiss them both," he said, moving his mouth downward.

"Go on...give it a kiss and take a little nibble too," she said, closing her eyes so she wouldn't have to watch him.

Henry kissed her nipple lightly, then slid his tongue over it, and Kira thought his tongue felt like a snail crawling slowly over the sidewalk on a hot day.

"How does it taste Henry?" She asked, opening her eyes.

"Delicious!" He replied. "I could spend all day doing this."

Kira laughed and moved back from him. "Well, you'll have plenty of time later, but right now we're going diving, and enjoy some of this beautiful weather."

Henry stood still while Kira finished undressing in front of him and put on another one of her tiny swimsuits. He never saw her wear the same one twice, and if it was possible, each one seemed to get smaller than the previous one.

"We're going diving already?" He asked, feeling teased and frustrated as usual. "We just got here and I haven't even unpacked."

"Well, get your skinny ass back to your cabin and get ready Henry," Kira snapped in her familiar dominating manner. "We're going diving now!"

Henry watched Kira brush back her hair and tie it into a pony tail.

"Get going!" She shouted, glaring at him in the mirror.

Henry slumped his shoulders, turned around, and left.

CHAPTER THIRTY-SEVEN

Paul Dickinson felt better after he had heard on the midday news that Willy Burk was charged with the murder of his brother. It was a big piece of the puzzle that had to fit if his plan was going to work. He was contemplating having lunch and where he would go when his cell phone rang.

"It's done already!" Paul said, surprised. "That was fast, but very happy it's done!"

"You said as soon as possible," his friend replied. "So I put one of my best craftsman on it and I'm sure you're going to like it."

"Great!" Paul said, checking the time. "How about I pick it up around one?"

"One is fine…I'll see you then…" And they hung up.

Paul Dickinson wasn't the only one thinking of lunch, Andersson and Stefani were ordering chicken salad sandwiches on home-made, country white bread, while, unfortunately, Shay Abisi was having a plain tossed salad with low calorie Balsamic dressing.

"You're not going to pull the starvation salad, trying to eat our sandwiches trick again, are you?"

Stefani asked.

Shay shook her head sipping her iced tea.

"No, I'm not. I'm determined to lose a couple of more pounds before your wedding next month and I keep bouncing up and down. I think it's my hormones."

"You're hormones are fine Shay," Stefani said. "It's those huge donuts you're eating every morning."

"Leave my donuts out of this Roxanne," Shay replied, defensively. "I compensate those calories with exercise."

"Well, you better start compensating a little more girlfriend," Stefani teased. "Because Erin and I are going to be looking real good…"

Andersson groaned.

"Are you saying I'm fat?" Shay retorted. "Because you better look again girlfriend, I'm a lot taller than you and weigh less…"

You're not taller than me Shay," Stefani shot back. "We're both the same height and for sure you don't weigh less than me…"

"Ladies please…and I use the term ladies, again, very loosely," Andersson said. "You're both very beautiful women and look amazing!"

Both Shay and Roxanne made a face at each other and said at the same time.

"Thank you Nicklaus."

"Now Shay since you're also a forensic Psychologist as well as a Pathologist," Andersson quickly changed the subject after his compliment. "We need some insight and perspective on the Willy Burk case."

"What are you thinking?" Shay asked. "It looks like Carson's got a very strong case against him."

"He does," Stefani said, sipping some of her lemonade. "But we want to keep an open mind and look at the possibility he's being framed."

"Framed?" Shay said. "Who would want to frame him?"

"Paul Dickinson," Andersson replied. "We think he killed Billy and planted the grenades in Willy's unit."

Paul Dickinson, the cop?" Shay asked. "I know Paul, you really think he would kill Billy Burk? What…for revenge?"

"We're just looking at the possibility," Stefani said. "Especially since Paul himself has been out in the open about being a good suspect in the murder."

"Paul's a very egotistical man and a perfectionist at everything he does," Shay said, matter of fact.

"Plus, his sense of justice is right or wrong…"

"Then why would he kill Billy Burk?" Andersson asked, just as their food arrived.

Shay waited to reply until the server set the food down in front of them and left.

"Because to Paul, it's not wrong…it's justice, and he's changing what was wrong into what's now right." Shay looked down at her no frills salad; really just a pile of lettuce on a plate then over to Stefani's chicken salad sandwich. "That looks a lot better than this rabbit food."

"Shay, you touch my sandwich and I'm going to need a new bride's maid."

Shay looked over at Andersson's sandwich just as he was about to take a bite.

"Forget it!" He said, biting and chewing.

"So, Paul Dickinson thinks what he's done is okay, since he's getting justice for Heather," Stefani said, before taking a bite of her sandwich.

"Yes, but he's also settling the score on a professional level," Shay said, tasting the salad. "He's solving the unsolved case, and that's how Carson looks at it too from another perspective."

"You think Dickinson knew how Carson would react?" Andersson said, wiping his mouth with a napkin.

Shay nodded. "We worked with Paul on numerous murder cases so I know him very well. He's smart enough to figure all the players out and how they would react in these circumstances. He also knows the political climate is perfect since Carson is looking to ride on Forbes's coattails to the White House."

"But if he's so smart why is he being so obvious he might have done it?" Stefani asked.

"I think he really wants everyone to know he did it because he wants the unofficial credit for it; but yet he wants you to try and catch him at it at the same time, while he hides in plain sight."

"You think subconsciously he wants to get caught?" Andersson asked, taking another bite of the sandwich.

"I don't think he really wants to be caught, although some part of him knows what he did was wrong," Shay said, forcing more salad down. "Foremost, Paul enjoys the game of it all. He's testing your skills against his own and seeing not only if you can figure it out but if you did, can you prove it."

"Bottom line, he really wants Billy and Willy to pay for Heather's death," Andersson said.

"One down and one to go," Stefani said.

Shay looked down at her salad in disgust. "This salad isn't working for me Nicklaus."

Andersson finished one half of his sandwich, gave Shay the other half and took her salad.

"There!" He said, when he was done switching plates. "Eat that and keep focused on what we're talking about."

Shay smirked a ha-ha at Roxanne and took a big bite of the chicken salad sandwich. "Oh god! This Is delicious and the homemade bread really tops it off…"

Stefani shook her head and watched Shay saw through several more bites.

"I think the bigger problem than trying to prove Paul Dickinson killed Billy, is going to be trying to prove that Willy didn't, Stefani added.

"You're right," Andersson said. "We don't have much on Dickinson but we got a lock on Willy."

"You need some grilled steak in this salad, Shay," Andersson said, taking another painful forkful.

"And some thick blue cheese dressing too…"

Shay laughed and wiggle the rest of the chicken salad sandwich in front of Andersson.

"I'm good Nicklaus," she said, "You need some grilled steak and blue cheese dressing…"

"Oh thanks for the advice, Shay," Andersson said, glumly.

"Cheer up, Nicklaus," Shay said with her mouth full. "I promise I won't order anything light ever again when I'm with you two…"

"Oh, so we're the source of your weight problem?" Stefani said, ready to bite into the other half of her sandwich.

"Weight problem?" Shay said. "I don't have a weight problem. I said I wanted to lose a couple of pounds for your wedding."

"So my wedding is the source of your weight problem?" Stefani said, with a ha-ha grin.

"Nicklaus!" Shay hollered, with a pout. "Tell her to stop!"

Andersson kept his head down picking through the salad again; still looking for more than lettuce to eat.

"Stop Roxanne!" He said, then held up his hand to one of the servers going by their booth. "Could you please have some grilled steak put on this…and add some blue cheese dressing too…"

He handed the plate to the server.

CHAPTER THIRTY-EIGHT

Paul Dickinson finished his small, deep fried calzone, and ordered five large ones to go. A fried calzone was fresh pizza dough stuffed with various combinations of meats, and cheeses, with or without peppers and onions, and some homemade sauce, then instead of baking it in the traditional style, it was deep fried. Paul ordered a couple with sausage, one with meatballs, another with salami and the fifth one without any meat, just cheeses, peppers and onions. They were still warm and ready to eat when he got to the Best Done Nails Salon. The place was busy with customers and everyone looked up from what they were doing when Paul walked in with the calzones.

"Who ordered lunch?" He shouted, looking around for someone who might be in charge as he spotted Pi sitting on a small stool way in the back of the shop, giving a woman a pedicure. "Five large calzones for the Best Done Nail Salon. I think the name on the order slip was Pi."

The owner came over to Paul and looked in the box Paul was carrying, turned around and spoke to Pi in Vietnamese.

"She said she not order any food," the owner said to Paul. "We're sorry and they smell so good too."

Paul handed the box of calzones to the owner.

"I was joking," he said, with a smile. "I bought them for the shop; there's enough there for the whole place including the customers."

"Why you buy for the shop?" The owner said, taking the calzones.

"Because I wanted to see Pi for a couple of minutes and I didn't want you to be mad at her for my Interrupting her work."

The owner smiled and said something again in Vietnamese and several of the other girls around her who were giving manicures, all began to chatter. Some even giggled the way Pi did and Paul watched the banter and laughter spread all the way to the back of the shop where Pi was working.

"I know who you are," the owner said. "I do not think she wants to see you."

"Please, I just need a couple of minutes," he said. "She won't return any of my calls and when I went to her parents apartment, no one would answer the door."

It was clear to the owner, despite Paul's pleasant demeanor and gesture with the food, he wasn't going to leave until he saw Pi.

The owner spoke to Pi again without turning around or moving from where she was standing in front of Paul. Finally, after much back and forth discussion, the owner spoke to Paul in English.

"I cut these up for everyone while you go back and see Pi," she said.

Paul approached Pi who kept her head down while she used a small cuticle scissors on the customer's toenail.

"I tried to call you several times Pi," Paul began, standing over her as she worked.

"I no want to talk Paul," she said, head still down as she carefully snipped the cuticle around the toe nail.

The woman getting the pedicure, who was an attractive rusty redhead, smiled at Paul and moved her hand in a downward motion. Paul got the hint and sat down on the low ledge where he could face Pi eye to eye.

"I'm sorry Pi," he said, softly with everyone else in the shop listening and not saying a word. "I'm sorry I sent you home. I was wrong to do that and I want you to come back."

Pi kept her head down and continued to work as some of the other workers who did not speak English well had someone else translate what Paul had said.

"No thank you Paul," Pi said, nervously, her eyes filling with tears. "Pi not come back."

Paul looked up at the woman and she nodded to keep going.

"I'm sorry I hurt you Pi and I hurt myself more. I really have feelings for you and I wanted you to know…"

Pi continued to work without having made any eye contact with Paul.

"I think about it…," she finally said. "…I have feelings for you too."

Paul smiled up at the woman who smiled back down at Paul and nodded.

"I'm going to go now Pi," Paul said, taking something out of his jacket pocket and handing it up to the woman. "Please accept this gift, it's something special I had made for you, and I want you have no matter what you decide."

Pi nodded and Paul left the shop. The woman in the chair told Pi to look at what he had left and Pi looked up. It was a heavy gold chain with a solid gold pendant, about the size of a quarter, which was clearly shaped like a pie. The woman held the chain out to Pi, and she took it in her hand. She ran her finger over it, and when she saw what it was, she smiled, and started to cry.

CHAPTER THIRTY-NINE

It was after eight o'clock when Henry and Kira finished eating dinner on the aft deck of the Escape.

They had fresh, grilled, red snapper with a wild rice pilaf, that Kira loved, and Henry did not, since he did not like fish; so the chef made him a cheeseburger and some French fries.

"You look tired Henry," Kira said, pouring herself another glass of wine.

"It's been a long day Kira, and I'm not used to all this physical activity," he said, holding his hand over his glass when she tried to pour time more wine. "The traveling was exhausting and then we made several dives on top of everything else."

Kira took a long swallow of the wine; it was her third glass.

"That's how these short dive trips are Henry," she said. "You need to get in all the fun you can."

Kira looked radiant and her skin was glowing from the sun while the white linen dress she had on only made her tan look more intense. She was truly a beautiful woman and had boundless energy. She thrived on this kind of whirlwind lifestyle, where

Henry seem to flounder. It was always the same thing, Henry thought. Kira tanned while he burned, her hair was soft and shining while his looked dull and dry as straw.

"What's the matter Henry?" Kira said, noticing his mood. "You look unhappy."

"I'm just not cut out for all this," he said. "I look at you and I don't even know why I'm here."

"You're here because you want to spend time with me," Kira replied, boastfully, taking another long swallow of her wine.

"But you don't really want to be with me," he said, with unusual candor. "In fact, knowing you as do Kira, I'm sure there's another hidden reason that I'm about to discover."

Kira set her wine glass down and looked seriously at Henry.

"Now that you bring it up Henry, there is something I want," she said, taking his hands in hers. "I want your manuscripts."

"My manuscripts?" he said, confused. "But you already have my manuscripts Kira. "You're my agent and my lawyer."

"I know Henry," she replied, drawing circles with her finger on the back of his hand. "But, think about this for a moment. You just said you're not cut out for this kind of life; that you don't have the energy or even the desire to be around people who are all about themselves."

Henry watched Kira's finger as she touched his hand and immediately he fell under her spell.

"Once those manuscripts are published Henry, people are going to swarm all over you like locusts," she continued, using her fingernail now on his skin and leaving white lines where she drew. "You're going to have to make appearances and give interviews too; do book signings. It's not going to be like the success you had with Gina Wells, where you can loiter in the background."

Henry could feel the difference in her using her fingernail as opposed to her fingertip and it was beginning to hurt; but he liked it none the less.

"I didn't loiter in the background Kira," he replied, his eyes fixed on her fingernail. "I just didn't seek any attention for my writings and to be honest, I wasn't really proud of what Gina Wells wrote."

Kira dug her fingernail deeper into Henry's skin just short of drawing blood and ran the nail up his arm.

"You like that Henry?" She asked, sensing the tension in his arm. "Gets you going, doesn't it?"

Henry closed his eyes, nodding, and the tip of his tongue peeked out at her.

"I want the manuscripts for myself Henry," she said, digging in her fingernail and causing more pain. "Let me publish them under my name and not yours. Let me take the credit for writing them."

Henry opened his eyes forgetting where he was and what he was thinking.

"Are you crazy Kira? Henry said. "Let you take my manuscripts…my writing…and say that they're yours?"

Kira tried to hold on to Henry's hand but he pulled away from her.

"Listen to me Henry," she said, reaching back for his hand. "Listen to me. You can still get the royalties for them once they're published but you're not going to able to handle the fame. I know you Henry, those manuscripts will be your end."

Henry recoiled, moved back onto the chair, drawing his legs up and wrapping his arms around himself.

"You're making it all sound so terrible Kira and you're scaring me," he said. "I thought you would be proud of me and happy with my success."

"Oh I am honey, mommy's very proud of her little boy, but I'm trying to protect you from the big bad world out there."

Henry was never more confused in his life and he needed to think but Kira was pressing all of his buttons at once and he was on overload.

"I need to go and lie down Kira," he said, pulling his hand away from hers, and abruptly standing. "I need to think about everything you've said and I can't think clearly when I'm around you."

"Okay Henry," Kira said, knowing she had pushed him too far. "Go to your cabin and think. It's been a long hard day for you and we'll talk more about this in the morning."

Henry nodded, again, feeling embarrassed and humiliated.

"Should I come to your cabin tonight?" He asked, weakly.

"No Henry, not tonight," she said, draining the rest of the wine from her glass. "Suddenly, I'm very tired and I need to get some sleep. Maybe after you've had some time to think and have come to a decision, maybe then you can come to my cabin."

Kira got up from the table and left, leaving Henry there, trembling all alone.

CHAPTER FORTY

I t took Henry several minutes to calm down enough to leave the aft deck and go to his cabin. The Escape was anchored and there was only a slight rocking sensation, not enough to make anyone feel it, but still it made Henry queasy.

Inside his cabin, Henry felt more alone than he did when he was up on the aft deck. He wanted to leave but he was trapped on a boat with strangers and he needed time to think clearly; to make an important decision. He lay on the bed and after a few seconds of thinking, he was sound asleep.

It was after two in the morning when Henry woke up with a start; he got out of bed, still dressed and looked at the time. Maybe he could go to Kira's cabin; perhaps she was still awake and they could talk.

Henry washed his sun burned face and thought about it again. He didn't want to talk with Kira, he wanted to have sex with her. He's wanted to have sex with her since they met and this is the closest he's been to fulfilling that dream. Henry stared at himself in the mirror and made his decision.

He opened his cabin door just a crack and peered out into the empty gangway, then stuck his head out and look up the other way. No one was coming and all was quiet, so Henry left his cabin and tip toed down to Kira's cabin.

He was about to knock on her door when he heard sounds coming from within. He looked around to make sure no one was coming and put his ear to the door. He listened for more than a minute before he heard Hanna whisper behind him.

"He's pounding her," she said bluntly, and Henry turned around to see her standing behind him.

"I was just going to knock…" Henry said, trying to hide his embarrassment.

"No, you were listening to them," Hanna said, putting her ear to the door. "Listen, you can hear them fucking."

At first Henry was repelled by Hanna's language, then she waved him closer to the door.

"Here, listen," she said again and Henry put his ear back to the door. "It's Captain Sam, he fucks her like that every time she's here."

Henry did not reply but kept his ear to the door, listening to them. The grunts, the groans, the moans and most of all, Captain Sam slamming himself into Kira, over and over.

"He's really killing her tonight," Hanna whispered in Henry's other ear. "I need to go back to the bridge, but you stay and listen to them finish; it's really something to hear."

Hanna left, but Henry kept his ear glued to the door, and despite the anger he felt for Kira, he was still very much aroused by what he was hearing on the other side of the door. There were shouts, dirty talk from Kira, telling Captain Sam what to do, then more slapping noises. Henry looked around for Hanna just in case she came back, but she was gone and he pulled himself out of his shorts, jerking like crazy.

More dirty talk from Kira, now frenzied, hurried, with precise directions for Captain Sam; a few more seconds, some screams, and all three of them finished at the same time.

CHAPTER FORTY-ONE

The next morning, Kira was already eating a huge breakfast of bacon, eggs and pancakes when Henry came up on the aft deck. Hanna was also there, pouring Kira a large cold glass of fresh squeezed orange juice.

"Good morning, Henry," Kira said cheerfully, sipping the orange juice. "Have some breakfast with me, the pancakes are the best ever!"

Henry gingerly approached the table and said good morning.

Hanna walked up to him with a carafe of hot coffee. "Good morning, Henry," she said. "Would you like some fresh coffee?"

Although Henry had slept for hours, he still felt tired and a little nauseous.

"I'll just have some hot tea Hanna, thank you," Henry replied, sitting down. "...any maybe a piece of dry toast..."

Hanna set the coffee carafe down on the table and left to get Henry his hot tea. Kira took the opportunity to speak bluntly.

"You could have brought a tissue with you last night Henry," Kira said, biting into a thick slice of crisp bacon. Captain Sam almost stepped in the little deposit you left at my door, and I must say it was a little deposit."

"I didn't have a tissue Kira, but I wasn't planning on doing what I did either," he said, too tired to deny it or even feel embarrassed. "I went to your cabin to talk and when I got to your door, I could hear you."

"I bet you could hear us," Kira replied.

"I got excited and I couldn't help it, I'm sorry."

"No need to apologize Henry, I'm glad you enjoyed hearing us, but just think about it, that could have been you."

"Yes, it could have been me and it will be me Kira," he replied, mustering a little gumption.

"Oh?" Kira said, stopping short of putting a forkful of pancake into her mouth. "Do I detect a decision, on the this beautiful morning's horizon?"

Hanna brought Henry's hot tea and set it down in front of him.

"Here's your tea Henry, and I'll have some dry toast for you in a couple of minutes," she said.

"Thank you Hanna," Henry replied and she left.

"She's so fucking jealous," Kira said, eating the pancakes.

"Hanna?" Henry asked."

"Yes Hanna," Kira said, "Who do you think ole Captain Sam is riding when I'm not around?"

"Oh...no wonder she's serving us breakfast and not some of the other staff," Henry acknowledged.

"She wants to keep an eye on you."

"Yeah, the bitch thinks her boyfriend might want a little more of Kira," she said, "Like he didn't get enough of me last night."

Henry sipped some of his tea, while Kira ate a couple of more bites of the pancakes, drank more orange juice, then looked him square in the eye.

"Well..."

"Here's the deal Kira," Henry said, succinctly. "You can have the manuscripts and publish them under your name. I'll be your ghostwriter and I get fifty percent of the royalties on each manuscript plus any movie rights."

"That's very generous of you Henry," she said, sipping some coffee. "I make more on those books than I did on Gina Wells."

"Yes, it is very generous, and not only that, but I will keep on writing more books after these three are published."

"Oh my," she said, hiding the touch of fear in her voice. "Fame and more fortune than I have now; how lucky can I be. What's the catch?"

"You know the catch Kira," he replied, sipping more of the tea and feeling better. "Sex is the catch."

"Sounds like a very good deal to me Henry," Kira said. "You get laid, and I get the Pulitzer Prize!"

Henry smiled his happy smile, as his nausea faded, and he began to feel some empowerment.

"Yes, I get laid, and you get the Pulitzer, as you say," he replied, with a couple more sips of tea. "But Kira, this isn't one of your, I-promise-to-have-sex-with-you-Henry-but-it-never-happens-deals. This is Kira's-best-sex-ever-for-Henry-and-on-a-weekly-basis-for-as-long-as-we-publish-my-work-under-your-name-deals."

Kira sat back in her chair and looked out over the ocean into the rising sun. Good thing, she thought, I'm wearing these sunglasses or Henry could see the disgust in my eyes at the very thought of any kind of sex with him. This insect of a person and he wants Kira's best sex at that!

"Once a week, during the week, on a day of my choosing," Kira replied after a long period of time.

"Since I usually travel to New York on three day weekends."

Henry was going to say something, but Hanna showed up with his dry toast, set it down and sensing they wanted privacy, left them alone.

"Okay, once a week with a scheduled day of either Tuesday, Wednesday or Thursday," Henry began, the second Hanna was gone. "That will leave Mondays and or Fridays for your three day business weekends…"

Kira picked up a long, thick piece of bacon and slid it into her mouth back and forth several times in a very sexually suggestive manner.

"You're beginning to sound like Gina Wells' Captain Sam, Henry," she said, biting the piece of bacon In half. "I can hear a ring of authority in your voice…"

Henry nodded, feeling a surge or new found power.

"It's a side of me you're going to see on a weekly basis Kira, but not the only side," Henry replied, watching her chew the piece of bacon and slide the other half into her mouth. "I want to explore both sides of the fence and I want to take charge at times."

"Oh really now," Kira said. "That would be a new twist…"

"Yes, it is," Henry said. "I want to take charge at times, and at other times, mainly at the end of our sessions; I want to be punished, degraded and humiliated."

Kira sat up in her chair and leaned across the table in Henry's face.

"You want to play the switch with me Henry?" She asked. "Both sides of the fence as you say…"

Henry nodded, barely able to contain his excitement at the endless possibilities.

Kira sneered at the prospect at sharing power with him, yet was intrigued as her evil mind flooded with depravity.

"Sounds like that could be an interesting proposal Henry," Kira said, reaching for another piece of bacon.

"Yes, it is, and who knows, over time you might even want to share me with some of your other kinky friends."

Kira smiled devilishly not wanting to say what she was thinking.

"Yes, all of that is within the realm of possibility," she replied. Good...so we have a deal?"

"Yes, we have a deal Henry," she replied, offering her hand.

Henry lifted his hand to hers with the same enthusiasm as if he was placing it inside a crocodile's mouth.

"It's a deal Kira and with absolutely no tricks," he said, shaking her hand firmly. "Any tricks with the sex play on your part, and the deal's off, and I go public with everything."

"No tricks Henry, just treats," Kira said, shaking his hand. "I promise I'll deliver, and in fact we can start tonight."

"Tonight?" Henry said, with butterflies in his stomach. "Really? Like Gina Wells' Captain Sam?"

"Yes, just like Gina Wells," she said, with the most sincere smile he had ever seen; but all the while she was wishing she could run to the side of the boat and heave her breakfast over the side. "But first, we have to do a couple of dives...the usual forty footers, then one final deeper dive before play time."

"Deeper dive?" Henry asked, with caution flags waving in the background. "I'm just getting used to the forty foot depth, do you really think I'm ready for a deeper one?"

"Absolutely Henry, and there's something special I want to show with the deeper dive," she replied, running her fingernail up his arm. "Besides, nothing gets me going like the excitement diving...if you know what I mean..."

Henry felt her nail dig into his skin and despite all the flashing, red, warning lights; he allowed the tingling between his legs to override them.

CHAPTER FORTY-TWO

Hank spent his Saturday morning as he had done for almost the entire last year; training with Rocco Stefani at his gun range. Rocco's long distance shooting skills were improving but had reached a plateau in recent months, especially at the one thousand yard mark. He could hit the target but not consistently nor with any relative accuracy. It was disappointing for him since he thought with more practice, he would improve. His best targets were hit at around six hundred yards which wasn't bad but wasn't even close to Hank's ability. Hank's sniper skills were simply amazing and Rocco had deemed him the best long distance shot in the world.

"I guess I need to keep my ranges down around six hundred yards and stick to combat pistol shooting," Rocco said, realistically.

"You do what you do best Rocco, and frankly as team leader, that's your real forte," Hank said, graciously.

"You always say that Hank and I appreciate it," Rocco replied, as they walked to Hank's Jeep.

"It's true and if you remember, when we first met, I wasn't much good with a pistol," Hank said, loading his guns and gear into the back of the Jeep. "But after you're mentoring and some help from Roxanne, I've become pretty good with various kinds of pistols."

"You're a lot better with a pistol than I am with a rifle," Rocco said, helping Hank load the gear.

"But I think since you made that unbelievable shot, you've accepted your talent. Hank, I'm sure you're the best long distance shot in the world."

"I'm not so sure about that Rocco," Hank said, modestly, getting into the Jeep. "There's at least a half dozen guys who can make the same shot. I've even heard rumors there's a couple of women now who can shoot at those distances…"

"I know there're other top shooters in the world and they're all at about the same level of skill," Rocco continued as Hank drove off. "They're great snipers in their own right but you're better than all Of them."

"Thanks for the boost in confidence Rocco," Hank said, turning onto the highway. "But there's only so much head room in this vehicle."

Rocco laughed. "Okay Hank, I'll give it a rest, but we need to sit down with Roxanne, and a few of the of the other players and get a serious plan for the future with these CAT teams."

"Okay, I understand," Hank said. "We need to meet soon, and we will, but I don't want any of this to overshadow our wedding. Once that's over, we can spend more time organizing things. Besides, Roxanne's got her hands full with this Burk case and I don't want to add to it."

"I know," Rocco said. "We're all feeling the political pinch on this one and I've talked with Andersson about using any of our resources if he needs to; but we need to be prepared for what's going to most likely happen on a larger scale."

"You mean more organized terrorists attacks worldwide?" Hank asked.

"That's already happening Hank," Rocco replied, woefully. "Every day more innocent people are coming under attack by militant extremists. It's not only limited to the Middle East with beheadings and burning people alive, but it's extended across the globe from Europe to Australia. We need to get ourselves ready for what's coming to this country…for what's already here…"

"You make it sound so ominous Rocco," Hank said. "Like there's no way around it…no diplomatic chance to resolve it."

"It is ominous, and it's way past any chance of a diplomatic solution Hank," Rocco said, bleakly. "My God, look what happened in Iraq, I mean, we spent ten years there, and countless billions of dollars, and almost immediately after we left the country, it's all but lost to terrorists."

"I know, you're right, and that's not even taking into account all the military lives lost, and those with permanent injuries of all kinds plus untold civilians."

"Exactly, and those so called coalition countries are a joke too," Rocco said, becoming agitated. "It's just giving them an added slap on the wrist and they laugh at us. We need to strike back hard and we need to organize, recruit, and train our own citizens just like they're doing. Then, when the time comes they rear their evil heads here, in the United States, we'll make the Gulf War shock and awe, look like yawn and stretch."

Hank drove for a couple of more miles to let Rocco simmer down.

"What's happened Rocco?" Hank asked, trying to change the subject. "Life was much simpler thirty years ago."

"People happened Hank," Rocco said, staring out the passenger window at the wooded countryside.

"Too many people, too many poor people, and too few other people holding all the wealth. It's what's been happening for two thousand years."

"I'm not one to advocate war, but with our track record; I think we need stronger, smarter, more decisive leaders."

Rocco laughed. "Hank, we haven't won a war since World War II and you want to know why? Politics. We got the politicians fighting the wars instead of the Generals."

"No one wants to be the bad guy and they all talk tough when they're running for office," Hank added, looking for the pub that they always went to for lunch or a beer, after shooting.

"They're not entirely at fault for that Hank," Rocco said, as they slowed down. "The media has a big part in shaping the political landscape since World War II. War is war and they make it like no one is supposed to die or get injured, especially civilians."

"So we really can't fight to win…"

"Hell no," Rocco said, as Hank turned into the pub's parking lot. "…and another thing, how long does it take to train an army to fight for their country and protect themselves?"

"I know," Hank said, parking the Jeep. "It seems like we could have gotten a lot more for all the time and money we spent in Iraq not to mention the lives…"

"Absolutely," Rocco said, getting out of the Jeep. "Here in this country, we take kids right out of high school or college and train them into the best military people in the world in six months or less. Those clowns over there couldn't get it right in ten years."

"It's crazy, isn't it?" Hank said, locking the Jeep.

"It's crazy about money, being politically correct and getting reelected," Rocco said, feeling better now that he had vented.

Hank put his hand on Rocco's shoulder.

"We're going to change things Rocco," Hank said, optimistically. "We're going to make our country safe; we have to and we will."

CHAPTER FORTY-THREE

Kira had Captain Sam move the Escape to another location where the water was deeper and she had found a ship wreck a few years ago. It wasn't a secret spot to dive, and it had been picked clean of anything of value years before. But now, its value was one of an artificial reef that drew some of the most beautiful and unusual marine life; both plant and fish alike.

A couple of hours after breakfast, Kira and Henry had made two dives, each one being deeper than the previous one. The ship wreck lay in ninety feet of water, which was twice the depth Henry was use to. He did feel good at the last dive which was at sixty feet, even with the added pressure and air usage.

Henry felt a new sense of energy and power after his ability to bargain favorably with Kira. The old Henry would have given her the manuscripts and relinquished the sex to boot; but that wasn't going to happen. For the very first time in his life, Henry was about to get his cake and eat it too; and what a piece of cake it would be. Henry was finally going to have a real woman, a very attractive and utmost a very sexual woman.

"Remember to stay close to me Henry as we go down," Kira said, as they sat on the transom of the Escape. "We'll go down to sixty feet like before and arc around the last thirty feet to the wreck. It'll take a little longer that way, and it's easier with the pressure adjustment, but we'll use more air in the process. Once we're down, we'll only have about ten minutes or so but it's such an incredible sight it's worth it."

Henry wasn't as sure about this dive since he wasn't happy about having to watch the time and be more careful about his breathing.

"I'm not that comfortable with the extra thirty feet Kira," Henry confessed, avoiding the word scared.

"I think getting myself to sixty feet was a big deal for me, and now I'm beginning to think about my breathing again..."

"You did super Henry, I was so proud of you," she said with a dazzling smile; her wet hair was slicked back and beads of salt water dotted her glowing face. "You know what they say Henry, the real confidence to do something only comes after you're already done it."

"I know Kira, and I want to do it, I really do," he said, with butterflies in his stomach growing bigger by the second. "But, I haven't mentioned it before, but my eyesight isn't good, and I'm concerned I might lose track of you."

"Oh nonsense Henry," she replied, careful not to lose her temper. "I'll tell you what Henry, you make this dive with me and I promise you'll never have to go any deeper. There's this little cave that had formed, after the boat went down, and whenever to come to the Keys, I come here to see it. You're going to love it."

"How about I make this dive once with you and go back to the forty foot ones where I feel more secure."

"Okay Henry," Kira said, with her captivating smile. "Make this dive with me, and show me what a man you are, then tonight, when we're alone, you can show me what a real man you are..."

Henry smiled the happy smile and his wiggled in his mouth like a newborn tadpole.

"Let's do it!" He said, taking in a deep breath, anxiously. "But, once we get to sixty feet, I'll give you the signal to continue or the signal to go up..."

"Of course Henry," she said. "If you don't think you can do it, just let me know. It's up to you and it's your safety first."

Henry started to take in deeper breaths as he put his face mask on and his rate of breathing had noticeably increased.

"Easy Henry," Kira said, putting her hand on his thigh. "Slow down and concentrate on the dive. Forget about your breathing and just follow me."

Henry took in his last deep breath of fresh air and placed the regulator into his mouth. Kira did the same, and they slid off the Escape into the water.

Going down to sixty feet felt the same for Henry as it did with the other two previous dives and he was near panic when Kira stopped and looked at him for his decision. He wanted to please her and more than anything, he wanted to hear her words of praise after he had accomplished it.

For a few long seconds, Henry just hung there, suspended in the water. He was afraid to decide no but he was more afraid to decided yes and Kira sensed his fear. In an instant, she slipped off her bikini bottoms and stuffed them into a small mesh bag dangling in front of her BC.

Henry was shocked at what she had done; but transfixed on what he saw after she had done it. Kira spun herself around to Henry twisting and turning in every direction while she exposed herself. She did not wait for Henry's decision and proceeded downward into the deeper water with Henry trailing behind.

The thirty more feet went quickly, and Henry forgot all about his breathing, while focusing on Kira's white ass cheeks like a beacon in the night. Once at the ninety feet, the wreck lay before them, no longer in the shape of a boat but rather it had become a natural habitat for all kinds of multi colored, salt water fish.

It was a beautiful sight as Kira had promised, but despite its beauty, Henry couldn't keep his eyes off Kira's naked bottom. He wanted to touch her, and when she motioned to him to come closer to her, he was more than happy to oblige.

Kira looked at Henry and her eyes had a twinkle in them. She looked happy, and maybe they were finally happy for him, he thought. She pointed to her watch and held up her hand indicating five minutes. Henry nodded, and Kira pointed to something at the reef, but at first, he did not see what she was pointing to, and moved closer.

Kira moved away as he approached, and she pointed to an odd formation in the reef, a small cave that had become home to a school of fish. Kira moved back from the opening and motioned to Henry to move up closer for a better view.

Henry swam up ahead of Kira and looked into the opening as the fish swarmed around him. He went to turn back to Kira, but before he could get fully around, Kira grabbed Henry's face mask and, tore it away while at the same time removing his regulator.

Instant panic and confusion!

Instinctively, Henry held his breath and tried to see, but without the facemask his vision was blurred, then suddenly, he was turned upside down. Kira had grabbed him by the ankle and flipped him into a summersault. Henry didn't know which way was up or down, and in those terrifying seconds, Henry knew his life was over. He was going to die and there was nothing he could do to change it. He forgot everything he had learned about diving and the burning in his chest only made him think more about taking his next breath.

As Henry came upright, he struggled to replace his regulator, and while he fumbled with it, he could see a foggy vision of Kira swimming away. Then, as Henry was about to give up, and take that fatal breath of water, he saw Kira stop, and turn around. He thought for a moment she was coming back to help him, but in his heart, he knew she had only turned to watch him die.

Henry did not want to have Kira be the last thing he saw, so he closed his eyes, and thought of his mother. He was happy now, this last second of his life and as Kira was watched him, making sure that he would drown; right before his last gasp, he waved to her. Goodbye Kira, goodbye, and Henry sucked sea water into his lungs.

CHAPTER FORTY-FOUR

Kira surfaced with just seconds of air to spare; she had timed it perfectly, gasping for breath, and screaming for help. A few more screams, something about Henry in trouble, and the entire boat, including Captain Sam, were on the run. Although Kira had enough air to make her ascent without any urgency, she took her time, put back on her bikini bottoms, and let her air run out.

"Help! Help me! Help me!" she hollered, as loud as she could, all the time thrashing in the water while she took in deep breaths of air.

One of the deck hands, a young, well built, male named Rick, was the first to hear her screams for help and dove into the water.

"Call the Coast Guard!" She shouted to him as he swam toward her. "I'm okay, but something has happened to Henry and he's still down there!"

Just as the deck hand reached Kira, Hanna and two other crew members were arriving on aft deck, followed right behind was Captain Sam.

"What happened?" Hanna shouted down to Kira as she swam the short distance to the boats transom.

"Henry's still down there," Kira shouted back, still in a panic state. "Get some gear on now! Henry is still down there by the cave and he's had a seizure or something!"

Hanna, who remained calm, despite the shouting of Kira and the other crew members, helped Kira back into the boat.

"Get some gear on Hanna and get another fresh air tank for me...we need to get back down there now!"

"Okay! Okay Kira," Hanna replied. "We're going back down there right now, but much time does he have left...?"

"Not long! We were just about to surface when he some kind of seizure, and suddenly he pulled off his face mask!"

Captain Sam was just finishing his call to the Coast Guard on the satellite phone when Maria ran up with scuba gear for Rick.

"Here Rick," Maria said. "Put this on, and Mark's on his way with your gear Hanna..."

"Hurry Rick! Hurry...hurry Hanna!" Kira cried frantically, creating a more stressful atmosphere. "Get me a fresh tank and I'll go back down too!"

Kira! Stop!" Hanna said, with both hands on her shoulders with a slight shake. "We're doing everything we can and as fast as we can! There's nothing you can do now but try and get a hold of yourself!"

Kira seemed to snap out of it with perfect timing.

"...but we need to get Henry, Hanna," she said, trying to focus and regain more of her composer.

"He's going to run out of air...if he hasn't already..."

"I know and we're going down to help him now..." Hanna replied, looking up at Captain Sam. "Go up with Sam Kira, we'll handle this..."

Kira still acted dazed but she did what Hanna said and went up on the aft deck with Captain Sam.

"Are you alright?" Captain Sam asked, hugging Kira. "What happened?"

"I'm okay Sam," Kira said, still physically shaking from the ordeal. "It's Henry, he's been down too long and I fear for the worst…"

"I know…I'm sorry Kira," Captain Sam said, holding her tight against himself. "Maybe you should get Into something warmer, you're shivering…"

"I'm okay," Kira glanced at her dive watch, then back over her shoulder as Rick and Hanna suited up and slipped under the water. It had been over fifteen minutes since she surfaced.

"No, you're not okay," Captain Sam said. "You go right to your cabin and change into something warmer. I've called the Coast Guard and they should be here shortly."

Kira smiled at Captain Sam and put her head back on his chest.

"You're right Sam, I guess I'm still in shock and I don't need hypothermia on top of everything else."

"No, you don't," he said, kissing her head. "Get going now. I have to stay here for the Coast Guard but I'll have one of the crew walk you back to your cabin…"

"Thank you Sam," Kira purred, in the safety of his arms.

Captain Sam waved over one of the crew members who was standing nearby and she walked Kira back to her cabin. Once at her cabin, Kira dismissed the crew member, and told her she would be fine.

Under protest, the crew member left, and Kira entered her cabin, took off her wet bikini, and got up onto her bed. At that moment, she never felt happier in her life, and she began to bounce up and down while chanting; Henry's dead…Henry's dead… Henry's dead…"

CHAPTER FORTY-FIVE

When the Coast Guard Cutter got there, which took over thirty minutes, Rick and Hanna were just reaching the surface with Henry's body. They had done their best to get down to him as fast as they could, but when someone is underwater, ninety feet down and not breathing, they had less than five minutes to reach him, which was impossible. They took over fifteen minutes to get down to where he was and they had no idea Kira had already taken another fifteen minutes before she came up.

Henry never had a chance from the moment Kira pulled off his face mask and removed his regulator.

Flipping him over to disorient him wasn't even necessary, but Kira wanted to be sure Henry would not somehow survive. Hanna and Rick found Henry were Kira said he had suffered his seizure; lying on his stomach at the bottom of the shallow cave.

The Coast Guard took Henry's body and all the equipment he was using back to Key West. They also took a statement from Kira, although she was clearly distraught the entire time she was interviewed.

Captain Sam, who was well known to the Coast Guard crew, assured them he would follow them into Key West where they would be met by the local police.

The circumstances surrounding Henry's death, from the preliminary standpoint, appeared accidental.

Of course, an autopsy would need to be performed and Kira said she would gladly stay until that was accomplished and she could fly back to Raleigh with Henry's body.

Ironically, since Kira was Henry's attorney, as well as his literary agent, she was also the executor of his will. It was something that would come in very handy when she met with Henry's mother.

"Why not stay on the Escape the next few days while all this business is cleared up," Captain Sam suggested to Kira. "I'm sure you'll be out of here by Wednesday, and in the mean time you can relax and enjoy yourself here."

Kira appreciated Captain Sam's offer, and she knew what he really meant by enjoying yourself, but Kira decided on staying at a hotel while the authorities went through the process of Henry's unfortunate accident. Kira would have loved to have stayed on the Escape with all the amenities it had to offer, especially Captain Sam's nightly visits of comfort; but she didn't want to look callous or inappropriate.

She needed to continue to look devastated by Henry's tragic death and that didn't include sweating, screaming orgasms in the middle of the night. She needed the police to sign off on all of this as simply what it was; an accidental drowning. Besides, there wasn't any crime scene to examine, no real tangible evidence, or DNA, and no motive, well, no motive anyone knew about.

Captain Sam accompanied Kira to the police station and was there with her when she gave her formal statement of what had happened.

"We had made a couple of earlier dives, the last one to around sixty feet and everything seemed to be fine," Kira said, dabbing the corner of her eyes with a tissue. She wasn't hysterical, or even sobbing, but she wasn't her unemotional, or totally in control self either, like normally. The tears were real and her dabs with the tissue seemed to punctuate the end each end of a sentence like a period. "He seemed in perfect health, in fact, I thought the diving had made him feel more fit, and he was excited to make the deeper dive to the wreck."

This might have been Kira's official statement, made formally, but it was definitely under informal conditions. Captain Sam was with her, holding her hand, and the investigator nodded at the appropriate times. He had already spoken with the Coast Guard, and had interviewed Hanna, and the rest of the crew; everything seemed to fit.

"Please go on, Miss Lake," the investigator said, politely. "I know this is difficult for you …"

"We got fresh air tanks and discussed our time table for the dive," Kira said, taking in a deep breath.

"I'm all about a safe dive…Captain Sam knows that…"

"Kira always follows the rules, Ed," Captain Sam, jumped in. "Well, heck, you know I run a tight ship; you crewed with me several summers when you were college…"

Ed nodded. "Yes, I did and I know you always ran things by the book."

Kira smiled weakly and let of couple of tears slide down her cheeks.

"We took our time getting to the wreck and I wanted to show Henry that small cave, you know the one Sam…," she said, stopping and looking at him for affirmation.

"I know what you mean Miss Lake," Ed said. "I've dived on the same wreck myself many times."

More dabbing.

"So we got to the wreck and found the cave without any trouble," Kira said, her voice choking up. "...and that's when it happened..."

"What happened Miss Lake?" Ed pushed her gently.

Kira shook her head, unable to speak and began to cry.

"I don't know...,"she whispered, between sniffles. "He just started to shake and pulled at his face mask like he was struggling to breathe..."

"It must have been horrible," Captain Sam, interjected, clasping Kira's hand tightly.

She nodded. "I tried to help him but he was in a complete panic..."

"You think it was a seizure of some kind?" Ed asked.

"Perhaps...I don't really know," Kira replied, trying to regain her composure. "I tried to go to him several times but he pushed me away."

"Did he seem like he was in pain?" Ed asked.

"He could have been," she said. "...but he seemed more confused...like he didn't know where he was and then he pulled the regulator out of his mouth..."

Kira stopped and put her hands to her face as if she was blocking what came next.

"It was the worst thing I've ever seen in my life..."

"I'm sure it was," Ed said.

"I tried one more time to help him but he pulled away again and retreated into the cave."

"He must have been so disoriented," Captain Sam added. "Maybe he was having a hallucination and somehow thought he was seeking safety in the cave...since that's where Hanna found him..."

Ed nodded in agreement with Captain Sam and Kira began to cry again.

"I think I have enough for now," Ed concluded. "Captain Sam tells me you're going to stay in Key west for a few more days."

Kira nodded still crying.

The investigator looked at Captain Sam for support.

"I'll be in touch. They'll do the autopsy tomorrow and things should be wrapped up by Thursday."

Captain Sam helped Kira up and thanked the investigator; and they left the station.

CHAPTER FORTY-SIX

Monday morning, while Henry Harris lie on an autopsy table in Key West; back in Raleigh, Andersson and Stefani were sitting in the conference room with the rest of the team. Over the weekend, everyone had put some extra hours in on the Burk case, especially Harper.

"I spent a lot of time at the storage facility going over their records and it looks like it's a pretty basic operation. You rent the units, pay the monthly fee, and no questions asked. From what I gathered it's low security for exactly that reason, they're not responsible for lost or stolen property, and you sign a waiver to that effect when you rent the unit. They do have insurance for fire or damage they cause, or personal injury, again it's standard and limited liability."

"I think the other reason they don't have cameras or more security, is because what they don't know happened, they don't have to defend in court," Stefani said. "Especially if the cameras proved the storage facility was somehow negligent."

"Alright, so what about the grenades," Andersson asked. "Anything to link them to anyone locally or where they might have come from?"

"They're American made and are from the Gulf War era, according to the ATF," Harper said. "How they got from point A to point B, is anyone's guess. There's no way to track who might have had these grenades in the first place and at what point they were stolen. Thousands of weapons and anything else you can imagine, goes missing or lost in combat, and is unaccounted for. Unless they can find someone who has other grenades that match these…it's pretty much a dead end…"

"What about Willy?" Stefani asked. "How's he doing?"

"He's been in solitary and on a suicide watch," Reynolds said. "Carson didn't want to take any chances with Willy getting into it with another inmate or hurting himself before he could get him into a court room."

"Good idea," Andersson said. "I know the media is having a ball with it and all the crime shows are bringing up Heather's death and trying to link it to Billy's…"

"Just like Carson knew they would," Stefani said, sipping more coffee. "Hank and I watched one last night that showed some clips from Heather's death and several experts debated whether or not Billy's death was related."

"Which anyone with a half of brain would come to that conclusion," Reynolds said, sarcastically.

"So really all we got is an eyewitness from near Billy's apartment who saw someone get out of an SUV right before the explosion," Andersson said, in summation. "Someone that could have been Paul Dickinson…"

"Who most likely got out of his vehicle because he saw the girl come out of Billy's apartment looking like she was going to get into the car with him," Stefani said.

"But...," Harper said. "The woman wasn't sure if the man who got out of SUV was going to do anything, or if it was just a coincidence that he pulled in, and was getting out of his vehicle. She said she was watching Billy and the girl and only when the man opened the door and light came on, did it catch her attention."

"I bet by the time Carson gets done with her, if the defense even calls her as a witness, she won't remember if the man got out of the car before or after the explosion," Stefani said.

Andersson laughed. "By the time Carson gets done with her, she won't even believe she saw the man in the SUV at all..."

CHAPTER FORTY-SEVEN

By late Tuesday afternoon Kira Lake was leaving Miami on a commercial airline, back to Raleigh, North Carolina. Henry Harris was going back to Raleigh too, but he was in the cargo section of the plane, and not in first class with Kira.

Captain Sam had notified Henry's mother of his death and got an unusual response from her. He expected her to collapse at the news, but Henry's mother did not scream or cry when Captain Sam told her, but merely stated she knew Kira Lake would be the death of her son.

Henry didn't know it, of course, but his death came as a shock to many people, especially the fans of Gina Wells. In fact, Kira was very surprised to see that a huge number of them had sent condolences to the publisher; many professing their love for Gina and her work.

After Kira arrived in Raleigh with Henry's body, she moved quickly to have him cremated and schedule a memorial service all in accordance with his wishes. At hearing the news her son had been cremated, Henry's mother flew into a rage, fell getting out of her wheelchair and broke two left ribs in the process.

Although she was sedated from taking pain medication, she did attend the memorial for Henry on Thursday, and after the service she spoke with Kira in private.

"Mrs. Harris," Kira said, entering the room with open arms in an attempt to hug her. "I can't express how sorry I am for the loss of your beloved son."

Henry's mother put up her right hand to stop Kira, while she held her left side where she had broken her ribs.

"Stop right there Kira!" She said, in a stern voice. "Don't touch me and shove your condolences!"

Kira sat down in a high back leather chair next to her and covered her face with her hands.

"I'm so sorry Mrs. Harris," she replied tearfully. "I know you must blame me for Henry's accident."

Mrs. Harris turned her head away from Kira and scoffed.

"You're dammed right I blame you for my son's death, and it was no accident," she said, forcing each word out as she winced in pain. "I don't know why you killed him, but I know in a mother's heart that you did it."

Kira leaned forward but did not raise her voice.

"I did not kill Henry, Mrs. Harris," she whispered. "We were very close friends as well as business partners and Henry even trusted me to be the executor of his will, which by the way continues to provide for you in the event you survived him."

"I know, I also have a copy of his will and of course he provided for me," she said. "After all I'm his mother and his only heir."

"I know you are, but Henry has made other bequests in the will as well, as I'm sure you're aware."

Kira replied, noticing how she held her left side and winced in pain with every breath.

"I want those manuscripts Kira," she said, bluntly. "Henry told me he gave all three of the original copies, along with the computer he used, to you."

"What manuscripts?" Kira said, with a flash of anger as she thought of Henry's promise that no one else knew he had written them.

"You didn't know he told me, did you?" Henry's mother said, noticing Kira's glint of anger. "I also know he stipulated in his will that all his written work, both published and unpublished, would remain under his name and could not be altered in any way, shape, or form. I want those manuscripts and I don't want you having anything to do with their publication. That work is the kind of writing Henry could really do; not that filthy trash you had him doing to make a lot of money."

"I'm afraid I don't know what you're talking about Mrs. Harris," Kira said. "All of Henry's work I represented was published under Gina Wells and if he was working on anything else, he didn't tell me about it."

"I don't know what your scheme is Kira, but I want those manuscripts, and they're not going to be published under Gina Wells. Henry had real talent and I'm determined to stay alive long enough to see them published under his given name."

"Forgive me Mrs. Harris, but you must be confused," Kira said, sliding closer to her. "There are no manuscripts…"

"I'm not confused and I know those manuscripts exist," she said, while in severe pain. "Henry was very proud of those manuscripts and spent many hours telling me about them."

"I have no idea what you're talking about," Kira replied, as she placed her hand lightly on Henry's mother's left side. "Did you hurt yourself?"

"Don't touch me!" She snapped. "I fell and broke some ribs!"

"I'm sorry Mrs. Harris," Kira began, but was cut off.

"You're going to be a lot sorrier, you bitch!" Henry's mother spat with a grimace. "I'm going to a see a lawyer..., a real lawyer, and get those manuscripts back form you!"

Kira's face tightened, and she pushed on the broken ribs with her hand, making the pain was so excruciating that Henry's mother couldn't take a breath, let alone cry out for help.

"Listen, you fucking old bag of bones!" Kira said, in her most hateful voice. "Your son was nothing without me! I made him what he was, and if you cause me any trouble, I'm going to show the world what a dick-less wonder he really was..."

Henry's mother tried to push Kira's hand away from her broken ribs but she pushed harder.

"Stop...! Stop...!" The words were barely audible. "...the pain..."

"I'm just getting started causing you pain," Kira said, with a sick smile. "I have videos of your beloved son, Mrs. Harris; real hot videos too."

"You're a pig...," she gasped.

Kira laughed. "Little Henry sitting in the bathtub while mommy gives him his bath...and I mean little, tiny, Henry..."

Henry's mother could barely speak the pain was so bad.

"You know his dick was about as big as my little finger," Kira said, holding up her left hand and wiggling her pinkie in her face. "But, now that I look at it, my little finger is even too big."

Henry's mother made a feeble attempt to push Kira's hand away but Kira only pushed harder.

"You say one fucking word to anyone about those manuscripts and I'm going to put those videos all over the internet," she said, pushing harder. "And if that doesn't work, I'm going to come back and push those broken ribs right through your heart."

Kira released the pressure just before Henry's mother was about pass out, stood up, bent over and grabbed her by the hair.

"Forget those manuscripts, and remember Henry as he was, or be prepared to have the world watch your son, the famous Gina Wells, jerk his weenie while his mommy spanks him."

CHAPTER FORTY-EIGHT

Another week went by, and Paul Dickinson hadn't heard anything from Pi. She didn't call or try to see him, and he left it at that; he had done his best to win her back, but it didn't work.

Stefani had two panic attacks right in a row, which surprised her since she was doing so well. Hank told her she was getting cold feet over their wedding, which was only two weeks away. She laughed, telling him that was the last thing to panic her since she was so happy to marry him and there was no doubt about her commitment.

Stefani did mention to Andersson that everything was all set with her wedding plans and he assured her that Governor Forbes was still attending. Stefani really hoped the Governor would change his mind since she still thought his presence would somehow turn her wedding into a political function.

"Did you see where Gina Wells died in a drowning accident in the Florida Keys?" Roxanne asked Hank, as he took a panful of roasted chicken and potatoes out of the oven.

"Who?" He said, swinging the pan around and setting it down on top of the stove.

"That smells great and I'm starved!" She said, tossing the salad. "Gina Wells, or I should say he, since she was really a he, and he died while scuba diving in the Keys."

"I'm afraid I don't know who that was," Hank replied, off-handedly, reaching for large platter. "What did he do?"

"Gina Wells was a writer," Roxanne said, picking a piece of tomato out of the salad, and eating it.

"From what I read his real name was Henry Harris, and he wrote a ton of erotic novels."

"Which of course you just happened to read."

"Of course, we all read them in college," Roxanne said.

Hank laughed and set the platter of food down on the large, hand crafted, dining room table his father had made.

"No wonder you're such a sexy woman," he said.

Roxanne blushed. "They were all the rage back then, you know, forbidden stuff everyone was reading, but no one would admit to."

"The rage must have happened when I was in med school, and the only thing I was reading were medical books."

"The newspaper article said he wrote up until the time of his death and his books were still very popular," Roxanne said, with a wink. "Perhaps I'll pick up a couple of his latest ones so I can read them to you on our honeymoon."

Hank smiled, poured some wine, and sat down at the table while Roxanne.

"Somehow I don't think we're going to have any time for reading," he said, with bravado.

"Well, if that's going to be the case, maybe we can write a few chapters of erotica ourselves," Roxanne said, putting a couple pieces of chicken on Hanks plate.

Hank handed a glass of wine to Roxanne and picked up his glass.

"To Gina Wells!" he toasted, with a big smile and they both took a long sip of the wine.

CHAPTER FORTY-NINE

Paul Dickinson was about to leave the office, and was planning to stop at Hot Rod since he hadn't been there since he met Pi, when his assistant knocked on the door once and entered.

"Paul, I was heading out the door when a man walked in and said he needed to see you."

"Who is he?" Paul asked, slipping on his suit jacket.

"I thought I had recognized him," she said, handing Paul the man's business card. "It's Casper Townsend."

"Oh my god!" Paul said, "I haven't seen Casper since I retired. Please, have him come in."

Casper Townsend was a tall, thin, sixty year old man, with close cropped white hair and a pointy beak for a nose. An avid hiker and lifelong bachelor, Casper had hiked the Appalachian Trail, from Maine to Georgia, four times. His skin was weathered and tanned from years in the sun and despite his underweight appearance, he was in remarkable physical shape.

Casper Townsend was an investigative reporter for one of the local television news stations and he had a reputation for being tough and cynical; yet persistent in the pursuit of the truth in a news story. Personally, he wasn't an easy man to get to know and often bragged about not having any friends. For being very successful at what he did for a living, he rarely socialized with his colleagues and hated all politicians. He was the champion of the underdog, both with two legs as well as with four.

Casper did like two people in the world and both of them for much different reasons. One of them was Paul Dickinson, from whom he had often gotten valuable inside information about cases Paul was working on, which gave him a jump on the competition. In turn, Casper would mention Paul by name in his reporting or pass a tip along exclusively to Paul before going public with the story. It was a back and forth, one hand washing the other type of relationship, that served them both well over the years.

The other person Casper Townsend liked and had followed his career since first meeting him in college when he was one of his creative writing students, was Henry Harris.

"Thanks for seeing me Paul," Casper said, shaking hands. "I was going to call first, but I thought I'd stop in, and finally get a look at the inside of this beautiful building, and see all the work you've done to restore it."

"Sit down Casper," Paul said, directing him to the same sitting area where he met with Andersson and Stefani. "Can I get you something to drink? I have a great single malt Scotch or how about a cold beer?"

Casper sat down and looked around the office, especially noting all the ornate woodwork and high ceilings.

"A cold beer sounds great Paul, and this place looks amazing!" Casper said. "From the moment I walked into the outer office, it was like turning back the clock one hundred years."

Paul went to a bar that was cleverly paneled in wood cabinets, one which was the refrigerator and took out two long neck bottles of beer. He popped off the caps with an opener and handed a frosty bottle to Casper.

"You even have old fashioned beer bottles made up?" Casper asked, taking the bottle from Paul.

Paul laughed, sat down across from Casper, and held up the bottle of beer to him.

"I know the guy who runs the microbrewery that makes the beer for Hot Rod, and he'll make up small batches of the beer for me with my business logo on the labels," Paul said, taking a long pull on the bottle. "It's good stuff too and people love getting a couple of cases of it as a thank you for hiring us…"

"I bet they do," Casper said, after tasting some of the beer. "It is good and I'm going to have to get on your Christmas list."

Paul held up the bottle again. "You got it Casper; how's five cases sound?"

Casper held his bottle up to Paul. "Sounds perfect and I can drink it all myself."

They each took another swig of the beer before Casper spoke.

"Paul have you ever heard of a guy named Henry Harris?"

"No, I can't say that I have. Should I know that name?"

Casper smiled as he rolled the cold bottle between the palms of his hands.

"No, I guess not, but you might have heard of a writer named Gina Wells."

Paul thought for a moment. "Sounds familiar but I can't place what she writes. You know it's the kind of name someone mentions to you at a party and says you have to read her book but never do."

Casper nods. "Well, not many people knew this, but Henry Harris and Gina Wells were one and the same person."

"Okay," Paul said, as he waited for the punch line.

"Gina Wells wrote what is now classified in the publishing world as erotica, but what some other people would say are just dirty books."

"Using the word erotica," Paul replied, sipping more beer. "is that something that might make it more appealing to women? Reading a sexy book written by a woman…maybe something about having an affair or some kinkier sex that most of them would likely never do for real."

"Something like that, but Gina Wells was very popular and had an almost cult like following. Her, or should I say, Henry's work, his writing, was exceptional."

"So, Henry Harris really writes hot, sexy books under the name Gina Wells," he said, wondering where this was all going. "Why didn't he write under his own name and become famous. I bet his love life would have been as popular as his books."

Casper laughed. "Not exactly Paul, you see Henry was a very odd man. Not only was he odd looking and I should talk, but he was strange acting."

"Therefore, not the best role model for someone who wrote dirty books that were extremely popular."

"Exactly," Casper said. "People are funny and not only women read his stuff but he had a large following of men as well."

"Maybe I should pick up a book or two," Paul remarked.

"From what I know about you Paul, I don't think you need any book to spice up your sex life."

Paul smiled. "True, now that you mention it," he said, getting intrigued about Henry Harris. "I know somehow this is going to involve me, but I bet I'm going to have to wait a little longer before I know how…"

Casper smiled and handed the empty beer bottle to Paul.

"You're right, but it's important you understand all the players first before I tell you everything."

Paul stood up, took Casper's empty bottle, and went back to the bar.

"In that case, it calls for another beer," Paul said, getting two another of beer for each of them, and sitting back down.

"Thanks," Casper said, taking the beer from Paul. "Now, the other reason Henry didn't go public with the fact he was Gina Wells was his literary agent, who was also his attorney, Kira Lake."

Paul thought for a moment. "I don't think I know her either…"

Casper tasted his second beer. "I'm a bit surprised you don't know her or have heard of her. I'd thought you two might have bumped into one another at some party."

"You mean by bumping into one another, in the sense of bumping into one another, over and over and over again?" Paul asked slyly.

"Yes, I do," Casper said. "Kira Lake is quite the woman in many ways, and she's extremely attractive, and rumors have it, shall we say, extremely provocative."

"Having told me about this Henry Harris character, and now Kira Lake, it's no wonder she wanted to keep his identity secret," Paul said "I'm sure it was also much better for their business."

"It was, and Kira took every advantage of it. She controlled every aspect of their arrangement with the Gina Wells books, and made a lot of money from it."

"Why didn't Henry find himself another agent, or lawyer for that matter?" Paul asked, crossing his legs.

"That's where the plot thickens in all this Paul, forgive the pun," Casper said, wryly. "Henry was in love with Kira Lake, totally, head over heels, and obsessively, in love with her."

"I see," Paul said. "and need I ask how she felt about him?"

"From what Henry told me, she did everything in her power to avoid him," Casper said. "…and having met Kira Lake twice, and knowing Henry, I'd have to say, more than likely, she hated him."

"So what happened to change that relationship?"

"I'm not sure the real reason, not yet anyway" Casper replied. "But it's so suspicious to me that she would barely meet with him in her office for five minutes, and then suddenly, invite him to dinner at her house; just the two of them."

"It does sound strange…"

"Yes, it does, and it gets better," Casper said. "So, after Henry goes to dinner at her house, she convinces him to let her teach him how to scuba dive."

"Scuba dive?"

"Scuba dive, Paul," Casper repeated. "Henry was overjoyed she wanted to spend more time with him, but at the same time, terrified, since he wasn't physically inclined in the least, and hated the water."

"You think she was she having sex with him too?" Paul asked, then guessed. "Maybe she was trying to get more money out of him…"

Casper shook his head vigorously. "No, I don't think so, since she has a lot of money," he said. "…and I know you're ready to say we all want more money; but I don't think all the money in the world would make Kira want to have a sexual relationship with Henry. No, in my opinion, for her to spend private time with Henry, it had to be something else she wanted."

"Did Henry take the scuba lessons?"

"Yes, he did," Casper said. "Kira's a Master diver."

"I bet," Paul said, with a grin.

Casper smiled. "After a few lessons, she takes him to the Keys, again just the two of them on a private yacht…"

"What was she after?" Paul pressed him. "Get to the point! You're killing me!"

Casper put his hand up.

"I thought you might have guessed by now, Henry's dead," Casper said. "Drowning accident while in the Florida Keys."

"Holy shit!" Paul said. "He died?"

"I thought you saw the obituary and article I wrote about him," he said. "And would put two and two together when I mentioned their names and all…"

"No, I was completely in the dark, and normally I would have seen your article of course, but I've been involved, well unofficially, in the Willy Burk case."

"I was wondering about that, but didn't want to mention it, since I've been preoccupied with Henry's death."

"It's cool Casper, and when I can give you something about the Burk case I will," Paul said. "So you believe Kira Lake killed him?"

"I do and so does his mother."

"His mother?" Paul said. "How does she know anything about this?"

Casper took another fifteen minutes and related all that Henry's mother had known up until Henry's death, which included the frightening talk she had with Kira at the memorial services.

"Sounds like Kira is not only black mailing Henry's mother to forget about the manuscripts, which she said didn't even exist, but she's also threatened her life."

"She did."

"Why doesn't she go to the police with all her suspicions and Kira's threats," Paul asked. "If it's already common knowledge Henry is Gina Wells, what's left to find out?"

Apparently, and Henry's mother didn't get into any details," Casper began delicately, "but Kira has videos of Henry performing degrading sex acts, and the tapes also reveal, other, more humiliating physical features of Henry she doesn't want to be made public."

"So if his mother goes to the police, Kira will go public with the videos…"

Casper nodded. "You have to remember too that Henry's mother doesn't have any proof of wrong doing on Kira's part, but when you know everything in total, the people, and what's happened the last few weeks, it all starts to fit together."

"I just don't get what Kira wants with those manuscripts." Paul said, confused. "Manuscripts, I might add, no one has seen but Kira Lake."

"I'm not sure Paul," Casper said, finishing his second beer. "She's got something planned for them."

"You're sure these manuscripts exist? Paul questioned. "Maybe Henry was making it all up just to impress Kira. Maybe this is all just some terrible accident after all…"

"I doubt it very much," Casper said. "I knew Henry since he was in college, in fact, I taught some of his classes and he could write, and I don't just mean erotica. I've read a lot of his other early work and he was a gifted writer, an exceptionally gifted writer."

"What about Henry's death? I assume it was officially ruled accidental."

"Yes it was," Casper said. "Of course Kira was the only witness, and she said Henry suffered a seizure of some kind at ninety feet of water, became disoriented, were her words, and drowned."

"You want me to look into it?" Paul asked. "Go talk to this Kira Lake and see what she's got to say about it."

"Yes, I would," Casper replied. "Something low key though and nothing about the manuscripts. That would send up immediate red flags so your investigation has to come from another angle."

"You mean my investigation has to be low key initially, don't you?" Paul said, with a flash of anger.

"Once I'm in, I'm in, and from what you've told me about this Kira Lake, she's not going to be easily fooled."

Casper thought for a minute about Paul's hidden meaning.

"Henry left me some money in his will and I did get a letter the other day informing me of that fact,"

Casper said. "Is that something you could use to make contact?"

Paul nodded. "I could say you're thinking of using the money to establish a writing scholarship in Henry's name but you wanted me to validate Henry's background and the circumstances of his death."

"Yes, that's good, Paul," Casper said, enthusiastically. "You can say I want to be sure nothing illicit happened that would taint his memory or embarrass the school."

"It's thin Casper, but I'm sure it will get me in to see her," Paul said, then he did his best imitation of Don Vito Corleone from the GODFATHER, I can always make her an offer she can't refuse."

Casper laughed at first then grew serious.

"You're kidding right Paul? Casper asked, staring at him.

"Yeah Casper, I'm kidding," he finally replied, breaking into a laugh. "But I had you going there for a second, didn't I?"

Casper didn't know whether to laugh or not, Paul had looked so ominous when he said the famous line. It was like he really meant it.

"Yes, you did Paul, you had me going there for a second," Casper said, nervously, standing up. "Paul please do what you can. Henry's mother is in a nursing home and she's given word to the staff not to allow Kira in to see her under any circumstances."

"What about the manuscripts?" Paul asked, standing up. "How bad does Henry's mother want them back?"

"She wants them back Paul," Casper said, extending his hand. "There's been enough injustice done to Henry and she doesn't want to lose those manuscripts on top of everything else."

Paul shook his hand and they moved to the door.

"It might all come out anyway Casper," Paul said. "I mean the videos of Henry too since I'm not sure that's something I can stop, at least, not conventionally."

Casper felt uneasy with Paul's phrasing and cloaked meaning. Paul sensed Casper's sudden urgency to leave and hustled him out through the outer office and out to the front door.

"Do what you can Paul," Casper said.

"You know I will," Paul said after him, as he walked down the stairs to his car. "It's why you came to me in the first place."

CHAPTER FIFTY

Andersson and Stefani were driving back from Michael Carson's office where they had gone over their investigation reports with him in preparation for Willy Burk's trail.

"That's the second time he's dragged us up to his office about our reports," Stefani complained.

"He's moving fast with Willy's trail date," Andersson said, weaving through traffic. "He's tried to get Willy on the docket, but his lawyers are blocking it, saying they need more time to prepare their case."

"I'm not sure any more time is going to make any difference," Stefani said. "Willy's alibi didn't hold up and Reynolds got the guy to admit he lied about the timeline. No one can verify where Willy was until he showed up at the bar at almost nine."

"Carson's got him nailed Roxanne," he said stopping for a red light.

"I know," she replied. "But we both know he didn't do it."

Andersson looked at her. "I'm not sure about this we, Roxanne," he said. "We might suspect someone else did it but we don't have any proof of it or even any reasonable doubt."

"Don't get me wrong Nicklaus," she said. "I'd like nothing better than to see Willy go to prison for the rest of his life but not for something he didn't do."

The light turned green and Andersson stepped on the gas.

"I think I feel a little differently than you do," Andersson said. "I tend to see Willy as a victim of his own doing."

"So it's okay to be part of his conviction?"

Andersson beeped his horn at another driver who cut in front of him but did not lose his temper.

"We're part of his conviction because it's the evidence we gathered during our investigation," he said. "We looked at Paul Dickinson and we don't have anything on him. Our job is to find the suspects and gather any evidence against them to make the strongest case for the DA to prosecute."

"I know. I know," Stefani said in frustration. "But if we found the missing grenade in someone else's possession, that could be considered an alternative suspect to Billy's murder and Carson would have to inform his defense attorney."

"That's true," Andersson said, stopping for another red light. "But we really don't know another grenade is missing, and if we did find it, that grenade would have to match the one used in Billy's bombing or the other two we found in Willy's storage unit, otherwise, it's just another grenade."

"Well aren't you full of good news," Stefani cracked.

"You're just a perfectionist Roxanne," he cracked back.

"Me?" She said. "You're the perfectionist, I just want to see things turn out right, as they should."

Andersson looked at her in astonishment.

"Did you just hear what you said?"

Stefani burst out laughing. "I'm sorry Nicklaus, you're right, I am a perfectionist."

Andersson laughed. "Look Roxanne, I don't want to fight about this with you, but sometimes, as you well know, these cases aren't all going to work out to our liking."

"I know," she said, sorrowfully.

"What's really bothering you?" He asked. "I know the way Carson is going after Willy bothers you. I get that, but you seem on edge. Is it the wedding?"

"No, it's not the wedding," she replied." Its Hank's involvement in the C-CAT teams; the Citizen Cells Against Terrorists or CAT teams for short. It's scary to me that he was in one in the past and now my father has gotten him back into the whole program."

"I know and the program is getting bigger and will have a lot more funding once Governor Forbes wins the election."

"I understand and accept the concept," Stefani said. "I'm just not that sure how they will work operationally on the larger scale."

Andersson pulled into Binky's parking lot and shut off the car.

"I thought we'd grab a breakfast sandwich and go back to the office. I'm swamped with writing performance evaluations."

"Fine," Stefani said.

Andersson hesitated to open the door.

"These CAT teams are the last defense," he said, staring out the windshield watching the steady stream of customers enter and exit Binkys. "We're going to need them just in case..."

"Just in case what?" She asked. "The end of the world? Total nuclear war?"

"Pretty much," he replied. "The CATs are our response to the terrorist's cells. They have secret cells and we have secret cells, small pockets of people who won't give up or give in to terrorism. We refuse to be governed by radical, fundamentalists, who make extreme acts of violence, a part of their religious beliefs."

"I just don't want Hank or myself to get involved in something that turns out to be nothing more than vigilantism in disguise."

"It's a gray area Roxanne," Andersson said. "There're going to be times when we're going to be unsure of the methods and the outcome of our actions. It won't be perfect, just like it isn't perfect with Willy's case."

"Sometimes, I wish Hank was just a regular doctor, taking care of his patients and I was at home with a bunch of kids. Nice and simple."

"Nothing is that simple any more, especially a bunch of kids," he said with a smile, as he watched a woman leave Binky's carrying a bagful of food in one arm, while holding onto her daughters hand, as they crossed the street. "Everything is much more complicated, and frankly, we just have to believe when the time comes will we end up doing the right thing."

CHAPTER FIFTY-ONE

After Casper Townsend left Paul's office, Paul spent a couple of hours on his computer, looking up anything and everything he could find about Kira Lake. By the time he was finished, he had quite a lot of information up to and including Henry Harris's drowning in the Florida Keys. Tomorrow, he would make some phone calls, and talk with the police in Key West, just to get the official version of what happened to Henry Harris, and if they had any reason to suspect foul play. Once he had done all his homework, he would make an appointment to see Kira Lake.

Right now it was time to get back into having a social life, although as he approached Hot Rod, he got a sick feeling in his stomach. He missed Pi now more than ever, and these feelings he was experiencing for her were no longer confusing, he was in love with Pi, and he knew it, but now she was gone, and he would live with the pain.

After he sat in his SUV for twenty minutes debating with himself whether or not to go into Hot Rod; he decided to go in, but sit at the bar. It was Thursday night, and maybe because the weather had gotten warmer, Hot Rod looked busier than on his usual Wednesdays when they did the drink thing.

"What's going on Emily?" Paul asked the girl behind the bar. "It's Thursday and the place is packed."

"Paul!" She said, leaning over the bar with a big smile and grabbing his hand. "Where the hell have you been?"

"Here and there," he replied, looking around. "It looks like Wednesday in here."

"We're doing the same deal with burgers we do with the drinks on Wednesday," she said. "It's our first time and it's been amazing!"

"Buy two burgers and give one away to someone else for free?" Paul asked, wedging himself between two people who were sitting at the bar.

Emily nodded and leaned over so he could hear her over the noise.

"People love it," she said. "We're selling more burgers than we ever have, especially on a Thursday."

Paul looked around again.

"I love it," he said. "Thursday was always kind of a down day here between the mid-week crowd and the college kids on Fridays."

"We kept your place in the back open, Cassie has been guarding it with her life and saying prayers you were coming back soon. Otherwise, I think she was going to have to get another part time job to make up her losses from you."

"Well, I'm back," he said, but I guess I'll have to stand awhile since it looks like the bar is full."

"Why not take your booth?" she said. "You never sit at the bar anyway."

"I know, but I want to take a break from it," he said, lamely.

Emily laughed. "Go on back Paul, it won't be the same with you up here at the bar. I'll have Cassie bring you a Prosecco."

"Okay, you're right," he said. "Besides, it's too noisy up here…"

Paul moved away from the bar, past the dance floor and around the back where his private booth was located. He just rounded the corner when he saw Pi sitting in the booth. She was alone. Paul stopped and Cassie came up to him.

"She's been here every night this week," Cassie said. "She drinks only coke and hasn't talked to anyone. I let her sit there since she says she's waiting for you."

Pi smiled when she saw Paul and he waved at her.

"I can tell you one thing," Cassie said, walking away. "She's not the tipper you are."

"Don't worry, I'll take care of you later and thanks," he said, and walked over to Pi.

Pi looked beautiful, and her smile grew wider, with every step Paul took closer to her.

"Pi come back," she said and hugged him. "I miss you Paul."

Paul hugged her tight. "I missed you too Pi and I'm sorry I sent you away."

"I stay with you Paul," she said, as a few happy tears fell from her eyes. "I not go again."

"No, you not go again," he said, pressing her head to his lips and kissing her.

They sat down in the booth and Paul kissed her again, this time on the mouth.

"I was happy you came to salon but I was afraid to say yes I come back," she said, snuggling closer to him. I no want to be on off…back forth…I not care you older…"

"I know," he said. "I was afraid to be with you Pi, not only because of the age difference, but I was guarding my feelings for you."

"I know…me too."

"You felt feelings for me?" Paul asked.

"What felt?" she said back.

"You know, like you have feelings for me…you like me…"

"Pi love you."

There was that word that Paul was trying to avoid, and had for so long replaced with lust.

"I love you from time I first see you."

Saw me…from first time you saw me," he corrected.

"No lesson Paul…I feel real happy," she said, pulling him closer. "I lose my English now same as nervous…"

"Okay Pi, no lessons," he said. "I'm real happy you're back and I love you too."

CHAPTER FIFTY-TWO

Paul was up early, and wanted to make love to Pi again, but she was sleeping so soundly; he got out of bed and went into the kitchen to make breakfast. A couple of hours later, Pi came into the room, still sleepy eyed.

"Why not wake me with you," she said, kissing Paul on the cheek. "I sleep late and I have to go in to work. No time for sex…"

Paul laughed. "I know Pi and its fine. You get some coffee or tea, and I'll take you home to change, and you'll still be there on time."

"Okay, I have coffee and bagel too, then we leave."

"I have to make some calls Pi," Paul said, while she helped herself to a cup of fresh coffee. "I'm working on a case and I'm going to be busy for a while."

Pi ran her fingers through her long black hair while she sipped her coffee.

"Why don't you bring some of your things here after work Pi," he said. "Then you can stay here and not have to spend the time going home to change for work."

"You okay with that Paul?" She asked, taking a sesame seed bagel out of the toaster. "Pi stay here and have her things in closet? Stuff for getting ready to work?"

Paul nodded without hesitation. "Yes, I'm okay with all that. I'll give you a key and the alarm code too. You bring whatever you like, I have plenty of room."

Pi smiled. "No worry Paul about future. We have what we have now."

Paul went to her and kissed her forehead. "You're right. I no worry."

Pi laughed.

"Eat your bagel before we go while I make a call."

While Pi buttered the bagel, Paul called the law office of Kira Lake. Only one ring and someone answered with a cheerful good morning.

"Good morning, I'm Paul Dickinson, I'm a private investigator, and I'd like to see Kira Lake today if possible. It's a rather urgent matter."

"Well, I'm sorry but Miss Lake is not available this morning and she's going out of town this afternoon."

"I'm sorry to hear that since this matter is of great importance and came to my attention only yesterday," he said nicely, but with enough key words to make the assistant pause.

"Can you hold for a moment?"

"Sure," he said, and waited a long minute, while the assistant no doubt was speaking to Kira Lake.

"This is Kira Lake, how can I help you?"

"Paul Dickinson, Miss Lake," he replied. "I'm a private..."

She cut him off. "I know who you are Paul. I may be a commercial lawyer, but I follow the criminal cases in this town as well."

"I hate to call you cold like this Kira," he said, flattered she had heard of him. "May I call you Kira?"

"Of course Paul," she said. "So what's the urgent matter and can it wait until Monday? I'm flying up to New York at two."

"I apologize Kira, but I'd really like to see you this morning if I could," he persisted. "I only need twenty minutes of your time and I'd like to discuss this face to face and not on the phone."

Kira thought for a second.

"If you come to my office now I can see you right away."

Paul paused like he was checking his watch.

"Yes, I can," he said. "I have to make a brief stop first but I should be there by nine."

"Very well," Kira said, trying to sound disinterested. "I'll see you at nine."

They hung up and Paul took Pi home then hurried over to Kira's office, getting there at eight fifty-five.

"That was fast," Kira said, when Paul entered her office. "I'm Kira Lake."

The shook hands and immediately Paul was taken in by her beauty, not to mention her spectacular ass he was trying to glance at while still looking her in the eye.

"Again, I apologize for the inconvenience, but I thought I would get this matter cleared up as soon as possible," he said. "My client wants to move forward with his plans for Mr. Harris and he asked that I personally take care of it for him."

"Oh, and what does your client have planned for Mr. Harris?" Kira asked, relieved he didn't say his client was Henry's mother. "You're aware I'm the executor of Henry Harris's will, and I also have limited power of attorney of his estate, despite the fact his mother is still living."

"Yes, I understand," Paul replied, sitting down right after Kira did. "I can tell you my client is Casper Townsend, and he wants to establish a scholarship in Mr. Harris's name."

"I see, and that was the urgent matter?" She asked, tersely.

Paul laughed. "Well, I must admit, after Casper came to me and told me all about you and Henry Harris, and his erotic books by Gina Wells, I had to meet you."

Kira's wicked smile appeared when Paul pushed her narcissistic button.

"So you really came here to meet me?" Kira said swinging slightly her chair," I wondered why the great detective…"

"…former, now retired, great detective…," Paul corrected, with his own wicked smile.

"Yes, I meant former, now retired, great detective," she said, with obvious flirtation. "would not be sending one of his underlings, and would be handling this himself."

"I'm sorry Kira, I don't mean to waste your time," he replied, humbly. "I know you're leaving for New York."

"Yes, I am," she said, assuming her role of importance. "I just got a new place there in Manhattan.

I'll use it for business, but this weekend, I must admit, I need some time away from the pain of Henry's death."

I can just imagine," Paul acknowledged. "It must have been horrible him drowning like that…"

"Yes, it was terrible," she said. "The worse thing I ever saw and I don't think I will ever get over it."

"I'm sure, but I'm here to ask you about Henry when he was alive," Paul said, wanting to remove any hint of suspicion he was inquiring about Henry's death.

"What can I help you with?" She asked.

"I just want to be sure, for my client's sake and reputation that, well, how should I say it?" Paul said, cautiously. "That Henry Harris wasn't leading some double life; some dark secret we should know about, that would embarrass Mr. Townsend, should it ever come out."

Kira laughed almost to the point of tears.

"Oh my god, no!" She finally said, with a small choke. "Henry Harris only wrote under the pen name Gina Wells for privacy and to make the public think a woman wrote those books. I can assure you Henry Harris, in real life, was nothing like his novels."

"I'm glad to hear that," Paul said, relieved. "Mr. Townsend never suspected anything different but he only knew Henry from the professional standpoint, so he really didn't know Henry."

"Yes, of course, I understand completely," she said. "It's always very difficult to tell what really lurks deep inside us all."

Paul nodded as they watched each other intently like two rabid wild animals about to attack one another.

"Henry was a quiet man, I guess who lived vicariously through his writing," Kira offered, in defense.

"Otherwise, he was very vanilla"

Paul's wicked smile returned when Kira seemingly slipped up and used the word vanilla.

"That's a word you don't hear often to describe someone sexually," Paul noted. "Vanilla, the word makes me wonder more about the person using it, than the person it was said about."

Kira's kinky button, which was sitting right next to her narcissistic button was just fully pressed.

"Yes," Kira purred or was it the start of a snarl. "one would wonder…"

Paul stood up and glanced at his watch.

"I think my time is up and I want to thank you for your time Kira," he said, offering his hand.

Kira stood up, moved out from behind her desk and shook Paul's hand.

"It was a pleasure to meet you Paul," she said, walking to the door with him. "But can I ask you why Casper just didn't call me himself? No offense to him or you, but I don't think he needed a PI, especially one of your stature to be involved."

"I guess he just wanted to have a third, independent party," Paul said. "All formal and such."

"Well, you can assure Casper there's nothing in Henry's background to worry about…no drugs and no kinky, scandalous sex…"

"There's that word kinky," Paul said, with a laugh. "but I think we'll define that when you get back from New York."

"Oh my goodness," Kira said, fanning herself, as if she suddenly got hot. "Aren't you the dominate one…"

Paul looked into Kira's eyes and saw nothing but emptiness.

"…or maybe it's you…," he said, opening the door.

"Perhaps we should find out," she said, as she walked away.

Paul did not reply, but turned back, and stared at her ass until she was sitting down behind her desk, then he the closed the door behind himself, and left.

CHAPTER FIFTY-THREE

Paul wasted no time after leaving Kira's office he called his assistant, told her he was on the way to the airport, and to book him on the next flight to New York. He also told her to send one of his associates to meet him outside the terminal and was specific in what items to bring to him. He had to beat Kira to New York, and he would, but he paid dearly for a last minute, first class seat at eleven.

In New York, Paul rented a small, white van and drove into the City. The midday traffic was heavy but not unusually so for a Friday. April had turned into May, and it was a clear, sunny and warm spring day. His travel gear was brought to the air terminal just as he had requested and it contained the specified clothing and equipment. It was a small bag, but something he checked anyway to avoid any issues getting through security and he wasn't carrying a gun. He could have filled out the paperwork to check one, but once in New York City, he wasn't licensed to carry it, so why take it, and risk getting caught. Besides, he had a plan, sure it was something spur of the moment, daring, and not completely thought out, but it was a good place to start.

Paul's first thoughts when he knew Kira was going to be out of town for the weekend was to gain entry into her home, find the manuscripts, and take them back. But, rethinking that, he considered the possible problems, the main one being the fact that Kira, most likely, had secured the manuscripts, and any other methods of storage such as a laptop, somewhere difficult to locate. The other thing was he didn't know what he was looking for in the way of physical appearance. With Kira being the literary agent and having many other clients, how would he know he was taking the right manuscripts. There could be dozens of them lying about in some office and if he took the wrong one, or even the right one, and it was incomplete, Kira would know they were on to her.

No, Paul needed some leverage on Kira, something he could use to blackmail the blackmailer. He didn't know what that leverage was, but if he was going to be successful, he was willing to take the chance and find out. The way Paul saw it, was Kira came to New York for more than business on a weekend and he suspected any fun Kira was having wasn't going to be vanilla, as she put it. He knew she had a place, she owned it and his staff had easily found the address. It was a one bedroom, one and a half bath apartment in a newly renovated brownstone with a total of eight apartments. All eight of the apartments were sold, and as far as Paul's staff could determine from the real estate agent, two of were still undergoing some construction. The agent was eager to show Paul's assistant the unoccupied units so she could give an idea of similar units she had in another building nearby, also undergoing renovation. Nothing in New York was inexpensive when it came to real estate, especially those places located in Manhattan. Now, every neighborhood was fair game, even those once unheard of as hot properties.

Paul found Kira's brownstone, and the street was busy with traffic, which was both good and bad for him. Good, his van would blend in and not be noticed, bad, there wasn't a place to park near enough to the entrance. He drove slowly past the front and noticed another couple of things in his favor. No doorman and the front security door was propped open for the workers to come and go without having to wait for someone to let them in each time they went out for something. Hustle and bustle, Paul thought, New York City, everyone in a hurry and no time to really pay attention to what someone else was doing.

Paul pulled away and drove around for several minutes until he found what he was looking for; a flower shop. It was two thirty and Kira's plane was in the air. He found a spot in front of the flower shop that was a loading zone only. He figured with the van and the amount of flowers he was going to purchase, the owner of the flower shop wouldn't mind him parking there and he was right.

He bought four of the largest bouquets of flowers that the owner had already made up and only needed to be loaded into the back of the van. One of them Paul had made even bigger, the owner added a dozen more red roses which drove the up the price for the four arrangements to over eight hundred dollars.

When Paul got back to Kira's place, it was almost three-thirty, and there were still no parking places, so Paul doubled parked right alongside another van, similar to his, which had a painting company logo on it. Sitting in the van for a minute, dressed in a khaki pair of pants, jacket and matching ball cap, he looked like an everyday deliveryman. He wasn't from one of the well-known delivery companies, nor did he want to impersonate one, he just wanted to be someone delivering a huge bouquet of beautiful flowers, taken from the back of a van, full of other bouquets of flowers. A normal, everyday, very forgettable delivery man, and if someone was about it asked later, all the person might remember is how beautiful the flowers were the man was carrying.

One of the painters, who was standing outside the brownstone smoking a cigarette watched Paul as he opened the back of the van and took out the huge flower arrangement.

"Somebody die?" The man, shouted and laughed heartily.

Paul swung the spray of flowers around, blocking the full frontal view of his face and replied.

"Naw, I think some big shot closed some deal or something… it's a congratulations…"

The man took a long drag on the cigarette.

"Must have sold the Empire State Building with that many flowers," he said, exhaling a large plume of toxic smoke.

"Mind if I block you in a few minutes while I bring these inside," Paul asked, from behind the wall of flowers.

"Block away," the guy replied, taking another puff. "We're going to be here for a few more hours."

Paul moved passed the man, still hiding his face, and glanced around at the beautiful brownstone, which had been completely restored to its former glory. He wished he had more time to take in all of the workmanship, but he had to get in, and out, of Kira's apartment as soon possible.

Paul went up the stone steps and easily slid through the front door into a lobby where the first four apartments were located. The apartments were two on one side of the corridor and two on the other, with Kira's the first one on the left, which faced the street. Paul took his time moving up to the door and stalled a minute while the painter finished his cigarette and was coming back to work. Just as the man entered, Paul pulled a piece of paper from his jacket and looked down at it as the man moved up the staircase behind him to the second floor.

Paul knocked on the door loud enough so the man could hear him as he ascended the stairs. He waited ten seconds, no answer, and knocked again, and again, no answer. Now, the critical time would begin, and with it, the most danger. Someone could come here at any minute and catch him going inside the apartment. That is, if someone other than Kira Lake was living here which he thought was very possible.

Paul took in a deep breath and let the rush of anxiety pass through him. Should he do it or not, it's now or never. He almost wanted to start laughing at how stupid this all might be in hindsight, but he just couldn't stop himself. He set the flowers down on the floor and took out his automatic lock pick gun. This wasn't just any old lock pick tool, but something a licensed locksmith or law enforcement person would possess, something, not just anyone could own, or use, at least not legally.

In less than a minute and wearing latex gloves, Paul was inside Kira's apartment, which was small, by any standards outside of New York City. It was perhaps nine hundred square feet, with a tiny powder room right off the entrance way that led into the living, dining, and kitchen area. At first impression, Paul thought the place was well-constructed, with elegant furnishings, and high ceilings; a feature alone that made the apartment appear bigger. Off to his left, in the living room, two large double windows sat side by side and looked out over the street. Kira's bedroom was down a short hallway but the inside could not be seen from where he stood. Overall, the place was very clean and neat, and to Paul, either no one lived there when Kira wasn't in town, or if someone did, they didn't cook often or entertain. Even given the fact it was all brand new, it felt sterile, all of it, and not something Paul would ever live in.

Paul looked at his watch and got right to work. He wanted to snoop around, but he didn't want to spend any more time inside the apartment than he had to since his time was limited and the flowers were sitting outside the door which might draw attention.

From inside his jacket, he took out two, small Wi Fi cameras built into smoke detectors that would replace the ones already installed in the apartment. The one in the living room could view the immediate areas which included the kitchen. The other one would go into the bedroom and neither of them should be suspicious to Kira. Paul could have used cameras hidden in clocks, air purifiers or even a tissue box, but they held more chance of being discovered.

After he was satisfied the cameras were well placed, and would offer the best view of any activity inside the apartment, Paul went to Kira's closet and opened it. There, he saw it was full of both men's and women's clothing and was excited that a man lived there.

Paul left the apartment in under ten minutes, making sure the door was relocked. He picked up the flowers, went back out to the van, and drove off. He laughed as he felt the rush of the break-in pass through him. His heart was racing, and he let out a long, deep breath as he drove to the end of the block and found a parking spot. He could barely see Kira's building in the driver's side mirror, but he knew where the painters had parked their van, and he used that as a land mark.

Now, he settled into the seat and a possible long wait, but very soon, the smell of all the flowers crammed into the back of the van started to make him nauseous, so he opened the window for some fresh air. After a while he felt better and took the time to call the office.

"It went smooth as silk," he said to his assistant, without saying exactly what he did. "Nothing like being well prepared with the best equipment."

"I'm glad you're okay," she said. "I was worried with these last minute trips that something would go wrong or the information I got for you wasn't accurate."

"No, it was fine," he said, keeping his eyes glued on the outside mirror. "The brownstone has been completely redone, inside and out, and the apartments are laid out just as you said they would be."

"And no trouble with alarm systems?" she asked.

"No, from what I could see, there were no indications of an alarm system, not yet anyway," he replied. "The flowers worked like a charm and I delivered them in five minutes."

"Good," she said and gave him the rundown of the other phone calls for him including one from Pi and another call from Casper Townsend.

He hung up, and thought Pi had probably tried to call his cell but it was off. He was glad he had told her he was taking an overnight trip to New York City for business but he didn't mention any of the details. He glanced at his watch and made a mental note to call her later when she was off work.

Two hours passed, and Paul thought Kira would have arrived by now, but she hadn't. The painters had left and Paul thought of taking the parking spot right in front of the brownstone but he feared Kira might see him, so he stayed right where he was.

Another hour passed, and Paul had spoken with Pi, drank a bottle of water, and eaten a peanut butter sandwich he had bought at a nearby shop, where he also got a chance to use the bathroom. It was thirty more minutes before a cab pulled up, and Kira and a man got out. It was still light out and he could see the man pay for the cab, and both of them walk into the brownstone.

Paul's van was about one hundred and fifty yards from the building, and his computer was already up and running with the cameras staring into an empty apartment. These Wi Fi remote viewing cameras were great, he thought, and they could be streamed live up to seven hundred feet from their sources.

A minute later, Kira and the man, who Paul could tell now was young and very good looking, entered the apartment. He couldn't hear what they were saying, but it looked like Kira was upset about something, and she was giving him a tongue lashing, and not in a good way.

CHAPTER FIFTY-FOUR

"I'm sorry Kira, but the booking for her shoot came last minute," Chris said, trying to calm Kira down.

"You know how it is in this business, you have to take the gig when they want you, especially when they're paying you a lot of money. You can't say no, you can't be sick, even for real, they don't give a shit what's wrong with you. You need to be on time, look great, and stay that way until they're done with you."

"I know, Chris! I know all about it!" Kira said, setting her purse down on the kitchen table. "I just needed to relax, and have some fun that's all, and now that bitch can't be here. Radhika... some fulfilment of desires she is! She's not fulfilling any of my desires, that's for sure!"

Radhika will be back tomorrow morning, she promised," Chris said. "She is ready to completely fulfill your desires Kira, believe me, she really wants to please you."

Radhika was a jewel, and a rare find, Kira knew this. The woman possessed all the qualities and passion Kira required, not to mention the stamina to keep up with Kira's intense sexual appetite.

"She's going to pay for it Chris, no matter how sorry she is," Kira said, turning to him. "You know I'm going to have to punish her."

Chris nodded, putting his head down. "I know, and I know I'm going to have to do until she gets here tomorrow."

"That's right, little man of mine, you are," Kira said, slipping off her blazer and tossing it onto the table.

"Should I get the flogger or single tail Mistress?" Chris asked, with such anticipation that Paul sat up in his seat and took notice. Even without the audio, he knew something was going to happen.

"No, I'm past that," she replied, unbuttoning her blouse and taking it off. Her black delicately laced bra could barely contain the fullness of her breasts. "I really need to hurt you…really hurt you…"

Chris nodded again and took off all of his clothes and neatly piled them up on the table next to Kira's blazer.

"Get that fucking wooden spoon over there, you stupid failure," Kira said, squeezing her breasts together so tightly, it looked like she was trying to pop them like balloons. "Bring it here, and use your teeth…don't you dare touch it with those pathetic, incompetent hands."

Chris turned immediately at her command, and went to the utensils sitting in a holder on the counter top.

"Hurry up stupid!" Kira barked, kicking Chris in the ass so hard with her high heel that Paul winced.

"Hurry up!"

Chris was built like a Greek god in every way but one. All those statues have men small, soft and flaccid, but Chris, well, what was between his legs, was, shall we say, impressive, very impressive.

"Get that spoon now!" Kira screamed, and Chris worked his mouth around the top of the large wooden spoon, and swung it back to Kira.

Paul watched in the van and whispered to himself.

"Someone's been a bad boy and now they're going to get hurt..."

Kira took the spoon from him, and slowly ran it between Chris's legs while Paul cringed in sympathy.

At first she teased him with the spoon, and then, in a blur, snapped her wrist several times, striking the spoon against him, over and over and over. Chris wanted to scream, the pain was so sharp, but he kept quiet and took it. Kira continued to beat Chris so long with the spoon that Paul had to turn away from the computer screen.

Finally, after what seemed like forever, Paul looked back and saw Kira had stopped, and was now rubbing some ice cubes all over Chris's very red, very swollen and very hard, enormous penis.

"All better now, Chrissy?" Kira mocked.

"Yes Mistress," Chris said, nodding. "I'm all better now."

"Good," she said, sliding the ice over him. "We don't want to make hamburger out of this beautiful piece of meat, now do we?"

Chris shook his head as tears ran down his cheeks. "No ma'am, we don't."

"No, we don't," Kira said, softly, kissing Chris's penis. "I think you're ready now and besides, soups on!"

Paul watched as Kira hiked up her short skirt, turned around, bent over, and set her elbows on the kitchen table.

"Finish me rough," she ordered, putting her head in her hands. "Don't cum or I'll beat your dick with my high heel!"

"Yes ma'am," Chris replied, moving into position behind Kira, and Paul watched as he slammed himself into her.

Ten minutes later, Paul could see Kira shudder violently, lay her head on the table, catch her breath, and look at her watch.

"Did you make us reservations?" She asked, getting upright. "Or did you fuck that up too?"

"Yes, I made the reservations," he said, standing there sweating. "I know you always want steak after a session."

"Yes I do," she said, kissing his mouth, which signaled the session was over, and they were to return to a normal acting mode. "All of this sex is so primal, so natural, that nothing completes the evolutionary cycle like another great, big, thick, piece of juicy meat."

"I know and I hope tomorrow I get a chance to finish too, I'm dying," he said, wiping his sweaty face with a paper towel.

"We'll see how well Radhika does and if I'm pleased, then maybe you will...," Kira said. "Now let's shower and get something to eat."

Paul watched them disappear into the bedroom, and when he followed them with the bedroom camera, both of them went right into the bathroom. He couldn't see what they were doing, but it didn't matter; for almost as fast as they went in, they came out, and both of them had showered. When they began to kiss, Paul thought it was the start of the second round, but they stopped, got dressed and left the apartment.

It was after ten o'clock when they came back and Paul was dead tired. They entered the apartment and Paul thought he was in for a long night of more sex, but he was wrong. Kira and Chris went straight into the bedroom, undressed, got into the bed and turned off the lights.

Paul waited another hour, watching only shadows on a dark screen, until he was satisfied nothing more was going to happen, then he left, and drove to his hotel. He figured he had about six hours before they would be up again, and he might as well get some sleep himself.

CHAPTER FIFTY-FIVE

The next morning, right before six a.m., Paul was back in front of Kira's apartment. It was Saturday morning, and with several of the surrounding buildings also under renovation, without any construction workers, there were a half dozen parking spots open. Paul parked the van closer than he did yesterday but it was still around one hundred yards away from the entrance, and he could still see it with the outside side mirror.

He was still tired, and could have slept a couple of more hours, but the five he got was better than sitting up all night in the van, and getting none. Paul figured Kira for a high energy person, and knew she was going to be up early, and out doing whatever a literary agent would be doing on a Saturday morning. Maybe she would meet a client or editor for a breakfast meeting or two, who knows, but as he sat in the van he began to wonder why he was even there at all.

Sure, Casper Townsend was someone he had gotten a lot of favors from, and in turn, had given them back tenfold. The one hand washing the other, the promise in a good faith relationship that worked well for both of them.

But, what Paul had on tape so far wasn't really anything that he would call leverage, not against Kira, for what she had on Henry Harris. He needed more and he wasn't sure he was going to get it. Yesterday's play time with her boy-toy-friend was definitely in the kinky category and out of the norm but it wasn't something she wouldn't want the rest of the world to know. Heck, he thought, to some people she was just having some downhome fun. Two consenting adults, exploring the fringes of the wilder side.

Maybe this whole thing was just a crazy idea he had, and he took a chance for nothing. There was no way he was going back into her apartment and retrieve those smoke detectors. He was lucky to get in and out the first time, no, he would play out the hand today and see what happened.

Anyway, who really cared about this Henry Harris? From what Casper told him, he sounded like a mama's boy and maybe he got what he deserved. Or maybe Henry did suffer a seizure while scuba diving and did drown accidently and Kira Lake was completely innocent.

Paul Dickinson knew better, and he knew he was really here for Kira Lake, and not for Henry Harris. He knew there were too many coincidences to be coincidences, like in so many murder cases. For instance, Kira changed years of a set behavior with Henry for a reason, and it had to be something she would ultimately be willing to kill him to obtain.

The mother said the manuscripts existed and very likely they do. A mama's boy isn't going to lie about that, especially to his mama. Henry Harris could write and according to Casper, he was a brilliant writer. Kira wanted those manuscripts, but why? What was the real reason?

Paul kept the whole thing spinning around in his head. Motive, method and opportunity; how many times had he seen it happen. Over and over, all for the same reasons; greed, money, sex and jealousy.

The four cornerstones of the house of murder; strong, heavy supports, that rationalized the taking someone's life. Just people, somehow now simply obstacles that needed to be removed, so the perpetrators could get what they wanted, needed, or were entitled to.

Paul had seen them all, and solved them all that came his way, well, all but one, Heather Burk's murder, at least he didn't solve it officially, not in the record books. It was down as an unsolved, still open, a cold case, something for someone else to try and solve. Well, not really, not any more, not in Paul's book, no sir, that baby was almost to bed.

He kept watching the computer screen but there wasn't any movement from the two people sleeping in the bed and Paul knew right then, somehow Kira would pay for what she had done. Sure, the victim didn't raise as much sympathy as a pregnant Heather Burk, and to Paul, that didn't matter. It was about bringing the person responsible to justice; the person who had thought they had committed the perfect crime; that one person above the law. Yes, Paul would get Kira, one way or another, and most likely, it would not be in a court of law.

CHAPTER FIFTY-SIX

At eight that Saturday morning, when Governor Forbes called the first meeting of what he deemed his future core security group, Andersson and Stefani didn't know what to expect. They had been involved many times in the past with his security issues; it was an ongoing process that constantly needed review.

They both knew it was SOP, standard operating procedures, when they walked into the specially prepared room, much akin to the White House situation room. They were more than a little surprised to see who was already there.

Governor Forbes and Mary Gordon were sitting in the middle of the long conference table when Forbes spoke first.

"Come in, sit down I'm sure you already know everyone else."

The faces came up like flash cards, one after the other; Michael Carson was sitting next to Mary Gordon, Rocco Stefani on the other side of the Governor, with everyone else scattered down on either side of them. Shay Abisi, Vanina Cruz down from Carson and Craig Reynolds, Lilly Harper and Jefferson

Culpepper flanking Rocco Stefani. Both Andersson and Stefani were about to say something at the same time when the last person they saw off to the far right of their vision made them speechless; it was Buster.

"Please sit down," the Governor said again, and Andersson and Stefani took the two chairs opposite everyone else. "I know everyone is probably shocked to see everyone else that I've asked here, but that's the way I wanted it. No one here knows any more than the other person and basically that's pretty much nothing, but we're just starting this program, and this is the first meeting as a group."

"Starting what Governor?" Roxanne Stefani spoke up first, asking the question that was on everyone else's mind.

"We're starting what's become something we hope we will never need," the Governor replied," at least on a massive scale, but we're going to be prepared just in case we do, and North Carolina is one of the first states to begin such a program."

Stefani looked at her father who smiled at her, and she smiled back. When she first saw him sitting there, she was surprised that Hank wasn't sitting next to him, but she was relieved when he wasn't.

"We're in a new world," Mary Gordon said, hardly able to keep quiet for more than two minutes. "Or I should have said, an old world with old wars and new rules, which are no rules and we're choosing up sides."

Buster laughed. "That's a good way to put it, Mary. I like that, choosing up sides."

"A few of you don't know Buster or have even heard of him," the Governor said, and you're not going to know any more about him than you do right now, but I can tell you he's with us from one of the Federal agencies. You might want to ask me which one, but I don't even know, and frankly I don't care."

"For now, I'm just an advisor and liaison between the Governor, the State of North Carolina, and the White House," Buster said, standing up and moving around the room. "We don't need a history lesson or a lesson on current events because we all know what's going on in the world and it's unorganized chaos."

Roxanne Stefani watched Buster as he slowly took each step in precise cadence which reminded her of how he moved during their training sessions. He made calculating steps with intent, his eyes darted around constantly, taking in his surroundings. He looked at everyone in the room and yet acted like he saw no one, Stefani knew he had already committed each their faces to long term memory.

"The United States is no longer effective, if it ever was, fighting in countries where wars are religion based," Buster continued. "We haven't changed anything in all the years we've been sacrificing our military men and women, not to mention unbelievable amounts of money we could have used in this country for other well intended purposes."

Governor Forbes continued. "Buster's right, we've torn apart those countries, removed dictators, and tried to help train internal armies to defend themselves against terrorist enemies which have become so confusing; no one really knows who they're really fighting anymore. Meanwhile, terrorist attacks are happening everywhere and anytime, even now in our own country."

"We don't want a military police state here," Rocco Stefani said. "and we're not pushing the panic button, but we need to change our policies, not only internationally, but here, internally. The term freedom has become a weapon against ourselves. Individuals, and even groups of people, think they can do whatever they want, and not be held accountable."

Forbes picked it back up. "People have the right to their freedoms, but we also have to take responsibility for our actions, especially those in positions of power."

"Even four star General Officers are finding themselves looking at possible Court Martials for breaking the rules, and if anyone should be the example for others, its them," Buster said.

"I'm going to play the devil's advocate," Andersson interrupted, "which doesn't mean I don't agree with everything you're both saying one hundred percent, but aren't we all talking about why nothing is getting done in Washington? Everyone with their special interests groups, the ultra-conservatives against the ultra-liberals; we don't have statesmen any more. We don't have anyone that can stand up and say anything that might offend someone in some way, and if they did, their political careers are over. How are we going to change that?"

"We need to take all that we've learned with being politically correct, and with diversity, and make it work for all of us," Forbes said, moving up the next step on his soap box. "We need to take this melting pot of people and begin to get to our roots as one nation. We need the rainbow colors of people and our beliefs to become the colors of the red, white and blue."

"We're under attack people," Buster chimed in, moving behind the Governor. "We're under attack from radically charged nations with radically charged religious groups who will stop at nothing to achieve their goals."

"My country tis of thee...sweet land of liberty...," Roxanne Stefani said. "We're all preaching to the choir here. What's the real deal, and how are our roles in law enforcement going to change to keep up with the demands?"

The room was quiet for a moment and that's just what Stefani wanted. She had heard enough rhetoric.

"Your rules aren't going to change, Roxanne," Forbes replied. "They're just going to be more focused."

"Focused how?" Andersson said. "We already focus on high profile crimes and report directly to you."

"That's right, you do," the Governor said. "You and Stefani will continue to do that, concentrating on high profile crimes, but you will also now investigate any possible connection to home grown terrorism. You and Stefani, and the rest of the team here, will officially work in concert with Rocco Stefani and our friend here Buster."

"What about my role in all this Governor?" Michael Carson asked pointedly. "I notice the State Attorney General isn't here and I'm just the Wake County DA."

The Governor smiled. "Are you looking for a promotion Mike?"

"Well…sir…no…I was just…I mean…"

"Of course you are Mike," Forbes said, not letting Carson say any more to embarrass himself. "The Attorney General is on board and he's ready to go along with whatever we decide warrants criminal prosecution."

Carson breathed a sigh of relief. "I'm glad to hear that, sir," he said, smoothing down his tie.

"By the way, if you didn't already get the hint with my warm up patriotic speech back there," Forbes said, confidently, "I'm officially announcing my candidacy for the President of the United States."

"Everything will remain the same for now," Mary Gordon said, "but we're going to be making some schedule changes as the campaign revs up."

"I know you all have a lot more questions, I'm sure," Forbes said. "but one thing I can assure you is we have the additional funding for this long term project. Therefore, we're all looking at bigger budgets to get our jobs done, and on a personal basis, you're all going to have more take home pay as well. "

The more take home pay part made Jefferson Culpepper and Lilly Harper show obvious smiles.

"You all deserve it and you've all earned it," Forbes said. "But I expect you all will continue to work just as hard and I might add, if for some reason you decide to no longer be a part of this special operation then you're free to leave it. Of course, you'll be reassigned back to regular duty with no hard feelings."

Anderrson and Stefani looked at each other when the Governor said, no hard feelings, and he noticed their skepticism.

"What?" he said smiling, "You don't trust me?"

And everyone laughed.

CHAPTER FIFTY-SEVEN

Paul left the van for twenty minutes, he went to a nearby restaurant and picked up some breakfast to go, when he got back, Kira and Chris were up, and someone else was with them. The images from the cameras he had placed were very sharp and crisp, but he was hard pressed to tell exactly what nationally the third person was, and at first glance, even what sex they were.

A few hungry bites of the bacon, egg and cheese sandwich, and his mind cleared, now he could definitely tell the androgynous person was female. She was very tall, and he thought a mixed white Hispanic, then possible a mix with Asian, but her skin coloring and exotic features, especially the eyes, brought him to India.

She seemed very calm despite the animation of Kira while Chris stood passively off to one side for what appeared to Paul to be another one of Kira's tantrums. Chris was wearing only a pair of very tight, black briefs, and Kira, just a lavender thong.

"When I'm coming to town, nothing else matters!" Kira ranted, her finger pointing, while she circled around Radhika like a hungry shark. "I don't give a fuck how much money they're paying you! I'll double it and don't tell me you can't give them any excuses! That's bullshit! Think of something, anything, but you don't ever miss a session with me again or we're done! Do you understand?"

Radhika nodded, without any sign of emotion or fear.

"Someone's going to get more than a wooden spoon," Paul mumbled through another bite of sandwich.

Kira slapped Radhika across her face with such a full swing that it would have sent a linebacker's head spinning, but Radhika just stood there, and put her head down.

"I'm going to change and get something very special for our bad little girl here," Kira said, turning to Chris. "and when I come out, I want her properly prepared. Do you understand?"

Chris nodded, Kira left the kitchen, and went back into the bedroom. Now, Paul had to watch both screens at once, scanning back and forth between what Kira and Chris were doing. Chris undressed Radhika, who was wearing only black, skin tight, ankle length leggings, a cropped black leather jacket and high heels. Leaving her high heels on, Chris had her stand at one end of the table, and had her bend back, face up. Unfortunately for Paul, the table was length wise to the camera, and he could only see Radhika from the side, still, there was little left to the imagination.

"Don't these people ever use a bed?" Paul said to himself, taking a drink of the cold orange juice.

Chris removed a long piece of clothesline rope from one of the kitchen drawers. He wound the rope around Radhika's right ankle to the right side of the wooden table leg, and when that was tightly secured, he moved to the other side of the table, and stretched her arms out as far as they would go over her head. Now, taking her wrists, he wound the rope around them at least five times that Paul could count, and pulled her arms out to the edge of table, then ran the rope down under the table to her left ankle. After lashing her left ankle; Radhika was splayed helplessly.

Paul was so transfixed on Chris's rope work that he missed Kira getting into a leather corset with so many buckles that it would have made Edward Scissor-Hands proud.

"Oh yeah! Showtime!" Paul said, sipping some hot coffee, and taking another bite of the breakfast sandwich.

Kira moved from the bedroom back into the kitchen and was carrying something in her hand that looked like an electric tooth brush but wasn't. It was a little larger than an electric toothbrush and Paul knew right away this wasn't something anyone would use to brush their teeth. It was a violet wand that sent an electrical current over someone's skin with varying degrees of intensity depending on the power setting and the discretion of the operator.

Kira turned on the wand and it glowed violet, hence its name, and like most stimulating devices which were really sex toys, they were advertised for personal use and relaxation. Additionally, along those same thought lines, with tools sold for any purpose, there's a handyman variety and there's a professional grade version. This wand was professional grade and it was in the hands of a professional.

The violet wand could be used to get a light tickle on the skin, or it can deliver a powerful jolt to very sensitive parts of the body, and one has to remember that even a tickle can become painful if prolonged.

Paul watched as Kira approached Radhika like a surgeon would a patient before make that first incision. She held the wand like a scalpel, delicately, yet when she began to move the wand over her and Paul could see Radhika react; this hurt, and it was going to get worse. At first Kira danced the wand over Radhika's skin in general areas, her arms, legs and tummy. She was careful not to place the wand directly over her heart, since the heart worked on a small electrical current of its own and any possible disruption of that vital rhythmic flow cold result in dire consequences.

"You like that?" Kira asked, as she placed the wand over Radhika's nipples.

Radhika nodded.

"Feels good, doesn't it?" Kira asked her again.

Radhika nodded again and Paul could tell from the expression on her face that what Kira was doing to her had a pleasurable effect.

"But we want it to hurt too, now, don't we Radhika?" Kira asked, as she dialed up the power setting.

Radhika nodded.

"Yes, we need to get to that fine line of pain and pleasure now don't we?" Kira said, jolting the nipples again at the higher setting.

Radhika nodded again, this time in stoic silence and Kira ran the wand down her body to in between her legs. Here, with plenty of moisture, Paul missed the crackling sounds when the wand made contact but he didn't miss Radhika's reaction. Her body jerked and heaved with each touch of the wand and Kira knew exactly all the right places too. Paul watched and as the session progressed, Kira changed the wand with different attachments and used them on Radhika until her orgasms were blurred into nothing more than blissful torture.

Time passed quickly and Kira used various pieces of other equipment besides the violet wand. Some of them Paul easily knew what they were and how they were effective. There were nipple clamps that Kira screwed down very tight with a chain that ran between them. Kira used a large massager with a round, vibrating head on Radhika while she jerked the chain which in turn pulled painfully on the nipple clamps. It was amazing to see how much of this type of sexual play Radhika could endure. To Paul, it looked more like work than play, but then again, he wasn't the one tied to the kitchen table.

For more than an hour, Paul watched as Kira prodded, pinched, probed, twisted, and slapped Radhika with everything she had and still, from Paul's perspective, and as sick as it might sound, it was just a lot of kinky fun.

Maybe Kira was feeling the same frustration Paul felt when he finally saw her move away from the table and say something to Chris.

"What the hell is going on now?" Paul whispered, as if he didn't want anyone else to hear him.

Kira took a large, clear, plastic bag while Chris moved up the table and began to have sex with Radhika. When Kira was satisfied with Chris's performance and they both seemed like they were really into it, Kira took the plastic bag and pulled it down over Radhika's head. Chris kept doing what he was doing and Kira pulled the bag snug enough you could see Radhika's facial features.

At first, Radhika seemed to enjoy it but after about a minute with the plastic bag over her face, Paul noticed she began to move her mouth. She was trying to say something to Kira but Kira ignored it, until Radhika began to struggle. Paul saw her hands pulling against the ropes, trying to get free, but all the while Kira shouted to Chris to keep going, harder and harder.

Another ten seconds and Paul could see Radhika's eyes bulging.

"Oh fuck!" Paul said, sitting up in his seat. "She's suffocating her!"

Full panic engulfed Radhika now and she shook the table violently trying to get free, but Kira kept the bag down snug over her face. Chris shouted something to Kira and stopped his movement and Kira only kept the bag firmly in place.

Now, Paul was in a panic of his own. Was Kira going to kill this girl? Should he intervene? But, just as he went to leave the van, Chris bolted to the other side of the table, pushed Kira aside, and ripped the bag from Radhika's face. Kira looked dazed and if in a trance as Radhika gasped for air.

"Are you fucking crazy?" Chris said. "She was trying to use her safe word and you just ignored it!"

Kira looked down at Radhika who was trying to catch her breath.

"I didn't hear her," Kira replied. "I was really into it."

"You didn't hear her because the more she tried to talk, the harder you pulled on the bag," Chris said angrily. "A few more seconds and she could have stopped breathing. You know how to do breath play, Kira, you're supposed to watch them closely, and any signs of distress you have to release them."

"I know, I know," Kira said, looking down at Radhika. "I'm sorry."

Chris untied Radhika, made sure she was okay, and helped her off the table.

"Is she all right?" Kira asked, as Chris wrapped his arms around Radhika who was still trembling.

Radhika nodded and pressed her head against Chris's chest.

"Oh man, this is just the stuff I needed," Paul said joyfully, tapping the computer screen. "But remind me to never eat on that kitchen table."

CHAPTER FIFTY-EIGHT

Later, while Paul was driving back to the airport, Roxanne Stefani, her mother, Shay Abisi and Erin Milson, were in a bridal shop owned by a young new designer Roxanne had make her wedding dress.

Roxanne could have had a world class design original, but when Lilly Harper's friend, who just got married, suggested Miranda, Roxanne said yes, and she was glad she did. Miranda, who had recently graduated from a well-known design school, had a special talent for the classical look, and created a beautiful wedding dress for Roxanne, as well as for the rest of the wedding party, Shay, Erin and Maggie too.

Roxanne's dress was simple, and something Miranda thought Roxanne could pull off, although Roxanne's mom wanted something more of a ball gown style. Miranda used Roxanne's height and slender, lean shape, and put her silhouette into a trumpet/mermaid design with a sweetheart neckline, a chapel train with fabric of organza and satin, finished with embroidered beading.

It was strapless, sleeveless, and had a lace up, zipper back, and the color was ivory.

"It looks perfect on you, Roxanne," her mom said, as Roxanne stepped up onto the pedestal. "I know I wasn't a big fan of the sexier look and I wanted that ball gown with a long train, but Miranda was right, you really look amazing."

"It does," Erin said, sitting next to Roxanne's mom. "Not many women can wear that type of dress and still make it look as elegant as you do."

"Thank you," Roxanne said, then looked at Shay Abisi for her approval, who was standing next to Miranda.

Shay did not immediately reply and kept staring at her.

"What?" Roxanne said.

"I'm not sure," Shay said, after a long pause. "I think it's too tight in your butt and my guess is all those trips to Binky's has finally caught up with you."

Roxanne quickly turned in the mirror and peered at her backside.

"It looks fine to me," Roxanne said, laughing. "But maybe Miranda can let your dress out a couple of inches for all those donuts you ate."

Everyone laughed, but Miranda, who thought they were serious.

"They're kidding, Miranda," Roxanne's mom said. "The two thinnest women in North Carolina, and they're always going at each other about their weight."

"Oh god," Miranda said, catching her breath. "For a second, I thought I was going to be working overtime at the last minute to get your dresses done on time."

"No, we're good," Shay said. "I think the dresses are perfect too."

Miranda beamed at her accomplishments. It wasn't easy to satisfy a woman's taste when it came to clothes, especially for bride's maids, who are notoriously difficult to please.

Now Maggie, Hank's daughter, will be here on Thursday," Roxanne reminded Miranda. "She's taking an early flight, so I should be able to bring her in around one."

"That's fine," Miranda replied, moving to check Erin's dress. "Maggie's dress is all done too, and I sent the dress up to her a couple of weeks ago, and her mom said it fit her well. She did grow a little since we first took her measurements last Thanksgiving, but nothing that I couldn't easily alter."

"Good, I'm glad," Roxanne said. "I've grown close to Maggie, and I'm excited she's going to be in her dad's wedding."

"I bet," Miranda said, knowing having a readymade family and trying to fit into a parenting role of some kind, isn't easy. "My sister married a man with a son and now that they have two kids of their own, it's been an adjustment for his son when it's his weekend for visitation."

"I can imagine," Roxanne said. "Maggie lives in New York, so we have her here at the holidays, and a few weeks in the summer. It's been a big plus that Hank and his ex-wife, Stephanie, get along, at least where Maggie's concerned."

"I hope when I get married I can have just one husband, and one family," Miranda said, wistfully. "No offense to anyone who is divorced, I guess I'm just old fashioned."

"It's a nice thought," Shay said to Miranda. "But in reality, half of marriages end in divorce and half of those who remarry, divorce again. There're too many people marrying for the wrong reasons, and for the most part, too young."

"I don't think everyone is suited for marriage or for having kids," Erin said. "I guess I'm a prime example. I was married, and divorced when I was younger, no kids fortunately, and now I'm gun shy."

"I don't think everyone is suited for marriage or for having kids for that matter," Roxanne said, heading into the changing booth to take off her wedding dress.

"Well, I'm hanging in until I'm sure," Miranda said.

"You'll know when it happens," Roxanne said, taking off the dress and putting on her jeans. "I knew the moment I saw Hank."

"Well, everyone can't experience love at first sight like you and Hank did," Shay said. "Sometimes It takes a while for those feelings to develop."

"You're right," Erin said. "Maybe that was my trouble when I met my ex, I fell too quickly, and really didn't see who he was until after we were married."

"Oh you saw it girlfriend," Shay said. "But you were just blinded by all that smooth romance."

"Amen to that," Erin said, with a laugh.

Roxanne came out of the booth with her wedding dress, and handed it to Miranda, who was patiently waiting.

"What do you all say since our dresses fit so well," Roxanne offered. "we go out to lunch and celebrate!"

They all did a high five, left the bridal shop, and went to Binkys.

CHAPTER FIFTY-NINE

Paul had a late afternoon flight back to Raleigh but he still got home around seven and the first thing he did was hug Pi.

"God, I missed you!" He said, pulling her tight to him.

"I miss you too Paul," Pi said. "It's like you were gone a long time."

"I know," he said. "It was like that for me too."

They kissed and hugged again.

"You want sex now with Pi?"

"No, I mean yes," Paul said quickly. "But I want to go to dinner first and talk."

"Okay," Pi said. "I just need to change from work clothes."

Pi went into the bathroom, undressed, and washed up. She combed her hair out, and put on a very short dress. It only took her fifteen minutes and when Paul saw her, she looked beautiful.

"I look good for you?" She asked, as she slipped on the gold pie necklace he had given her.

"You look wonderful Pi," he said, noticing the necklace. "I love that necklace on you Pi."

"Me too Paul," she replied. "I wear all the time."

Paul stared at her for a moment and she noticed the glint of dismay on his face.

"No worry Paul," she said cheerfully. "We have today."

"Yes, we do," he said, taking her hand. "I guess our ages still makes me feel insecure at times."

"No worry Paul," she said. "I love you."

"I love you too Pi."

They left the apartment and went to a new Asian restaurant that had just opened.

"This place is very expensive," Pi said. "It not food most Asians can have money for in my country."

"Afford," Paul said, as they slid into the elegant cozy booth. "It's not something most Asians can afford in your country."

"Yes, cannot afford," Pi said, snuggling up to him.

The waiter came over to them and said good evening. He was a middle aged, Asian male dressed in a tuxedo. He suggested some items from the menu, some specials, and Paul ordered a full bottle of Prosecco.

"We celebrate tonight?" Pi asked.

"Yes, we celebrate tonight," Paul replied.

"Good, I like celebrate," Pi said, with her familiar giggle. "So what do in New York Paul? Can you tell Pi or is big secret."

Paul laughed. "No, it's not a big secret and yes I can tell you. I just can't tell you who the people are that are involved."

"Okay," Pi said. "I not know them anyway."

Paul nodded, and told Pi an abbreviated version of the story that Casper Townsend had told him. He didn't even get to the part about his trip to New York when the waiter came with the Prosecco and two fluted glasses. After the waiter opened the Prosecco, and poured the first glasses of the sparkling wine, they toasted each other, and Paul resumed the story.

"You could have brought Pi to New York Paul," she said, when he got to the part about getting into the apartment and waiting in the van. "I could have sat in van with you to keep company."

"I know and I would have loved to have you there with me, but having you with me would have drawn more attention and somebody might have called the cops to check it out."

"Pi understand Paul, I smart to go to University, but cannot afford," she said, using her new word.

They ordered many different dishes, tasted each one and commented on how delicious they were and Paul kept saying they had ordered too much.

"No worry Paul, we bring home and Pi eat it for next meal."

"Yes, I'm sure you will," Paul said, swallowing a piece of shrimp that was in a hot sauce. "If you had the money could you go to school?"

Pi nodded. "Yes, I could go, but Pi now use money to take English."

Paul talked more about what happened in New York. More food came during the conversation and they would stop talking, eat, then Paul would resume where he had left off.

"Why the lady play that game with bag over girl's face?" Pi asked, confused. "How she breathe?"

"She doesn't, that's the point," Paul replied, taking another mouthful of a dish with rice, vegetables and pieces of spicy chicken which was not as hot as the shrimp. "These sex games some people play are on the edge and sometimes can be dangerous."

"What edge are they on?" Pi asked, taking some of Paul's food from his plate with her chopsticks.

Paul laughed. "The edge of crazy sex play."

"Like fetish? You tell me before."

"Yes, something like that," Paul said. "But it's even more extreme. This lady who had the bag over the girl's face looked like she could have kept it there."

"You mean kept on her face until she die?" Pi asked, with her chopsticks full of Paul's food.

"I don't know," Paul said, remembering the look on Kira's face, and the panic when Chris realized she might not release the bag. "It was pretty scary to watch, especially since I couldn't really help her, well not at that moment."

"Pi not like that game Paul," she said, putting the food into her mouth. "I do lots of sex for you, but not bag over me."

Paul nodded, watching her eat. "No, Pi, no bag games for us."

The waiter came back several times and asked if everything was alright with the food and they both said they loved it.

"What happens with this lady now Paul?" Pi asked. "You tell police?"

Paul shook his head and set his fork down.

"I'm full," he said. "No, she didn't commit any crime unless the girl claimed assault, which would be difficult to prove since they all were willing participants and frankly I think, in the end, the girl got something out of it."

"What do you mean?" Pi said, continuing to eat. "She almost die."

Paul took the last of the Prosecco and divided it between them.

"Hard to explain Pi," he said, after a thoughtful minute. "It's like she dodged a bullet and got a super thrill from it that was extremely sexually arousing. I watched them have sex after everyone calmed down and it was like nothing had happened. They had a great time.

"They sound crazy Paul," Pi said, sipping some tea instead of her Prosecco.

"I guess they do, but I also guess someone can say I was crazy for what I did too," Paul said, watching Pi continue to eat more and more food. "But I'm hooked now on the case, on the lady too, and for the first time in my life, I'm not only feeling the thrill but also the fear."

CHAPTER SIXTY

"It sounds like you had a great day, and got a lot done," Hank said to Roxanne.

"Yes, I did, and we're all set for our wedding on Saturday," Roxanne said, getting into bed with Hank.

"Shay and Erin are a lot of fun and I'm glad she came down early and stayed with us."

"Me too and Maggie will be happy she's in the wedding too," Hank said. "Stephanie's a good mom, but lately she's been traveling a lot with her husband, and Maggie gets left behind with a nanny."

"Maybe she can spend more time with us," Roxanne suggested. "She's getting older, and pretty soon those dreaded teen years will be upon her, and those years can be tough for a girl."

"I know, you're right," Hank said. "I also know we're probably as busy as Stephanie in a lot of ways, maybe more so."

"It's one thing to be busy during the day, and still have time for your kids," Roxanne said.

"That's true," Hank said. "I guess we can look further into the future regarding her visit times and see if we can make any adjustments."

"When will Luis and his wife arrive?" Roxanne asked.

"Thursday too, same as Maggie," he said. "I thought they could stay here with us. Even though Erin is here and Maggie, we still have another bedroom and bath for them."

"Sure, as long as they know I don't cook," Roxanne said with a chuckle.

"No problem, I got you covered," Hank said with a laugh. "I'm taking a couple of days off to be here for Maggie, so I'll make everyone a big breakfast and we can do dinners out."

"Sounds great, just don't make the dinners too early," Roxanne said. "We're still working on the Burk case."

"I thought that was air tight, and Carson was itching for an early trial?"

Well, it is, at least to Carson, but Andersson and I still don't think he killed his brother," Roxanne said. "We're pretty sure we know who did do it, but we have nothing solid that would give any doubt for Carson to consider."

"So what are you going to do?"

"Not sure, we have another witness, someone who was at Hot Rod the night Burk was killed that might help us with the time-line," Roxanne said. "It's kind of a long shot, but we're still going to talk to him just for the record, if nothing else."

"So, how did your meeting go today with Forbes?" Hank asked, changing the subject.

Roxanne sat up. "You knew about that?"

He nodded. "I was invited, but your father thought it would be better if only he went. He didn't want to have you walk in and see both of us sitting there."

"Frankly, I was more surprised you weren't there," she said, putting her head back down on his chest. "I'm just not sold on this whole idea…not yet anyway."

"I know, the whole idea seems paranoid and confusing, but this type of citizen involvement worked well in some areas of the country with gangs and gang violence," Hank said. "But, I'm not sure how it will work with terrorists, especially when you don't know who they are or when or where they might strike."

"I just don't want anything to happen to you," Roxanne said.

"I know and I feel the same way about you, but we need to be part of this and see where it goes,"

Hank said, decisively. "Forbes has a plan, at least for North Carolina right now."

"I know you're right and I know my father is right, and I trust everyone who was in that room," Roxanne said.

We've left the Middle East," Hank said. "The United States is no longer going to be able to fight those wars again, not in the conventional sense, those countries are going to have to protect themselves, one way or another."

Roxanne nodded, hugging him tightly. She knew just as well as Hank, that tens of thousands of people, from many different Middle Eastern countries, were fleeing to the United States. They no longer could live in countries that were in constant states of war or threat of attack by random suicide bombings.

Most of the people who came here are good people, who only want to live in peace, be safe and care for their families. It's like that with all the people of the United States, we have different national, cultural, and religious backgrounds, and most of the people have the same basic life values. But, they're are those who are radicals, American citizens, who hate our government, our freedoms, world power, and our lives of what some consider capitalistic, unfair, and immoral.

It's really the same old story that been told for thousands of years in different way, but it's the same old scam. Men who want control, their power, their way but the same access to the riches they pretend to despise. They're men who always suppress women in every way possible. Men who commit atrocities in the name of God. The war is here in our country, as it is in many other countries, and the people may look like us, speak like us and even act like us at times, but it's still the same war.

Many will stand up and fight, others will run and hide, while some will even change sides, but in the end, and perhaps the bitter end, we will win, win, win.

CHAPTER SIXTY-ONE

Kira Lake got home from New York late Sunday afternoon, and except for the disappointing start, she felt she had a great time. She was still riding the sexual high she always got from her play time, as she like to call it.

It was addictive, and as with any addiction, it must have its fix, its temporary reprieve, before the next round of compulsive behavior. But Kira did not have any rationalization for her desires, they were just her. A driving force within herself, a force she had known all her life.

She had just killed someone, but for a good reason in her mind. Did she plan to kill Henry during the trip to the Keys, sure, of course she did. She knew it would come to that, right from the first moment she knew she wanted his manuscripts for herself. Her needs were first, and at some point in all the twisted, deductive process that went on in Kira's brain; it was the fact that Henry was going to prevent her from obtaining that goal.

She knew him too well, but she knew herself even better. There was no way he was going to leave her alone, and no way she was going to forget the manuscripts. That was never going to happen, if Kira wanted something; she got it! The methods and means to those ends were irrelevant.

Only now, since she had that brief, yet unsettling meeting, with Paul Dickinson, would she even have given pause to her plans. She would have been on to the next phase; the publishing of her books, but she didn't believe Paul Dickinson for one second. His lies to deceive her! Who did he think he was trying to fool her anyway? Maybe that was the better question. Who was he?

She knew of him, and knew his reputation, he was a celebrity of sorts. A police officer, a detective, okay, a damn good one, but he was a cop, now a successful private investigator, and it was that word that was most troubling to Kira about him, investigator.

Thirty years of nosing around in other people's business. Going on fact finding missions, like some little kid on his first Easter egg hunt. Who did he think he was playing with her? Like she believed that corny story he was looking into Henry Harris's background for Casper Townsend; no chance. Paul Dickinson was sticking that nose where it didn't belong, and he was probably already putting two and two together, maybe even three and three, or even all the way up to four and four. She was safe on what happened in the Keys with Henry, and nothing could change that, but Paul Dickinson could be a life sized fly in the ointment when it came to the manuscripts.

Kira kept thinking about it, as she took out her favorite ceramic tea pot her that grandmother had given her shortly before she died. It was a rare teapot, came over on the Mayflower, or something like that, and Kira's grandmother was never close to her daughter, Kira's mom. So, when it came time to pass the teapot down, the grandmother skipped over her daughter, to Kira. Nothing much was said about the old teapot, but it was worth quite a bit on the antique market, something Kira's mom never knew. Kira should have kept the teapot in a cabinet or some-thing, and not used it on a daily basis, but she didn't.

She took the teapot, and filled it with filtered, spring water like always. The sexual demons were quiet now, tucked away for the time being, perhaps a couple of days before they needed to come out again, but her anger began to stir. It was a deep root-ed, fear based, anger, yet a vicious anger when released.

She could destroy the manuscripts, the sex tapes of Henry, and that would be the end of it all. Or would it? Would someone like Paul Dickinson care about her motive, the reason Henry had to be eliminated?

The fact that Henry was sexually blackmailing her? Would Paul Dickinson really care about all that? About her?

No, Paul Dickinson was coming after her, she knew it, and she could feel that anger within herself ready to burst out in a violent rage, and before she could stop, Kira smashed her be-loved teapot down on the granite countertop. The teapot broke into a thousand tiny pieces, cutting her hand in the process, and she screamed. It was a long howl, which thankfully, no one could hear, but if they could hear it, they would have been afraid.

"Now look what you made me do, Paul Dickinson!"

CHAPTER SIXTY-TWO

Willy Burk wasn't doing well in the County lockup, but there was little he could do to change it, when he tried to get bail, he was laughed out of court. He was charged with first degree murder, plus, had a prior felony conviction, and was no doubt, an immediate flight risk if he did get out.

He was still on a suicide watch, and isolated from the general population, which didn't bother him as much as being confined. He hated prison, and he hated not being able to ride his motorcycle. That was the worst thing of all. He loved his motorcycle, and the way he felt when he was on it. Open. Free.

Careless about life.

He laughed at the suicide watch, and teased the Correctional Officers about it; he wasn't going to kill himself. He didn't do anything wrong to be in here in the first place. He didn't kill his brother; that was for sure no matter what that crazy DA said. He could stick all that so called evidence right up his ass.

Willy was being framed for a murder he didn't commit, and he said this over and over again, but no one was listening. Okay, so he did plan, and kill Billy's pregnant wife, Heather; but she had to go, and that was a totally different set of circumstances. Heather wanted Billy to settle down, to take responsibility for her and his child; I mean, was she crazy or what?

Willy told her a hundred times that Billy was a fun guy, but he was lazy, and he was always going to be lazy. He also told Heather, over and over, that Billy's not going to hold a job for more than a couple of months at a time. He'll work, get some cash, and then go party until it was gone. He won't worry about paying his bills either until their overdue, and you're getting calls day and night for payment. Marrying Billy was one thing, having your dad help him get a job to start you two off in life, was another, but throw a baby into the mix and Billy was going to bolt.

Willy's advice to Heather was get rid of the kid and that's how he told her too. 'Get rid of it!'

She refused.

Heather wanted to be married, she wanted a family, and she wanted Billy to change. Heather also blamed Willy for a lot of Billy's failures since he the enabler. He always came to Billy's rescue from the time they were kids, and many times for good reason, but as Billy got older those continued rescues only made Billy more dependent.

Heather also didn't like the fact that Willy was involved in criminal activities, which included dealing drugs and stealing motorcycles. She told Willy, warned him too, keep doing what you're doing, and you're going to end up in jail again. Willy would laugh at her, tell her he was off the radar, and just dealing small time. After a few months of back and forth, right around the time Heather got pregnant, Willy had enough, and told her point blank, stay out of his affairs and stop trying to put a wedge between Billy and him. He told her many times, that shit ain't happening. Then it was, stop Heather, stop, or else!

That's how it all went down, and then Heather has to hint around to Billy, that maybe if Willy got caught, and went back to prison for a while, everything would be better for all of them. Big mistake, and Willy told Billy, she's done it to herself. What's got to happen, has got to happen. He told Billy, and remembers the time very clearly, he's family, and she's just a bitch carrying a kid you don't even want.

She's got to go, he said, and he kept telling Billy how many times, before that dumb ass really got it.

No, all that Heather stuff was different. He didn't kill Billy, and no way was this frame up for his murder right. No way. Besides, Heather's death was really her own fault to Willy's way of thinking. Okay the insurance policy was a bonus, but that was an afterthought; and why not benefit from what had to happen. I mean, why not?

No, the law was the law and Willy knew the law.

CHAPTER SIXTY-THREE

I f Mary Gordon was a juggler, you know, the kind that can really juggle, not the three oranges kind of thing, the ten things in the air kind of juggling, then Mary would be the best juggler ever. She was that good. She could handle anything, and everything that Governor Forbes threw at her. Of course, Mary Gordon expected anyone associated with her juggling act to be as good as she was, and if not, well, that person was juggling in another show.

Nicklaus Andersson was a good juggler in Mary's opinion, and that meant Governor Forbes thought Nicklaus was too, but Mary didn't know all the things that went on between Forbes and Andersson and sometimes that bothered her, and other times, she was glad she didn't know.

This is one of those times. Forbes was running for the Presidency of the United States, and she told him, you have to be extremely careful about what you say, how you say it, when you say it and especially to whom you say it. The media, as well as your everyday person was always watching, always listening, always ready to record on their cell phones. They wanted something controversial, anything that could or would cause a stir or better yet, an embarrassment, and it would be crisis time. Even a slip of the tongue, a whisper on an open microphone, which has happened before to many an unsuspecting politician, could lead to disaster.

Does he take her advice? Yes, well, no, he doesn't. He takes her advice about what he says, how he says it, and to whom, but he still insists on talking to Andersson alone at times. It bothered Mary before and it bothers her now.

"I'm so paranoid since I announced my run for the Presidency that I don't like to talk on the phone anymore and Mary is constantly warning me about what I say."

"Yes sir, I can understand that," Andersson said, closing the door to his office.

"But, then Mary got me one of these encrypted satellite cell phones that are pretty much impossible to penetrate," Forbes said. "Ha! Ha! You know how that goes. It seems something is safe until it's not and I don't dare type this in an email or text."

"Yes sir, Mary's right about security," Andersson replied, beginning to wonder if someone was listening in on the his end of the call. "There's never enough, and what you have is probably soon to be compromised. I could come over to your office if you like."

"No, that's not necessary, Nicklaus," Forbes said. "Mary would really get suspicious about why I had you come here, and not let her sit in on the conversation. I'm lucky I can make this private phone call to you."

"Yes sir."

"Nicklaus we're off the record again, okay?"

"Of course sir."

"I'm going to need you to meet me Friday night around midnight, can you do that?"

Andersson thought well before he answered, and to say he was taken off guard by the Governor's request, would be an understatement.

"My son has the wedding rehearsal for Stefani's wedding, and there's a dinner after, but I should be done by ten at the latest."

"I hate to impose on you, especially with Roxanne's wedding, and all, but it was the only time I could make it all happen, and it was extremely difficult to arrange even with all my magical powers."

Andersson wondered if Forbes meant good or evil magical powers, and did he even want to know.

"Well, whatever it is sir," Andersson said. "It must be important, and of course I'll be there, where ever that is."

"Good man, Nicklaus," Forbes replied, never doubting that Andersson would say yes, or continue to ask more questions making an uncomfortable situation even more uncomfortable. "And since we're talking about strange meetings in the middle of the night, is that something you can help me with in the future? I mean, when I'm busy with the campaign?"

"I guess so," Andersson said. "Is this something to do with the CAT teams?"

Forbes took an audible breath.

"No, not this Friday anyway," he said. "But there will be other times in the future that it could be or should I say will be. I hate to sound so vague Nicklaus."

"Can I speak freely sir?" Andersson asked, always remembering his military bearing for rank.

"Yes, of course," Forbes said. "You know when we meet privately or chat on the phone like this, I welcome your opinion and especially your candor."

"I just want to mention Stefani sir," Andersson said. "If I'm going to be out of town, or meeting you at odd hours, she's going to notice and ask questions."

"I understand, and I've thought about her as well," he said. "She is going to notice and I'm prepared to make her aware of our activities when the time is right but not entirely make her aware of all our meetings."

"Okay sir," Andersson said, still confused, but trying to sound agreeable. "I have to trust your judgement on that, but I want to be clear since you appreciate my candor. I don't want to deceive Stefani if it's going to change my partnership with her, especially on the professional level."

"No, you won't be doing anything that should change your professional relationship," Forbes said, quickly. "This is more of a personal favor between you and me."

"Okay sir, I understand."

"And speaking of personal favors," Forbes added. "I have another one to ask of you and Stefani as well."

"What's that?" Andersson asked, hoping this favor would sound less complicated than the Governor's first one.

"I had a phone call from Casper Townsend," Forbes began. "Which I unfortunately had to dodge and Mary took, but he declined to tell her the nature of the call. "

"He's the investigative reporter right?" Andersson asked.

"Yes, he is, I thought you would know him," Forbes said. "Great guy, and he's been a huge support to me both politically and financially. Anyway, after the call, I run into him at the private fund raiser the other night and he asked me if I would have someone look into what he called a suspicious death of a friend. The guy's a writer, drowned in the Florida Keys few weeks ago, writes under another name, a female name."

"In Florida sir? Andersson asked. "How are we going to investigate that?"

Forbes laughed. "How the hell do I know? The guy's name is Harris."

Andersson laughed, this was one of those times he wished he wasn't the Governor's top, special, now, meeting in the middle of the night, investigator.

"Any details you can give me?"

"No, I don't know or remember, sorry," Forbes said. "But I do know Casper asked Paul Dickinson to look into it as well."

"Why did he ask you if he's got Dickinson involved...of all people..." Andersson asked, shocked.

"All I know is Casper is covering all the bases," Forbes said. "He said, he asked Dickinson on a personal note for the family, but then thought he should have someone official in the background as well."

"Sounds like Casper wants us in the background if the shit hits the fan, so none of it gets on him."

"I know, but I couldn't say no to him. He's done a lot for me already and I'm going to need him even more in the future."

"Okay, I'll call Casper first thing Monday morning," Andersson said, avoiding mentioning anything about the Willy Burk case. "Stefani's going to love this."

"I know, but just take a look at it so Casper thinks we're really doing something," Forbes said, lightly.

"Don't stress over it."

"Okay sir," Andersson said. "I'll be in touch."

They hung up, and Andersson took out some Chiclets, and popped a handful of the gum into his mouth. He needed a good chew, and he needed to think; and two Chiclets weren't going to cut it.

"Let's see," he said, as he thought to himself. "We got a guy in jail for the murder of his brother, who didn't do it, but did kill his brother's wife for profit, and we can't do anything about either case.

Now, the guy we do think killed the guy's brother, a former cop, turned private eye, is investigating a suspicious death of another guy who drowned in Florida, that we don't know anything about, but we're supposed to take a look at as a political favor, and on top of that, I have to meet the Governor at midnight, on Friday night, for unknown reasons, right before Stefani's wedding on Saturday morning."

"No, fuck no, I'm not going to stress over anything..." Andersson said, as he chomped on the wad of gum.

CHAPTER SIXTY-FOUR

Monday morning, bright and early, phones were ringing all over the country; well at least in North Carolina and Florida. Andersson called Casper Townsend, they talked for half an hour, and when they finished, Andersson had Reynolds, Harper and Culpepper burning up the phone lines or cell towers, or whatever they use nowadays, then, Andersson called Stefani.

"Why did Townsend call Dickinson and not us in the first place?" Stefani asked.

"My exact words," Andersson said. "But apparently from what Townsend said, and he's backpedaling now, so keep that in mind, he wanted to keep it low key, and off the radar. He told me this Henry Harris, the writer who drowned in Florida, his death was ruled accidental, and he's been cremated."

"Henry Harris?" Stefani asked. "You mean Gina Wells?"

"Yeah, he wrote under that name, erotic stuff," Andersson said. "You know him?"

"No, I don't know him," Stefani said, not personally. "I knew her, I mean, I read some of his writings in college. It's so odd,

I was just talking to Hank about it when I saw in the newspaper that he had died."

"Okay, well, Dickinson is looking into Harris's background for what Townsend says is about some scholarship he's funding in Harris's name. He wanted to be sure there was nothing hidden in his past that might embarrass the newspaper."

"Okay and…"

"Sounded like bullshit to me, and there's another reason he called Dickinson, and not us, but he won't tell me."

"You're right, that's the real reason he got Dickinson and the background story is bogus."

"Yeah, and I also think Townsend might be having buyer's remorse since he got Dickinson involved."

"How so?"

"Townsend only gave me a few bread crumbs to follow, but not enough to lead us anywhere,"

Andersson said. "He told me what he thought happened in the Keys, and he gave me the names of the only two people he knew, besides himself, that were close to Harris. One was his mother, who's not in good health, and in a local nursing home. The other person is Harris's attorney, and literary agent, Kira Lake."

"I don't know the name," Stefani said.

"I do, and I knew her maybe ten years ago, or more," Andersson said. "I got Harper on her, and Reynolds and Culpepper are talking to the police in Key West."

"Sounds good to me," Stefani said, trying to dodge what she knew was coming next. "You know I've pretty much taken most of the week off…"

"I do."

"You don't really need me on this one," she said. "Sounds like a wild goose chase."

"I know, but I thought maybe you could come in around one, and we could both hear what everyone has to say and then you're done. In and out, an hour tops"

"Okay sure," Stefani said. "One o'clock."

"Thanks, and look Roxanne, the Governor said not to stress over it."

"Oh great, thanks Nicklaus," Stefani said, with a long depressing sigh. "I wasn't stressing over it until you told me that"

And she hung up.

CHAPTER SIXTY-FIVE

Paul Dickinson took his time getting ready, since his appointment with Kira Lake wasn't until eleven.

When he called her office earlier, and spoke with her, he could tell she wasn't happy to hear from him again, but yet seemed very anxious to know what he wanted to see her about. Paul said it was something that developed since they met a few days ago, something personal, and it needed to be discussed in person.

Paul was wearing his best battle dress uniform when he walked into Kira's office right on the dot at eleven a.m. He was wearing a deep blue, tailor made, three button suit, with a crisp, white designer shirt and red silk tie. Kira, also ready for battle, had on a designer cut, form fitting, black two button blazer and pencil skirt, with a low cut white silk blouse.

Kira tried to be cordial, but when they shook hands it wasn't friendly, more like two boxers before the start of a fight.

"Take a seat," Kira said, heading for the back of her desk, there was no offer of coffee or other refreshment.

Paul sat down in one of the leather wing backed chairs that he thought weren't a nice or as comfortable as the ones in his office.

"I appreciate you seeing me privately, Kira," Paul began feeling a bit defensive when he wanted to be more on the offensive.

Kira folded her hands into a steeple up in front of herself. She was clearly annoyed.

"I have to ask you Paul," she said directly. "Are you somehow recording this conversation?"

"What?" he said off guard. "No, I'm not, are you?"

Kira smiled. "This is my office and you're my guest by invitation. I don't have to prove anything to you."

Paul felt a tinge of anger, at not only her remark but at the tone of her voice.

"Open your shirt!" she ordered. "Let me see!"

Paul stood up and took of his jacket, loosened his tie and unbuttoned his shirt.

"See, no wires or recording devices," he said.

"What about that pen in your pocket?" She asked.

"Just a pen," he said. "I'm not recording us, and frankly, I don't want our conversation recorded."

"Come over here," Kira said. "Come around here so I can check for myself."

Paul said nothing, but did as she requested. He walked around to her side of the desk and stood there waiting for her next move.

Kira smiled up at him, and slowly ran her hand over his bare chest and around to his back.

"You stay in pretty good shape," she said. "...for an old guy."

Paul laughed. "Yeah, for an old guy. I know you like them a lot younger."

"Oh?" Kira said, squeezing his ass. "And where did you hear that?"

"Are you having fun?" He asked, as her hand continued to slide over his body. "Let me know when you're done."

Kira laughed again. She liked playing with him and it was her way of taking control.

Well, you seem to be telling the truth," she finally said, after her hand started down the front of his pants. "Perhaps you should take your pants off too."

Paul grabbed her hand before she could grab him.

"I'll take my pants off," he challenged. "If you take your skirt off."

Kira removed her hand from his pants and slid back in her chair, lifted her left foot up on the waste paper basket, and spread her legs just enough to make him look down.

"So that's how this can go?" She asked coyly. "You show me yours and I show you mine."

Paul stared between Kira's legs and could just see a hint of red silk. He wanted to kneel down in front of her but he knew once he crossed that line with Kira there was no going back.

"If you're satisfied I'm not wearing a wire," he said. "I'd like to dress and get back to the real reason why I'm here."

Kira smirked at him, closed her legs and slid the chair back up under the desk.

"Go ahead," she said. "Dress up, sit down and let's put our cards on the table."

Paul buttoned his shirt, tightened his tie and sat back down.

"Henry's mother want those tapes and she wants the manuscripts Henry wrote!" Paul said, flatly.

Kira's hands went back into the steeple.

"So that's what this is all about?" Kira asked. "Henry's demented mother and her crazy ideas about some non-existent manuscripts. I told her when I was kind enough to meet with her after Henry's passing, that there were no manuscripts, probably just some fantasy idea a son told his dying mother who was confined in a nursing home."

"I know you have those manuscripts Kira, and I know you threatened her with exposing Henry on video performing deviant sex acts. Which I'm also sure you set up for him."

"Once and for all, there are no manuscripts and there are no sex tapes."

"So this is all some big mistake?" Paul asked. "Some made up story Henry concocted to make his mother happy. Is that your answer?"

Kira nodded.

"You know what I think Kira," Paul stated. "I think Henry's drowning in the Keys, his scuba diving with you, I don't think that was an accident at all."

"Oh?" Kira said, her jaw tightened along with her steeple shaped hands. "So now you're accusing me of having something to do with Henry's accident?"

"I'm not accusing anyone," Paul said. "I'm just wondering why someone, who for years had only a professional relationship with their top money making author, a relationship that never included anything of a personal nature, would give him diving lessons, and invite that same man, who she could never tolerate in her presence for more than a few minutes, invite him to an intimate dinner at her house, just the two of them. How does that happen?"

"It's really very simple," Kira said, relaxing her jaw and hands. The last thing she wanted to do, which she really wanted to do, was jump over the desk, and begin to pound Dickinson's handsome face into something unrecognizable. To grab the nearest, weighted object, and feel his delicate facial bones crush under the enormity of her first blow. She wanted him to fall out of the chair onto the floor, semi-conscious, but still be able to see, and still feel her spiked, high heel, as it hammered away until she was no longer able to raise her hand. "Henry Harris was sexually blackmailing me. His literary contract was due for renewal, which we did every three years, but this time he threatened to leave and go somewhere else unless I slept with him."

"That's an even better motive for Henry not to come back from the Keys," Paul pointed out.

Kira's features softened and she suddenly had an emotional collapse. She was completely and totally pissed off at this James Bond wannabe sitting across from her, but she was beginning to enjoy the game he was trying to play with her. Her! Kira Lake! Him! Paul Dickinson! Oh Please!

"It's true, whether you believe me or not," Kira said, as real tears flowed from her eyes. "I didn't want to lose Henry, I admit that, but I had known him for so many years, I never saw him as a romantic interest."

Paul was taken aback by Kira's breakdown. If she was faking it, just acting, she was doing a great job, and if he hadn't seen her in action, in New York, he might have fallen for it.

"...And the winner is..." he said, clapping his hands. "I have to say you had me there for a split second, but then I remembered the look on your face when you had that plastic bag over that girl's face..."

CHAPTER SIXTY-SIX

Kira stopped crying as fast as she had started, and in a reactive flash, stood up and screamed.

"How dare you invade my privacy? Get out! Now!"

Paul sat still and the door to Kira's office burst open.

"Are you okay?" Kira's assistant asked, to her visibly shaken boss.

"She's good," Paul replied for Kira. "She's practicing her lines for a play, and we're having a bit of creative differences, but we're good, aren't we Kira?"

Kira was in a rage, which wasn't something new for her or her assistant.

"I have more to say with my part, and I'm sure Kira wants to hear it," Paul said. "Don't you Kira?"

Kira's rage was well beyond tantrum level but she did want to know everything Paul had to say.

She has been exposed to him in every imaginable way. He had seen her naked, sexually aroused, but most of all, he had seen her, the real Kira Lake. He had seen her as only a select few people have, and they were submissive to her. They wanted and needed what she gave them, allowed them, her control.

"I'm fine, thank you," she said, sitting back down, and forcing a smile. "I was just over reacting, but really, I'm fine."

Her assistant left the office.

"Obviously, you broke the law over the weekend, and somehow were able to see what happened during a consensual sex game. I'm not sure how you did it, but I would say either you gained entry to my apartment or paid one of the low life workers that have been milking the finishing work on our brownstone. In either case, I hope you enjoyed yourself and I'm sure you have made a recording of it as well."

Paul nodded and spread his hands out in front of himself taking full credit.

"Yes, I did see you playing, what you call a consensual sex game, which on video, to someone of a more conservative lifestyle, would look like attempted murder."

Kira scoffed. "Radhika would beg to differ Paul and I mean she would really beg to differ."

Paul was still amazed at how fast Kira could change her personality, and so completely. It was like there were triplets of her, each with separate degrees of mental illness. Let's see, there was almost sane, functionally insane, and most concerning, there was psychopathic, sexually sadistic, and straight jacket certifiably, shit house rat crazy.

"What do you really want Paul?" She asked. "Just tell me, and perhaps we can come to some agreement."

"He wanted to say, I want to see you getting a lethal injection, no wait, I want to see to strapped into the electric chair for what you did to Henry Harris but that wasn't going to happen.

"I want those sex tapes, and more importantly, I want those non-existent manuscripts that really exist. I want them back so Henry's mother can see them published before she dies. That's what I want."

Kira stiffened at the mention of Henry's mother, and thought how she should have pushed that broken rib right into her lung when she had the chance, and none of this would be happening. It would have been so easy, and even enjoyable, to see to see that interfering old bat in the throes of such well-deserved pain.

"And what do I get in return Paul?" She asked, politely as she was imagining Henry's mother gasping for her last breath.

"You get a free pass on Henry's death and as a bonus, I give you the tapes from your New York performance."

"Not much of a deal for me," Kira said. "I lose a lot more than I really gain."

"Not really Kira," Paul said. "I think the tapes of you in action really speaks volumes, and the circumstances of Henry's death if leaked in vicious rumors might have some people think there's more to Henry Harris's untimely death than meets the eye. I think in the final analysis it would keep you out of jail."

"Yes, that's all they would be is vicious rumors," she said, arrogantly. "Nothing that would ever lead to any real charges, let alone stand up in a court of law."

"Maybe, maybe not," Paul teased. "There's been other cases where people have drowned suspiciously on vacation trips and even honeymoons. A new husband tried the same trick you pulled on Henry, and when the whole series of events were laid out and looked at, he was ultimately convicted of her murder."

"Oh stop Paul!" Kira leaned back in her chair confidently. "You're scaring me."

Paul stood up. "I think enough has been said for the both of us. Let's take a couple of days and think about all this, and we'll meet again, say, Wednesday or Thursday."

She did not reply and Paul left her office. Once he was gone, Kira began to smash things; things that ironically had just been replaced from her last rampage.

CHAPTER SIXTY-SEVEN

When Andersson and Stefani got together with the rest of the team at one o'clock, they were using one of the smaller conference rooms located on the second floor of the State Office building. They could have used the larger conference room at Raleigh Police Headquarters since Chief Poole was always willing to accommodate the Governor's special investigators, but it wasn't necessary.

Andersson was impressed with all the work that was accomplished in such a short period of time.

Even Shay Abisi had time to thoroughly go over Henry's autopsy report that was faxed to her from the Key West Medical Examiner's office.

"From what I read about Mr. Harris's cause of death, it seemed consistent with a drowning," Shay began. "His lungs were full of water, and there were no other signs of trauma to his body."

"Any way to tell if he had a seizure just prior to the drowning?" Andersson asked.

"No, there isn't," Shay replied. "Except the seizure was witnessed by the woman he was diving with, Kira Lake, and when most people suffer a grand mal seizure, most of them don't recall the event, therefore, a witnessed seizure is usually the only way we know someone had one."

Stefani had come into the office an hour earlier than the scheduled time and had a chance to review the autopsy report as well as the statements obtained from the Coast Guard and the Key West Police.

"According to his medical history, he had no prior history of seizures nor was he ever on any anti- seizure medication," Stefani said, "From I read he was in general good health."

"Yes, that's right," Shay answered. "The autopsy report, as well as his medical history does indicate Mr. Harris was underweight and lacked good physical condition for his age. He did have an anxiety disorder, had depression and was maintained on medications related to those conditions."

"Could he have had a seizure based on the medications he was taking?" Andersson asked. "Maybe he took too much because of the stresses of the trip or he forgot to take it…"

"His toxicology screen came back positive for the medications he was prescribed and at appropriate blood levels. In addition, there were no illegal drugs or any alcohol present in his system."

"So it's possible he had a panic attack, became confused and pulled off his face mask and breathing device?" Stefani asked Shay.

"Sure," she said. "I guess anything is possible when someone is an experienced diver and becomes confused underwater. Even experienced divers have drowned when something goes wrong and they panic."

"Then someone with Mr. Harris could witness his panic attack, and mistake it as a seizure?" Andersson asked.

"Yes, they could, depending on how he was reacting," Shay added. "In fact, he might have had both, even a small focal seizure could lead to someone being disoriented and panic."

"What about the woman who was with him, Kira Lake?" Stefani asked, directing her question to Harper.

Of course Harper had Kira's biography poised in front of her, and it went back to Kira's Grammar School days.

"I'll spare you her early developmental years which seem to have been privileged to say the least; best schools, top of her class though college and law school. She was very athletic, and according to one Lacrosse coach I talked to, she was exceptional on the field, and very aggressive, but wasn't a team player. I asked him if she had any history of violence, and he said she once used her stick on another player who blocked her shot and she broke her nose. After law school, she practiced locally a couple of years, but with a four contempt of court violations for screaming at judge after being warned several times how she was presenting her case. She left Raleigh, and moved to New York City, and developed a literary practice managing successful authors as their agents. Henry Harris, aka, Gina Wells, was her biggest catch and both of them had done extremely well financially. She moved back to Raleigh a few years ago but recently just bought a new apartment in Manhattan."

Sounds like despite being successful, she can have a bit of a temper," Stefani said.

"Or if we want to stretch it, maybe even a personality disorder," Shay said.

Harper continued. "No criminal history of any kind and I checked New York State as well, not even a parking ticket."

"Culpepper," Andersson said. "what do you have?"

"I stayed away from her office staff since we didn't want to tip her that we're looking into her life," he said. "But, I did talk to a couple of people at the diving club and training center she belongs to. No one wanted to say anything negative about her since one kid said she was demanding but a big tipper. He did say she was an expert, Master level, certified diver, and knew her stuff. I got him to tell me who was on duty when she was giving Harris his dive lessons and he steered me to a college kid who will be graduating in a few weeks and not coming back to the job.”

“I bet he was more forth coming than the others since he doesn’t need the job anymore,” Andersson said.

“He was, and in fact, he offered a lot more than I thought he would,” Culpepper said. “For one thing, he just didn’t get the connection between Kira Lake and this Henry Harris. He told me Harris seemed reluctant about the diving and especially about going to the Keys and being out on the ocean. He said a couple of times when he was watching them at a distance; it seemed like Harris was upset and Kira would tease him sexually to distract him and it seemed calm him down.”

“Did he over hear any of their conversations?” Stefani asked.

“No, that was another thing he mentioned,” Culpepper said. “He said, Kira seemed very careful about what she said to Harris when he was around, but always seemed to make a point of how concerned she was about his safety.”

“Isn’t that her job though?” Andersson asked. “As his diving instructor she should be concerned about his safety.”

Culpepper nodded. “It is and at first the kid thought she was just being over protective since Harris seemed geeky and uncoordinated, but after a few days of it, it seemed like an act for the kid’s benefit.

He said, it was hard to explain, but it was like a parent who keeps warning their child about falling off their bicycle until they really fall and you end up telling them, I told you so.”

“What else?” Andersson asked, looking at Reynolds.

"I spoke with Harris's mother and she could barely speak," Reynolds said. "Besides being sick, she seemed reluctant to talk to me, and I thought she acted scared. I tried to press her for more information, especially about her son and Lake, but all she would say was she wasn't happy he was writing those kinds of books. I asked her if she thought Lake had done something to her son on the trip to the Keys, and she went silent. The next I knew the nurse came on the phone and told me Mrs. Harris was too weak to continue but I think she's worth an interview in person."

"We'll go see her tomorrow morning," Andersson said, looking over to Stefani.

"I'll call and set up an appointment for you and Stefani," Reynolds said.

"I'm going to be off Craig," Stefani pointed out. "Maybe you can go with Andersson."

"I'd really like you to be there with me, Roxanne," Andersson said, with a wink. "You know one woman to another. We'll be in and out, and you'll be all done for the week."

"I thought today's meeting was in and out and done for the week?" She asked.

"It is, we're almost done," Andersson said. "and you'll be out."

"So that's a yes?" Reynolds asked Stefani.

"I guess it is," she replied.

"What about Key West?" Andersson said, deferring back to Reynolds.

"I located the captain of the boat they used or should I say private yacht. A guy named Sam, who had nothing but nice things to say about Kira Lake and what a tragedy it was about Henry Harris's unfortunate drowning. He was quick to tell me the Coast Guard found nothing suspicious, and they took a few statements, did the autopsy and closed it out."

"What about any of the yacht crew?" Stefani asked. "They always seem to know what's going on with the guests."

"Most of the crew was getting the boat ready for the next charter when I called," Reynolds said.

"So after I spoke with Captain Sam, I had a conversation with his first officer, a chick named Hanna."

"What did she have to say?" Andersson asked.

"Hanna clearly didn't like Kira and she said she had chartered with her several times. An interesting point I found out when I was talking to Hanna was she was one of the two crew members who went in for Harris after Kira surfaced screaming for help. I thought from talking with the Captain, that the Coast Guard had recovered the body, but Harris was already recovered when they got there."

"That is interesting," Andersson said.

"It is, and Hanna goes on to say how strange it was that Kira would make a deeper dive with a rookie, and they would stay down so long that when she checked Kira's air tank, it was empty."

"What's so strange about that?" Andersson asked. "She could have stayed down to try and help Harris."

"I asked her the same thing", and she said, "she just didn't think Lake and Harris were getting along as well as she tried to portray and in fact, she thought Harris wanted something sexual and Lake didn't. Hanna also said she caught Harris standing at Lake's cabin door in the middle of the night like he was planning a visit, but from what they both could hear going on inside, she was busy."

Stefani and Abisi looked at each other and said at the same time.

"Captain Sam!"

Reynolds nodded with a big grin.

"Yeah, Captain Sam, then I asked her again about Lake's air tank and she said Lake told her Harris had a seizure and pulled off his regulator. She said Lake tried to help him but he pushed her away and she went for help. Even with Lake staying with Harris and trying to help him, she thought Lake would have had more air left in her tank."

"She have any conclusions to why she didn't?" Andersson asked.

"Not really conclusions, but her theory was maybe Lake took her time getting back to the surface and timed it just right," Reynolds said.

"Adding to the drama of the situation," Stefani said.

Reynolds nodded.

"Did she mention any of these things to the Coast Guard or Keys Police?" Andersson asked.

"The crew, including Hanna were only interviewed by the Coast Guard, and the Keys Police Interviewed just Lake and Captain Sam, but Lake was the only one the police took an official report. Hanna didn't mention anything to the Coast Guard about Lakes air tank."

"We need something more than all this, especially since we don't have a crime scene, body, or motive," Stefani said.

"Not to mention jurisdiction," Andersson pointed out. "This happened in the state of Florida and they signed off on it as accidental drowning."

"Even if Kira Lake confessed to killing Harris," Reynolds said. "Without any physical evidence, we'd be hard pressed for a conviction."

"And you know if she did anything wrong, she doesn't seem the type to confess to it," Stefani said.

"But, if Harris's mother tells us what's really going on, we might have something to at least get a search warrant for..."

"What about Dickinson?" Reynolds asked. "You said Townsend got him involved too. You think, we could approach him on this Lake, and see if he'll give us anything?"

"You can try him, Craig, if you want, but it's got to be off the record since we got a conflict of interest on the Burk thing," Andersson replied. "But I don't Paul being cooperative anyway, especially since our visit to him about Billy didn't go well."

"I think you're right, but I'll give him a try anyway," Reynolds said. "He might just throw me a bone for old time sake."

"Anything else?" Andersson asked looking around the table. "Okay, I appreciate what everyone did in such a short time. Let's meet again same time tomorrow, right here, but you can call me anytime if something breaks. We'll give this a couple of more days and then we're done."

CHAPTER SIXTY-EIGHT

Monday evening Paul picked up Pi after she was finished with work, but he wasn't in a good mood.

Craig Reynolds had called him twice, and the first time he let the call go to voice mail, but when Craig called again, he picked up. Craig tried to be nice but Paul could hear that catch in his voice. It wasn't like it was when he visited Reynolds at the station house; this call was different and both of them could feel the tension.

Reynolds tried to make small talk, but Paul was cool, and after a couple of minutes, Paul asked him straight out what he wanted. When Reynolds mentioned that Andersson and Stefani were asked to look into the Henry Harris death, Paul was furious, but he didn't let Reynolds know. He told Reynolds he was looking into Harris's background as a personal favor to Townsend, and it had nothing to do with Harris's death.

Reynolds asked Paul if he had spoken to Kira Lake, and if he did, did he think she was hiding something. Paul told Reynolds he spoke to Lake briefly, but just from the perspective of Harris's literary background, and that Lake was cooperative.

The phone call was maddening for Paul and it seemed like his world was closing in on him. He wanted to stop everything that was going on his life, and just forget about Billy and Willy Burk. He also wanted to forget about Kira Lake, but he couldn't.

"What's wrong Paul?" Pi asked, as they walked into his apartment. "You say nothing in the car. You mad at Pi?"

Paul went into the kitchen and threw his keys on the counter top with Pi following close behind.

"Paul?" she said. "You okay?"

"What?" he said, clearly distracted. "I'm not mad at you. I have that case on my mind."

"The New York one?" she said. "The lady with the bag, I remember."

"Yes, the New York one and the lady with the bag," he said. "And I wish I never got involved."

"Tell Pi what is wrong," she said, with a hug. "I can listen and help."

Paul smiled, hugging her back. He wanted to tell her everything that had happened from the time he left her at Hot Rod, to watching Billy Burk blow up to framing his brother Willy for the murder, up until meeting Kira Lake. He wanted to tell Pie all of it, from start to finish, but he couldn't; no one could ever know what really happened. He loved Pi, and he knew he could trust her, but he also knew the moment she knew he had killed Billy Burk, things would change. Maybe not at first, but later; that's how it was with secrets. They were better off staying secret.

"I'm worried she might hurt someone playing those crazy sex games," he said, lying.

"What can you do?" Pi said, moving to the kitchen cabinet. "You want tea Paul?"

"Yes, okay," he said, and he watched as Pi made some tea for them. "I only used to drink coffee and tea when I was sick before I met you Pi."

Pi smiled. "Tea is good, helps calm down."

"Yes, it does."

"You think police should know?" Pi asked.

"There's nothing they can do Pi," he said. "but do you think someone should stop someone if they think they might hurt someone?"

Pi took out two cups out and placed them on the counter.

"How you stop her from hurting someone?" she asked. "You say hurt her?"

"Maybe, but what if she had already killed someone, and there was no way to prove she had done it?" Paul asked. "What should someone do?"

"The lady in New York kill someone?" Pi asked. "How you know?"

"Let's just say she did," he replied. "Just pretend she did. Should she be punished?"

"By arrest and court, no?" Pi said.

Paul shook his head. "What if there was no arrest or way she could go to court?"

Pi shrugged. "I do not know how you mean."

"Should someone be punished for a crime they committed by someone other than the court, if the court cannot punish them?" he asked, knowing he was confusing Pi but wanting to hear her agree with him.

Pi thought for a moment as she finished pouring the tea.

"Once older girl hit me at school," Pi said. "She slap my face hard, and my sister go back to her and slap her face. You mean like that?"

Paul sipped the hot tea. "Yes, something like that," he said. "Your sister hitting her for you but also protecting you from her doing it again or worse."

Pi pondered his statement. "What then her older sister hit my sister?"

"I know Pi," he said, defeated. "It never stops and it can go on and on…"

Pi tasted her tea and smiled at Paul's sad face.

"War like that Paul," she said. "No different when girl slap me and my sister slap her."

"I know Pi, but sometimes there's nothing you can do to stop someone, but to slap them back."

CHAPTER SIXTY-NINE

Andersson and Stefani arrived at the nursing home where Henry's mother resided, and there had been a change in Mrs. Harris's heath status, a significant change for the worse.

"She developed a blood clot and had a massive stroke over night," the charge nurse said, matter of fact, as she led the way to Mrs. Harris's room.

"How come she's not been transferred to a hospital?" Andersson asked, following the nurse down the corridor.

"Her wishes," the nurse replied, stepping up the pace into more of a march. "She's made it clear both verbally and in writing, of course, she doesn't want any extraordinary care done to her in the event of something catastrophic."

"Can she speak or understand?" Stefani asked.

The nurse, who was in her fifties and heavy set, stopped, turning to them.

"She's in a coma," she said. "She's unresponsive, but breathing on her own. There's nothing we can do but make her comfortable."

"We knew she was ill when we called yesterday," Andersson stated. "The other nurse we spoke with thought despite Mrs. Harris's weakness, we should be able to see her for a few minutes."

"Yes, I know, and Mrs. Harris agreed to see you, but things can change on a dime, especially when someone is elderly and in poor health," the nurse said, picking up the pace again.

"We're sorry to hear that she had a stroke," Andersson said. "We wanted to ask her some questions about her son's death."

The nurse walked past a couple of rooms and stopped.

"Here's her room," she announced, walking in. "As you can see she's unaware of her surroundings."

Andersson and Stefani followed the nurse into the room and looked at Mrs. Harris. She looked like she was sleeping, but her breathing wasn't normal, it was labored and she made gurgling noises when she exhaled.

"We're suctioning her to keep her airway open, but beyond that we're limited in what we're allowed to do," the nurse said, walking up to the bedside and picking up a framed picture that was sitting on the nightstand. "This is a favorite picture of Mrs. Harris and her son, Henry. As you can see, she was a lot younger and Henry was around twelve."

Andersson walked over to her and she handed him the picture.

"You know he was a successful writer?" The nurse asked. "Made a lot of money writing sexy books so I'm told. Did you know that?"

"Yes, we knew he was a writer," Stefani replied, looking at the picture. "They seemed happy."

"Oh my yes!" The nurse said, taking the picture and replacing it back on the nightstand. "She loved Henry like no mother could love a son. All she talked about was her Henry and how good of a son he was to her."

"Did she ever say anything about his literary agent Kira Lake?" Andersson asked.

"Well, I'm not one to pass gossip on to the next person," she began. "But Mrs. Harris did not like Miss Lake at all, and she talked about her all the time to us. She hated how Miss Lake treated her son, even though he was making her a lot of money. She went on and on about her, until the day of Henry's memorial service."

"Then what happened?" Stefani asked.

"Don't know," the nurse said. "Mrs. Harris came back from the service, and said she never wanted to see Miss Lake again, and she didn't want to talk about it."

"Was she upset with Miss Lake about something in particular?" Stefani asked. "Maybe Mrs. Harris confided in someone she was very close to."

The nurse moved toward the door.

"She was very close to me, but no, she didn't tell anyone what happened at the service, but we all knew something definitely happened."

"You think it might have been over money?" Andersson asked. "Or something that might have involved his writing?"

"Maybe," the nurse replied, walking out of the room, assuming Andersson and Stefani were done.

"But Mrs. Harris was not only upset about what had happened, but she also seemed afraid."

"In what way?' Andersson said. "You think she was afraid of being without her son?"

"No," the nurse said, marching back down the corridor the way they had come. "She was very proud of Henry, and although she would miss him dearly, she was very happy for the time they had together. No, she was afraid for herself, for her life, like she had been threatened."

"By Miss Lake?" Stefani said.

"Yes, by Miss Lake," the nurse replied.

CHAPTER SEVENTY

K ira's alarm buzzed at six, and she must have turned it off without even knowing it, since it was seven-thirty when she finally woke up, and she was still groggy from the sleeping pill. It was one of the worse nights of her life! Nothing went right, and twice she wanted to shred the manuscripts, but she simply couldn't do it. She even turned on her industrial strength shredder, a massive machine that could turn cardboard into dust, and she was all ready to feed its hungry teeth, but stopped.

She wasn't ready to give up on something she had worked so hard to obtain. Why should she allow someone like Paul Dickinson interfere in her finest achievement. She deserved to have these manuscripts published under her name and there was no way anyone could prove Henry had written them.

She had transferred the documents from his computer to hers, totally erased all the remaining data, removed the hard drive, and recycled his outdated unit. There was nothing left to ever indicate Henry Harris had written these manuscripts, nothing but that pain the ass mother; a very loose end that need-ed to be tied off.

It was after ten when Kira arrived at her office. She had called she would be late, but she wasn't happy when she saw who was waiting for her when she opened the front door.

"These two people are from the State Police and have been waiting for you," her assistant said.

Kira looked at the two tall people who were admiring the one wall of her office that was lined with photographs of Kira with various celebrities. Some were famous, and easily recognized, others not so much, and even one with Governor Forbes. That one Andersson was sure the Governor would never remember having taken thousands of photos with his many campaigns. To note, there were none of Kira with Henry Harris.

"They just showed up about twenty minutes ago," the assistant continued. "I told them you would be late and best to make an appointment."

Kira ignored her assistant's attempt to apologize and smooth over this unwelcomed intrusion.

"Good morning," Kira said, even more cheerful than her as-sistant's greeting. "How can I help you?"

Andersson and Stefani made the introductions and showed Kira their identifications. If Kira was surprised by these two State Police Investigators showing up at her office, or if she was anxious, upset, or feeling threatened, she sure wasn't showing it.

"Let's go into my office," she said abruptly, walking to her office, and avoiding any conversation about the wall they were looking at.

Andersson and Stefani followed her into her office, and after they all had sat down, Kira offered them some coffee, but they declined.

"Thank you for seeing us," Andersson began. "We're looking into the Henry Harris death and touching base with anyone who might have known him. You know, family, friends, people who he worked with in his professional life."

"I see," Kira said, without any sign of being uncomfortable. "I guess I'm confused why you would be looking into his death at all, since he drowned accidently in the state of Florida, which I'm sure you already know."

"Yes, we do," Stefani said. "We have copies of all the formal reports and documents regarding his death. We just had some questions for you on a personal issue, since you were Mr. Harris's attorney, agent, and I'm sure closest of friends."

Kira stared at Stefani, and had a barrage of intrusive thoughts. She had recognized her the moment she saw her, and recalled the line of duty shooting she was involved in, her Medal of Valor, and all of it. Now, though, she wondered after seeing this beautiful woman in person, what was she like sexually.

Kira had seen her on television, in news reports, and photographs of her in the newspaper, but seeing Roxanne Stefani in the flesh was something different all together.

"Miss Lake?" Andersson said, jarring Kira back into reality. "You were confused why we were looking into Henry Harris's death…"

"Yes," she replied, as she tried desperately to dismiss the flood of sadistic thoughts coursing through her brain. "It was just off putting to hear Henry's name, and I had a flash back to his drowning."

"Are you all right?" Stefani asked.

"Yes, I'm fine," Kira said, with a smile.

"I think I misspoke," Andersson said, "To be blunt, we had a request to look into allegations that you possess manuscripts that Henry Harris wrote, and have refused to give them back to his estate."

"Did Henry's mother tell you that?" Kira asked. "Because if she did, she's confused. Henry always had a dream to write books other than the erotica that he wrote under the name, Gina Wells. He would tell me that many times and he would tell his mother even more times, since she never approved of what he wrote."

"So, the manuscripts don't exist?" Stefani said. "They're just fantasies that Henry made up to make his mother feel better?"

"Exactly," Kira said. "I'm sure if you talk with Henry's mother a couple of more times, you'll get a couple of different versions of what Henry was supposed to have written. What did she say the manuscripts were about?"

"She didn't," Andersson had to admit. "She lapsed into a coma overnight, and we were unable to interview her. It's why we had to come see you. Had she denied or was confused about the manuscripts, then we could have dismissed the whole thing as a mistake."

"Oh my god!" Kira said. "I knew Mrs. Harris was ill but a coma, how awful."

"Yes, it is," Stefani said. "We don't like to act on hearsay and rumor, but we thought with you being Mr. Harris's attorney, and handling his estate, you would welcome our looking into it."

"Of course," Kira said. "I'll have to contact the nursing home, and get an update on her condition, since, in the event of her death, other provisions of Henry's estate will go into effect."

"We understand," Andersson said," I wonder if I could ask you a personal question Miss Lake?"

"Sure," Kira replied, openly. "Go ahead."

"Why did you convince Mr. Harris to learn how to scuba dive when from what we knew about him he wasn't, how would you say athletic."

Kira smiled, of course, I have the ready answer. "Henry need-ed to build some confidence in himself, from the physical stand-point, not from the professional. He wanted to find someone to have a relationship with and frankly, he didn't have clue how to begin. He never really dated and I'm sure you heard that Henry was infatuated with me, but I had made it clear many times, I wasn't interested in having a physical relationship with him."

"I can understand not having a relationship with someone for several reasons," Stefani said. "But why teach him scuba diving and take him on a trip to the Keys just the two of you?"

"Exposure!" Kira replied. "I wanted Henry to not only learn a sport that almost anyone can do, at any age, but a sport he could take with himself all over the world. I thought he would be able to meet all kinds of people who possessed the love for diving and it could be a common bond which might lead to more."

Makes sense to me," Andersson said. "I guess no one could have foreseen what was going to happen to him. It was just something tragic; the wrong place at the wrong time."

Kira nodded at Andersson. "Yes, you're so right," She said. "It was just a tragic accident. Had it not happened, I think, despite some early misgivings, Henry would have grown to love diving."

Andersson marveled at how slick Kira was with her responses. Not only was she ready with the correct answers, but she was anticipating some possible follow up questions she thought they might ask. She knew this wasn't about manuscripts, but more about Henry's death and Andersson knew she knew it. Kira volunteered more information, but was careful not to sound overly helpful.

"Seeing Henry have that seizure or panic attack, was very disturbing," Kira said.

"I'm sure it was," Stefani said. "and there was nothing you could have done."

"No," Kira said, with tears welling up. "I tried to help him, but he seemed so confused the poor dear."

Andersson and Stefani waited while Kira blotted her eyes with a tissue and wiped at her nose.

"I'm sorry, Miss Lake," Stefani said, after a few seconds. "But, I have only one more question, then if Lieutenant Andersson doesn't have anything else, I believe we would be done."

Kira sniffled. "What's that?"

"Forgive me and I know this may sound crude," Stefani began. "But did Mr. Harris somehow think he was going to have sex with you on the trip to the Keys?"

Kira laughed. "Oh god yes!" She replied. "Henry's always thinks he's going to have sex with me. That was Henry and his wild imagination. It's precisely what I was trying to explain about those manuscripts."

"Yes, the non-existent manuscripts, and now Henry's non-existent love life," Stefani said, wryly. "and that one night when he went to your cabin in the middle of the night, like he was expecting to meet you, but apparently someone was already fucking you."

Kira mouth twisted, but finally made its way into a smile at Stefani's remark to irritate her.

"Now that was crude, but I'm sure necessary," Kira said, lightly. "Yes, I was with someone, Captain Sam, and apparently, Henry was listening at my door."

Andersson hoped Kira would have been offended by Stefani's well placed remark, and have lied, but she hadn't bitten.

"We apologize, Miss Lake," Andersson said, standing. "I'm sure as an attorney, you can understand we have to be thorough, and sometimes we have to ask tough questions."

Kira stood and moved our from behind her desk.

"Of course," she said, avoiding eye contact with Stefani. "Ms. Stefani was just doing her job."

"Yes, she was," he said. "I hope we can communicate with you again if necessary."

"Absolutely," Kira said, walking them out of her office.

After Andersson and Stefani had left, Kira walked back into her office, her staff thought they might hear her breaking things, but it didn't happen. Kira had been concerned when she first saw Andersson and Stefani when she arrived, but now, after hearing Henry's mother was in a coma, the news couldn't have been better, unfortunately, the good news was going to be short lived.

CHAPTER SEVENTY-ONE

Steward Dobson had been a Correctional Officer at the Wake County lockup for over fifteen years, and he had his regulars. The repeat offenders, those who committed crimes for a living; the ones who were in and out of jail as a lifestyle. He knew them all over the years, and he knew Willy Burk.

Stewie, as his fellow officers called him, was a fair and God fearing man. He prided himself on treating prisoners the way they ought to be treated, according to the crimes for which they had been convicted. Child molesters, and sex offenders were at the bottom of the pile, and were dealt with by fellow inmates. He usually had nothing to do with them unless they crossed his path by some chance happening. Murderers and people of violent crimes faired only slightly better within the system, depending on the nature of those violent acts, and who they were perpetrated against.

In general, Stewie felt if a prisoner followed the rules and didn't hassle anyone, especially the COs, then that was okay with him. But, make trouble, break the rules, and god forbid, harm a CO, and he was going to be your worst enemy.

"I could tolerate your small time drug dealing ways, Willy," Stewie said, as he stood with Willy, who was shackled while two other officers searched his cell for contraband. Willy had a visitor, who came with his lawyer, and Stewie took no chances that somehow, someway, someone slipped Willy something. "But killing your own brother for insurance money, and burning him like that, well, that's like a blasphemy. That's Cain and Able stuff, Willy, its unnatural, and straight out against the laws of the Bible, and you're going to hell as sure as shit."

"I didn't kill my brother," Willy said, wearily. "I didn't do it, I didn't kill Billy."

"You can say that all you want Willy," Stewie said, shaking his head. "But I heard they got a real air tight, and I mean snug as a bug in a rug tight, no wiggle room case against you, and you can dig up Clarence Darrow and throw in Johnnie Cochran while you're at it, and you're still going up to the State Prison death row."

"I didn't do it," Willy protested, while he watched the two other Correctional Officers look in every nook and cranny of the tiny cell. "I loved Billy and I would have done anything for him."

"You better try and work a deal with the DA Willy," Stewie advised. "I'm telling you the gospel truth on that one. You go and get yourself convicted on a murder one, and you're headed for the death penalty."

"I'm not going to get convicted of murder one, since I didn't kill Billy," Willy said, trying to bring his cuffed hands up but stopping short by the chain belted to his waist.

"My brother in law works up at State, and he knows people who work the death row, and it's no picnic, no sir, Willy boy. You're not sippin corn whiskey on the front porch and eatin no Carolina barbeque. It's lock down twenty three hours a day by your lonesome and it's a long ass grind for the con and longer one for the CO."

"I'm not going to death row," Willy said, as the other two officers left his cell without finding any contraband.

Stewie unshackled Willy, and secured him back in his cell, but gave him a last bit of advice before closing the door.

"You better tell that fancy lawyer of yours to call the DA, and make a deal, before it's too late.

If not Willy, you better get used to being alone, and you best learn how to pray to the Almighty."

CHAPTER SEVENTY-TWO

Kira never thought that hearing someone suffered a massive stroke could make her so happy, but it did. In fact, she was very happy when Andersson had told her, but she was elated after she got off the phone with the nursing staff. The news now was that Mrs. Harris was barely breathing, and wasn't expected to live more than a couple of more days. There was no chance she would recover, and Kira could hardly contain her joy when she began to chant.

"Yes! Yes! Yes!"

She was almost ready to leave for lunch, and was planning to go back to a new place she had found with the cutest, young waiters, when her phone rang. It was her private line that bypassed her assistant and it was Captain Sam.

"Hi Sam," Kira said, cheerfully, still riding her joyful high. "What a pleasant surprise to hear from you."

"What the hell is going on Kira?" Sam snapped, like the mouth of a Florida gator. "I've been on the phone all morning, bouncing back and forth between calls from that private investigator Dickinson, to some female North Carolina state cop named Harper."

"What?" Kira said, as her happiness came to a screeching halt. "I don't know who Harper is, but I do know Dickinson. Why are they calling you?"

"That's what I'd like to know," Sam said. "I had to delay my departure, and the charter was royally pissed off about it."

"I'm sorry Sam," Kira said. "What did they want?"

"They both kept asking me about the Harris death," Sam stated as he tried to calm down. "It was like they both were reading from an investigative template of questions."

"What did you tell them?"

"I told them just what I know, and what I thought had happened," Sam said, getting upset again. "I said the Coast Guard took a report, and the Key West Police ruled it an accident."

"I think it's got something to do with Henry's mother," Kira said. "She's been very upset with me over Henry's accident, and feels I'm somehow responsible, but I don't think she is going to be bothering anyone, anymore."

"Why?" Sam asked. "What do you mean?"

"She's had a devastating stroke, and she's not expected to live much longer," Kira said. "I just got off the phone with the nursing home."

"I'm not sure that's going to stop that Dickinson," Sam said, his voice finally below the level of a shout. "That Harper was persistent, but polite, on the other hand, Dickinson kept pushing me with one question after another, like I was a suspect or something. I didn't like that at all, and I told him so too."

"I know just how you feel Sam," Kira said. "He's been to see me twice, and someone needs to clip his wings."

"I hope they're not looking to file a wrongful death suit," Sam said. "I'm just starting to make some real money with the Escape since I've paid off my share of her."

"No worries Sam," Kira assured. "I'm the attorney for the Harris estate, and we're not going to be filing any lawsuits. Henry's death was an accident…no matter what anyone says…"

"I want your business Kira," Sam replied. "You've been a loyal customer, and have sent me other charters; I'm not forgetting it."

"I know you're not Sam," Kira said, thinking of those bonus middle of the night sexual trysts. "I'm going to take care of things on this end and put a stop to Dickinson's so called investigation."

"I appreciate it Kira," Sam said. "He's not a nice man."

"No, he's not Sam," Kira agreed. "Let me send you a nice big retainer, call it a deposit if you will, for my next charter."

"That's not necessary," Sam said, but didn't mean it."

"No, it is, and I'm going to write the check the moment we hang up," she said. "I think twenty-five thousand dollars sounds like I should be able to book a fun weekend on the Escape."

"That's a very generous deposit Kira," Sam said. "Let me know when you want to come down, and of course, that includes all the extras you've been accustomed to while on board the Escape."

"Of course Sam," she said with a giggle, taking his mind of Dickinson. "You know how I just love the special attention."

"I know," he said. "and you know how much I enjoy providing it too."

"Thank you Sam," she said. "and don't take any more calls from Dickinson or the State Police for that matter. Tell them I said to refer all calls regarding Henry Harris to me. From now on I'm your attorney of record."

"You think I should do that Kira?" Sam replied, cautiously. "I don't want to piss anyone off in the law enforcement community, and perhaps stir up the local cops in the process."

"It's not going to come to that Sam," Kira said, supportively. "They're just spinning their wheels."

"Okay Kira," Sam said. "I want to forget all that ever happened with the Harris thing. People who depend on the tourist trade don't like a lot of bad publicity, especially the kind associated with someone dying."

"I know they don't," she said. "Just worry about your charters Sam, and let me take care of things on my end."

"Okay Kira," he said relieved. "I trust your judgement."

"I'll talk to you soon Sam, and let you know when I'm coming down."

Sam wanted to talk longer, but Kira needed to go, and begin her offensive game; she was tired of playing defense.

CHAPTER SEVENTY-THREE

Monday afternoon's wrap up meeting with Andersson and Stefani went on longer than either of them had anticipated, but everyone had a lot to say. When it was over, Stefani hung around to speak with Andersson alone.

"I think when you start to look at all the players in the Harris case, and the chain of events, things begin to raise more questions than answers," Andersson said, pouring himself a fresh cup of coffee.

"Want some?"

Stefani nodded, changing the subject. "I'd love a cup, and that reminds me to ask Hank what time Luis and his family are arriving on Thursday. I want to make sure I'm there to greet them."

Andersson handed her a cup of coffee with some cream in it.

"Oh yeah, don't do anything to offend our coffee supplier."

"I won't," Stefani said, sipping her coffee. "I'm looking forward to meeting Luis and his family, as well as Hank's best man."

"It's going to be a great wedding," Andersson said, tasting his coffee and sitting down. "So the Burk case still on your mind?"

"Yes, it is," she said, "but right now this Kira Lake has pushed Burk into second place."

"Is she a piece of work or what?" Andersson said. "I thought she was going to come over the desk at you when you made that remark about Harris coming to her cabin in the middle of the night."

Stefani laughed. "You mean my crude remark? I know, I thought for sure I had insulted her and she would go off on me."

"Me too."

"She tensed for a split second," Stefani said. "Just in her shoulders, like a big cat does before they're ready to leap."

"I missed that," Andersson said. "She was good I have to give her that."

"She was," Stefani said. "Real smooth."

"So what do you think?" Andersson said, after a minute of quiet coffee drinking.

"I think we got three murder cases," she said. "The Heather Burk case, with Willy as the mastermind, and I use the term loosely, plus his brother Billy, as the accomplice."

"That's one," Andersson said, holding up his index finger, then adding his second finger. "Number two is Paul Dickinson blowing up Billy Burk and framing Willy."

"Right," Stefani said, pressing her thumb down over her little finger, and holding up the rest. "Three, is Kira Lake drowning poor Henry Harris."

"I agree," Andersson said, "she set him up with the diving lessons..."

"...and baited him with sex..." Stefani said.

"Which, I might add, he never got."

"Right, and she lures him down to the Keys where he has his so called accident."

"But why?" Andersson asked.

"For those non-existent manuscripts, that's why."

"But why not just publish them and make a lot more money," Andersson said. "What's the point of just keeping them?"

"She's going to publish them under her own name," Stefani said, spontaneously.

"Bingo!" Andersson said, toasting Stefani with his coffee cup.

"It has to be that!" Stefani said. "Henry's always written erotica and then out of the blue, he writes something completely different."

"And they turn out amazing!"

"Yes, totally!" Stefani said, excitedly. "He shows them to Lake, perhaps even trying to impress and she reads them."

"They're beyond anything she can even imagine him writing," Andersson said, sharing Stefani's excitement. "She sees well beyond the potential of publishing them under Henry Harris, and she wants them for herself."

"Exactly!" Stefani said. "The perfect ending to their professional relationship. Goodbye Henry Harris, hello Kira Lake, literary genius."

"First the money and now the glory," Andersson said.

They were both quiet for another minute, and sat thinking of that they just said, with empty coffee cups.

"Well, we solved those three murders," Stefani said, triumphantly.

"I know," Andersson said. "Too bad we can't prove any of them."

"We sure did stir up the pot though. Maybe we can get a break and something will shake out."

"Maybe," Andersson said. "But I thought you were off this week, remember, you're getting married on Saturday."

"I remember," Stefani said. "But, I'm going to be in and out… like you said."

"That's right…in and out…and then you're done…"

CHAPTER SEVENTY-FOUR

Tuesday morning was no better than Monday was for Kira, although Andersson and Stefani weren't standing in her office waiting room when she arrived, but Paul Dickinson was and he was still in a bad mood.

"I thought we agreed to take a couple of days and talk on Wednesday," Kira said, walking to her office with Dickinson trailing right in behind her.

"I couldn't wait until Wednesday," Paul said, sitting down in the chair, while Kira took up her familiar postion behind her desk. "I was up most of the night."

"You look like shit," she said, not feeling much better on probably as little sleep.

"Forget that," Paul said, then spat out the words at her, like pebbles from a sling shot. "I know you murdered Henry Harris!"

"Oh, so now I murdered Henry," Kira said, ready to attack him with her bare hands, she could see herself clawing and biting his face; ripping and tearing at his miserable flesh.

"Yes, you did!" He said.

"Of course you can prove this," she said. "Or would you rather I confess and turn myself in?"

"That would be easier for all of us if you did confess," Paul replied, in an agitated voice.

"Fine, call your buddies, Andersson and Stefani," Kira said. "Tell them I'm ready for make a full confession, and throw myself on the mercy of the court."

"They're not my buddies," Dickinson shot back. "I did all this on my own and I don't need their help."

"Oh that's right, you're the best of the best, I forgot," she said with mocking praise. "The almost perfect record with solved murder cases, all except that elusive Burk case."

Paul looked surprised and Kira gloated.

"You're not the only one who's been doing some investigating," Kira said. "I've been investigating you too, and I must say it's amazing how much people are willing to say, especially when a stack of Ben Franklins are doing the asking."

"Big fucking deal!" Paul said. "You think you can scare me off with some empty threats?"

"I don't think I can scare you off at all Paul, but I do think you have enough common sense to know when to back off."

"I don't back off!"

"That's fine, but what's going to happen if people get all confused about time and space and where they were the night Billy Burk was killed?"

"So what?" Paul said. "How's that going to affect me and what you did to Henry Harris?"

Kira leaned back in her chair.

"I heard the police only looked at three people; Heather Burk's father, Willy Burk and you."

"They looked at me because everyone knew I was a possible suspect," Paul said. "It's good police work and they should have looked at me, but then they looked back at Willy"

"Maybe they didn't look at you close enough before they went back to Willy or spoke with Ollie."

"Ollie doesn't know shit and they went back to Willy because of the insurance money," Paul retorted, noting her remark about Ollie. "The insurance money, I might add, they got from killing Billy's wife."

"So you say," she said. "and it's funny how we keep coming back to Billy's wife death, and right back to you too." Kira snickered. "That's one case that got away from you in an otherwise perfect record."

"You better start worrying about yourself Kira," Paul said ominously. "We're way past those manuscripts and sex tapes. You're going down for Henry Harris."

Kira laughed. "Think about a deal Paul," she said, licking her lips. "I'll give you what you want and you give me what I want. Who knows? We might even end up becoming close friends. You can be the hero in all this; get the tapes, even those non-existent manuscripts. It will be a shame though that Henry's mother won't be able to see her son's work published."

"What do you mean?" Paul asked. "What's happened to Mrs. Harris?"

Kira's hands went into the steeple and she put her fingertips to her mouth before replying.

"Oh that's right," Kira replied, moving one of her hands to her forehead and making a popping sound.

"She had a big blow out, so I'm told and she's totally unresponsive."

"That's a shame."

"Not really," Kira said. "But there's still time to make Casper Townsend happy as well as the rest of the literary world."

Paul got up and went to the door, he had lost the last round to Kira. He needed Henry's mother and now that leverage was gone.

"I'll let you know about the deal," he said and he left.

CHAPTER SEVENTY-FIVE

Andersson had left his office early, and was driving home when his cell phone buzzed, startling him.

He pulled the phone from his pocket and saw it was Stefani.

"Hang on," he said, "I'm driving, and I have to pull over." "No, I'm not on the highway, I just left the office."

Stefani was excited. "I just got a call from Cassie, the waitress from Hot Rod."

"What's up?" Andersson said, letting the car idle at the curb while the air conditioning ran.

"She said she heard that Ollie was back in town."

"Ollie?" Andersson said, thinking. "You mean the biker Paul had an argument with before leaving Hot Rod?"

"Yes," Stefani said. "Cassie said a friend of hers saw him with a couple of his pals at another bar last night."

Anyone know where he's staying?"

"No, Cassie said all she knows is he's back in town and she expects him to show up at Hot Rod, most likely tomorrow since it's Wednesday."

"Okay," Andersson said. "Tell Cassie to call us the second he shows up and we'll or should I say Reynolds and I will go over and talk with him. We might as well cross that t."

"What do you mean Reynolds and you?" Stefani said. "I'm going with you."

"But you're done for the week," he said. "Remember, I promised."

"Yeah, well forget it," Stefani said. "I want to be there and hear what this guy's got to say. We'll be in and out, and then I'm done."

"I think I've heard that before," Andersson said, with a laugh.

"I know," Stefani said. "Me too."

"Hang on, I'm getting another call," Andersson said, looking at the phone.

"Take the call," Stefani said. "I'll call Cassie."

"Okay, bye." Andersson replied, picking up the call from Mary Gordon. "Hi Mary."

"Hi Nicklaus," she said. "Where are you? Can you talk a minute?"

"Sure," he said, adjusting the vent so the cold air wouldn't blow on him. "I'm pulled over and was talking to Stefani when you called. What's going on?"

"That's what I was going to ask you," she said. "What's going on with Forbes?"

"What do you mean?"

"He's acting differently," she said. "He's excited about something, I can tell, but I don't know what it is, and It's driving me crazy. I know it's not about the campaign; this is something else. Did he mention anything to you?"

"No, the last time I spoke with him, it was over business," Andersson replied.

"Well, something's going on with him, and he's been evasive about Friday night," she said.

"Friday night?" Andersson said. "Oh, I might know Mary. A couple of us are taking Hank Milson out for a drink after the wedding rehearsal dinner, and he said he would like to join us."

"It's not going to be a bachelor party, is it?" Mary asked, her thoughts going to strippers and scandal.

"No, nothing like that," Andersson said, knowing Mary was thinking the worst.

"Just a few guys, his best man, Luis, his coffee friend from Guatemala, and Forbes and I were going to stop by."

"Okay," she said, and seemed satisfied. "That must be it, but he could have mentioned that to me."

"Probably slipped his mind," Andersson said. "I'm sure he's got alot going on."

"Maybe, and yes he does," Mary said, without elaborating. "Thanks Nicklaus, see you at the wedding."

She hung up, and Nicklaus called the Governor on his direct private line, which was only for emergencies, and this was an emergency.

CHAPTER SEVENTY-SIX

Tuesday night Kira was exhausted, but couldn't sleep. She worked all day and felt pretty good, especially after putting Dickinson in his place, but still she was anxious about him. He wasn't someone to trust, even if they did agree and made a deal. A deal my ass, she thought!

She tossed and turned, and wanted to take a sleeping pill, but hated how she felt the last time she took one. Maybe she should call Chris and then she remembered; she hadn't heard from him in days.

That wasn't like Chris, and now she wondered why. She picked up her cell phone and called him.

"Chris? It's me baby," she said. "I know it's late, but mommy can't sleep and she needs to relax."

I'm done Kira!" Chris said, without any warning.

"What are you talking about?" Kira said. "You're done with what?"

"Us, this whole thing!" He replied, like he had been waiting for her to call and had planned what he would say. "It's gone too far, and for me it's well beyond fun anymore. That last scene on Saturday that we played with Radhika, it was way over the edge. You almost killed her!"

"Oh nonsense!" She said, hardly recalling what he was talking about since she had blocked it right after it had happened. "I pushed her a little too far and I misjudged when she would climax, that's all.

You know how this stuff works once you start pushing the limits; it's never enough"

"I understand, Kira," he said, shaking. "But it's like an addiction too, a drug. It's not just a fun high now, you're close to that lethal overdose."

"Chris look," Kira said, trying to be rational. "I'm under a lot of stress here since Henry Harris died and I didn't call you to fight over some silly little sex game."

"It's not silly, Kira," Chris said, trying to control himself and not back down. "I'm done with all that."

"What are you talking about?" She said, beginning to take him seriously. "You love being my submissive."

"I told you," he said. "It's not fun anymore, and I'm really not submissive. It was something I played with you to have threesomes."

"Bullshit Chris!" Kira said, losing the tiny bit of temper she had left. "You're not going to leave me over that one slip up and nothing happened."

"Nothing more happened Kira, because I was there to stop you, and I'm sure you've conveniently forgotten the others. Radhika wasn't the only one."

"What are you talking about?" She said, dumbfounded that this conversation was even taking place.

"The other model I brought you a few months ago," he said. "The one you burned with the hot wax."

"She kept saying, lower, lower...hotter..." Kira said.

"Yes, she did, but then when it was right at the point where she was enjoying it," he said. "You kept going, lowering the hot wax until you were pouring it directly onto her skin."

"She loved it," Kira said. "She was screaming in ecstasy."

"She was screaming in severe pain that was caused by second degree burns," he replied. "You were the only one in ecstasy."

"She healed up fine, and I paid for the time she missed at work, big deal!"

"It was a big deal Kira," Chris challenged her. "She's a model, and she can't wear anything that shows her back since it's covered with thick scars."

"That wasn't my fault, Chris," Kira said. "The wax was hotter than I was used to using."

"That's just an excuse," he said. "You're supposed to know what you're doing, remember, the sub trusts you."

"So you're going to leave me over that?"

"They're other times Kira," Chris said. "How about the make-up girl you picked up, and you talked her into a gangbang."

"Those guys got out of control and wouldn't stop," Kira said.

"She agreed to three and you brought eight."

"She ended up with a massive infection and had to have a hysterectomy," Chris said. "She was twenty three and can't ever have a child."

"Who want's kids anyway?"

"I'm all done with this Kira," Chris said, firmly.

"You can't leave me!" Kira screamed, in her hellish voice. "I'm not done with you!"

"Well, I'm all done with you!" Chris screamed back.

"Then get out of my apartment! Now!" She said.

"I already did," he said. "I left right after you did on Sunday and moved in with Radhika."

"What?" Kira said, smashing her fist down on the bed repeatedly. "You left me and went with that slut?"

"She's not a slut Kira," Chris said. "Radhika is a wonderful woman. She's smart, educated and has done very well in her modeling career. She doesn't need you and neither do I."

"Why you ungrateful bastard!" she said, seething with anger. "You're both a couple of jokes! The two of you are used up play things!"

"Goodbye Kira," Chris said, as she continued to rant. "Get some help before it's too late!"

And he hung up.

"Chris? Chris?" Kira said, although she knew he wasn't there. "Chris, mommy needs you, please, Chris, don't go; don't leave me."

Kira was completely worn out, and too tired to smash anything. Tonight, now, everything was gone, and she only had enough energy left to cry herself to sleep.

CHAPTER SEVENTY-SEVEN

Pi found Paul pacing the floor at three in the morning, and he was talking to himself. He only had a few hours of sleep in the last couple of nights and he was living on coffee.

"Paul, come back to bed," Pi said. "I hold you and make you feel better."

"I have to stop her before she kills someone else," he mumbled over and over to himself.

"Paul, talk to Pi," she said, pacing alongside of him. "Let the lady go, and tell police."

"The police can't help me Pi," he said, stopping. "and I worry about you too, that she might find out about you, or maybe she does already. Maybe I should make the deal Pi..."

"What deal Paul," Pi asked, concerned. "Why worry for me? The lady not hurt Pi."

"I don't know," he said, turning to her. "I feel like leaving, packing some things, and just taking off with you, and never looking back."

"Okay Paul," Pi said, hugging him. "Let's go now."

Paul wanted to leave with Pi but he knew once they got to where they were going, no matter where it was, Kira Lake would be there with him. Paul stood with Pi for the longest time, holding her in his arms, and never wanting to let her go.

"Pi you didn't see that big guy I had the argument with leave after you went back into Hot Rod?

Paul asked, wondering if Ollie had followed him that night he went to Billy's.

I not know," she said. "I go back in but leave out the front. Why are you worried about him too?"

"No, no, I'm not worried about him," Paul said, but he was concerned why Kira mentioned him.

"He not bother me Paul, but I have not seen him since that time," Pi tried to calm Paul's fears.

"I have to make the deal Pi," he finally said. "I have to save myself, save us, before I can save anyone else."

CHAPTER SEVENTY-EIGHT

Paul finally fell asleep wrapped around Pi, and felt better when he woke up late the next morning. He dressed, had something to eat, took Pi to the nail salon, and went into the office.

Kira didn't do as well as Paul, and ended up taking a sleeping pill, which under the stressful circumstances caused her to have vivid nightmares of torture and stabbings. They were brutal scenes of her murdering Chris and Radhika; long, detailed, and almost comical in her memory this Wednesday morning.

Curiously, Kira wasn't upset or feeling any remorse about these murderous thoughts, in fact, they seemed to have given her new energy. She experienced relief, that in her mind, she could work through her feelings of betrayal and hate so easily. It had been therapeutic for her to symbolically kill them in her dreams, and she turned their screams and begging for mercy into happiness.

Paul finally called Kira late in the day and could her the satisfaction in her voice.

"Let's meet tonight," he said. "I want to get this over and behind me."

"Sounds good to me," she said. "You bring your laptop with those tapes you made of me in New York, and I'll bring what you want so we can make the trade."

"Okay," he agreed. "I'll have everything and no copies will exist."

"Same for me."

"Where and what time?" he asked.

Kira thought for a moment. "Let's meet at Hot Rod, since you know the place so well."

"And everyone knows me too," he said.

"That's right," she replied. "I know the place too and I'll feel safe with those people around."

"What time?"

"You pick," she said.

"Eight o'clock?"

"Fine, eight o'clock," she said. "and Paul, no tricks. Let's put this to rest and we both can move on."

"No tricks Kira, and that goes for you too."

"Of course not, no tricks."

They hung up, neither of them trusted the other any more than they did before they made the the the deal, maybe less.

CHAPTER SEVENTY-NINE

Eight o'clock sharp Kira pulled into the overflow parking lot across the street from the back entrance to Hot Rod. The evening was unusually hot and humid; even for North Carolina in early May. People were milling around outside, sitting on their cars, drinking beer, and a few were revving their motorcycle engines. The music was loud, and Kira could hear it the moment she pulled in and parked her car.

She took her time walking from the parking lot to Hot Rod and enjoyed the attention she got from the young men along the way. Some of them made cat calls, eyeing her sexy outfit, and a couple of them offered to buy her a drink.

Once Kira was inside, she was almost sorry she had picked this place to meet Paul, since it was so packed. It took a couple of minutes for her to walk from the back entrance around to the main bar. Paul said he would be sitting at the bar, but when she scanned it, he wasn't there. She looked at her watch and it was six after eight, when she looked up, Paul was coming through the front door, and carrying his laptop.

"You're late," she said, as he walked up to her.

"Sorry, I had to park several blocks away," he said, timidly. "But, I have my laptop, where's your stuff?"

"It's in my car and it's staying there until I see what you have on me."

"No problem," he said, moving over to the corner of the bar where the servers picked up their drinks. It was busy, but it was the only area Paul could stand with Kira.

"Let's see the tape," she said, wedging herself close to him so his back was against the bar. "Then we'll go to my car and make the trade. There was too much to carry in one trip."

"Okay," he said, opening the laptop and turning it on.

Just then Cassie came up to them while picking up a tray of drinks.

"I see you met your friend, Paul," Cassie said, with a grin. "Did she surprise you?"

"Yes, she did," he replied. "Thanks."

Cassie went to leave then stopped.

"Your other friend is here too," she said, jerking her head to the back of the place.

"What?" Paul said, looking at where she had indicated. "Who do you mean?"

"Ollie," she said. "You know the asshole you got into it with that time you were leaving with Pi."

"Oh yeah," he said, spotting Ollie standing with one of his buddies.

Cassie left and Kira spoke while Paul clicked up the files.

"Don't blame her," Kira said, as she watched him moved the cursor. "She thought I was an old friend of yours and I told her I wanted to surprise you here."

Paul nodded, and turned the laptop toward Kira.

"Here you go," he said, as the screen came to life.

Kira watched it for a minute while Paul held the computer in his hands.

"I've seen enough," Kira said. "You must have used high quality cameras Paul, I look pretty good, don't I?"

Paul smiled, closing the laptop.

"You're very photogenic Kira," he said, sarcastically. "Perhaps you missed your calling as a porn star."

"Very funny," she said, sliding her hand into the small cross body purse she was wearing. "Let's go to my car and finish this…"

They both turned to leave and had only walked a few feet when they both froze. Andersson and Stefani were standing side by side with their backs to them, talking to Ollie.

"What's this shit Kira?" Paul accused. "I thought we agreed no tricks and now you double cross me."

"I didn't tell them," she said. "But, maybe you did."

"I didn't call them," he said, trying to remain calm. "and they would only be here talking to Ollie if you told them."

"I didn't tell them about Ollie Paul," she said. "I was using him for leverage on you."

"Well it worked," he said. "We can't stop now or they'll see us…let's just leave."

"Fine with me," she said.

They left the bar area, and started for the back entrance, when Paul noticed Kira's hand was still in her purse.

"What are you carrying?" he whispered.

"A Kimber 9mm, and I know how to use it too," Kira said. "I don't trust you and especially now."

"Nice little weapon," Paul said smoothly, shifting his laptop into his left hand. "Perfect for a small purse or a pocket, weights about a pound doesn't it?"

"Seventeen ounces," she said, tightening her grip around the gun as they wove through the crowd of people. "They have their backs to us, so walk right past them. I know you're carrying a weapon Paul, so don't even think of trying anything stupid or I'll start shooting."

"I'm cool Kira," he said, as they approached Andersson and Stefani, and went right out the door.

Once they left Hot Rod, with Paul in front of Kira, they ran smack into Pi. Pi saw Paul and was just about to say something, when he shook his head slightly, and mouthed the word, no.

"Keep going Paul," Kira said, negotiating the people to keep close to him. "My car is across the street."

"Okay Kira," he said, relieved Pi did not acknowledge them and they were moving away from the rest of the crowd.

Once they were across the street and approaching Kira's car, she removed the gun from her purse.

"Do exactly as I say Paul, and we'll both be survive this."

"I'll do whatever you want Kira," Paul said, walking to the driver's side of the car.

"What are you doing?" She asked, pointing the gun at him.

"I thought you wanted me to drive," he said, decisively. "We're leaving aren't we?"

Kira reacted without thinking. "I'll drive and I want you to take your gun out carefully with your thumb and forefinger pinching the grip."

"Okay," Paul said, moving away from the driver's door.

He reached slowly behind his back and under his linen shirt.

"Easy Paul," Kira said. "Just take it slowly, and set it on top of your laptop, then hold onto the laptop with both hands."

Paul did exactly as she said.

"Now what?" he asked, holding the laptop out in front of him-self with the gun resting on top.

"I want you to walk around to the passenger side and set the laptop and the gun on top of the roof."

Paul did what she told him.

"Now, pick up the gun and cock it, then set it back down on the laptop," she said.

Paul picked up his semi-automatic, racked the slide back, cocking the gun, then he set it back down on the laptop.

"Okay Paul, pick up the laptop with both hands and hold it out as far as you can until I get around to the driver's side of the car. Don't move an inch until I tell you or I'll shoot you."

Inside Hot Rod, Pi, frantic with fear for Paul, had found Cassie, who took her right over to Andersson and Stefani. Once Pi was coherent enough for them to understand what was going on, they were both out of Hot Rod, and scanning the parking lot. Pi was told to stay inside, but she left as soon as they were out the door.

"When I tell you Paul," Kira said, still pointing the gun at him across the roof of the car. "Hold the laptop with your left hand, open the car door with your right one, and get inside as fast as you can. If you hesitate or try to run, I'll shoot you."

"I got it," he said.

Kira unlocked the car with her fob, and put her hand on the door handle.

"Ready?"

"I'm ready," he said, moving his hand to his door handle.

"Now! Open your door and get in! She shouted.

In one fluid movement, Kira and Paul opened their doors and began to slide into their seats, but before Paul was sitting, he dropped the laptop outside the car, and began to roll out. Kira was sitting down in her seat when she saw him roll and fired three shots. The first shot was hurried and missed him, the second shot hit his right shoulder as he rolled over, and the third one hit the edge of the open door jam, ricocheting down and through his back. In the four seconds it took for all this to happen, one other process was also occurring.

The door, the hanger, the safety pin, and the striker handle, oh yeah, and the gas too.

Boom!

CHAPTER EIGHTY

The gun shots and the explosion brought Andersson and Stefani on the run, along with a hundred other people. Kira's car was on fire, and fully involved, while Paul was lying on his back about ten feet away. Since his car door was open when the grenade exploded, not only was he shot twice, but he had been hit with pieces of shrapnel.

Three off duty Raleigh Police Officers who were working security at the Hot Rod, immediately went into action with crowd control and securing the crime scene. When Andersson got to Paul he was barely conscious, but opened his eyes when Andersson kneeled down beside him.

"Paul, its Nicklaus Andersson," he said, quickly trying to assess Paul's injuries. "What happened? Who's in the car?"

"Hey Nicklaus," Paul said, mustering a smile. "Kira's in the car and I've been shot twice."

Andersson saw the blood now seeping from Paul's shoulder and back as well as his mouth.

"It's not good," he said. "I'm bleeding inside, fast, I can feel it…"

"Hang on Pual," Andersson said, trying to roll Paul to apply pressure to his wounds. "There's an ambulance on the way."

"Forget the ambulance," he said, glassy eyed. "Is Pi here?"

Andersson looked up and saw Stefani holding on to Pi's arm.

"She's here," Andersson said.

"Good," Paul said. "I want to see her for a second if I could but first I want to ask you something."

"Sure Paul, what is it?"

"You remember the movie CASINO, with DeNiro and Pesci?"

"What? CASINO?" Andersson said. "Yeah, I think so…"

Paul coughed, and pink, frothy spit bubbled from his mouth. Stefani released Pi's arm, and she kneeled down on the other side of Paul.

"Paul! Paul!" she said, leaning over him. "It's Pi…"

"I'm sorry Pi," Paul said, trying to raise his hand to touch her. "I'm cold Pi, real cold, baby."

"I take care of you Paul, no worry," she said, crying, her pie shaped pendant touching on Paul's chest.

"Okay Pi," he said, knowing he had less than a minute to live. "It's a deal, but let me ask Nicklaus a question first."

"I'm here Paul," Andersson said.

"I can't see you, man, but I can hear you," he said, staring up blankly at Andersson.

"What's your question?" Andersson asked, feeling the heat from the car fire, and now hearing the sirens in the distance.

"What was Pesci's character's name?" Paul whispered.

Andersson thought a second.

"Nicky! His name was Nicky."

Paul smiled. "That's right…Nicky. What a crazy guy…"

"Yeah, he was," Andersson said. "Paul what happened with Kira Lake? Tell me, we can take it as a death bed statement."

"I know what you mean," he replied, barely able to touch Pi's pendant. "Just let me say something to Pi, you know privately, and I'll tell you…"

"Okay," Andersson said, standing up next to Stefani knowing Paul was in the final seconds of his life.

"I'm going to call the team," Stefani whispered to Andersson as she watched Paul say something to Pi. "I think we might have solved two of those three unsolvable cases, and now there's just one left to go."

CHAPTER EIGHTY-ONE

It was a repeat of Billy Burk's murder scene and even the same fire department was there. The team arrived shortly after the fire was out, everyone was there working for several hours, but left in time to get some sleep. Andersson set the meeting for ten o'clock the next morning, it gave Shay Abisi some more time to get the basics done on the two autopsies.

"A couple more of these car bombings and I won't even have to show up," Shay said, to everyone at the conference table. "I'll just change the name on the form and fax it over to you."

"Just like Billy Burk's right?" Andersson asked. "A grenade."

Shay nodded. "Yes, a grenade and the gasoline too, just like Billy. Kira Lake died the same way he did, and Paul Dickinson from the gunshots. The one that went through his back clipped several major vessels and he bled out."

"Can we tell if that grenade matched the one from Billy's car or any of them from the storage unit?"

Stefani asked.

"Not yet," Shay said. "ATF has it and they're working on it."

"How did Paul know where Kira's car was parked and rig the grenade before they met?" Andersson said. "Assuming Paul rigged the grenade and not someone else, since he never admitted to anything before he died."

"I think I know," Harper said. "We found what was left of a GPS device attached to back underside of Lake's car. We also found the GPS tracking program on Paul's laptop."

"He was tracking her car when she pulled in, left Hot Rod, attached the grenade and came back to meet her," Stefani said.

"Yes, that's how we feel he did it," Harper said. "Jefferson and I ran the times ourselves, and it only took about five minutes."

"We're still fuzzy on why Kira shot Paul in the first place," Andersson said. "But knowing now they were on a collision course, she had to kill Paul before he killed her."

"That's probably the best guess," Harper said. "Paul's weapon was cocked when we found it. She must have made him cock it before getting into the car, to give the impression he was going to shoot her, and she had to shoot him in self-defense."

"But Paul was one step ahead of her," Stefani said. "He must have anticipated that she would try something, and one way or another he was going to get her for killing Henry Harris."

Andersson whistled. "Those are some big leaps and bounds to a conclusion, but it all works for me."

"We found those manuscripts at Kira's house, but not anything else of Henry Harris's," Reynolds said. "No other personal items, like a laptop he used to write them."

"She got rid of them when Dickinson showed up in her life," Stefani said. "But hung on to the manuscripts when we told her Henry's mother had the stroke."

"She should have destroyed the manuscripts and just moved on," Culpepper said. "That's what I would have done."

"You wouldn't have taken the manuscripts in the first place," Andersson said. "People like Kira Lake feel they're entitled."

"It got way beyond entitlement last night with Lake," Shay added. "Last night, her personality disorder had a psychotic break." .

Reynolds, not one for the psychological aspects of criminal behavior changed the subject.

"What about Willy Burk?" He asked. "What happens to him now?"

Andersson looked at Stefani before answering.

"We spent some time this morning talking with Michael Carson about Willy," Andersson said. "He's not going to do anything different at this time. If the grenade matches the one used with Billy's bombing, then that could be used by the defense as an alternative theory and other perpetrator."

"What if they don't match?" Culpepper asked.

"He's prepared to continue with the charges against him and his defense attorney can argue it in court," Stefani said.

"Carson can say it's a coincidence that both bombings were done with grenades," Andersson said.

"It does raise some indication that someone else killed Billy, but that single piece of evidence alone, might not raise enough reasonable doubt to acquit Willy"

"But, we still think, collectively, at least as a team," Stefani said. "That Paul Dickinson killed Billy Burk."

"What a mess," Harper said. "It's possible Willy could get the death penalty for a murder he didn't commit, but in a way deserves for another murder he did commit."

"We'll have the results of the grenade analysis by tomorrow," Shay said. "We can see what they find, and if they match, give the results to Willy's attorney."

"I wish Dickinson had given us a deathbed statement that he killed Billy and it would be a done deal," Andersson said.

"He wasn't going to do that," Stefani said. "If he did that, then Willy would have walked on Heather's death too."

"We're going around in circles with this," Andersson said. "We need to wait and let the system do it's thing."

"Maybe not," Stefani said. "Maybe we can get Willy to make a deal."

"Why would he do that?" Andersson asked. "He said he would never say he killed his brother no matter what the consequences."

"Right," Stefani said. "But perhaps he would admit to killing Heather if the deal was sweet enough."

"How sweet are you talking?" Andersson said.

"Drop the charges for Billy's death, take the death penalty right off the table," Stefani said. "If he pleads guilty to Heather's death."

"He's not going to do that for life without parole," Andersson said. "That's like a death sentence to Willy."

"We'll have to offer him something where he can have the chance for parole at some point," Stefani said.

"Carson's never going to agree to that," Andersson said, dismally. "He's got a high profile case and will roll the dice and take his chances with the jury before he makes that deal."

"Maybe not," Stefani said. "Arrange a meeting with Willy and me as soon as possible, and let's see what he says."

"I can't arrange a meeting with Willy for you behind Carson's back," Andersson said.

"It doesn't have to be behind his back," Stefani said. "Get him to agree to it, and let's see what Willy decides. Given the opportunity to get out of prison with some of his life left, he might surprise us."

Andersson shook his head. "Carson's not going to agree."

"I bet he would agree if someone got the Governor to get the Attorney General to make Carson agree," Stefani said coyly. "Carson can still come out of this smelling like a rose if we can get Willy to plead to Heather's murder."

"Now, who would be the person to get the Governor to help us?" Andersson said, with an evil smile.

CHAPTER EIGHTY-TWO

Stefani thought the meeting with Willy Burk would never happen. Andersson contacted the Governor, the Governor spoke with the Attorney General, who called Carson. As expected, Carson argued against the meeting, but after much wrangling back and forth between Carson and Willy's defense attorney, the meeting was set.

Only one problem for Stefani, the meeting was going to take place Friday afternoon at four o'clock, two hours before her wedding rehearsal. Still, she was there at the County Jail at four o'clock sitting across from Willy Burk.

"Thank you for meeting with me," Stefani began, just the two of them in an otherwise very stark, small room.

"I didn't kill Billy and I'm not going to work a deal," Willy said, his wrists handcuffed, and his ankles chained to the floor.

"I'm not here about a deal for Billy's death," Stefani said. "I'm here about a deal for Heather's death."

"Heather?" Willy said, with a grin. "I haven't been charged with her death."

"Let's cut the shit Willy," Stefani said. "And wipe that grin off your face, or I'll wipe it off for you."

Willy was going to say something, but he knew Stefani meant what she said, and he stopped grinning.

Here's the deal," Stefani began. "You admit to killing Heather with your brother Billy, and you get fifteen years to twenty. You have to serve the minimum of fifteen years before you come up for a chance at parole. If you don't get paroled, you serve the other five and you're done."

"I do fifteen for Heather's death," he said. "And what about the charges for Billy?"

"They're dropped," Stefani said. "It's a gift Willy, fifteen years, is like serving a sentence for manslaughter."

"Maybe I should still take my chances on Billy's and get an acquittal," he countered.

"This isn't a negotiation," Stefani said, leaning over the table. "You take this deal or you take a trip to death row. You and your lawyer may think you're going to beat it, but you're going down for Billy's death. Carson's going ahead with the trial"

"Maybe," he said cockily. "We might get a break on the grenade."

"The grenade used in this most recent car bombing did not match any of the other ones, not the one used on your brother or the ones found in your storage unit."

"Those were planted there by Dickinson," Willy said, sharply.

"So you say Willy," Stefani said. "You got any proof of that?"

"I didn't kill Billy."

"Yes, I know, but you did kill Heather and her unborn child," Stefani said, staring him in the eyes.

"And you're going to pay for one of these deaths. It's either Billy's or Heather's; take your pick."

"I don't want to go to jail for fifteen days let alone fifteen years," Willy said. "I hate jail."

Stefani stood up.

"I guess its death row..." She turned to leave.

"Wait!" Willy said, yanking on his handcuffs. "I'll take the fifteen for Heather's death."

Stefani turned around.

"You'll have to admit to killing Heather and say what you and Billy did to her in open court."

Willy nodded.

"We'll set it all up with the DA and your lawyer," she said. "You should be in court next week."

Stefani glanced at her watch and exhaled; she would be on time for her wedding rehearsal after all.

CHAPTER EIGHTY-THREE

The wedding rehearsal, and the dinner afterward all went well. Everyone got to meet everyone else, and by the end of the dinner, they all seemed like they had become good friends. Stefani left with her mother, Hank's sister, and Hank's daughter Maggie, while Rocco Stefani, Hank, Hank's best man, Luis and Andersson all left together.

It was after eleven when they all said goodnight and went home, all except Andersson. He drove to a private airstrip and got there at ten minutes to twelve. Buster met him at the gate, got into Andersson's car, and at his direction, drove to the end of the runway where a private jet was parked.

"Where is everyone?" Andersson asked, looking around.

"They're here, you just can't see them," Buster said.

"Where's Forbes?" Andersson asked.

"He's on board the jet," Buster said, pointing. "The pilots and crew left with the Governor's driver, and will be back when we're done."

Anderrson sat quietly with Buster for a few minutes, and stared out the window into the darkness.

There were no outside lights this far down the runway, plus there was a large stand of trees about a hundred yards away from where they were parked, that made it seem even darker.

"So you're doing private security for the Governor?" Andersson asked, to break the deafening silence.

"I've always done the private security for the Governor," Buster replied.

Buster always made Andersson uncomfortable, since he never knew what he was thinking and Buster wasn't much of a talker.

"He's ready now," Buster said, glancing down at his cell phone when the screen lit up.

Andersson opened the door and got out while Buster just sat there.

"Aren't you coming?" he asked, leaning back in.

"No, he wants to see you alone," Buster replied.

"Okay," Andersson said, and left.

He walked to the jet, the cabin door was open, the stairs down, and when Andersson went into the plane, he immediately saw her. The Governor was sitting next to her and he had a wide, happy smile on his face. It wasn't his usual plastic political model, that he used for the public, but rather one much less posed and fake.

"Nicklaus," Forbes said, remaining in his seat. "Come in, I want you to meet someone. This is Myra."

Andersson stood frozen and speechless. He knew who she was the moment he saw her since he had seen her pictures many times during the Richard Blaine case.

"Well, don't just stand there looking surprised," the Governor said, waving him over. "Come in and sit down with us."

Andersson finally found his mobility, walked to one of the large leather chairs opposite them, and sat down.

"I'm Myra," the beautiful woman said, extending her hand.

Andersson was still reeling and wanted to scream out to the Governor. 'Are you crazy?' but he didn't and slowly extended his hand to meet her.

"Pleasure to meet you Myra," he said, shaking hands.

"I know this is a shock for you Nicklaus, Forbes began. "We don't have a lot of time left now, but I wanted you to know Myra will be around from time to time…"

"Oh," Andersson said. "You mean during the campaign?"

"Yes," Forbes replied, placing his hand over hers. "There's a lot to explain, and I'm sure you have a thousand questions."

"More like a million sir," Andersson said, before he could stop himself.

Both Forbes and Myra laughed.

"I'm sure you do," the Governor said. "But there's not time for that now. Myra's on her way back to Palm Beach and I'm going home, but I wanted you to meet Myra."

"Okay, and now that I have sir?"

"We'll talk about that later, but soon," Forbes promised. "I don't want any secrets between us, especially during a very busy campaign; but don't worry, I'm not going to have you lying for me, at least not on the record."

"Sir? Lying?"

"Later Nicklaus," Forbes said, glancing at his watch. "The pilots and crew are on their way back.

You ride back to the gate with Buster, and I'll call you as soon as I can."

Andersson stood up, looked at the Governor, then to Myra.

"Myra," he said, with a nod.

"Nicklaus," she replied, also with a slight nod.

Andersson turned and left, walking robotically, as if in a dream, hardly believing what had just transpired. He had just been with, very likely, the future President of the United States, sitting with his mistress, on a private jet, in the middle of the night. He heard Buster start the car in the distance, and a chill ran down his spine.

CHAPTER EIGHTY-FOUR

I t was a week later, and Stefani was leaving on her honeymoon with Hank that evening. They were going to Paris for a four days, then on to Rome for a few more days before returning home.

Right now, she and Andersson were sitting in court, and Willy Burk was just finishing his allocution. It was just like everyone had always known had happened that fateful night. Billy wanted her gone, and Willy concocted a plan to kill Heather, and make it look like a traffic accident.

Willy spoke without any emotion, as if he was telling a make belief story he had heard, something that wasn't real, at least in his mind. He told the court he was sorry, but his apology wasn't sincere, and no one believed him, especially Heather's father, who sat in the front row surrounded by three burly deputies.

When Willy finished speaking, the judge asked Heather's father if he wanted to say anything to Willy, and Al shook his head no. Heather's mother and sister wasn't there, neither one of them could bear to hear the details of what was done to Heather before she finally died two hours after Willy had hit her with his pickup truck.

The judge reviewed the terms of the plea agreement with Willy, and after he was done, passed the agreed sentence, fifteen years to twenty. The whole process took about twenty minutes and the court was adjured. The three deputies that hovered near Heather's father, left, and took Willy away.

"Well, there goes number three case closed," Andersson said, watching the suddenly scared looking Willy leave the court room.

"He might think he's going to serve just the fifteen and he's done," Stefani said, standing next to Andersson. "But, I can become the queen of Mars, and I'm flying back for his parole hearing. He's going to do the twenty."

Andersson laughed. "I thought you already were the queen of Mars."

Stefani laughed too. "I am, but please don't tell anyone."

"Oh great! Just what I need, more secrets," he said, turning to leave.

"Sounds like you got the weight of the world on your shoulders," Stefani said, leaving with him.

"I do, I do," Andersson said, noticing that Heather's father had left. "That's funny, Al's gone, and I thought for sure he would have something to say to us."

"I know, me too."

"Oh before I forget, I heard from Casper yesterday that Henry's mother passed away, and he was going ahead with her wishes to have Henry's manuscripts published."

"Great!" Stefani said, as they walked outside into the bright sunshine. "I'm going to stop by the nail salon on my way home and see Pi. She called me a couple of times this week and said Dickinson had left her some money for school. I thought I'd keep in touch with her and see how she makes out."

Andersson stood on the court house steps for a few seconds without replying, then suddenly took hold of Stefani's arm.

"Wait! Listen!" he said.

"What?" she replied, startled.

"There!" He said, releasing her arm. "It's gone now."

"What was it?" She asked.

"Everything was perfect in the world, just for a moment," he said.

Stefani smiled, and walked down to the sidewalk with him.

They hugged.

"Have a wonderful honeymoon," he said, as they embraced like a father and a daughter would. "See you when you get back."

Stefani turned, then stopped.

"Don't look now," she said. "But there's Heather's father by the curb.

"Hey Andersson! Stefani!" Al shouted to them. "Look at me! I'm dancing in the street! I'm dancing in the street!"

ABOUT THE AUTHOR

Tony Cerminaro is a Nurse Practitioner in Oncology and a re-tired Lt Colonel from the United States Air Force. He resides in Central New York with his wife Corinne, daughter Gretchen, and two dogs, Bella and Buster.

www.ingramcontent.com/pod-product-compliance
Lightning Source LLC
Chambersburg PA
CBHW070614260626
47161CB00007B/2432